GAYLORD

# BLISS, REMEMBERED

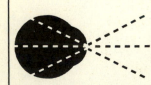

This Large Print Book carries the
Seal of Approval of N.A.V.H.

# BLISS, REMEMBERED

## FRANK DEFORD

**THORNDIKE PRESS**
*A part of Gale, Cengage Learning*

GALE
CENGAGE Learning·

Detroit • New York • San Francisco • New Haven, Conn • Waterville, Maine • London

LARGE CORE
F
DEFORD, F
3  1257  01928  1301

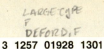

**LIBRARY OF CONGRESS CATALOGING-IN-PUBLICATION DATA**

Deford, Frank.
  Bliss, remembered / by Frank Deford.
    p. cm. — (Thorndike Press large print core)
  ISBN-13: 978-1-4104-3153-0
  ISBN-10: 1-4104-3153-3
  1. Swimmers—Fiction. 2. Reminiscing in old age—Fiction. 3.
Triangles (Interpersonal relations)—Fiction. 4. Large type
books. I. Title.
PS3554.E37B57 2010b
813'.54—dc22                                          2010030568

Published in 2010 by arrangement with The Overlook Press, Peter
Mayer Publishers, Inc.

Printed in the United States of America
1 2 3 4 5 6 7 14 13 12 11 10

*for Scarlet & Adam*
*Lauren & Christian*

# ACKNOWLEDGMENTS

It's always tricky to place real people into a fictional work, but in inserting some of them into Sydney's story I tried to be as faithful to their true selves as possible. It did help me that the two main historical women who play significant roles as characters — Eleanor Holm and Leni Riefenstahl — are people whom I actually met. Both were old women when I spent time with them, but they were both still very much vibrant and distinctive personalities, and it was easy to imagine what they had been like in the 1930s.

I am particularly indebted to Mary Lou Petty Skok, who swam in the '36 Olympics, and Marilyn Sahner, a member of the Women's Swimming Association back then, for their first-hand remembrances. Adolf Kiefer was also a member of the '36 U.S. swimming team — he won a gold medal in the hundred-meter backstroke — and he too recalled the Berlin Olympics for me.

Angela Leuker, a wonderful old friend, was invaluable in supplying me with the right German expressions, as Mackey Dutton and Al and Georgianna Evans were so helpful in providing me with background detail of Chestertown and the Eastern Shore (although it's a place where I've spent a lot of time myself). Lest anyone from Washington College question where the school's indoor swimming pool was, I'm sorry, that was simply a necessary invention. Sydney had to swim somewhere in the winter, and so I gave the pool to the college. Otherwise, I believe I held literary invention to a bare minimum. The Germans did indeed, for example, land a spy from a U-Boat off Bar Harbor. Goebbels threw that party. Adolph Kiefer's meeting with Hitler at poolside happened exactly as I described it. I just inserted Sydney into the scene. The best women swimmers really did wear those sexy bathing suits. Who knew?

Karen Crouse of *The New York Times* and Bob Duenkel of The International Swimming Tennis Hall of Fame steered me to good contacts, and the Westport Public Library and the New-York History Society library provided, once again, valuable research resource assistance.

8

Aaron Schlecter did a fine job of improving my manuscript, as Samantha Weiner, his colleague at Overlook, first disected it so lovingly. Sterling Lord has been my agent for forty-five years. It seems to work pretty well.

— FRANK DEFORD
*Westport, Connecticut*
*January 24th, 2010*

■ ■ ■ ■

# PART ONE:
# ELEANOR

■ ■ ■ ■

The summer after my mother found out that she was dying of cancer, she asked me to come visit and watch the Olympic swimming on television with her. It was 2004, when the Games were in Athens. Mom had been on the United States swimming team in the Berlin Olympics in 1936, when she was eighteen. While she never talked about that experience — she was, in fact, mysteriously silent on the subject — she would say, "That's the only thing of any real consequence I ever did in my life." That wasn't true, but it was very much like her to speak so modestly. To put this in perspective: my mother was one of these people who gave much unto the world, brightened the lives of those around her and left us all better for her having been here among us.

You can be sure I understand if you think I am prejudiced, and I am, but nonetheless, that all happens to be the God's truth.

Of course, she also could be herself, which was a handful.

She was an awful lot of fun; she had a way about her. Unlike most old people who seem to withdraw unto themselves, she became more expressive and confident of herself (and her opinions) as she grew older. She had developed an uncommon facility about the past, wherein she discussed herself back then with a certain out-of-body quality, as if that girl was someone else altogether. And while she certainly maintained the courtesy and graciousness that had always marked her, she felt less compunction to suffer fools. In particular: woe to the poor person who called her a "senior." Mom, I think you could say, went out — well, if not with a bang, then certainly with a lot of sizzle.

I was, then, not altogether taken aback when, after I told her that I'd be delighted to come see her, she said, "I'll have something in the nature of a surprise for you, Teddy." But, although I pressed her in a good-natured way, she wouldn't tell me what it was, and I had all but forgotten about it until I arrived, a few weeks later, at her garden apartment in Eugene, Oregon. After Daddy died and she sold the house in Montana, she came to Eugene because she

14

had heard it was a nice place to live, and it was a college town, and while she wanted a more benign climate, she didn't want to go to the Sun Belt and "play bridge with a bunch of old hags like myself."

She made a lot of good friends in Eugene and enjoyed her years there, stirring the pot. She told me she was accepting of death, although her one wish was that she would not die while George W. Bush was the president of her country. Unfortunately, much to her chagrin, she would be denied that hope.

Mom, whose name was Sydney Stringfellow Branch, threw off her mortal coil, going on eighty-seven, on January 11, 2005. "Well," she said, a few days before the end, when the die was cast, "at least I won't have to be around for that damn fool's second inauguration." And she added: "You know, Teddy, I've always wondered what comes next, but at least I can die positively knowing that as long as Bush is president here, I'm guaranteed to be going to a better place."

Anyway, it was the previous August when I visited her. I came by myself, for although Mom adored Jeanne, my wife, I could tell that she wanted to see me alone. So I'd left home, left behind Jeanne, left our empty nest (well, save for our dog, Elsinore), and come to Eugene at the time when the Olympic swimming started. Mom and I would watch it every night. She adored Michael Phelps, all the more so that he came from Baltimore, because she had grown up nearby, across Chesapeake Bay, on the Eastern Shore of Maryland. "I wish he'd swim in the backstroke," she said. That had been her specialty.

"You can't swim everything, Mother."

"He can. He's amazing."

"I never asked you: why did you swim backstroke?"

"You really wanna know, Teddy?"

"Yeah."

"Because when you're on your back you don't have your face stuck in the water. You can see the sky. I liked that."

"Who woulda thunk it?" I said.

"Now, it's not so good when you're in a race in an outdoor pool, because if the sun's out, it's in your eyes, but me just swimming the backstroke in the river, why, if the sun got in my eyes, I just turned over for awhile. You've got to remember, in the beginning, I just swam for the hell of it because the river was out our backyard. I imagine if I'd lived in Nepal, I'd've climbed mountains and been a Sherpa."

"Aren't the Sherpas all men?"

"For God's sake, Teddy, don't be so literal. Is this any better: if I'd grown up in Las Vegas, I'd've been a whore."

Mom made certain to find out when the women's hundred-meter backstroke would be shown. That had been her event when she'd made the U.S. team. "I want to tell you all about that," she told me.

"You do? I could never get a word out of you on that."

"Well, there was a reason."

"What was that?"

"That's what you're gonna find out, antsy-pants. But things were connected."

"I don't know what that means."

"It means I didn't ever want to talk about the Olympics because that was connected to other stuff, which I didn't think was any of your damn business."

"Till now."

"A woman can change her mind. So can a man, but most of you are too stubborn ever to do that."

That reminded me. "I thought you had something for me."

"I do."

"What is it?"

"Teddy, just hold your horses." She shook her head in despair at me — which was not

17

uncommon, although I usually couldn't imagine what exactly it was that Mom held me in despair of. "Nobody can wait anymore," she said in exasperation. "One of the great technological advances in this world, which is actually a terrible step backwards, is cameras."

At times like this, I had no idea where she was going. "How so?" I asked. Mom liked a straight man.

"Much of the fun of taking pictures was not knowing how a picture came out. You took a picture and then had to wait till you got the roll back from the drugstore to find out how good the pictures were. And when you found out one of them — even only one of them — was a honey of a picture, it made your day. Now, with all this digital nonsense, you can see the picture right away. What fun is that?"

"Well, there's something to be said for getting something right, isn't there?"

"Oh sure," she said, in that world-weary way, which I took to really indicate a weariness of me and my questions. "But the point is — the larger point, Teddy — is that there are no surprises left. You can tell on the phone who it is before you pick it up. All the children are on that Facebook thing, so there're no blind dates left. Just peek-a-boo

18

dates. Everybody has to know what sex their child is hardly before they're out of bed and through conceiving. No, no, no, we think we're so clever, but we're a poorer world without surprises."

Still shaking her head at the folly of us all, she got up and went over to her little antique desk, opened a drawer and pulled out one of those large acetate envelopes. It was a bright purple — violet, her favorite color. I instinctively reached out my hand for the folder. You would've thought that I'd have learned by now. "No, no, no," she said. "Not yet. In fact, I've decided that I'm gonna tell you the first part of the story."

"This is a story?" I asked, pointing to the envelope. "You've written a story?"

"No, no, Teddy. Not a story story. It's the real story that happened to me long ago that I want you to know about."

"To you?"

"My story, yes."

"At the Olympics?"

"That's part of it." She grinned — and rather mischievously, I thought. "That's a lot of the part I'm gonna tell you."

"Why do you wanna tell me that part?"

"Well, the first part is a lot of fun, so I decided I'd enjoy telling you that." As she stood before me, she gently rapped the

19

envelope on her thigh. "But the second part is more important, so I better let you read that to make sure it's absolutely clear."

"All right, I got it."

"But Teddy: prepare yourself now. There's some sex."

That took me aback a little. "There is?"

"I hope you can abide that, Teddy. I promise not to offend your delicate sensibilities."

"I'll try not to blush, Mom."

"And I'll try not to spell it out."

"Okay, it's a deal."

Her expression changed then, and in a voice so different that I thought at first she was putting me on, she spoke softly: "Some violence, too."

I watched her closely before I realized she was serious. Even then, I wasn't certain. "Violence? Really, Mom? Violence?"

"One day, yes." But quickly, then: "Only let's not get into that now. That's a ways off."

"Okay."

She put a smile back on her face, reached into the envelope, pulled out a little tape recorder and handed it to me. "You gotta use this."

"But you said you've already got it all written out in there." I pointed to the acetate envelope.

"That's true, but I'm sure I'll flesh it out some in the telling, so it'll be a fuller picture. Probably more scintillating, too."

"You want me to get this transcribed afterwards?"

"You can if you want, Teddy. After I'm dead and gone, you can do whatever you want." She sighed. "That's the point."

Mom wasn't fey when she said that. Rather, her voice was suddenly very trenchant, and, of course, it made me all the more curious. "What is the story, Mom?"

"That's what I'm gonna tell you. You don't need a preview of coming attractions. Can you work this gizmo?"

I may not be a technological wizard, but I knew enough to push the start button, and I said, "Testing, testing," and stopped it and pushed the little backwards arrow and played it back. Sure enough: "Testing, testing."

"I got it," I said. "Whatta guy."

"Let's go outside," Mom said, leading me out the French doors to where she kept a pretty little garden — flush with rhododendron, which had always been her flower of preference. It was a soft summer's day, terribly quiet. She sat down and smiled at me in something of a conspiratorial way. It even left me a little uneasy, because it was obvious she had something up her sleeve. Sex, okay. But violence? My mother?

"When does the story start?" I said, laying the little tape recorder down on the table next to her.

"Nineteen thirty-four," she said. "When I was sixteen, on the Eastern Shore. But, really, Teddy, you'll see that this moves on from the damn Depression and becomes the last story about the war."

"World War Two?"

"Yeah. It's the absolute very last story about World War Two. I gotta believe all the others have already been told by now."

Truth be told, I never knew all that much about my mother's life Back East. She and Daddy moved to Missoula, Montana, when she was still carrying me, and so I — and, too, my younger sister, Helen — simply had no connection with that part of her life, where she was brought up, in Chestertown, Maryland, which is on the Chester River off the upper reach of the Chesapeake Bay.

Even if she wouldn't talk about it, Mom was proud of having been on the Olympic team. Of course, she was always quick to add: "I wasn't good enough to win a medal" — and that invariably concluded the conversation. As I got older and learned more about Hitler and the important political implications of those Nazi Games, I asked her more about them, but she always managed to be evasive on the subject. The one time I really pressed her on it was when I was in high school and was assigned to write a composition about something interesting that somebody in the family had done. But she brushed me off again. "You gotta remember, Teddy, I was only a wide-eyed little girl from the Eastern Shore, and I couldn't've cared less about the politics."

It rather left me in the lurch, though, because what I really wanted to write about was how my father had been wounded at Guadalcanal in the summer of 1942. However, Mom had always told me that, like so many of the men who'd fought in the war, Daddy wanted to forget about it, and so I was instructed never even to approach him on the subject.

So, Guadalcanal was out and the Nazi Olympics were out, and I ended up writing my paper on how my grandfather, whom I'd never even known, had won a music contest when he was a boy, playing the accordian. I didn't even appreciate the significance of this achievement. Mother had to explain it to me, how everybody always looked down on the accordian, and disparingly dismissed it as a "squeeze box." Apparently, however, my grandfather was a downright whiz with the instrument, and when he came up against all those other kids playing their fancy pianos and violins and cellos, the judges were unable to deny

him his due. It was a big deal in Chestertown at the time, and it remained prominent
in my mother's family folklore, but frankly,
to me, it seemed awfully insignificant compared to the Berlin Olympics and Guadalcanal. But, there you go: any port in a storm.

Once Mother got me settled in her garden
and was convinced that I was actually
capable of operating the little tape recorder,
she went back and fetched a pitcher of iced
tea. It was obvious to me by now that she
was laying in for the long haul. Before she
began talking, though, she looked over at
me and broke into this glorious, even
beatific smile.

"What's so funny?" I asked.

"Oh, nothing really. I'm just remembering, and it makes me happy." She stopped
and pointed again at the tape recorder.
"Now, you sure that's working?"

I left nothing to chance. I played the
rewind: ". . . makes me happy. Now, you
sure that's working?"

Satisfied, then, Mom sat back and began.

Teddy, the house I grew up in wasn't right
in Chestertown. It was a few miles out of
town, toward the Bay. The lawn backed
right down onto the river. The Chester
River. This long, sloping lawn. Lord, but it

was a wonderful place to play. We had a dock there, and Daddy always had a boat. We had some land, too. I can't remember how many acres, but Daddy sold most of it when I was a little girl. See, my father's side of the family had a little money, and he didn't want to bother with farming. You had to look after the tenants, the tenant farmers.

There was an old house on the property where the tenants had lived. You wouldn't have known it was there, that old tenant house, tucked away behind where the river bends. After Daddy sold the farmland, we just stored stuff in there, but when the hard times came, the Depression in '29, there was an old colored man — excuse me, we called the black people colored then, and it just slipped into my conversation, remembering . . .

*"I understand, Mom. I won't stamp you as a racist."*

Well, Teddy, isn't that white of you . . .

*We both laughed, and she went on:*

There was an old black man . . . an African American. Well, he seemed old to me. Probably wasn't over sixty. Certainly nowhere near as old as I am now, that's for sure. And maybe not even as old as you. His name was Gentry. That was his first

26

name, Gentry. Gentry Trappe. There was the town of Trappe, Maryland, farther down the Shore in Talbot County, and I suppose Gentry Trappe's family had been slaves way back and just took that name, or there were people named Trappe they named the town after who owned his ancestors when they were slaves. Anyway, Gentry Trappe was a wonderful old fellow, quite distinguished in his way. I always called him "Mr. Trappe." Poor man — his wife had died in the flu epidemic of 1918. You familiar with that?

*"Oh yeah, sure."*

Terrible thing. It was right about the time I was born. Well, Gentry Trappe never remarried and his children grew up, and then he lost his job in the Depression. Daddy had known him forever, and so he said, "Gentry, why don't you come and live in the old tenant's house on my place?"

And he said, "Oh, Mr. Robert, I couldn't afford anything like that."

But my father explained that he thought it'd be a good idea to have someone in the house, just to be on the property, to look after the two of his ladies — that's my mother and me — when he was away on business. Your grandfather was the sweetest man, Teddy. There was no justice in such a model of goodness being killed. We always think of the mother's milk of kindness, but I believe, if there's any kindness in me, it came more from my daddy than Mom.

Daddy knew Mr. Trappe would want to plant a little garden, and all he asked in the way of rent was that when the sweet corn crop came in, he'd give us a dozen ears or so, and some peaches and maybe a dozen of those good Eastern Shore tomatoes. One thing I remember about my father. He'd dig into a tomato like it was an apple. Just take a big bite. All that juice and those little orange seeds running down his chin. I can see that now. I was never that partial myself to tomatoes. I like tomato soup and tomato sauce and tomato ketchup more than plain tomatoes themselves. Must have somethin' to do with rememberin' the juice runnin' down Daddy's chin.

Anyway, that was the deal Daddy struck with Gentry Trappe. A little produce would be rent enough if he'd keep an eye on the two gals. So he lived there on the property during all this time I'm tellin' you about.

Sorry, Teddy, I'm getting off the track. It's your job to keep me on the straight and narrow here.

*"I'll do my best, Mom."*

Thank you. Daddy's family did have a little money. My grandfather had started a nice little insurance office in Chestertown, servicing most of Kent County and some of Queen Anne's, too, right across the river. It was thriving — you know, for that neck of the woods. And Daddy followed in his father's footsteps. Stringfellow and Son Insurance, it became. Right there on Cross Street, the main drag in Chestertown. And the main drag was about the only drag then.

Now, Mother, her family didn't have a pot to piss in. They were farmers. Corn. The Eastern Shore corn is a sweet white corn, and it's the best there is, but the De-Havenons didn't have that much land, and I suppose it wasn't the best, either. All during the Depression, Mother had to help her folks out. But Daddy understood. We were very fortunate — relatively. I think everybody was more understanding, more generous, during the Depression. And the good thing about insurance then was that it was the one thing — well, after their mortgages — that people would try their damndest to keep up. Your insurance. If nothing else, if you had a life policy, it would pay for your funeral. You'd be surprised how that mattered to a lot of folks.

*"How did Grandmother meet Grandfather?"*

*She sipped her ice tea, then shook her head at me.*

29

Here, I ask you to keep me on point. That's what they say now in business, don't they — "on point"?

*"I believe they do, yes."*

Well, I urged you to stop my digressions, and promptly, Teddy, promptly you encourage them.

*"Okay, never mind about Grandmother and Grandfather."*

No, even a blind pig finds an acorn now and then, and come to think of it, that was a pretty good question. It was apropos.

*"I'm glad to be on point, Mom."*

Well, Mother was a couple years behind Dad at Chestertown High, and I'll bet he had his eye on her even then. Mother was what we call "upwardly mobile" now. She didn't want to marry some damn corn farmer like her mother. And she was smart as a whip, Mom was, and she learned how to type, and Daddy hired her as the receptionist and what-have-you for the office. Otherwise, I think she would've taken off for Wilmington or Baltimore, for the city. My mother was not going to be some farmer's wife. But once Daddy got her in that office, she snared him pretty quickly. Or, I'm sure, he let her snare him. And it was a good marriage, Teddy. It was full of love, just like my own. As far as I could tell,

30

Mom even liked it when he played that damn accordian of his.

*"You didn't care for that?"*

No comment, buddy-boy.

I think the only sadness in their marriage was that after me, Mom couldn't have any more children. I never understood exactly why. She couldn't. And, of course, Daddy had wanted a son. So I became more than just Daddy's little girl. I did more things with him. He'd take me out in the boat, fishing, throw a baseball around with me, go swimming with me, take me dove-hunting.

*"You shot little birds?"*

Oh, don't be such a nancy boy, Teddy. We all did. Why, Mr. Andrews, the next farm over, he'd grow a whole field of sunflowers just because doves like sunflower seeds So Daddy and me would go over there and fire away when the doves would pop down for a meal. Then come the fall, he'd take me duck-hunting, when the mallards flew down south over the Bay.

*"Blew those poor devils to kingdom come, too?"*

Listen, Teddy, you're not going to get up before dawn and sit out there in that blind, freezing your heinie off, and not shoot. That was the whole point: to shoot. Daddy and the other men would bring a little rye to fortify them, so at least they had something to pass the time with, waiting for those damn ducks. So you bet I shot 'em when the chance presented itself.

*"Ever hit any?"*

Did I? You think a girl can't shoot? Teddy, I was a regular Annie Oakley.

*She brought out an imaginary pair of six-shooters, pretended to fire them off and then blew cool over the top of one make-believe barrel.*

*"Hey, no offense, Mom. It's just that I never ever saw you have anything to do with guns."*

*She paused for a moment.*

Let's simply say that I decided to lay down my firearms when we left the Shore. But I always had a wonderful time, just being with my father, whatever we did. He called me Trixie.

*"Trixie! Oh yeah. Now why was that?"*

It started off because he said I was so full of tricks, and then it stuck. All the way through school I was Trixie Stringfellow. I rather liked it, to tell you the truth. I was one of a kind, among so many names that were dime a dozen — and the fact that Trixie was my father's name for me made it seem even more special. He was just a honey of a guy.

*Mom stopped then, sighed, and took a swal-*

*low of the iced tea. When she looked away
then, I was fairly sure what was coming next.
She swallowed and said:*

And then Daddy was killed.

*"Yeah."*

He was going over to Sudlersville, over
near the Delaware line, to handle some sort
of a policy, and coming back that night
there was a truck that wandered over the
line, and it hit Daddy almost square on, and
you know what cars were like then. They
weren't much more than old tomato cans
with wheels. It was June, Teddy, June 26,
1934. I still remember. And I'll tell you
something, if it hadn't been June, been summer, my whole life would've been different,
because I was so upset, and what did I start
to do? I started swimming a lot. I'd go out
in that river and swim my heart out. It got
me through things. Mom had the agency. It
wasn't Stringfellow and Son anymore. It
had become The Robert Stringfellow Insurance Agency. And she threw herself into the
work. I remember. But me, I just swam all
that summer. I don't know why, but the
Chester River always seemed warmer, and
it seems like I could stay in it forever.

I can see Gentry Trappe now coming by
and watching me out there in the river, and
he'd say, "Miss Trixie, you swim better than

33

any fish I ever did see." I just swam. All the time.

Mom had already become like the office manager under Daddy, and after he died she'd hire young men to be agents. Remember now, this is '34, the depths of the Depression. There were good men dying for work, anything at all, so she had her pick, and they'd work all on commission. She'd service Daddy's old accounts herself. She kept that agency going just fine. My mother was not going back to farm work.

And I swam. Out there off the dock in the Chester River. That's why I liked the backstroke so much. I could swim and look up at the sky, and think some — well, when I wasn't trying to swim lickety-split. You can't think, Teddy, when your head's down in the water and all you're doing is comin' up for air. The Chester River was a little brackish, too, so the salt taste could burn your lips after a while.

Nobody had any pools then, private pools, you know, but some of the bigger towns on the Shore had community pools. Easton had one. It was the swankiest town around.

*"How far away?"*

Oh, I don't know. Thirty, thirty-five, maybe forty miles. But of course the roads were all terrible, so it was a haul. It was a haul to go anywhere then. That made the Eastern Shore even more like a little kingdom unto itself. Across the Chesapeake Bay, over to Baltimore and Washington, that was another world. That was Oz. I guess the other side of the Bay was the western shore. After all, it was the western side, and it was a shore. But nobody called it that. Only our side was identified that way: The Eastern Shore. We were one. Everybody knew everybody. You take the people where we lived, in Maryland, we felt a lot more in common with the people from Delaware and that skinny tit of Virginia that stuck down on the other side of the Bay than we did with the rest of Maryland. In fact, they called us Delmarva, like we were a real state. I guess they still do. It's been so long since I was back there. So long.

You know what Delmarva was really like?

*I shook my head. I didn't know where Mom was going, and I liked hearing her reminisce.*

We were like those countries in Africa that the great powers split up along political lines without taking the tribes into account. We were one big tribe, Delmarva, and they didn't have any business divvying us up, willy-nilly, between Maryland and Delaware and Virginia. Yeah, we were tribal — very independent people. Very insular. Very suspicious — especially if you came from across the Bay.

I remember Mom telling me there was this one big account that was in arrears. I mean, the grace period was about up. This was after Daddy died, so she had to go out there herself. It wasn't like these folks were poor, either, but she said they behaved like it was an imposition that she was expecting them to pay the bill on time so they could keep their insurance up. The man said: "I don't think you understand, Mrs. Stringfellow. You are new to doin' bidness, but everyone on the Shore knows that we Carneys never pay our bills on time." It was that sort of place, the Shore.

*"What happened?"*

What happened what?

*"To the Carneys, to the people who wouldn't pay their bill?"*

Oh, I believe Mom just told them that she was sorry, but the Aetnas didn't live on the Shore, they lived up in Hartford, Connecticut, and the way it worked in Hartford was, you had to pay, at least by the time the grace period was up. Mom left with the check.

So anyway, Easton. They had a community pool, and somehow I heard that on Labor Day they had this swimming tournament, and I decided I was gonna go. Even though it was a haul, all the way down in Talbot County. It was all so strange, Teddy. I mean, I'd never been in any sort of real race. Nobody had any swimming teams. Well, for that matter, there weren't any girls' teams in anything. But I told Mother about the meet in Easton, and she said she'd drive me down.

*"Even though you said it was a veritable haul?"*

Yes, and don't be a wisenheimer. I think she was just so glad to see me excited about something — anything — she'd've taken me anywhere. I was still so depressed about losing Daddy.

And so we drove down. We had a new Ford, because us being in insurance, we had insurance on the car my poor father had been killed in. It was totaled. So we had a new Ford. We drove down to Easton, and right away I could see it was a bigger deal than I'd ever imagined because, as I told you, Easton was a swanky place (well, by Shore standards), and they had a country club, and all the kids from the club had come over, expecting to win all the ribbons. They'd been practicing all summer, racing against themselves at their pool. They even had a coach, and all of them had the same trunks on. I'll tell you, one look, and it was very . . . imposing.

*Mother stopped suddenly and smiled her great big gigantic moon of a smile again.* "What's so funny?" I asked.

*Without losing that grin, she gestured toward the tape recorder.*

Turn that off a second, Teddy.

*I obliged. Mom leaned back in her chair and crossed her arms.*

Well, pardon my French, but I whipped all their asses.

The phone rang. It was my sister, Helen, calling from outside of San Diego, where she and her husband lived. She's my kid sister, but we're placed in completely different birth categories. I'm a war baby, but she's a boomer, born just after the war, when we were settled in Montana. Helen was coming to see Mother in a couple weeks. It made more sense for us to take turns being with her than for the two of us to come together.

"What're you and Mom up to?" Helen began, naturally enough.

"Well," I said, "we're sitting here having an iced tea, and she's telling me a story." But when I said that, Mom had a conniption fit, mouthing "no" and running her hand back and forth across her neck to cut it out. So when Helen asked, "What story?" I mumbled something innocuous about stories in general, and how we were getting ready to watch the swimming that evening. Finally, with great relief, I passed the phone to Mom.

When she hung up, I said, "Why don't you want Helen to know this?"

"It's more important for you to know, Teddy. That's why."

"Can I tell her?"

"I told you: after I'm dead, sure."

"I wish you'd stop saying that, Mom."

"Teddy, I'm eighty-six years old, I have terminal cancer, and I'm done with the chemo, so I'm gonna die in the not too distant future. Now, let's not be ridiculous."

"Well, I just wish you wouldn't bring it up. You're too direct."

"That's my Delmarva upbringing, I suppose. We are not creatures of subtlety."

"But then I can tell Helen?"

"Teddy, for all I give a hoot, you can sell it to television as one of those god-awful reality shows. It's damn fine reality. It's a good story, and there's a love interest. Everybody likes a love interest."

"Yes, ma'am," I said.

"I wish you wouldn't call me 'ma'am.' How old are you?"

"I'm sixty-one."

"Well, it's ridiculous to have a sixty-one-year-old man calling anybody 'ma'am.' "

40

"Come on, Mother, I can't help it. I've called you ma'am all my life. Daddy told me to call grown-up men 'sir' and grown-up women 'ma'am.' "

"Well, your father was very old-school, very, uh, continental, and I'm glad the apple didn't fall far from the tree, but if you would drop the ma'am now, and just call me Mother or Mom, I would definitely appreciate it."

"Could I call you Trixie?"

"No, that's out."

"Why?"

"I'll tell you later. I'm gonna take a nap now, because I want to be fresh for the swimming tonight. Natalie Coughlin's in one of the heats of the one-hundred-back."

Pointedly, she picked up the violet acetate package and took it with her. She stumbled just a little bit as she got to her feet, and I instinctively began to rise up, but Mom caught herself immediately and didn't look back. She knew I was watching her, so she made sure to walk especially carefully the rest of the way to the door as if nothing could possibly be wrong with her.

There was an odd dichotomy to her. On the one hand, she spoke so blithely of her impending death, but on the other, she was determined not to let me notice any of her distress — although it was obvious that she was occasionally in discomfort, even some pain.

How well, though, did I know that type of behavior. I think I always admired my mother as much as I loved her. She had never been a whiner, and now, if she understood so well that death approached, she was not going to bide her time in the waiting room. She was going to enjoy her last days, enjoy my company, and she appreciated that I couldn't reciprocate if I was worrying about her. So she pretended that she was much better than she was, and I pretended that I didn't know she was pretending.

But she knew what she was doing; we had much more fun this way.

That evening, Natalie Coughlin did win her heat, which absolutely invigorated Mother; she so wanted an American to take the gold in her old event. "Actually," she explained, "I think the two-hundred was my better distance, but they didn't have that in the Olympics then."

"Why not?"

"Because the asinine Olympic pooh-bahs thought women were dainty little vessels who were too fragile to endure two hundred meters. Ridiculous! The first time I raced Eleanor Holm was the two hundred yards. And I wasn't even tired." As if to relive that moment, she raised herself up out of her chair energetically and cried out, "Well, hooray for Natalie. This calls for a drink. Will you have a drink with me, Teddy, or are you an old stick in the mud?"

"I'm on, Mother."

"That's the stuff. Fix me a G and T, and don't go light on the G, mister. You make me a good stiff one, and I'll tell you about that time I went down to Easton to swim."

So I made two gin and tonics, and after we both took a swallow, upon her direction, we raised our glasses high and Mom cried out: "To Natalie Coughlin and the old red-white-and-blue!" Then she settled back. "Where did I get us to in Easton?"

"Not very far. You just told me you whipped all their asses."

She chuckled. "That's the God's truth, Teddy. Those gals from Easton were Custer, and I was the Injuns." She sipped her drink again. "You make a good G and T, Teddy. Just like your father."

"Well, the apple didn't fall far from the tree," I said.

Mom smiled at that and began again.

For a kid who'd never even seen a swimming meet before, it was pretty exciting. There were maybe a hundred people watching — course, most of 'em were just parents — and lotsa swimmers. It was age divisions. I was in the oldest — senior division. There was even a little stand where you could buy lemonade and hot dogs. Let me tell you, Teddy, I was mightily impressed.

There was a table where you signed in, and the man in charge there asked me my age and where I was from. That got a rise outta him. "All the way from Chestertown?" he asked.

I said, "Yes, sir."

And then he said, "Well, you understand now, the swimmers from Talbot County come first."

So I asked him, "So, what races are still open for me?"

He looked at his papers, and he told me,

"Well right now, there's a spot in all the races in your division except the hundred-yard freestyle. That one's filled up."

So I asked, "So exactly what all's left?"

He said, "Which races do you want, young lady?"

I turned to Mother and shrugged. It was all foreign to me. I said, "I guess you can put me down for all of 'em."

"All right," the man said. "Unless you get bumped, you'll be in the hundred-yard breaststroke and the hundred-yard back-stroke and the five-hundred-yard freestyle. That's the girls' longest race of the day. You sure you can do that?"

I shrugged. I thought I could. I knew I must've swam that far regularly in the Chester River. But just so I understood what an absolute marathon I was getting into, he said, "It's ten lengths of the pool."

"I can do that," I told him.

So he wrote me down for all those races, and Mom and I found a place to sit, and we waited. Pretty soon, the races started — the little kids first. The first one for girls in my division was the hundred-yard freestyle, which was the one I couldn't get in, but I stepped closer to watch — you know, Teddy, to check out my competition.

The gals from the country club looked

very impressive. They all, the boys and girls alike, had these very snappy maroon suits with white piping, and the girls had maroon caps that matched. I didn't even have a swimming cap, my hair flowed all out, and my suit was white — well, more kind of cream — with red roses on it. And those roses had seen better days. As a package, I don't imagine I looked especially imposing.

Well, I was standing there, watching, and the girls lined up. There were four of them from the country club and three others, which meant one lane was open. When I saw that, I looked around, and when I saw nobody else was approaching, I ran over to the man at the table and asked if I could fill in.

He said, "I don't see why not," so I ran back and took the empty lane, which was the one by the side of the pool. We didn't have starter's blocks or anything, just divin' in from the edge of the pool, and the starter raised his pistol and said, "Take your marks." I was kinda lookin' to the side at this girl next to me, to see the proper way to take my mark, when the gun went off. It took me a moment to collect myself, and by the time I dove in, everybody was ahead of me.

So I just started swimming, Teddy. As fast

as I could. Like I told you, I was in the last lane over, and when I breathed I was looking away from all the other swimmers, and so when I got to the end of the lap I had no idea where anybody was. I was amazed to see that I was way ahead. I didn't really know how to turn around properly, so I lost some of my lead there, but then, that second lap, I just aired it out and won goin' away. The four country-club girls all came in after me, second, third, fourth and fifth, and you could tell they were really PO'ed. The best one was named Edna, and she was downright furious.

I hopped out of the pool and was standing there in my cream bathing suit with the faded roses when Edna and this man who I suppose was her father went over to the table and carried on some. After a while, the man behind the table called me over and said, "How old are you, young lady?"

I said, "I'm sixteen."

And Edna, who was fuming, said, "Well, can you prove it?" I mean, the whole thing was ridiculous, Teddy. The senior division was fifteen through eighteen, and there was no way in the world I looked nineteen, but I said, "As a matter of fact, I can," because I had passed my drivers test a few weeks before, and my mother had my wallet, so she showed them the license.

The man behind the table examined it and said, "Earl, she's fine. She's only just sixteen."

But Edna and her father still weren't mollified. He said, "It's like a ringer, someone comin' down here all the way from Chestertown."

But the man behind the table, who was sort of getting annoyed at all this nonsense even though he was obviously from Talbot County himself, said, "Earl, there aint no geographical limits here. We had that boy come up from Salisbury two years ago."

Earl just shook his head. "Well, it just doesn't seem right," he said. But there wasn't anything he could do. I was perfectly legit, and so the starter called out, "The winner is Trixie Stringfellow, all the way from Chestertown."

That did not endear me to the crowd, Teddy. That is, the part about "all the way from Chestertown." I would say I got only scattered applause when he gave me the blue ribbon. Extremely scattered.

But you know, I didn't give a hoot. I was so excited to win that blue ribbon. I'd never gotten anything like that before, and I was downright exhilarated. It was the first time I'd really felt good about things since Daddy

48

got killed. Plus, I was pretty irritated, let me tell you, about Edna and her father trying to get me disqualified. So, by the time my next race came, which was the breaststroke, I had developed what you might call a killer instinct, as well.

*"And you whipped their asses again,"* I said.

Destroyed them, kiddo. Left them in my wake. Watch my smoke. I won from here to yesterday. I'd watched the senior boys race to see how you made a turn, so I was better at that. Poor old Edna didn't know what hit her.

Even better, when I climbed out of the pool, the senior boys were coming over for their race, and the cutest one, who I'd certainly taken note of — he made a point of going over to me and saying, "Nice race, Trixie." And I could see that PO'ed Edna even more.

And trust me, Teddy, I could tell he wasn't just interested in my athletic prowess. I wasn't bad to look at then, Teddy. You know, girls grow up fast, and I was full grown, and if I must say so myself, I had developed a very nice pair of bosoms inside that cream bathing suit with the faded red roses. Boys called them "bazooms" in those days.

*"They called your bosoms 'bazooms'?"*

No, smarty pants, they called everybody's

49

bosoms "bazooms" then. Boobs didn't come in until later. A boob then was just a dopey person. Whaddya call 'em now?

*"Whaddya call what?"*

Boobs.

*"We call 'em boobs."*

Nothing new? You men usually have a new one.

*I gave it some thought. "Rack."*

Rack?

*"Yeah, like check out the rack on her."*

*Mom shook her head, both in wonder and some admiration, I thought. She said:*

I never heard that one, Teddy. And it's usually in the plural. I'm just not up on the new lexicon. But I must say, it's not unexpected. It's amazing how you men always keep coming up with a new way just to say "tits."

*"Well, Mom, I think it's kinda like the Eskimos have a hundred different ways to say 'snow.' "*

I don't know if that's a good analogy, Teddy. The Eskimos are surrounded by snow. You men just wish you were surrounded by tits.

But, anyway, keeping with that train of thought, it was obvious that Frankie had an eye for mine, whatsoever you might call them. Neither did I particularly try to discourage these attentions. Somebody even called over, "Come on, Frankie, stop flirting with Chesty-town and take your mark." Oh, it was very obvious. I was reveling in it. Reveling.

" 'Chesty-town,' huh?"

Yeah, that made me blush, but tell you the truth, I kinda liked it.

"Reveling?"

Reveling.

"Was Frankie the best swimmer of the boys?"

No, no, just the cutest. And he could be comical, too. The best was a big, strong, tall boy named Carl. He won all the boys' races, like I won all the girls'. And he was full of himself, Carl was. I won the backstroke next. And, you know, that was my best. That was an absolute rout. After the boys raced, Frankie asked me if I wanted a lemonade, and so we chatted awhile, and he said if ever I came back to Easton, he'd love to go out with me. And I said, well that was unlikely, but why didn't he make the effort to come up to Chestertown sometime?

It was all very flattering, and then came the grand finale, the long one, the ten laps freestyle. To be honest with you, Teddy, when I got goin' in that, I was so far ahead, I eased up. I mean, by this point, I even showed some mercy to that awful Edna.

So I got my fourth blue ribbon, and Mom was ready to leave, but I said I wanted to see the boys' long race, too, although actually I was only interested in maybe having a little more of a tête-à-tête with Frankie.

I don't think I was fooling Mom any, but she was so proud of me, and she was so happy to see me happy again, so she let me stick around. Of course, Carl won the race, but when he got his blue ribbon, standing there all full of himself, Frankie called out, "Hey Carl, I'll bet you can't beat the girl." And everybody looked over at me, and I blushed, but people began to clap and say, "Yeah, yeah," and Carl got his dander up.

"I'm not racing any girl," he said, but Frankie came right back and called out, "You're scared of her, aren't you?" and all his friends hooted at him. "Carl's scared of the girl!" — that sort of teen-age stuff. So Carl was a rat caught in a trap.

The starter called out, "Shall we have a match race of champions?" And everybody cheered. Now nobody'd even asked me anything, and so Mother whispered, "Do you wanna do this, Trixie?" and I said, "Sure," and Carl cried out, "I'll give her a head start," and that really frosted me, and so I stepped forward and said, "I don't need any head start," and everybody cheered some more. Carl might've been the hometown boy, but I was the underdog, and everybody roots for underdogs, even if, as in this case, they're from faraway Chestertown.

The starter said, "Well, we'll give the young lady the choice of weapons. What stroke do you wanna swim, Trixie?"

That's what they call a no-brainer today. "Umm, the backstroke," I said, playing dumb, you understand.

*"Like a fox."*

Exactly, Teddy. So Carl nodded, and the starter said, "All right, what say we make it four laps — two hundred yards? Is that okay?" I said sure, and Carl agreed, all smug, and everybody moved closer to the pool. I mean, I guarantee you, nobody was leaving. Well, maybe Edna had gone. I'd lost interest in her by now, so I don't know.

*"How'd you feel, Mom?"*

Never so calm in all my life. I knew I should beat him, and if somehow his pride got his adrenaline up and he beat me, then it didn't really matter, 'cause everybody'd say I was just a girl and so what? I knew all the pressure was on him. And just before we jumped into the pool — you know, you start the backstroke in the pool — Frankie called out, "If he beats you, Trixie, he gets to kiss you."

And everybody cheered some more, but I was really feelin' my oats now. I'd never been in a spotlight before, and I'd found I enjoyed it. So I called over, "And suppose I beat him?"

And Frankie called back, "Then you get to kiss me." Oh, he was fresh, that Frankie. They don't say "fresh" anymore, do they?

*"No, they stopped that awhile ago."*

So, let us say Frankie could be inappropriate. Unfortunately, that's what they say now. Inappropriate. Awful word.

But like I said, I was feelin' my oats, and I called back, "In a pig's eye!" And everybody roared.

And so we jumped in, and the gun went off, and I just lay out on my back and pretended like I was on the river, with nobody around, and I just started moving my arms in that windmill way and kicking my feet nice and easy, taking my breaths, and it was such a breeze, Teddy, just me skimming along, looking up at the blue sky.

*She stopped and smiled, cocked her head, remembering.*

It was a year or so later when I first met Eleanor Holm, and she told me how there wasn't anything as grand as moving through the water on your back. She told me, "Yeah,

I like to be on my back in the water and on top in bed," but I was so young, I really didn't know what she meant. I just said something foolish like "yeah." That Eleanor Holm, she was a piece of work, lemme tell you . . .

But there you go again, lettin' me wander. Poor Carl. I got ahead of him halfway through the first lap, and it was all over but the shoutin', because then he began to panic, flailin' his arms and choppin' his legs too hard, so he started to wobble and even weave outside his lane. It was like with Edna earlier. I actually began to feel sorry for him. But I didn't let up, Teddy. I wasn't gonna go easy on any boy — especially one as stuck up as Carl. I beat him better'n a whole lap.

*"You whipped his ass."*

Yes, indeed. He could barely bring himself to shake my hand. The people were cheering. Some of the little girls jumped right into the water with me. This girl had beaten a boy, and they were all simply ecstatic. Now remember, Teddy, this is a million years before Billie Jean beat Bobby Riggs. I was one big heroine. Yes sir, on the Eastern Shore anyway, the women's movement began that day.

But, best of all, as Mom and I were leaving, this bald man came up to me. He said he was the coach at the country club. Honestly, I think he was more like some kinda glorified lifeguard, but he was awfully nice. He said, "Trixie, how much coaching have you had?" and I told him none, and he said he thought that was the case, but he just couldn't believe how good I was. He told me, "If you ever get coaching, you could be really good."

I said, "Really?" And he said, "Yeah, really. You're a natural, Trixie." A natural. Is there anything better anybody can tell you but that you're a natural? I don't think so.

He asked if I knew that there was an indoor pool at Washington College, which was in Chestertown. I told him, no, I didn't, but he told me there was. He also said there was an old guy named Wallace Foster who had been a real good swimmer himself, who swam at the pool up there, and he was gonna call Wallace Foster long distance and get him to start coaching me some. Which he did. Mr. Foster started to teach me what he knew. I mean, he wasn't a real coach, but in the land of the blind, the one-eyed man is king, so I swam all that winter indoors, and I got faster and faster, and I knew I was good. It's an amazing thing to be sixteen years old and realize you're truly outstanding at one thing in the world.

*Mom stopped abruptly and pointed at the tape recorder.*

Well, you can turn that off now. A girl's gotta get her beauty rest.

*"Wait a minute, Mom. First, you gotta tell me about Frankie. Did he ever take you out?"*

Yes, he most certainly did. I told you: I was pretty pert then, easy on the eyes. And he came up from Easton in his father's very stylish Pontiac. Remember now, he was one of the country-club boys. Frankie's family was doin' all right, even in the Depression. He picked me up in that Pontiac, and he was cute as a button and a barrel of fun. But all Frankie wanted to do was monkey around with my bazooms, and I wasn't ready for that sort of thing yet. In fact, he's the only boy I ever slapped. I mean actually hauled off and slapped him right across his face.

*She pantomined that. With vigor.*

No, Frankie wasn't used to bein' told no. Just so full of himself, so fresh.

He was killed at the Battle of the Bulge. I was living in Missoula by then, and my mother mailed me the obituary. But even if he was fresh, I thought about him fondly. To tell you the truth, Teddy, if I was going to start letting boys feel me up, I think I

57

would've begun with Frankie, but I was getting into swimming at the time, and I didn't want any physical distractions of that nature.

Poor Frankie. Just his luck.

The next morning, Mom came to breakfast dressed up in a printed silk dress that Helen had given her for her birthday. "You going out?" I asked. She still drove, even though I wished she wouldn't.

"I'm just gonna get something." And, anticipating me, she said, "And, no, I can get it by myself quite well enough. I'm not dead yet." I didn't rise to the bait, but just kept eating my eggs and bacon. "Well, you don't know what day it is, do you?"

I knew August 23rd couldn't be the complete answer, so I had to say no.

"Well, this is the day Jimmy died. Seven years ago."

"Yes, ma'am." She didn't correct me when I said ma'am. "I'm sorry I've forgotten."

"No, I didn't mean to chastise you, Teddy. It wasn't a test of your love. We remember the days when people were born, not when they die, and that's the way it should be."

"It doesn't seem like it's been seven years," I said.

"I know. Once you're gone, it's amazing how fast everything moves on. You miss a lot very quickly when you die."

I had to chuckle. "I never quite thought about it that way."

"Well, I'm dying, so it occurred to me." She rose from the table. "But, of course, I'd rather remember all the wonderful things your father and I shared. You remember, I dragged him to the Olympics in Los Angeles in '84."

"He liked it, didn't he?"

"Oh yes, but I made him sit through all the swimming. He would've preferred a more varied fare."

"Well, Daddy was always very agreeable."

"Yes, indeed he was. He was the sweetest husband a woman could ever want."

"Sweetest father, too," I added. And for just a moment, I thought Mom might cry, but she kissed me on the forehead and moved on with dispatch, snapping up the car keys. As she approached the door, though, she suddenly swung around and looked directly at me. "How much do you think you could do for love?"

That came right out of the blue, and I was completely taken aback. "You mean me in particular?"

"Well, anybody."

"What in the world made you ask that, Mom?"

"It just occurred to me."

"It's awfully hypothetical."

"So that's your escape clause?"

"Well, all right. People have made the supreme sacrifice for love. They've died to save someone they love. That's the answer, isn't it?" I was still rather puzzled by the whole exchange.

"Yes, I suppose. Or if we do something completely out of character —" She paused. "Even something illegal . . . We do that to help someone we love, maybe that's an even greater sacrifice."

"A greater sacrifice than dying?"

"Under some circumstances, I think."

"You have anything particular in mind?"

She shook her head. "Well, Teddy, let's just say: not right now."

"Okay, Mom, I'm sorry, but I just never really gave the subject much thought. You have a habit, you know, of springing things on people."

"Well, keep it in mind, and we can talk about it some other time."

"All right," I said, if only to be done with the matter.

But it seemed to satisfy her enough and, promptly turning the conversation back a ways, she said, "Now, speaking of your father, I'm gonna get some flowers, Teddy. I feel guilty that I can't put 'em on his grave —"

"Come on, Mom, it's back in Missoula, so you can't very well —"

"Exactly. So I'll get some flowers in honor of Jimmy, and we can look at 'em here."

"What're you gonna get?"

"Oh just some cheap bunch at the supermarket. Your father never cared much for flora. I don't think he could tell a gladiola from a gardenia, so there's no sense going whole hog on a bouquet that wouldn't impress him, anyway. Is it?"

"No, we should be consistent. On the other hand, if we raise a toast to Daddy tonight, it better be a good bottle of wine, or he'll be ticked off."

"A point well taken, Teddy. I will stop by the grog shop too."

And off she went. I must say, times like this, when all the medications were working, it was absolutely impossible to tell that she was dying. She was thinner, yes, but all her hair had fallen out during the chemo, so she had a very nice wig on, and what with her lovely new dress and her usual cheerful demeanor, it all seemed so out of joint. I called up Helen then and gave her an update on Mom's condition, and reminded her to call in the evening. "Do you know what day this is?"

"No."

"It's the day Daddy died, seven years ago."

"Oh my god, Teddy. Who ever remembers the day when people died?"

"Yeah, I agree with you, but if you call up Mom tonight and mention it, it'll make a big hit with her, and then she'll go to her grave loving you much more than she does me."

"All right," Helen said. "Under those circumstances, I'll certainly do it."

We always got along well, Helen and me. We shared much the same outlook and had quite the same wry sense of humor. Curiously, I, the male, looked more like Mother, while she, lighter in coloring, favored Dad, but it was not pronounced in either case. As a family, right along into the next generation of our own children, we're not much into spittin' images. In terms of personality, though, Helen is more of a risk taker than I've been, and in that sense, she took more after Mom. She went back East to college, while I stayed close to home — Montana State, down in Bozeman. Then after col-

lege, she flew for Pan Am as a stewardess —
that's what you called them then: stews —
so she saw the world for several years. She
was libertine and married a pilot who had
the look of eagles and a voice of authority
when he assured passengers that the turbu-
lance was nothing at all to fret about — only
"some chop."

That helped our relationship, too. We both
liked each other's spouses. As a matter of
fact, I liked all of Helen's husbands, and
never could understand why she kept changing them. After the pilot, there was a plastic
surgeon, and then the one now, whom I'm
pretty sure is the finale. He's a retired stock
brokerage president, which means that he
is, at the least, "well heeled." Certainly, from
all outward appearances, Helen and Buck
live a very well-heeled life in Rancho Santa
Fe.

Helen likes Jeanne, my wife, a lot. "She's
very good for you, Teddy," is what she said
from the beginning — although I've always
been a bit dubious about that analysis. I
like to think that you want someone who's
good with you, rather than for you. But
then, maybe I'm splitting hairs. In the event,
Jeanne and I do get along absolutely wonderfully, just as Mom and Dad always did.

I'm a school teacher. I've been that all my

life. I taught English in high school and was in charge of dramatics, as well. Theater's been my passion. I always directed as many plays in school as I possibly could, and now that I'm retired from teaching, I still work with a little theater group in Great Falls. I started teaching in Butte right out of college, but I went to a high school in Great Falls three years later, strictly because I could run the dramatics. And I've been there ever since. Jeanne was a teacher, too, and we met there. History was her subject. And she coached the girls' tennis. Sounds terribly dull, doesn't it? But I've just never been the sort to move around or change when things seem to be going reasonably well, and Jeanne, being good for me (as well you know), went happily along. We had three children, all grown now, all healthy, all spread to the winds, the way Americans are supposed to.

After Mom left for the flowers and wine, I could not help thinking about Daddy. The apartment, of course, was rife with his pictures, and I studied them all. Daddy as a young man at the bank, Daddy holding baby Helen in his arms, Mother and Daddy on vacation, posed here and there at various ages and holidays with the two children, then Daddy later on with various grandchildren. I especially paused to study the one on Mom's little desk of the two of them in front of the swimming venue at the Olympics in Los Angeles. Daddy was approaching seventy then, but he had a little tan and that wonderful smile of his, and I'll bet no one would've thought he could've been much past fifty.

Understand this: Daddy was simply terribly handsome — so much so that men were as inclined as women to acknowledge that. Before his hair turned gray, it was a soft sandy shade, and he had wonderful blue eyes and dimples and the sort of features that only a few people have that simply all work together. That is, everything was exactly the right size and not the least bit out of place. People who met him were always comparing him to some heartthrob actor. When I was a kid, it was Richard Widmark in particular. One of my first girlfriends thought Troy Donahue. The next generation thought Robert Redford, and even when he was an old man, I heard somebody say that if he were younger he'd be a dead ringer for Brad Pitt. As much as I loved acting, if I'd had Daddy's looks, I would've tried Hollywood. More's the pity, no?

In fact, when I got out of college, I thought

66

about going to New York and trying my luck at acting. It probably says more about my parents than me, that my mother's response was, "What the hell, Teddy, give it a shot. I went to Berlin all by myself when I was much younger than you." But Daddy said that while it was my decision, and he didn't want to discourage me because for all he knew I might be one terrific actor, he didn't think I was sufficiently built for that challenge.

"I don't mean to be critical of you, Ted, but New York's tough, and it's even tougher trying to make it as an actor. You'll have to suffer a lot of rejections, and you haven't got the thickest of skins."

"Yes sir, I know. That's what worries me."

"Now, it's nothing to be ashamed of. I've always thought that the American Dream can be a terrible onus on people."

"The American Dream is terrible?"

"No, I didn't say that. I said it can be a problem, because it suggests that everybody can succeed if they just try hard enough or want it hard enough. And, of course, that's nonsense. The good side of the American Dream is implicit in that, okay, there is no ceiling on hope in this country. But the dark side is that dreams are not reality — not even American dreams — so if Americans do not succeed in their quest they tend to be weighted down with a greater sense of failure. Then they come to my bank and ask to borrow money. Or, rather, they expect to.

"Expectations can be cruel, Ted. Someday, you know, the United States is not going to be top dog anymore. I don't mean the Communists are going to beat us. The Communists are frauds. But they're mean bastards, like the Nazis were, so they get away with it. For now. But someday the rest of the world will simply catch up with us. That's not a prediction; that's just the way history works. And it'll be especially hard for us, because we've been conditioned to think that we must be the best and so we deserve the best. We won't handle that disappointment particularly well."

"Does anybody, under the circumstances?"

"That's a good point. Every country can get a pretty good ride out of that national pride stuff. But America is different from all the other empires, ever. You see, Ted, nobody else was ever brought up to believe that they're living a dream."

After thinking about it, I didn't go to New York, and while I don't know if my father's advice was pivotal to my decision, I do know that it comforted me. And I do know that

68

once I made up my mind I was never dogged by that sense of might-have-been, probably because I enjoyed what I did do with the life I chose, and I was so very happy at home with Jeanne and my family.

In fact, on the occasion of my fortieth birthday, Daddy told me how pleased he was for me that I had found such joy in my work. It made me wonder. "Haven't you liked your job?" I asked him. He was about to retire as a vice-president at the First Montana Savings and Trust.

"Well," he replied, "I can't say I get up every morning anxious to get down to the office, but it's been satisfying enough. And I've improved over time; I think that's significant. Perhaps that means more than merely liking your work. When you only like something, I'm not so sure you work hard. You can drift along then, enjoying the ride."

"I never thought about that," I said, "but it makes sense. Of course, I was never in a war, Dad. I never had to go through anything like you did, being wounded and all. I guess it's affected the way you've thought about things."

"Yes, I'm sure that would be true, Teddy," he said, but he refused to take the bait. Even after all those years, that remained off-limits.

Mom came back with some posies, to remember Daddy by. She put them in a vase and placed it on top of the television set. But instead of wine, she'd brought a bottle of champagne. "How'd you happen to do that?" I asked.

"Well, I was in the liquor store, and it occurred to me that I might never have another reason to celebrate something and drink champagne again before I die, so I might as well do it tonight."

"What are we celebrating?"

"Well, if Phelps wins the butterfly tonight, I think that's a very valid cause for celebration. You know, when I was swimming they hadn't come up with the butterfly yet, so —"

"It didn't exist?"

"Well, yeah, somebody had dreamed it up, but it wasn't an official race until sometime after the war. I always liked to swim lots of ways myself, but when Mr. Foster started coaching me, he told me, 'Trixie, concentrate on the backstroke. That's your best, and you know, as good as you can be, you're getting into this kinda late. You're already sixteen, so let's just master the one thing.'

Look, Eleanor Holm was on the Olympic team when she was fourteen."

"Fourteen?"

"That's right. In '28, in Amsterdam. I had some catchin' up to do."

It had warmed up nicely by now, so Mom and I went back down to the garden, and I turned on the tape recorder and she resumed her story:

The first thing Mr. Foster had me do was get a new bathing suit. I didn't even know you were supposed to call them "swimsuits." On the Shore, we just said bathing suits. But the only one I had besides that faded cream number was light blue with some kind of overlapping red and green circles. Mr. Foster said he couldn't take me seriously in those get-ups, so Mother and I found a proper black one. It was wool, the way they made them in those days, very modest of course — high in the front and, well, high in the back, too, with kind of a little skirt. It was constructed more for modesty than for speed.

But, of course, everything is relative. "Now," Mr. Foster said the first day I showed up in it, "you look like you mean business."

And so I began to work out with him. Like I told you, Teddy, he wasn't a real coach.

He'd been a good swimmer in college and a camp counselor and what-have-you, but, still, he sure knew more about swimming than anybody else around, so I counted myself lucky. He also had an instructional primer, which he consulted. And he gave it to me, so I could take it home and read it myself. I won't go into any of the who-shot-John about what he taught me. Suffice it to say that I followed his advice and what the book said, and I could tell right away that I was getting faster. I could tell that I was pleasing Mr. Foster, too. He was some kind of administrative officer at the college, and working with me gave him an interesting hobby. But he didn't let me get carried away. I think you could say he was circumspect.

Most importantly, though, I kept improving, and one day right before Thanksgiving, he said, "Trixie, does this really matter to you?"

I said, "Yes, sir. I want to be good."

"Well, if you keep working as hard as you have, and you stay dedicated, and you don't get too involved with some boy, I honestly believe you can make the Olympics."

I was flabbergasted. I barely knew what the Olympics were, and I certainly had no idea where they were taking place. I thought maybe they were permanently situated in Los Angeles, like Hollywood was, because I knew that's where they'd been last time, in '32. I knew that much, and that Babe Didrikson had been the big star, which I thought was neat, because she was a woman. I'd never heard of another woman in athletics. So, Mr. Foster was satisfied with my enthusiasm, and he told me there was something called the Eastern Interscholastics in March up in Philadelphia, and we were going to point for that.

I worked so hard at my swimming that I kinda irritated my friends. Every day, after school, I'd have the bus drop me off at my mother's office downtown, and either she or one of the agents would run me over to the pool at the college, or I'd take her car and drive over myself.

Either way, I became something of a lone wolf.

My best friend was Carter Kincaid. She was the most grown-up girl around — hot stuff. Carter had her wits about her, too. Her father had a large farm, and so he was weathering the Depression better than most, and Carter was determined to go to college. She wanted to become a teacher. In those days, there wasn't all that much a girl could do, apart from being a secretary. Well, then there was teaching or nursing. That was about it.

Carter was gonna go to Towson State Teachers College. There was a college on the Shore, Salisbury State, but Carter was like my mother. She wanted to be hell and gone from the farm. In fact, Carter wanted to be hell and gone from the whole Eastern Shore. Towson State was right outside of Baltimore, and so she had her sights set on the bright lights of the big city. Baltimore might as well have been Paris as far as we were concerned.

Our junior year in high school — that's when I started swimming — Carter began going out with Tommy Witherspoon, who was very cute and the captain of the baseball team. Tommy's best friend was Buzzy Moore, and he was cute enough too, and he had a mad crush on me, and Carter and Tommy wanted us to double-date all the time. If it was going to a party or a movie at the New Lyceum Theatre with Buzzy, that was fine, and I'd let him kiss me goodnight, but that was pretty much the extent of it.

"Buzzy'd really like to neck with you, Trixie," Carter told me. This came as no surprise to me whatsoever, but I told Carter it just wasn't on my agenda. We didn't say "agenda" then, but that was the idea. I think then we said: it isn't in the cards.

"Well, look, I'm not planning to settle down with Tommy Witherspoon either, but it is kinda fun, Trixie."

"I know, Car. But I guess I'm just too wrapped up in my swimming."

We were over at her farmhouse, in the parlor, having this conversation one Sunday after church. I remember it very distinctly. I can see the Kincaid's parlor as plain as if it was right here in this garden, Teddy. But I'll spare you the details. It's just that I remember so clearly that Carter leaned forward in her chair, and with this really queer expression on her face, she said, "Trixie Stringfellow, what are you up to?"

Well, I told you she was my best friend in all the world, and so, given that, I just told her flat out, "I wanna swim in the Olympics. That's what I'm up to."

"The Olympics?"

"Yeah."

If I'd said I'd just come down from the moon, she couldn't have been any more surprised. "You mean *the* Olympics? The ones in Berlin?"

*I looked at Mom strangely. She'd said Berlin, like to rhyme with Merlin, King Arthur's magician. She saw the expression on my face and laughed. Then she repeated it the same way:*

Berlin. Exactly. There was this town on the Shore down in Wicomico County, and everybody knew it, because the road went through there on the way to Ocean City, which was the big seashore resort. Everybody on the Shore went to Ocean City sometime, to the boardwalk and the beach, and they'd all go through Berlin on Route 50 over from Salisbury. And it was spelled just like the one in Germany — B-E-R-L-I-N — only it was pronounced the way I just did. Not Ber-LIN. But —

*"BURR-lin," I said.*

That's the way we said it on the Shore. So it threw me off when Carter mentioned Berlin. "Berlin?" I said, thinking she meant the one in Wicomico County. "No, not Berlin, Car. The Olympics. I think Los Angeles."

But, as I said, Carter was smart. She was well read. She didn't know how to pronounce Berlin the way people did off the Shore, but she knew that's where the next Olympics were. "No, Trix, they're in the Berlin in Germany." She said that as if people around the world were regularly mixing up the two Berlins. But at least she had the right info.

"I didn't know that. I just know they're the summer after next, after we graduate."

"And you think you can actually go to Berlin, Germany and be in them?"

"I think I got a chance. The man who kind of coaches me up at the college, Mr. Wallace Foster, he keeps my times, and he says if I keep getting better, maybe I can make it."

"Wow," was all Carter said.

Then I panicked. "But Carter, you gotta swear to me you'll never tell a soul, not even Tommy. Nobody."

Carter nodded and stuck out her hand, and very solemnly, she said, "I promise, Trixie." Then she just shook her head. "I had no idea. When did this come over you?"

"Oh, just when I realized how fast I was."

"A girl doesn't wanna be known as fast," Carter smirked.

"You know."

"Yeah."

"Well, when I found out, I thought that maybe to be real good at something, maybe even the best of all, that that was something not very many people could shoot for, and I'd be lettin' myself down if I didn't at least try. And I'd be lettin' my Daddy down, too, if he knew." And I misted up a little, and Carter came off her chair and put her arms around me and hugged me.

"It's okay, Trix. I didn't realize you were amazing."

So I really cried some, thinking about Daddy, but after that, Teddy, after I'd actually told someone the way I felt, it committed me all the more. All the rest of the fall and the winter, all I thought about was those Eastern Interscholastics.

Mr. Foster took care of all the registration work. I believe he used the college lines to call long distance, because he had to make several calls before they allowed me to swim in the Eastern Interscholastics, and it would've cost him a pretty penny otherwise. You had to go through an operator for long distance then. It was terribly expensive. Just to get a long-distance call was an exciting thing. Now, I know Mr. Foster was an honest man, but let's just say he cut a corner here when it came to getting me into the Eastern Interscholastics. It was all for a good cause, though.

It seemed like all the other swimmers were from private schools, the ones with indoor pools. Also, it was mostly boys. There were only three events for girls: the hundred-yard freestyle, the breaststroke and the backstroke. The boys, now, they even had relays.

At first they weren't even going to let me

in because I didn't have any record to substantiate myself, except for that one meet down in Easton, and nobody had kept the times or anything there. It wasn't sanctioned. That's a big word for people who run these things. Sanctioned. Because they do the sanctioning. It did help that Mr. Foster was calling from a college. That gave him some authenticity, and he laid it on a little thick by saying that I was preparing for Washington College myself, which was ridiculous, because they didn't even have a swimming team — not even for boys. But who knew that up in Philadelphia? It was a harmless enough fib. As I said, Teddy, all for the greater good.

The hardest part was getting the meet director to believe what Mr. Foster told him about my times that he'd clocked. They were too good. The meet director said, "If that time is right, she could be in the nationals." To make sure there'd been no mistake Mr. Foster timed me again that afternoon, and I'd actually improved some, so he reported that I had even faster times. So, the Eastern Interscholastics agreed to let in Trixie Stringfellow from Chestertown High School to compete against all the swells.

The Interscholastics were held at the Penn Athletic Club pool, which was right on Rittenhouse Square, a very fancy address in Philadelphia. They gave Mr. Foster the schedule, which had the girls backstroke going off at two o'clock, so we knew we had plenty of time to drive up. Still, we left at the crack o' dawn to be sure. We went in Mother's car, the maroon Ford we'd gotten from the insurance to replace the car that Daddy was killed in. Carter'd been dying to watch me race, but I let her come along only if she promised — cross her heart and hope to die — not to tell another soul about it. Frankly, Teddy, I was scared to death.

Now, we got there in plenty of time, hardly past noon, but wouldn't you know it, they'd screwed up when they told Mr. Foster that the girls backstroke would be at two o'clock. Instead, it was the breaststroke at two. The backstroke was going at twelve-thirty. And here I was still in my street clothes, and I had to pee terribly, and this man, who was the meet director, came running over and said, "Are you the girl from the Eastern Shore? Where have you been?" And so forth and so on, wailing like a banshee.

Well, Mr. Foster explained about the time confusion, but, of course, the meet director wouldn't believe that he was the one who'd made the mistake, so he didn't have any sympathy at all, and he just told me to go to the locker room and get into my suit if I wanted to swim. Teddy, by the time I got back to the pool there couldn't've been but about two minutes before my race. All the other girls were standing there, cool as cucumbers, and here I was completely frazzled.

*"I hope at least you'd peed."*

Thank you very much for that line of inquiry, but, yes, I did have time to take care of that, and, you know, the Lord works in wondrous ways. Maybe it was good that I didn't have time to sit around and get all nervous. I didn't even realize I'd left my bathing cap in the locker room. It was all happening so fast. I just jumped into the pool and took my position. There were six of us. The other five girls all seemed to know each other. And the gun went off, and I just pushed off and won easily. Piece o' cake.

*"You whipped their asses."*

Yes, I did — but I think we've beat that dead horse enough. In fact, there was a great flurry of excitement because my time was so fast. You've got to understand, the pool in Chestertown was just a regular old pool. This one at Rittenhouse Square was built more for competition. It created less waves and all that. So I swam faster than ever before.

*"What was your time, Mom?"*

Oh, I don't remember exactly, and it gets all confusing because we swam most of our races in yards, and already back then, the races in the whole rest of the world were meters. The Olympics was all meters — and, of course, like most Americans I didn't know a meter from Adam. Be that as it may, I think I did the hundred yards in about a minute and thirteen, maybe twelve-five. That was lickety-split for that crowd.

So Mom and Carter and Mr. Foster were all congratulating me when the meet director came bustling over and pulled me away for the victory ceremony. It wasn't much, just me and the girls who finished second and third stood there by the diving board. They both had their school sweatshirts on. I just had a towel around my shoulders. And then, suddenly, out of the blue, this beautiful little young woman materialized with the ribbons. It was just ribbons, no cups or anything. But I was thrilled. And she gave out the yellow and the red, and then she handed me the blue ribbon, and I thanked her.

I was already grown to my full height, Teddy. I think I've shrunk a little now, but I was about five-six, and I was taller than she was, even though she had heels on. She was

84

really snappy, though, very fashionable, in a tailored worsted suit, and just absolutely gorgeous. I could see Carter even stopped looking at all the cute boys in their bathing suits to check her out. We didn't encounter that sort of style down on the Shore. I shook her hand, and I thought that was that, till she pulled me aside and said, "How long you been swimming, honey?"

"Oh, I don't know, I guess all my life."

She shook her head a little. She had a sort of a bob cut, very stylish then. Brown hair. "No, I mean how long competitively?"

"Oh," I said, thinking back to Easton. "Since Labor Day."

"You mean this last Labor Day? That's all?"

"Yeah. I just took it up."

"I was wondering why I never heard of you." Then after she lit a cigarette with a long holder, like the one President Roosevelt used, she asked me, "How old are you?"

"Sixteen. Well, I turn seventeen next month."

"You started swimming late."

"I don't know," I said. "I don't know when you're supposed to start."

It was probably a pretty stupid thing to say. I was so naïve. The woman laughed, but it was a nice laugh, not mocking. "Well, most of us start younger. I won my first Nationals when I was thirteen."

That rocked me. "No foolin'?"

"No foolin'." She paused then. "You don't know who I am, do you?"

"I'm sorry. Am I supposed to?"

"Well, they introduced me earlier, but I guess you weren't here."

"We just got up from the Eastern Shore."

"Oh," she said. It was apparent she didn't have the foggiest where the Eastern Shore was, but she let that go and just stuck out her hand. "Well, I'm Eleanor Holm . . . Jarrett."

"Hi. I'm Trixie Stringfellow."

"Well, Trixie, I'm the world record holder in the hundred-meter backstroke. I won the Olympics in '32."

"You did? What are you doing here?"

That was another stupid question, but she only laughed nicely again. "Well, when you get to be a champion — and I can tell already, honey, you're gonna be one — they expect you to do things."

"Who does?"

"The stuffed shirts who run swimming. I call 'em 'the blazers,' 'cause they always wear blazers with fancy shields on their pockets. And you have to play ball with them, or there's hell to pay. Of course, we're amateurs, we're just doing this for the love of it, so we don't get paid, but they still expect you to do things . . . for the good of the sport."

"Oh."

"So I happen to be over in Atlantic City for a week. My husband is Art Jarrett. He's a singer with the Ted Weems orchestra. You know him?"

"The band with the fellow who whistles?" She nodded. That was Ted Weems' signature: he had a guy who just whistled along with his band. It was a weird specialty, but it worked for Ted Weems, and he milked it to death. That guy could whistle just about anything. "I've heard him on the radio, on the Jack Benny Canada Dry Program."

"Well, my husband's not the whistler, but he's the vocalist in Ted's band, and so you've probably heard him. He's a swell singer." Actually, Teddy, it was just the whistler I remembered, not any singer, but I certainly didn't clarify that. However, the lady was delighted that she thought I remembered her husband, the vocalist. "We're playing at the Claridge Hotel for a week. I sing a little myself, too. So when the blazers asked me to come over here and hand out ribbons, I agreed to do it."

"Oh, I see."

"Yeah, you gotta stay on the good side of the blazers."

"I'll remember that, Mrs. —"

"Mrs. Jarrett. But I'm just Eleanor, okay? Because if you get a little bit better, you're gonna be swimmin' against me before too long."

"Really? You think so?"

"Honey, you're that good. And you'd be even faster if you'd wear a bathing cap."

"Oh, I know. I was so rushed when I got here I completely forgot about it and left it in the locker room."

"Well, don't do that again. That hair of your's probably cost you another half-second, maybe more. Course, it didn't make any difference against these gals, but when you start swimming nationals, that's the difference between winning and losing."

"I won't forget again. I promise."

"Okay, honey." She started to step away, and then she turned back. "Now, I'm sorry, what's your name again?"

"Trixie Stringfellow."

She pondered that. I thought she was confused about my last name, because Stringfellow is an unusual name. You can just imagine some of the variations the wiseacres in school made up, including some off-color versions. But Stringfellow wasn't the issue. Instead, she said: "That . . . Trixie. Is that your real moniker?"

"My what?"

"Your moniker? Your real name?"

"Oh no, my real name is Sydney. I'm just called Trixie. When I —" I was going to explain about how my late father gave me the name, but she interrupted.

"Sydney? Where I come from that's a boy's name."

"Well, not where I come from. And it's spelled with a *y* which is different from the boy Sidney."

Eleanor considered that for a moment, and then she said, "Well, a little piece of advice. Ditch the Trixie."

"What?"

"Honey, if you're gonna be a champion, if you're gonna swim in the Olympics, you don't wanna be Trixie. Names like Toots, Babe, Chickie . . . Trixie. No offense, but you don't want names like that when you're standing up there and they're playing 'The Star-Spangled Banner' for you. You want a grown-up name. Not something some cheap dame gets called."

"I never thought of that."

"Yeah, well, if I were you, even if most people think it's a boy's name, from now on, I'd be Sydney."

And you know what, Teddy? I was, from that moment on.

Well, Michael Phelps did indeed win again that night, and so Mom asked me to pop the cork on the champagne, and we raised our glasses high to him. "You mark my words," she told me, "that boy will do even better in 2008."

"That's a long way off," I said.

"Yeah, but he's young, and you can tell how much he wants to win. That's the way I was. And he can make the big bucks, too. It was all amateur back then. The rules were insane. The next time I saw Eleanor Holm, she told me how she could've made a whole lot of money in Hollywood swimming in movies, but if she swam in movies, the American Olympic Committee would declare her ineligible. Of course, that's what everybody wanted to see, though. Everybody wanted to see Eleanor swim — especially since she couldn't act her way out of a paper bag. But she was pretty as a picture.

They were always posing her in these sarong-type things and putting her next to giant clamshells to show that it was, you know, marine."

"Prettier even than you, Mom?"

"Oh yeah. No contest."

"Now, Mom. Is that modesty compelling you to say that?"

"Oh no, I could be as vain as the next one, sure, but Eleanor was a real doll. Ziegfield wanted her to be one of his girls on stage. Now, Teddy, all right, I could turn some heads when I had it all going for me, but nobody was giving me any movie contracts to sign. I'll tell you, though, we weren't a bad-looking group, us swimmers. It wasn't very fashionable then to be a girl athlete. They said it gave you all the wrong muscles, and a lot of people assumed we had to be dykes." Mom paused a moment. "I know that's out of line to say now, but I'm just quoting what people said then, you understand. They said 'dykes.' So I'm just quoting."

I told Mom I understood where she was coming from.

"They also called us 'naiads?' "

"What?"

"No, I didn't imagine you ever heard that. It's spelled n-a-i-a-d-s."

"Naiads?"

"Right. First time I saw it in the newspaper, I didn't know what to think, and I didn't want to ask anybody for fear of looking like a naïve little girl from the Eastern Shore —"

"Which you were."

"Which I was. But I suspect there were a lot of sophisticates from Park Avenue who didn't know what in the Sam Hill naiads were either."

"Well, I give up."

"I looked it up in the dictionary. It turns out to be some kinda water nymph in Greek mythology. I've sorta forgotten now, but I think we naiads were supposed to guard the brooks and rivers and such from ogres and trolls and what-have-you. There, I'd been a naiad all my life swimming in the Chester River, and I never even knew it. I think the newspapers thought it was some kind of compliment. They always called the men swimmers 'mermen.' "

"But they didn't call you 'mermaids'?"

"No, I think they thought that would be an insult to mermaids naming a bunch of dykes after them. So we were naiads."

"But the naiads weren't insulted?"

"Evidently not. But I'll tell you, Teddy, it was a bad rap they gave us. There was this prejudice that all girl athletes had to be ugly. And that was nonsense. Lemme tell you, Eleanor wasn't the only looker in our crowd."

"Would you get the silver medal?"

"For looks?" She rubbed her chin very thoughtfully. "No, but maybe the bronze. We had a diver named Dorothy Poynton. She'd won a gold at Los Angeles, and after Berlin — she got the gold there, too — Dorothy figured to make hay while the sun shone. She had all sorts of contracts signed to dive professionally. Dorothy didn't even want to be photographed in our team suits. After she'd finish diving, she'd rush back and change fast into a real snappy number, with this kind of bandanna she wore, and then she'd come out and pose for the photography boys. And before she dived, she'd sashay all around the pool in gold lamé high heels. She was very sexy."

"But you'd get the bronze for looks?"

Mom simply smiled, and let it go. In fact, I think she regretted that she'd so quickly given the silver to Dorothy Poynton. So she raised her champagne glass again. "And to your father, too, Teddy. Seven years. Seven years gone. My Jimmy."

I raised mine too. "Why'd he never talk about Guadalcanal, Mom? Was it that bad?"

"It must've been."

"He talked to you about it when he came back, didn't he?"

"Not, uh, extensively. There were a lot of them that way, the boys in the war. You get shot, I don't suppose you want to dwell on it. Who in their right mind wants to talk about getting shot . . . or shooting someone else, for that matter? Could you shoot someone, Teddy?"

"Well, maybe if I was a soldier. You know, in a war."

"Yeah, maybe," she said. "But maybe not everybody could."

"I guess I don't know, Mom."

"No. No one probably knows till they're confronted with the situation." She stopped abruptly then. "But that's enough of that. The point is, your father got his honorable discharge, and then he made it plain to me that that chapter was concluded, and it was not something he wished to discuss, and I was happy to comply with his wishes. Why not? Your father and I always had plenty of happy things to talk about."

"I know that. But after all those years . . ."

"Like someone said, Teddy: War is hell. War must be hell. Jimmy wanted to let it go." She looked back at the television, even if it was a commercial. It was apparent, as always, that my mother didn't want to talk about my father's experience in the war any more than he had. But then, after she'd given it some thought, she turned back to me and said, "Well, there's a bunch of that in the story. I told you: it's the last story about the war."

"The story in the purple acetate folder?"

"Yeah. That'll tell you more than enough. So be patient."

"Okay." I shrugged, and raised my glass again. "Well, to you both. I couldn't have asked for a better mother and father." I went over and kissed her.

"Thank you for that, Teddy," she said, but I could tell that she'd grown tired. Sometimes now she wore down more quickly, and sure enough, before long, she started to nod off, even before all the swimming races were over. There was a women's relay she'd been really looking forward to, but she couldn't last, so I helped her to bed, and when she was settled, I brought in the flowers that she'd bought in honor of Daddy and put the vase by her bed. I took one, though, a little yellow one — like Daddy, I've never been very learned about "flora" either — and stuck it in one of my shirt buttonholes. She liked that. She touched it. "Bachelor button," she said.

"No, Daddy button," I said, and kissed her good-night.

As I was leaving, she called me back. "Teddy." I turned around. "Would you be upset if an old lady threw humility to the winds?" I shook my head. "Well, maybe I was the silver medal. Dorothy Poynton was very pretty indeed, but she had all those fancy get-ups. I was still just a kid swimming in a plain black suit. But it showed me to good advantage, I think. And I always made it a habit to rip my bathing cap off as soon as the race was over, so my hair could tumble down."

I said, "You always had pretty hair, Mother."

"You don't have to gild the lily. I knew how pretty I was. But I'm thinking now of a time in Germany when I got all gussied up in a beautiful gown, and when I saw myself in that, I suppose that made me think I had the edge on Dorothy."

"I'm sure you turned a lot of heads."

Mom smiled deliciously. "One in particular," she said. "And we'll get to him soon enough."

Unfortunately, Mom woke up the next morning feeling poorly. She had, as she simply called them, "her days." I wanted to drive her over to the doctor's, but she absolutely forbade me to even call him. "Teddy," she said, "some mornings I just gotta roll with the punches. You wait, by the afternoon, I'll be fine and dandy — relatively, of course." Sure enough, she took some kind of pain pill, lay down awhile and by the afternoon she emerged with a smile on her face. "Get that machine goin' mister," she told me.

"You sure you want to, Mom?"

"Well, Teddy, either I sit here and tell you more of my story or I'm goin' over to the Chippendales' matinee."

"You're what?"

"It's a joke, Teddy. It's a joke. Come on, let's go."

So I put a new tape in and she immedi-

ately took up her story again.

In those days, you didn't have a lot of national meets. The best swimmers couldn't just take off and fly around the country, willy-nilly, like pashas. You stuck pretty much to your territory, your region. Besides, we had to be amateurs, and it was still the heart of the Depression, so nobody much had the money to travel hither and yon just to swim. But after I did so well at the Inter-scholastics, Mr. Foster realized that I needed some good competition. I mean, I couldn't improve if I just practiced all the time, even though basically that's all I did do, because there wasn't a whole lot to do on the Eastern Shore in 1935 except possibly neck with Buzzy Moore, which I didn't much want to do except just enough for him to take me to the movies and what-not. And eventually, in fact, when Buzzy realized that the candy store really was closed, that was the end of that. So I just swam more and more, especially when the weather got warmer and I could go back to swimming off the dock at our house in the Chester River, like always.

Sometimes Carter would come over and keep me company, swimming. We'd race some. I'd give her a head start and she'd swim freestyle, and I'd try to catch up with her swimming backstroke. But it was just fun. The best part, then, was we'd lie there on the grass and talk about what we were gonna do with ourselves. Nobody — especially kids like us — envisioned a war. Who did in the United States? Mostly, we just imagined the Depression stretching out forever and ever, all our days. After all, it'd been everybody's way of life for years, and it was hard to picture the world without it.

Our senior year was coming up, so even if I hadn't gotten myself all worked up about swimming, everything was necessarily gonna change in just another year. It was time to start thinkin' ahead. Carter knew she was going to Towson State Teachers and find a husband in Baltimore and make a life there. "Does Tommy know this?" I asked her.

"Tommy doesn't think much beyond next week," Carter replied. She was just gonna cross that bridge when she came to it.

So we would talk like that, and this one time — it must've been late in June after school let out, I suddenly said, "You know, Car, I'm gonna have to leave, too."

"Leave here? Leave the Shore?" I nodded. "Gee, I didn't know that, Trix. That's great. I just figured you'd stay and help your mother at the office."

"Well, I figured that, too, but if I'm gonna be a swimmer, I have to go somewhere where there's a swimming club."

You see, Teddy, if I'd been a boy, I could've gotten some kind of scholarship to swim on a college team somewhere, working at a job on the side. But there wasn't anything like that for girls. There weren't even any girls' teams in college. Girls swam in clubs. By now, I had found this out, because I'd been to one seniors meet. Understand, "seniors" doesn't mean what it does now — that god-awful "senior citizens." It was just the difference between juniors and seniors. It was like the major leagues, seniors.

The seniors meet Mr. Foster had taken me to was down in Washington. It was sanctioned. It was run by the Shoreham Hotel Athletic Club, which some of the best girls belonged to. And understand this, too, Teddy. When I say girls, I mean women and girls. They just called us all girls then. Like they called us naiads. But then, we called ourselves girls. I don't remember anybody much being a "woman" then, Teddy. Unless maybe if you were a cleaning woman. You were a girl unless you were a young lady, until you became a lady. And then you finally became an old lady.

*That lexicon being squared away, I asked*

101

*Mother how she did in the meet down in Washington.*

Well, as a matter of fact, I did very well. I was moving up in competition here, Teddy. I finished second in both the one-hundred-yard and the two-hundred-yard backstrokes, which amazed everybody because nobody'd ever heard of me. Here I was swimming in the seniors, and I wasn't even in a club. I swam what was called "unattached." Almost everybody else was associated with some club, but I was just "Sydney Stringfellow, unattached," and there was only this one girl who beat me in both races — and barely that — but she was really grown-up, maybe twenty-five or something, so, as Mr. Foster told me, at that advanced age, she wasn't gonna get any better. In fact, driving back home, when we were on the ferry goin' across the Bay and we went to the lunch counter, he told me that someone from the Shoreham Hotel AC had asked him if maybe I wanted to come down and swim for them when I finished high school.

He told me, "Trixie — I mean, Sydney." (See, when he had met me, I was Trixie, but then I asked him to change that after Eleanor Holm advised me against being Trixie, so he would forget sometimes.) "Sydney, you might make it to the Olympics in

Berlin. You've got a chance, I would imagine, if you keep improving, but it's gonna be tough. Nobody's gonna beat Eleanor, and there's two or three other gals who're pretty good. You couldn't beat 'em now, but maybe by next year. I will say you should be at the height of your powers for the next Olympics, in '40. But if you're gonna do that, you have to go somewhere and swim with a club. I just can't help you that much anymore."

So that's why I told Carter I had to leave Chestertown and go out into the big, wide world. Her first reaction was, "That's great, Trix, you can join a club in Baltimore, and we can get a place together."

I said, "I don't think so."

"Why not?" At that point Carter started to take her straps down, and she said, "Come on, let's get the sun on our backs like the boys do." And just like that, she yanked the top of her suit all the way down to her waist. It was absolutely scandalous, even if it was just the two of us girls alone in my yard. But, as I told you, Carter was always out in front of the rest of us. Today, I suppose, you'd say that she'd be ahead of the curve. Anyway, she just pulled her suit down and lay on the towel.

*"Did you do it too, Mom?"*

Well, for a moment I worried that Gentry Trappe might be around, but he certainly wasn't the sort to be a peeping Tom, and it was an absolutely gorgeous day, so yes indeed, I pulled my top down, too, and laid on my stomach with the sun on my back. Teddy, I felt absolutely debauched, but the funny thing was, I think it made it easier for me to think about goin' out in the world. I mean, if a girl could take her top down outdoors, even if no one was around, it made you feel grown-up.

So I explained to Carter, "Well, there isn't any swimming club I know of in Baltimore."

"So where else?"

"Well, there's a lotta choices. There's that Shoreham Hotel AC in Washington and the Carnegie Library Club in Pittsburgh and the Broadwood AC in Philadelphia and . . ." I know I paused here, Teddy, because even as absolutely wicked and grown-up as I was with my top down, it was still hard to imagine it: ". . . the Women's Swimming Association of New York."

It struck Carter the same way. "New York!" she said.

"That's what I want: the Women's Swimming Association." I got so excited I raised up on my elbow without even thinking, exposing my one side there for all the world to see — even if Carter was all the world that was looking at me at that particular moment — and I told her how Eleanor Holm herself belonged to the Women's Swimming Association, and that next month when Mother and Mr. Foster were takin' me up to Jones Beach for the national championships, I was gonna ratchet up my nerve and ask Eleanor if I could get into the Women's Swimming Association.

"You think you can?" Carter asked me.

I got hold of my enthusiasm sufficient to restore decorum and laid back down on my stomach. "I'll be honest with you, Car. I don't see why not. I'm startin' to understand how good I really am. I've only been serious about my swimming for a little while, but that time I made in the hundred down in Washington a couple months ago — Mr. Foster told me it was the ninth best in the country. In the country, Car!"

"The whole country?"

"That's what I'm saying: the whole country, the United States, and I'm already ninth best. And if I just get a little better in the next year, if I'm third best, I can go to Berlin, to the Olympics, next summer, and even if I don't make it, if I get to join the Women's Swimming Association, I know I could be the very best by the '40 Olympics.

They give out gold medals if you win the Olympics, Car. I could get a gold medal in Tokyo."

"What's in Tokyo?"

"That's what I'm tellin' you. The 1940 Olympics are in Tokyo, Japan."

"Wow," Carter said. She processed all that. "So, let me get this straight. If you join this Women's Swimming Association, you'd live in New York?"

"Yeah. I would. I'd get a job."

"In Jones Beach?"

"No, that's just where the nationals are. The Women's Swimming Association is right in the city. They have their own pool and everything. You could come up from Baltimore on the Royal Blue" — that was the fancy B & O train then — "and stay with me in my apartment. I'd have my own apartment."

"Wow," Carter said again. "But you gotta look out for the men in New York, Trix. Men in New York can't be trusted."

"Come on, Car. Not all of them. There's some good men everywhere, I'm sure."

Carter agreed I had a point. Possibly. She was silent for a long time, then. This was a lot for her to take in from her best friend, especially when she thought she was the one who was so daring, going off to big, cosmopolitan Baltimore. But after a bit, all of a sudden, do you know what she did? She sat up and said, "Come on, Trix, we're halfway. Let's go skinny dippin'."

If Carter Kincaid had suggested we rob the Queen Anne's County Savings and Trust, I couldn't've been any more shocked. "But, Car, it's the middle of the day."

"There's nobody around."

"Maybe Gentry Trappe."

"Well, then it'd just be his lucky day," Carter said. Teddy, she'd made up her mind. She was already pullin' her suit down over her thighs. I could see, there was no stoppin' her. And you know what?

*No, I don't, Mother.*

I went right along. In another minute, I was naked as a jay bird, too, and here we were, in broad daylight, runnin' down to the river and out on the dock and divin' in. And the water never felt better, Teddy. You've been skinny dippin', haven't you?

*A time or two, yeah.*

Doesn't it feel just wonderful?

*I agreed that it did.*

Yeah, we splashed around and swam underwater some, just like little girls, and I remember, I came up and I was treadin' water, and I said, "You know what the Women's Swimming Association bathing

107

suits look like?" It was sort of strange to think about a bathing suit when I didn't have one on, but it came to me. Carter, of course, didn't know. "There's like a shield here," I said, drawing it with one hand, right in the middle of my chest. "And right in here" — I pointed to my cleavage — "there's this big S."

"S?" Carter asked.

"Yeah, S for swimming. And there's a smaller capital W on this side and an A on the other. I could just see myself in that." There I was without a stitch on, and I could visualize myself in the best swimming club in America, with the likes of Eleanor Holm herself, wearin' that suit. It's funny, Teddy, this was before Superman —

"With the big S on his chest."

Exactly. But years later, whenever I'd see him taking his shirt off in the phone booth, I'd think back to the dreams of me wearing my own big S on my chest. I don't know, maybe whoever it was that dreamed up Superman had seen Eleanor Holm with her S, and that was his inspiration. Any man who saw Eleanor in a bathing suit, even just a picture, was gonna stop and dwell on her. I can assure you of that. I wouldn't be the least bit surprised if Superman got that S on his chest that way. Because of a girl.

And so we swam around a little longer, the sky so perfectly blue, the sun beating down on us, and it was as if I could see the future, all laid out for me. It was like Daddy had never been killed and there was no Depression, and I was gonna make the U.S. team and go to Berlin, and then I was gonna come back and leave the Shore and move to New York and join the Women's Swimming Association, with the big S right there on my chest, and Eleanor Holm would be gone by then, off making movies or singin' and whistlin' along with Ted Weems, and I'd be the star of the backstroke, gettin' ready to win a gold medal in 1940.

It was absolutely amazing how clearly I could see all the tomorrows stretched out before me, Teddy. In fact, I don't think I ever had another day like that — one when I'd ever been so sure of things ahead of me — until maybe right now when I know I'm going to die pretty soon, and there's not a thing I can do about it.

We watched the swimming from Athens again that night. It was an especially important evening for Mom because the finals of her old event, the hundred-meter backstroke, were on. With grand expectation, we settled in before the TV set. "You know what they called us then?" she asked me.

"Naiads."

"Well, that's right. I told you that. But that was all the girls who swam. I meant what they called the backstrokers?"

"Just the girls?"

"No, the girls and the men."

"Mother, you know I haven't got the foggiest idea in the world."

"They called us 'dorsal swimmers.' "

"Excuse me?"

"Dorsal swimmers. Dorsal means the back or something like that."

"There's dorsal fins on, like, sharks, aren't there?"

Mom nodded. "I don't know whether it was the fin or just the back in general, but they called us dorsal swimmers. It was pretty dopey." I nodded in agreement. "We never called ourselves dorsal swimmers, that's for sure."

It was, however, evidently going to be awhile before the swimmers came on. Instead, NBC was showing the girls' gymnastics. The floor exercises were on, and it was terribly boring. At Mom's request, I muted the sound. "They're so little they're creepy," she said, scrunching up her nose. "None of 'em have any boobs or heinies."

"I haven't heard anybody say 'heinie' for a long time," I noted.

"Well, it's better than 'butts,' don't you think? You say heinie, you know exactly what you're talking about. Butts are cigarette butts and gun butts and butt in and butt out and all that. Heinie's a good old word that isn't ambiguous. Anyway, those little gymnasts don't have any, whatever you want to call 'em."

I let that pass. It was not a subject that had previously engaged me. Anyway, suddenly Mom clapped her hands and cried out, "Let's get the damn swimmers out here. They look like real women." Natalie Coughlin was the favorite in mother's race, and since she was an American, Mom was particularly interested. "That Natalie, she could even give Eleanor a run for her money in the looks department."

"She is good looking," I said, agreeably, remembering her from the trial heats.

"Get outta town, Teddy. Are you losin' it in your old age? She's a real fox, that girl."

"Nice heinie," I said.

"There you go," Mom said. "You're still my red-blooded American boy."

"Okay, so to really get my blood racing, tell me more about Eleanor," I said. It was like she was just waiting for her cue.

Well, Teddy, never mind how pretty she was, she was also the nicest thing to me before my first big race. Did I tell you about Chicago?

*I shook my head.*

Well, if I was gonna try for the Olympics I needed one major meet under my belt, so to speak. There were really only two big ones each year during the Depression. There was the national indoors and the national outdoors, and that was about it. For us girls, anyway. The outdoors were usually at Jones Beach, and the indoors were always in Chicago in April, and in '36 I had to go out there. I simply had to. I couldn't start off and try to compete nationally the first time in the Olympic Trials themselves.

But, of course, Chicago was a long way from the Shore, and it cost a lot of money. Mr. Foster was wonderful. He couldn't afford to go himself, but he had an old friend who lived in Chicago, and they agreed to put me up, so all we needed was my train fare. And I remember: I had $18 spending money.

*"That's all?"*

Broke the piggy bank. My mother gave me ten bucks and some sandwiches and a thermos, and Mr. Foster, bless his heart, gave me a five-dollar bill — a Lincoln, we called it. Of course, in the Depression, money went a long ways. You remember that song, "Brother, Can You Spare A Dime?" Can you imagine that, anyone panhandling for a thin dime?

I was scared to death. I mean, for me, Chicago was like going to, uh — she glanced at the screen — Athens. Why, I'd never even been on a train before except to go up to Wilmington.

*"They had a train station in Chestertown?"*

Sure, most every town did then. It's like every town worth its salt nowadays has a mall. Mr. Culver was the station master, and twice a day there was a train to Wilmington. We called it "The Bullet." Facetiously, you understand. So off I started for Chicago on the Bullet.

Mr. Foster's friends in Chicago — they were named Simms — they met me at the station, and the next day Mrs. Simms took me down to where we swam. It was downtown, smack on Lake Shore Drive. In fact, it was called the Lake Shore Athletic Club. It was this absolutely gorgeous building, in Beaux Arts style. I mean, Teddy, I was used to swimming pools. This was like swimming in the Taj Mahal. My gracious, you came into the lobby, and there was this huge foyer. The ceiling must've been forty feet high, with marble steps. I could imagine Bojangles himself dancing down those steps. When I got back to Chestertown, I think I bored poor Carter to tears just describing the lobby. And the pool — Teddy, the pool was on an upstairs floor. In all my life, I'd never heard of that — an upstairs pool.

Mrs. Simms appreciated how nervous I was, so that first day, when we could practice in the pool, she not only rode with me on the streetcar to the club, but she stayed with me till I got registered. And she promised to wait down in the lobby till I was finished practicing, too.

But after I left Mrs. Simms, there I was,

Teddy, all alone in this beautiful locker room, and I didn't know a soul. And these were the crème de la crème of the girl swimmers in America. I told you I'd been to the Shoreham Hotel AC in Washington and the Broadwood AC in Philadelphia, but the girls swimming there were mostly, you know, just local yokels. These were the indoor nationals.

Well, I found a place over in the corner, and I think I was blushing all over as soon as I even contemplated taking my clothes off. And this, even though I was turned away from everybody. Probably none of them so much as noticed I was there, either. I mean, of course, it was just girls, but girls aren't like boys. I know the way you all are, a bunch of exhibitionists, all runnin' around with your whatzits flyin' in the breeze, thinkin' you're Greek gods, snappin' towels at each other's behinds and so forth, but girls . . . well, we value a certain amount of privacy. We don't parade around, showing off our private parts to one another. Now, maybe they do now. Things have changed so much. Girls have become so much more assertive nowadays, so I couldn't attest to what it's like in a girls' locker room today, but in my time, it was a place where modesty prevailed.

So, you've got to picture this. I am in the corner, and after I took off my shoes, I took my bathing suit out of my little traveling bag and laid it at my feet.

*"Why would you do that?"*

I was preparing for a record-setting quick dress.

*"Okay, I'm catching on. You're shy."*

Shy is not a word that would have done me justice.

So, with my bathing suit perfectly positioned on the floor, I then discreetly sat down on the bench and reached up under my dress — because no respectable girl would be seen in a city such as Chicago in anything but a dress — to undo my stockings —

*"Stockings?"*

Of course I had stockings on, Teddy. I doubt very seriously whether Mrs. Simms would've even agreed to take a girl out in downtown Chicago if she didn't have stockings on. Of course I had stockings on. This is 1936, Teddy. For goodness' sake.

*"Mother, remember, I wasn't born yet in 1936."*

Well, yes, you do have that as an excuse. But anyway, after I rolled down my stockings, I unbuttoned my dress, and when I was absolutely ready, I stood up and turned away, like a child who was being disciplined in the classroom, and I pulled off my dress, and without looking, laid it back on the bench behind me, and then, just as quickly, pulled off my slip. Yes, a proper young lady in downtown Chicago on Lake Shore Drive in 1936 would have most certainly had a slip on. And that accomplished, I reached round to unhook my bra. Teddy, now we are approaching the moment of truth. I hang onto my bra — although we still called them brassieres at this point in time — I cling to my brassiere, then drop it and grab for my panties. I am prepared to take off my panties — we referred to them as un-mentionables then.

*"Unmentionables? I won't ask."*

Thank you. I am prepared to strip myself of my panties, then to quickly scoop up my bathing suit, yank it on, stuff my bazooms in and then turn around as casually as if I was standing on the street corner waiting for the red light to change. And so it was, that at that exact instant, at that one mo-ment when my unmentionables no longer covered this earthly vessel of mine, in that split second before I could toss them aside and pull up my bathing suit, in that one unguarded moment, I felt a hand upon my back and heard the words clear and loud enough for the whole locker room to hear: "Hey, Sydney, how are ya?"

It was, of course, Eleanor Holm. Well now, naturally, I should've immediately just reached down and pulled up my bathing suit, but I was so discombobulated, I felt like I had to be polite and say hello, which I did, and that would have been mortifying enough, but then Eleanor took it upon herself to introduce me to everyone.

There I am, standing there in my birthday suit, blushing all over — I mean all over, I'm sure — and Eleanor is saying, "Girls, say hello to Sydney —" Only then she couldn't remember my last name, so it prolonged the agony.

*"But, Mother, why didn't you just reach down and pull up your suit?"*

I really don't know, Teddy. I just froze. Eleanor didn't seem to be fazed by me being naked, so I figured I better just go along. I don't know, maybe I thought it was sophisticated. After all, Eleanor was the very height of sophistication. So I just stood there —

*"What did you do with your hands?"*

You know, it's odd that would occur to you, Teddy, but I'll admit: it's a good question. I really don't remember, though. Maybe I used them to cover something up, like Botticelli had Venus do. I just don't remember.

*"Maybe you fiddled with your hair. Women are always concerned about their hair."*

Well, yes, that's fair. We are hair-conscious, but that's when we have our clothes on. At this particular juncture, though, my hair was not the paramount body part on my mind. I just said, "Stringfellow."

"Yeah," Eleanor said. "This is Sydney Stringfellow." Then she swept her arm around, pointing out the other girls. "This is Mary Lou Petty and this is Dorothy Forbes and this is Katherine Rawls and this is Margie Smith . . ." and so forth. It seemed to take an eternity. It was like those introductions at the head table of some luncheon that can go on forever, although, to this point in my life, Teddy, I don't believe I had ever attended any function fancy enough to have a head table.

But I finally got my wits about me and began to pull up my suit. I was still so rattled, though, it's amazing I got my legs in the right holes. And, anyway, Eleanor made it worse, because she lit a cigarette then and started going on about how great I was, how I was going to replace her as the queen of the backstroke — she actually said that: "the Queen of the Backstroke" — when she left the amateurs after Berlin. And I know a couple of these girls, like Dorothy and Margie, are also backstrokers —

*"Dorsal swimmers."*

Exactly. You're paying good attention, Teddy. I knew some of them were my putative rivals, and you can just imagine how that made them feel having Eleanor introduce this kid they never heard of before as her annointed successor — her heiress, for God's sake! — especially with me standing there, buck naked, like an idiot. I mean, in all my life, I've never been so mortified.

But, I'll say this for the girls. They were very nice to me. Probably from sympathy. Mary Lou Petty even went out of her way to take me out to the pool. She was a freestyler, so it probably didn't offend her when Eleanor announced that I was the budding queen of the backstroke. So we all practiced, and I even grew a smidgen more comfortable. Then, after practice, Eleanor asked me where I was staying, and I told her, and also how Mrs. Simms was waitin' in the lobby, so she came down with me and introduced herself.

"What are you and Mr. Simms and Sydney doing for entertainment tonight?" she asked. I think Eleanor assumed that everybody did something every night in the entertainment line.

Mrs. Simms replied that there was actually no organized entertainment on their plate this particular evening, that we would probably just listen to the radio. She said, "Sydney needs her beauty sleep if she's gonna be ready to swim her best."

And Eleanor replied, "Oh, we don't have the meet for another two days, so Sydney oughta paint the town red tonight. I want you all to come to the Palmer House and be my guest for the show at the Empire Room."

Now, Teddy, let me back up a minute. Here is what had transpired since I'd first met Eleanor in Philadelphia, when her husband was performing with Ted Weems in Atlantic City. Her husband — do you remember his name?

*"Well," I said, "it was Jarrett. Because Eleanor was Mrs. Jarrett."*

That's correct. And his first name was Art. He was a vocalist.

*"I thought he was a whistler."*

No, no, no. That was another fellow, the whistler. Art Jarrett was just a vocalist. We didn't call them crooners yet. I forget when vocalists became crooners. But, in any event, by now Art Jarrett had left Ted Weems to form his own band. This was, by the way, the best thing that ever happened to Ted Weems, because Art Jarrett was no better than your garden variety, run-of-the-mill vocalist, and to replace him, Mr. Weems hired an unknown — an absolute nobody — named Perry Como, and the rest is history. But that's another story and doesn't involve me.

What did involve me was that now that Art Jarrett had his own band, he could have Eleanor sing regularly, too. Probably, in fact, she was an even bigger name than he was. And so on this occasion, the Art Jarrett Orchestra was performing at the Empire Room of the Palmer House, which was generally thought of as the grand dame of Chicago hotels, right off the Miracle Mile itself, and here Eleanor was inviting us to be her guest.

Well, Mrs. Simms hemmed and hawed, said she and Mr. Simms couldn't possibly, etc., etc. But Eleanor said she wouldn't take no for an answer, which was what Mrs.

Simms was hoping to hear her say, so Mrs. Simms pretended to say yes reluctantly, and we all put on our Sunday best and after dinner, off the three of us hied to the Palmer House. There was a table reserved for us right up front. Of course, Teddy, while I didn't know the first thing about the Simmses, I could tell this was not their usual night out. I think an evening at the neighborhood bowling alley would've been more their idea of an occasion. Let's just say that they were overwhelmed, but trying not to show it.

*"Sort of like you standing there in the buff amid all the other girls in the locker room."*

Yes, Teddy, that would be an apt analogy. Very good. And hardly had we taken our seats when the waiter appears with a bottle of champagne, compliments of Mrs. Jarrett. The waiter pours me a glass, too. Honestly, I don't know if there was a drinking age in Chicago, but if you recall, Chicago was a pretty lawless town back then — home of the St. Valentine's Day Massacre, for example — and so I think it's fair to say that none of the gendarmes in the Windy City were particularly concerned with teen-age girls drinking champagne in the Empire Room. So Mr. Simms said, "Go on, Sydney, you may take a sip."

Well, of course, I'd heard plenty about champagne, but it was not the beverage of choice on the Shore, so I was surprised when it burned so. Champagne is very sharp, you know. You'd think something with bubbles would be sweet, but, of course, that isn't the case at all. So I believe I made a face, but luckily, the lights dimmed and here came Art Jarrett and his orchestra, taking their places — and, well, there was a little dance floor, but the whole band was no more than spittin' distance from our table.

Then right away, after the opening number, Art Jarrett came over to our table and, leaning in very closely to Mrs. Simms, he sang "You're The Top." You know, you're the Louvre Museum, you're the Tower of Pisa —

" 'You're a melody by Strauss.' "

Very good. And Mrs. Simms just swooned. As we used to say then, she didn't know whether to spit or wind her watch, and everybody in the Empire Room was looking at her, figuring she must be somebody famous. Art Jarrett just laid it on thicker. "You're the top . . . You're Mahatma Ghandi, you're Napolean Brandy —"

" 'You're Mickey Mouse.' "

Teddy, you and I could give Art Jarrett a

run for his money. But, trust me, it was a sketch, and I believe Mrs. Simms would've fainted dead away with the attention if Art Jarrett finally didn't finish "You're The Top" —

*" 'You're cellophane —' "*

All right, all right. This is still my story. Because then he finished singing and turned to me and introduced me as — well, you can see this coming: "the princess of the backstroke." Eleanor wasn't going to let that go. So I had to actually stand up, and Art Jarrett took my hand and kissed it, which was absolutely the first time anybody had ever done that, and everybody cheered to beat the band, even if they didn't know me from Nutsy Fagan. I sat back down and dove back into that champagne.

*"How'd it taste this time?"*

Lemme tell you, Teddy, a girl could get to like that stuff. So peace and quiet reigned at our table again, and the band played a couple more numbers, and then Art Jarrett took the mic once more, and he said, "Ladies and gentlemen, you've met the princess of the backstroke, who will be swimming at the Lake Shore Athletic Club this Saturday, but now we're gonna raise the bar, and introduce you to the queen of the backstroke, a lady you know as the

Olympic gold medalist named . . ."

*Mom moved her hands up and down.*

Drum roll. And then he all but shouted, "Eleanor Holm . . . but whom I'm proud to call . . . Mrs. Art Jarrett." The Empire Room exploded in applause. And here came Eleanor.

Teddy, she was all in white. She had on white high heels and a white bathing suit and a little white shawl kinda thing, and a huge white cowboy hat.

*"Cowboy hat?"*

Ten gallons. Because you see, this was her signature opening number, "I'm An Old Cowhand From the Rio Grande." It was pretty rousing. But as the wags would say: as a singer, she made a good naiad. Not bad, Teddy. Not all that bad. But let's face it: I think it's fair to say that it was the outfit that sold the song. I mean, the Empire Room, or any other respectable night club, was probably not used to having any girl singer dressed so skimpily. Gowns. You wore long, beautiful slinky gowns if you were a girl vocalist. If Ted Weems, for example, had brought out a girl vocalist dressed like a stripteaser, it would've been a scandal for sure, but since Eleanor was a swimmer, no one batted an eye. Especially the men. And she got rid of the hat and sang a couple more numbers. One was "On The Good Ship Lollipop."

*"Continuing the maritime theme."*

Exactly. And then "Up A Lazy River," which allowed Eleanor to take off her little shawl and toss it into the band, when the lyrics went "throw away your troubles . . ."

*"I get it."*

And then she finished up with "The Isle of Capri." It wasn't a bad little act, and the crowd was very appreciative. Then, while Art Jarrett and the band resumed their musical stylings — that's what they called them back then, "musical stylings" — Eleanor retrieved her little shawl and came over to our table. This time, I thought it was Mr. Simms who was gonna have a heart attack. He couldn't even bear to look at her, he was so nervous being in the close company of such pulchritude. Eleanor chatted with them awhile, and since some people had begun to dance now, she told Mr. and Mrs. Simms that they had to. "If you don't, Hilda . . ." That was Mrs. Simms name; it just came to me now. "If you don't get up there with that good-lookin' husband of yours, then I'm the one who's gonna take him out on that floor and trip the light fantastic." Well, Mr. Simms grabbed the missus pretty quickly then. I don't think he was prepared to take Eleanor Holm into his arms. That would've been entirely too much for the poor man's beating heart.

So Eleanor poured herself a glass of champagne. "Well, Sydney, whatdja think of my act?"

I said, "It was really swell. I didn't have any idea you could sing that good."

"I'm workin' on it. Art doesn't think I'm quite ready for ballads yet. Just the up-tempo stuff."

"Well," I said. "It really works swell."

"Yeah, you'll see, I do one chorus of a ballad. It's a start. And once the Olympics are over, I'm gonna concentrate completely on my show business." She nudged me. "Then you can win all the gold medals."

I kinda rolled my eyes at that, Teddy. Eleanor looked down at my drink. "Hey, have some more champagne."

"I dunno, Eleanor. I wanna stay in shape."

Eleanor just roared at that. "Honey, I train on champagne and caviar. Don't pay any attention to those blazers. They'd have us all living in a nunnery between races. A little champagne is not the end of the world." I took a polite sip. She poured more into my glass. "I think the European swimmers drink this stuff for breakfast." Then she picked up Mr. Simms' pack of Lucky Strikes and took one out. "Reach for a Lucky instead of a sweet," she said. That was the famous advertisement then. So she offered me a Lucky, too.

"No thanks," I said.

Eleanor lit up. "Actually, I don't smoke all that much. Just to be sociable, you know. And in the locker room. I can see the faces on all the other girls when I light up a coffin nail. They're thinking: she not only beats us, she smokes, too. What could she do if she took care of herself? See, that's the mental part, 'cause I'm playin' around with 'em. Now don't you let on." She kinda nudged me and winked. I was not only the queen-in-waiting; now I was her confidant, too.

She went on: "You'll see how much of a game the amateurs are, Sydney. I mean, it doesn't make any sense at all. The Hollywood people want me to swim in the pictures, but I can't do that because of the blazers. Especially that Avery Brundage — what a pompous jackass. He's the worst. Of course, he can be, because he's the boss — he's the head of the AOA."

AOA — I toldja, Teddy: that's the American Olympic Association.

And Avery Brundage really did drive Eleanor nuts.

She said, "Brundage says if I just jump in some pool in a movie lot and swim to the other side with a rose in my teeth, then I'm a professional swimmer. Isn't that ridiculous?"

I agreed that it was. Which, in fact, it is.

"But I can get up here and sing in a bathing suit, and that's no problem. Even though I'm gettin' paid for singin' in a bathing suit, that doesn't make me a pro. I can dance in a bathing suit. No problem with the blazers. I can act in a bathing suit. No problem. I swear, Sydney, Avery Brundage wouldn't care if I came out and screwed in a bathing suit so long as I didn't swim in a bathing suit. Well, you can't screw in a bathing suit. So dry hump. Avery Brundage wouldn't care if I dry humped in a bathing suit right here on the dance floor of the Empire Room as long as I didn't swim in one."

I agreed, Teddy. I just agreed. This was all a bit much for me. But Eleanor wasn't finished.

"Of course, they expect us all to be good little girls. The blazers don't like any of their girls being married like me, because that means I'm actually having marital relations! Well, since I married Art, you think that's slowed me up any? As a matter of fact, I'm faster. My world record for the hundred —

131

the hundred meters — is one-sixteen and three, but whaddya think I did in practice just a couple months ago?" I shook my head. "One-fourteen and six."

"Good grief," I said. I actually swooned at that. "That's really fast." It was, Teddy. That was unworldly.

Eleanor took one more drag on her Lucky Strike and squashed it out. "Tell you the truth, I like to make love the night before I swim a big race. Art and me'll make love tomorrow night. I think it helps."

"You do?"

"Sure. It relaxes you, and for goodness' sake, it doesn't take that long. Then you just have a cigarette and go off to dreamland. And all these other gals are lying in bed alone, tossin' and turnin', worryin' their pretty heads about the race. Now you just tell me: who's getting better preparation?" And then, as I pondered this, hoping it was a rhetorical question, Eleanor asked, "You have a boy friend, Sydney?"

Actually, Teddy, I'd been going out some with a sophomore at Washington College. He was a great improvement on Buzzy Moore, and I liked him enough, but he wasn't anything special. "Well, not really," I told Eleanor.

"Gee, someone as pretty as you should

have a fellow. Now, I'm not asking you to do anything you wouldn't feel comfortable about, but in the future, you remember what I said."

"I will, Eleanor. I will." That occasioned me to take a good long swallow of the champagne, and just about then Art Jarrett wrapped up the dance numbers. The dancers could tell the set was ending, because there was a flourish from the band, and that meant the showoffs on the dance floor did a lot of dipping, the women swaying back as their partners held them.

Eleanor drained her champagne glass and patted me on the knee. "Well, there's my cue. I'm back in the saddle again."

And that was when Art Jarrett grabbed the mic and began singing "Did You Ever See a Dream Walking?" Only, of course, he kept looking over at Eleanor sitting next to me while he sang, and when they got to the second chorus, she stood up and threw that little shawl off again and started moving toward him, only like she was swimming.

*"Don't tell me it was a backstroke, Mother."*

No, she swam over freestyle. And I had to wonder what the blazers would think about that, if pretending to swim in a bathing suit on dry land made her a professional. But I guess not. Anyway, when she got to Art,

133

they put an arm around each others' backs and sang the last chorus together. That was the part of a ballad he let her sing — only, of course, she sang "Did you ever see a dream walking?" and he sang "Did you ever see a dream swimming?" It wasn't a bad show, really. It really wasn't.

Mom shook her head, smiling at the memory. Then she glanced over at the television set, but the gymnasts were still the attraction. They were on the balance beam now. "Aren't they ever gonna get rid of those damn little imps and get the swimmers out here, Teddy? I'm an old lady, I wanna see Natalie Coughlin swim the hundred before I fall asleep."

I looked at my watch. "It can't be much longer now," I said, "but come on, don't leave me hangin'. How did you do when you raced a couple days later?"

"Actually, not bad. I told you, we were still swimming yards then in the United States, a hundred yards and two hundred yards, and I got my best times in both. But still, I was fourth. And not all the best girls were at the Indoors. If I was gonna make the Olympics at the trials in New York, I had to get third. I had to get a little faster."

"How did Eleanor do?"

"Oh, my gracious, she not only set a new world record in the hundred, she did it by more than a second."

"Wow."

"Oh yeah, it made me think: Hmmm, if I can just figure some way to get laid in New York the night before the trials, I could make the Olympics."

"Come on, Mother."

"Oh, don't be such an old woman, Teddy. Of course I wasn't serious. I was still such a sweet little virgin then, I didn't even know what a dry hump was. But . . ." She paused. "But, no, honestly, I certainly didn't forget what Eleanor said. To make love to the man of your dreams, and then sleep in his arms and get up and beat all the other girls the next day and stand there on a podium with a gold medal round your neck and 'The Star-Spangled Banner' playing . . . well, Teddy, life couldn't get any better than that. My gracious, queen of the backstroke . . ."

When I was a child, it seemed so strange listening to my parents talk about their lives before I was born. I mean, however irrational, in a way it just didn't seem possible that they were around before I arrived on the scene. In my parents' cases, too, it was even more difficult, because I grew up in Montana, and they'd both come from Back East, and for those of us from Out West, Back East might as well have been The Mysterious East. That made it that much more confounding to hear of times past that had transpired in such alien territory.

Actually, it wasn't just the war that my father didn't care to talk about. He was reluctant to bring up his childhood, too. I gathered enough to appreciate that it had been a terribly sad one for him. His family had been hard on one another, lacking much love, and they were poor, too, and as things had grown so terribly hard in the Depression, Dad simply saw no reason to bother any longer with the blood he'd been dealt. The best I could glean from him, one lovely summer's day after high school, he just said good-bye, took off from home, which was upstate New York, and started looking for work. It seems that his folks hardly missed him; he certainly didn't miss them.

As near as I can tell, he was a hobo for a while (although he was ashamed, I think, ever to say that in quite so many words), then he got into the CCC, the Civilian Conservation Corps, and that seemed to give him both hope and purpose. Dad was bright and self-confident. It was a bit odd, but whereas Mother would sometimes drift back into the rural argot of the Eastern Shore, Daddy — who'd come from far worse circumstances — always spoke with the finest diction. It was as if he was determined to leave that dispiriting youth of his completely behind. You could say Daddy remade himself.

Certainly, he began to improve his lot after he left the CCC, if only little by little. By that time, two or three years later, when he somehow happened to run into my mother, he'd already transformed himself into a young man of some evident potential, who had his eyes fixed on the main chance.

Now, mother was certainly more forthcoming about her upbringing. There were funny little stories, silly adventures she'd had with Carter Kincaid, tales of struggling in the Depression and, always, fond memories of her father. The only perplexing omission was that she'd never bring up her swimming in any detail.

Mother's mother would also visit us periodically, bringing the latest breaking news from the Shore. Mom would listen to Grandmother's reports, but she never seemed that engaged about the old homeland. I guess both Mom and Dad were like so many Americans. Once they'd left Back East and moved Out West, they simply didn't look behind them, and without other family to connect them to the past, soon the tides of time washed over their earlier lives.

When Grandmother died in 1978, Mom returned for the funeral. Daddy had always been close to his mother-in-law, so it surprised me that he didn't go, too. But Mom went alone, and I suppose because she hadn't been back to the Shore for so many years, it made her, when she was there by herself, that much more sentimental. She told me, in fact, that she'd cried as much standing by her father's grave as she'd wept for her Mother's death. "All this time, Teddy, all this time he's been gone," she said. Part of her was really crying about her own past, about how it had all drifted away.

I asked her, then, if she'd stayed in touch with Carter. "No," she said. "Not after we moved to Missoula."

"But you were so close."

"Oh, Lord, yes. When I was a girl, I never had a better friend than Carter Kincaid."

"But you lost complete touch with her after she went to Baltimore?"

"No, I saw her there," she said. "Well, the once."

"But . . . ?"

Mom paused awhile, not so much to consider a response, I thought, as she did to use this occasion to remember Carter. She smiled broadly, fondly. Finally, though, she just said, "It's complicated, Teddy. It was just too complicated."

I had to assume there must've been some sort of falling out. In my experience, when there are sad ruptures among old friends, it usually has to do with new husbands or wives. Perhaps Carter's husband didn't get along with Mom. Whatever it was, I could tell that she didn't want to discuss it, and so, reluctantly, I had to let the matter drop and consign Carter Kincaid forever to Mom's childhood.

Like that, once Grandmother died, the Shore was, for my mother, gone for good. There was nothing Back East but cemetery plots, so thoughts of that past only surfaced again when Mom knew her own death was approaching — which also happened to be at the same time that Michael Phelps came out of Maryland, storming the Olympics and triggering the memories of swimming and all that went with it, way back then.

Mom slept late the next morning. She always ate a good breakfast, although one of the few tedious things about my mother was that all too often she'd go on (and on) about how she missed having scrapple for breakfast. They'd had that growing up on the Shore. "Most people don't even have a clue what scrapple is," she'd whine. They certainly didn't in Missoula, Montana, or Eugene, Oregon — and, I assume, in most other places. "Just as well, I suppose," she would then add. "I never was sure what was in it, but I think it was all the stuff that wasn't good enough for sausage."

"Not good enough for sausage? I thought

you shouldn't even ask what went into sausage."

"Yeah, Teddy, scrapple is probably just nasty scraps, but it sure was good. We'd pour maple syrup on it."

"I've never heard of anyone putting syrup on meat."

"Well, we did on scrapple on the Shore, and it was delicious. For all I know, maybe they don't even have scrapple anyplace but the Shore. All I know is, I sure do miss having a choice of scrapple for breakfast."

But this morning, after her scrapple-less Oregon breakfast, when she found me out in her garden, she was raring to resume reminiscing. Mom was still in a good mood from the night before, because late in the evening, when she'd despaired that NBC would never desert the teeny little heinie-less gymnasts, they'd switched to the swimming. Then, not only did Natalie Coughlin win the hundred backstroke — hooray! — but Michael Phelps also won another gold medal in something or other.

It was a gorgeous morning in Eugene, and I'd sort of drifted off in the sun, reading the newspaper. Mom took it off my lap and turned right to the sports pages, looking for the certification in print of what she'd seen with her own eyes on TV the night before.

141

She searched the agate. "I just can't get over it, Teddy. The time."

"What time?"

"Natalie Coughlin's time. Just thirty-seven hundredths of a second over a minute. Remember what I told you Eleanor swam it in — a minute, sixteen and something. Imagine that. And now they're down to almost a minute."

"That doesn't make Eleanor or any of your crowd look very good, does it?"

She glared at me with eyes that suddenly seemed much younger than the rest of her. Angry eyes. The veritable headlights people always have that poor, clichéd deer caught in. "That's both rotten and ignorant of you, Teddy Branch. Jesse Owens was running in those Berlin Olympics, and his times look pretty slow now, but would anybody think the less of him?"

"No, I'm sorry, you're right, Mom." I realized I'd waded into rushing waters and had better try to negotiate my way safely back to shore. But too late. She snapped at me now:

"The artists — the painters and the writers don't get any better, do they?"

"What?"

"What? There's nobody around today who's supposed to give Shakespeare or

Rembrandt a run for their money, is there?"

"No, that's for sure."

"Are any of the current would-be geniuses any smarter than Leonardo da Vinci was?" I shook my head. I saw where this was going. "So just because athletes have better times now doesn't mean they're intrinsically better, does it?"

"I see your point, Mom."

"Well then, you're not as ignorant as you let on. They're swimming today in those skin-tight suits that look like something out of science fiction. Put me in one of those new-fangled suits!" She paused to consider that for a moment. "I don't mean me now, of course. Me then. And the pools weren't so streamlined either, so there were waves that would wash back on us. And in the backstroke, my stroke, the rules made it much more difficult to make a legitimate turn. You had to touch with your hand, like you were playing tag. You saw Natalie last night. They can just sort of flip around." She threw her hands all around in some representation of a backstroke flip turn. Mom had gotten herself quite worked up. "Hell, Teddy, that in itself is whole seconds right there." She shook her head in despair at me again. "Besides, there wasn't any money in it then. The blazers wouldn't allow it. These kids today can work at it all the time. I don't imagine Natalie Coughlin is working nights singing at any Empire Room —"

"Or training on champagne and cigarettes."

"Exactly. There I was, going to the Olympic trials, and I'd never even had a real coach. Just Mr. Wallace Foster in Chestertown, Maryland — and he was learning how to coach me out of a damn book."

I held up my hands. "All right, all right. So, Mom, tell me: how in the world did you improve enough after the Indoors to finish in the top three and make it to Berlin?"

She looked over at me strangely. "Well, it wasn't quite that way."

"It wasn't?"

She shook her head. "Get me another cup of coffee, Teddy, and grab that tape recorder, and I'll explain."

So I got her a cup, and she sipped at it and, like Scheherazade, began again.

The Trials in '36 were held in New York, but this time they weren't out at Jones Beach, but at a pool in Queens, right off the East River in a neighborhood called Astoria. You know New York, Teddy?

*"Just the parts everybody knows. Not Queens."*

So you don't know the Triborough Bridge?

*"Not really."*

Well, the Triborough Bridge was a big Depression project to put men to work, and the very day of the Trials — the exact day — it opened up, right near where we were swimming. The pool was new, too. It was another Depression project, so they wanted to show it off. That's why we were there instead of Jones Beach. So every Tom, Dick and Harry with a car drove out that way to see the new bridge. Now at this same time, there was an ungodly heat wave that hit the whole country. People were dropping like

flies. Remember, this is pre-air conditioning. Or AC, as everybody says now. Why in
the world can't we just say the words for
things, Teddy? Does it really take that much
longer to say "air conditioning" than "AC"?
Well, does it?

*"I'm sorry, Mom, I thought that was a rhetori-*
*cal question."*

You mean an RQ?

*Mom had lost me. "A what?"*

An RQ — a rhetorical question. We might
as well give up the good fight and just use
initials for everything.

*I ratified that with an "OK."*

Notwithstanding, Teddy, it was hot as
Hades, and we didn't have any air conditioning. Now, listen, it gets pretty darn hot
on the Shore, so as Br'er Rabbit used to
say, I was born and bred in that briar patch,
but let me tell you, it was plenty uncomfortable for all us gals, regardless of our prov-
enance.

The girls who made the team were going
to ship out to Germany only three days after
the Trials ended. They had space reserved
on the SS Manhattan, New York to Hamburg, but the American Olympic people had
the shorts. Right up until the last minute,
they didn't know how to pay for all the
athletes they wanted to take to Berlin. They

had to appeal to the public for funds. But that was the Depression, Teddy. I don't think anybody nowadays can imagine it, unless they're old and decrepit like me and actually lived through it.

Why, there was so little money for the swimming team that when the men had swum against the Japanese in some dual meet a few weeks before, they had bathing suits made with both flags on 'em — you know, the stars-and-stripes and the rising sun — and there were some left over, and that's what some of our swimmers wore at the Olympics. I'm not kidding, Teddy, swimmers representing the United States of America actually wore bathing suits with rising suns on them in the Olympics. And what was it, five or six years later, that the little buggers bombed Pearl Harbor . . . and then shot your father at Guadalcanal right after that. But here we were wearing bathing suits with their flag on 'em because we didn't have enough money to buy our own.

But it was the Depression.

I don't think anyone was as PO'ed as Eleanor. See, here was the deal. The AOA had bought space for our athletes on the SS Manhattan, but it was all down in the bowels of the ship. Third class — the cheapest cabins possible. They used to call that

147

steerage. Eleanor said, "The blazers'd put us all in hammocks if they could."

But you can probably guess the rest. The blazers themselves, and the newspaper men and all the other swells in the Olympic party were booked in the better cabins, up top. Oh, they were gonna have a nice, smooth ride across the Atlantic. But the athletes, the people competing, for goodness' sake, they had the most uncomfortable accommodations.

So Eleanor goes to the AOA and says, thanks, but no thanks, I'll pay my own way over in a first-class cabin. But they wouldn't let her. If you're an athlete, you have to ride with all the others down in steerage. Keep that in mind, Teddy, because it becomes important to the story . . . and to me — me in particular.

Eleanor was still fuming at the Trials. Plus, it's at least a hundred degrees in Astoria, Queens, and every car in New York is spitting out fumes, checking out the opening of the fantastic Triborough Bridge. But I'm determined to beat some of those gals I'd never beaten before and get to Berlin. We were staying at the Paramount Hotel, which was just off Times Square, and the day before the Trials, a bunch of us went out and got passports, because the SS Manhattan was going to sail right afterwards. I was that confident, Teddy — not cocky, but I thought I had enough of a chance that it was worth going over and getting a passport, even though it cost two dollars and change and I didn't have much more than that with me.

The day of our race Eleanor arrives as jaunty as ever, talkin' about how she went out night-clubbin' the evening before. She had on her Women's Swimming Association suit, with the big S in the middle of her chest. Everybody but me had some affiliation or other. I was still just Sydney Stringfellow, unattached, with my plain black bathing suit and black cap.

But I did have a new bathing suit. After swimmin' at the Lake Shore Club, I saw I had to get one. You see, at the meets that really counted, all the swimmers wore silk suits. If I was gonna compete in the top echelon, you had to have a silk suit, because that could mean maybe a whole second or two better time in a race. I mean, let me tell you, Teddy, those silk suits were so light they were a marvel of their age. It felt just like another layer of skin.

But here was the problem. Once you got wet in those suits, which, of course, you did, inasmuch as the whole idea was to swim in them, they really were like so much skin. I mean, they left almost nothing to the imagination.

*"Get a load of this."*

Exactly. And remember, now, this is the 1930s, when people were not regularly publicly visible in the buff in movies and whatnot. The newspaper photographers — especially the tabloid boys — were always shooting us innocent little swimmers because it was a way of sneaking pictures of girls in bathing suits into the paper without appearing lascivious, or upsetting the U.S. Post Office, which didn't tolerate dirty pictures being sent through the mails. Us modest little swimmers, us naiads, were the nakedest women this side of the burlesque theaters — and even those ladies had to wear little things over their —

*She pointed to her chest. "Nipples," I said.*

Thank you for dotting the *i*s and crossing the *t*s, Teddy. But trust me, it was scandalous. The suits did have a little extra piece across down here — and, no, I don't believe you have to verbalize that territory for my benefit. They were known as "modesty panels." That's why they were called "panel" bathing suits. If they hadn't had that, we would've been banned in Boston, I can assure you. So here is your demure little mother and these other girls of much the same modest comportment performing in the closest thing to the au natural.

It was so shocking that helpers were stationed at the end of the pool with either robes or large towels at the ready, so you could pop out of the water and cover yourself up before you treated the entire assemblage — especially the tabloid boys with their Speed Graphics — to a pretty good viewing of your private parts. Well, some of the girls were quicker at the coverin'-up business than others. Eleanor, as you might imagine, took her own sweet time puttin' that robe on.

Now, of course, as well you know, Teddy, with the backstroke you start in the water, so at least, being submerged, I didn't have to concern myself about these issues of modesty beforehand. But when I saw how we were supposed to line up for the race, I just about died. The way the luck of the draw had it, I was in the very next lane to Eleanor.

Now, I'm no Alibi Ike, Teddy, but I think that was my downfall. I was so in awe of her. Nowadays they would say she was my "role model," which is a term I detest only slightly less than "senior citizen." It is so sappy: role model. It sounds like some

151

sociologist thought it up. Let's call a spade a spade: Eleanor was my hero. But, of course, whereas I was quaking in my boots, Eleanor was just taking care of business. Once we jumped into the pool and took our positions, I'm sure she didn't know if it was me or the Queen of Romania next to her. But I was so self-conscious, I got a terrible start, and then, of course, I was painfully aware of the fact that Eleanor was pullin' away from me.

Now, understand, I knew very well that I couldn't beat Eleanor. I was swimmin' for second or third place, but it's hard to stay cool in a situation like that, and it was so discouraging knowing that she was gettin' further ahead, and so I tried to swim faster, and all that did was screw me up some more, and, frankly, I never had a chance. I wasn't even close to qualifying, Teddy. I think I ended up fifth or sixth. A girl from California named Edith Motridge came in second after Eleanor, and Alice Bridges came in third, which was nice. I knew Alice a little bit. She was one of the girls I'd gone to get a passport with.

Well, when I finally touched out, Eleanor had already yanked her cap off, so everybody could see her better, especially if there were any newsreel cameras around, and right away, she said, "I'm sorry, Sydney, I don't think you made it."

I shook my head. This was one time I didn't take my bathing cap off myself. I wasn't sure I even wanted anybody to see my hair, let alone any other part of me. "No, I didn't do well at all."

She patted me on the shoulder. "But don't let it get you down, honey. Four years from now you'll beat all these gals as bad as I beat them today, and you'll win the gold."

About then, people started coming over to congratulate her. I hoisted myself out and grabbed the towel from the person there responsible for my modesty and wrapped it around me as quick as I could. I was starting to slink off and get into my clothes — I just wanted to disappear from Astoria, Queens, New York — when I heard Eleanor calling my name. I looked back, and there are all these people surrounding her, but there's one gentleman in particular that she's talking to. Hot as it was, he still had his tie and his suit jacket on. Eleanor beckoned me over.

"Sydney," she said, "I want you to meet Avery Brundage."

I was absolutely flabbergasted. Avery Brundage was not only the biggest American blazer of them all, but eventually, he'd become president of the whole international Olympic shebang. Also, if you don't mind my saying so, Teddy, he was a total horse's ass. Of course, he had a lot of company in that particular regard in the AOA.

He kept taking his hat off to mop his bald head with a handkerchief, and when he shook my hand, he kept this sort of disdainful expression on his face before he went back to mopping. I mean, he was a real sourpuss. He might've been head of the AOA, but I don't think he liked athletes. It was like being a veterinarian and not liking dogs. We were just sort of necessary evils to him.

I said, "How do you do, Mr. Brundage?"

He kind of grunted back.

Eleanor picked up the ball then. "Avery," she said, and you could just see him turn up his nose at that, because everybody under the sun deferred to him and called him "Mr. Brundage," which Eleanor knew, which is why she called him Avery. It irked him even more that it was Eleanor, a girl, addressing him that way, because he pretty much thought that sports weren't ladylike, that girls shouldn't be competing. Of course, if you will excuse me, Teddy, Brundage didn't mind girls being un-ladylike in bed. He was a rampant womanizer.

Eleanor wasn't fazed; I guess she was used to the old goat leering at her. "Avery," she said, "you should know who Sydney is, because she's my successor in the back-stroke."

"Is that so?" he said.

"Yeah, she didn't do very well today, and it's a shame she can't go to Berlin, because she's got more natural talent than all these other gals." He looked at Eleanor like she was a buttonhole salesman trying to peddle him a bill of goods. "You see, Avery" — and he grimaced again — "Sydney hasn't had any coaching at all, and here she just missed qualifying by a second or so."

That interested him. "No coaching, young lady?"

"No, sir. There's no real coaches where I live."

"And where's that?"

"Down on the Eastern Shore." And since I wasn't sure that registered, I quickly added: "Maryland."

He just nodded.

Eleanor jumped in again: "But Sydney's gonna move up here and join the Women's Swimming Association, and you just watch, in three or four years time, she'll have every one of my records."

"My gracious, Eleanor, I've never heard

such an expression of humility from you before."

"Well, Sydney's just a natural, and you fellas in the AOA ought to help her out. That's all I'm saying."

"And what's your name again, young lady?"

"Sydney Stringfellow," I said. "Unattached."

"I shall remember that," he said. And he did repeat my name. "Sydney Stringfellow." (He didn't bother to add the "unattached," though.)

"And, Avery, Sydney's the nicest girl around. She'll make America proud."

"Well, it's been my pleasure, Miss Stringfellow."

"Good," Eleanor said — and then brusquely: "Now, let me ask you again about me getting a better cabin on the Manhattan —"

Whatever grace he had mustered up on my behalf immediately disappeared. Hot as it was, you could feel the frost coming off him. "I have told you, Eleanor, that subject is a dead letter."

"Avery, it just isn't fair."

"What isn't fair?"

"That all the athletes, the actual ones representing the United States, have to travel down in third class with the rats, while you officials get first class."

"Eleanor, I will not dignify that with an answer," Brundage said, and without another word, he turned and walked away.

I just said, "Thank you, Eleanor."

"Aw, Sydney, I only hope those creeps treat you better than they did me. Another month, I'll be done with 'em."

Actually, Teddy, as it turned out, it'd be a bit sooner.

So I went back to the Shore, and tried to salve my wounds. I didn't want to hear anything about swimming for a while. I did read in the paper that the financial appeal that the AOA made raised enough money to get all the athletes on the Manhattan, and off it sailed for Hamburg. So, Teddy, bon voyage sans moi.

What I didn't know, but should've figured out, was that Eleanor Jarrett, nee Holm, just wasn't gonna tolerate stayin' down there in steerage. There was a ten o'clock curfew, but every night she'd dress to the nines and find her way up to the fancy part of the ship and drink and smoke and play cards and generally carry on with the newspaper boys, and it was way past ten o'clock before she'd turn into a pumpkin and go back down to the room she shared with Mary Lou Petty. The blazers warned her about it, but you couldn't get that particular leopard to change her spots.

So, about a week later, out of the clear blue sky, this arrives for me at the house.

*With that, Mom reached into that purple acetate folder and pulled out a telegram. I hadn't seen a telegram in I don't know how many years, but I recognized that particular pale yellow paper right away. She handed it to me. It had the message pasted on, in lines of copy, the old-fashioned way. It read:*

POSITION SUDDENLY AVAILABLE ON US TEAM STOP MUST LEAVE NY 26 JULY ON SS DEUTSCHLAND, HAMBURG-AMERICAN LINE, 4 PM DEPARTURE STOP IF CAN COME WIRE BACK STOP TICKET AT PIER, WEST 44 STREET STOP WILL ARRIVE HAMBURG 3 AUG AND BE MET STOP ADVISE IMMEDIATELY STOP AVERY BRUNDAGE

*"So that's how you made the team."*

Exactly. What happened is that when the ship stopped over in Cherbourg, Eleanor spent the whole afternoon playing cards with some of the newspaper boys. In fact, she pretty much cleaned them out. Then she really hung a toot on. It didn't help, either, that there were stories that she was getting a little too cozy with Charley Mac-

Arthur. He was a famous writer who was married to Helen Hayes. You remember her, the actress?

*"Sure."*

Well, Mr. MacArthur's missus was not on the ship and neither was Mr. Art Jarrett. I don't know whether there was any truth to that rumor. I thought Eleanor was happy with Jarrett at the time, even though they divorced a few years later when she started runnin' around with Billy Rose.

*"The theatrical guy?"*

Yeah, him. He made Eleanor the star of his Aquacade at the World's Fair in 1939. But once again, Teddy, you're lettin' me get ahead of myself. What mattered here is The Year of Our Lord 1936, and Avery Brundage had had enough of her shenanigans on the Good Ship Lollypop and threw her off the team. It was a huge story. As soon as I got the telegram, I called Mother, and she brought the newspaper home, and the story was headlined.

Now what Eleanor told me later was that she simply didn't believe Brundage was serious — especially after he got a petition signed by about two hundred of her teammates pleading with him not to expel her. She was sure he was bluffing, but when she went to appeal to him, he told her he meant business. She said, well then, she at least hoped somebody else would get her place. See, the swimming didn't start till the second week of the Olympics. So there was plenty of time for another backstroker to get to Berlin to compete.

Eleanor told me she just said that off the top of her head, but Brundage took hold of it, and he asked her who'd finished fourth. Eleanor replied, "Oh, don't send her, Avery, she hasn't got a prayer for a medal. But if you send that girl I introduced you to at the Trials, that Sydney Stringfellow — now that kid has the potential to maybe put it all together and win something."

Actually, Eleanor told me, she still thought Brundage was going to come to his senses and back down, but he was dead serious. Why, he threw Jesse Owens himself out of amateur athletics a little later — hardly a week after Jesse was the toast of Berlin — just because he said he might turn pro. You see, as far as the Olympics were concerned, Brundage pretty much made up the rules on the fly, so he just went ahead and fired that telegram off to me.

Well, Teddy, Mother was terrified. "Trixie," she said, "are you really prepared to go up to New York and get on a foreign ship, where they'll be speaking German —

not the king's English, mind you — and go off to Hamburg all by yourself and trust that someone can get you to Berlin? You really are brave enough to do that?"

The fact is, I was scared myself, but it was such an amazing opportunity, so somehow I got my courage up and told Mother I was prepared to go. All by myself. She took a deep breath and said, "All right, Trixie, if you can promise me your father won't roll over in his grave."

That made me think about Daddy and all the things we'd done together, out fishing, shooting ducks and doves, playing ball — and, Teddy, that just evaporated any fears I had. Stoutly, I told Mom, "I'm sure Daddy would want me to be his girl and go."

So she drew in a deep sigh and said, all right, she'd ride with me on the Bullet up to Wilmington, where I'd catch the train for New York. We called Western Union and wired Avery Brundage that I'd be on my way. It cost, I think, ten cents a word, but Mother splurged, because she added one more sentence, seventy cents worth: "PLEASE BE SURE MEET AT HAMBURG PIER."

That was all that really worried me, getting off the ship in a foreign land. The rest seemed pretty easy. After all, Teddy, at this point, I was gettin' to be quite the veteran traveler, a regular Baedeker. Why, I'd been to Chicago and New York City, and I'd ridden in subways and called for taxi cabs, and now I was goin' back up to New York and then across the ocean all by myself. But sometimes, it isn't that you grow up. Sometimes I think it's just that you've already grown up, only you don't realize it till something faces you down.

That's what happened to me that summer of '36. If I'd looked back then, say in September, I would've hardly recognized that girl I'd been a few weeks ago. So much had happened to me. I wasn't a different person, you understand. And it wasn't a matter of just changing my name from Trixie to Sydney. It was all of me. But, of course, I didn't look back, because by then I was looking forward. That's the whole point of growing up, isn't it?

It's funny, isn't it, Teddy? Here Eleanor gets thrown off the team, but it turned out to be a terrific thing for her. She told me that herself. By the time I got to New York, she was on all the front pages. You don't get that no matter how pretty you are and no matter how fast you can swim backstroke. So Avery Brundage was the best thing that ever happened to Eleanor. And me, too, of

163

course. He changed my life for forever and a day. You'll see.

But then, if you'll excuse me, Teddy, he was still a total horse's ass till the day he died.

■ ■ ■ ■

# PART TWO:
# HORST

■ ■ ■ ■

Well, sure enough, Teddy, I got to Berlin without any difficulty at all. The ship sailed across the ocean blue, and, as promised, I was met right at the pier in Hamburg and taken directly to the women's dorm. We were kept separate from the men. They had a large village about five miles away, but no girls were allowed in. As far as I know, the only woman who ever got into the village was Leni Riefenstahl. Do you know her, Teddy?

*I shook my head, though the name sounded vaguely familiar to me.*

Oh, she was a piece of work. She'd been a big German movie star, and Hitler was crazy about her.

*"You mean they had an affair, Hitler and . . . ?"*

Leni Riefenstahl. I'm surprised you never heard of her, you being in the theater. Well, yes, there was some scuttlebutt about that,

167

but the general consensus was, no, they were never lovers. Now, the Nazi bigwig all the movie stars had to worry about was Joseph Goebbels. Certainly you've heard of him?

*"Oh, sure."*

He was the head of propaganda, so he got involved in movies, and he had what they used to call the casting couch.

*"I think they still call it that, Mom."*

Well, Goebbels was a creepy little guy with a limp. Now, please, Teddy, I'm not a mean person. I understand some very nice people have to limp, but it just added to his, uh . . .

*"Creepiness."*

Exactly, there's just no other word for it. Now Hitler himself really wasn't impressive. You know, he had that foolish mustache, and he wasn't very tall, but he wasn't creepy. He didn't put you off. You certainly never thought: well, this fellow is the absolute personification of evil. I mean that just didn't cross your mind when you were around him.

*"Wait a minute, Mom. You were around Adolf Hitler?"*

As close as I am to you right now. I was at Goebbels' house, too. Well "house" doesn't do it justice. His estate on an island. And there was a beautiful movie star there and everyone whispered that she was his mistress. Understand, Goebbels' wife was right there, too. The movie star was named Lida something, and I kept trying to imagine her climbing into bed with that little creep, and it made my skin crawl. I thought, if you have to do that to be a movie star, well —

Dammit, Teddy, you've got me off the track again. I was talking about Leni Riefenstahl. She'd made this propaganda film for Hitler a couple years before, and now she was shooting one about the Olympics.

She'd just burst right into the men's village to shoot her movie. She was crazy about men's bodies. Not that I have anything against men's bodies, Teddy. Even as old and decrepit as I am now. But Leni Riefenstahl — her whole movie featured men's bodies, including a number of them in the altogether — carrying the Olympic torch, in the sauna, what have you.

Yep, when it came to Leni Riefenstahl, rules were made to be broken. I never saw a woman who could get men to do whatever she wanted better than she could. She'd cajole, she'd threaten. She could cry on cue. Well, of course, she was an actress.

She actually got a lot of the athletes to repeat their performances for her camera, pretend to run the whole damn race again, the total rigamarole, so she could get close-ups and so forth. Whatever Leni wanted. Of course, sometimes it was a two-way street. The American boy who won the decathlon — his name was Glenn Morris. After she finished shooting him, she got him into her bed. Of course, I don't think Glenn fought very hard to avoid that particular destination. It would not be in the least bit fair to say she seduced him.

*Mom stopped then, and a funny little smile played over her face. At moments like this, I knew enough to just let her remember whatever it was that had struck her, so I let the tape run silent. She started again after awhile, but speaking more wistfully:*

She did try to seduce Horst. Here he was only twenty, and she must've been thirty-five if she was a day, and she tried to seduce him. Now he told me she didn't succeed, but, honestly, I couldn't have blamed him, Teddy. It would've been very hard to reject the blandishments of Leni Riefenstahl. Especially for a young German boy. I mean, it would be like gettin' into bed with the Queen of Sheba if you were a Sheba boy — a . . . Shebanese? Right?

*"I really don't know, Mom."*

Well, you get the picture. Now, I wanted to believe Horst when he said he'd managed to say no, but there was always a part of me — well, a very considerable part, to tell you the truth — that thought this one time he was fibbing. But I would've forgiven Horst. It was before he met me that she tried to seduce him, and, as I said, Teddy, no man could say no to Leni Riefenstahl.

*I stopped her. "Mom, excuse me: who's Horst?"*

Yeah, you're right. What's that word they always use now for that sort of thing?

*"What sort of thing?"*

You know, when you move from the one thing to another. Wait, wait. It'll come to me. . . . Segued! That's the word. I don't ever remember people saying "segued" until very recently. Well, just now I guess I segued into Horst, through Leni Riefenstahl, but that's appropriate, because it was because of her that I met Horst. His name was Horst Gerhardt.

*Mom stopped and smiled that special smile that I recognized only comes from bliss, remembered. In fact, as she kept sitting there, musing, blissfully, it didn't seem that she was going to pick up the thread. So I finally spoke up. "Well, who was Horst Gerhardt?"*

He was my gold medal, Teddy.

*She beamed.*

Horst was my gold medal.

*She paused again. My curiosity was up.
"Well, tell me about him," I asked. Instead,
Mom rose abruptly.*

No, not right now. Before I get into Horst,
I have to assemble my thoughts.

*And she left me right there, with the tape
still running.*

She had acted so precipitously that when she went into her bedroom I began to fear that she might've experienced some sort of crisis, or perhaps was in pain. But on the contrary: when Mom emerged, she seemed downright chipper and blithely suggested we go out to lunch. "I'll treat," she said. She had a favorite little restaurant in mind, one where we could sit outside in a pretty, covered courtyard. Very green; very northwest. As soon as we sat down, she called the waiter over and, bingo, ordered two Bloody Marys.

"You didn't even ask me," I said.

"If I'm going to be fortified, I want you to be, too," she replied.

"You need to be fortified? Against what?"

"Well, it's not fortified against, Teddy. It's just that I wanna have all my ducks in a row."

"Because of this Horst?"

"Exactly. I sorta got ahead of myself back there. Let me back up now and get a running start into Horst."

"All right. Where do you start to run from?"

"Well, get out that tape recorder, Teddy, and lemme see."

Dutifully I obeyed, and Mom pondered for only a second before she launched back into her tale.

Well, I'll begin at the women's village. Of course, it wasn't a village. Not like the men's. Now that was a village. It was way out of town, in Doeberitz, set in these lovely birch woods with ponds and all sorts of animals. They even had a kangaroo or two to make the Australian boys feel at home. And the sauna, of course. That's where Leni got her film of the Scandinavian boys all runnin' around naked as blue jays. That was avante garde for the time, Teddy. Very avante garde. I can assure you, you didn't get to see that sort of thing at the New Lyceum Theatre in Chestertown.

But as for the Olympic girls — well, there simply weren't enough of us competing then to have a village. We just had a dormitory — the Friesenhaus they called it — and it was mighty spare, lemme tell you. They turned it into military barracks after the Olympics were over, and I'll bet you dollars to doughnuts it wasn't for officers.

They'd just finished the place, too, and because it was so damp and cold when we first got there —

*"In August?"*

Exactly. All the Germans were saying it was the first time they'd ever had April in August. It was so raw that the plaster was still wet. And the beds. The mattresses were filled with straw, I think. Oh, they were awful. But I was lucky, Teddy. By the time I got there, the other girls had already been there a week, and they told me the food had been so bad at first, almost nobody could eat it. Green apples, brown bread, all that heavy Teutonic stuff. There'd been so many complaints, though, at least it was edible by the time I arrived. And you know how it is: when in Rome. Why, I even got to like pickled cabbage and cucumbers —

*"What the hell, Mom. You also like scrapple."*

Well, I suppose. Anyway, the cuisine was definitely improving. I got there on the third. Monday, August the third, 1936. Things had started on the first. The track and field especially. Jesse Owens was already the talk of the town.

There was two of us to a room. I got put

in with Mary Lou Petty, because Eleanor had originally been assigned as her room-mate. I think it was Olive who said, "It was convenient for Eleanor that she got thrown off the team on the boat, because she'd've left this place first night."

And Iris said, "If I'd've known what this place was gonna be like, I'd've run around with Eleanor on the boat and gotten thrown out myself."

But we were just gripin', you know. It's the nature of the beast, Teddy. And nobody much expected a great deal then, in the way of accomodations. I mean, it was the Depression. You were grateful for a roof over your head and three squares. You know what we use to do for amusement in the dorm? We'd bowl oranges down the floor at Coke bottles. Nowadays, none of the young people can amuse themselves unless they have something electronic.

*"Video games."*

Exactly. But you had to make your own fun in the Depression. And, anyway, we were all just a bunch of gals away from home. It was exciting just to be there. And the Germans — the interpreters they had livin' with us — they were the nicest ladies. Later on back home people would say, "What about those awful Nazis over there,

Trixie?" and the first person who would come to my mind would be Elsa, our interpreter. I never met a nicer person on the Eastern Shore than Elsa. It's the personal things you remember much more than the general picture. Even the matron we had, she was an old biddy, with pearls hanging down with her jowls. She'd been royalty — Baroness Von Wangenheim was her name — but she wasn't so bad. They had a high wrought-iron fence around our dorm, but I don't think that was so much to keep us girls in as to keep any boys out. And the Baroness was formidable enough to handle that without any fence. So we were certainly not under any house arrest, I can assure you.

*"But how did you get to meet Hitler and Goebbels?"*

Teddy, I told you I needed a running start. For goodness' sake, let me get warmed up.

*That was when the Bloody Marys came, complete with limes and celery stalks. Mom and I clinked glasses. Then she took her celery stalk out. She explained:*

Always gets in the way of my nose.

*"I can work around it," I said. We both took good long sips.*

Nobody says "wet your whistle" anymore, do they?

*"No, I don't think so."*

Well, this sure wets my whistle, Teddy.

*So she took another sip and sighed and said:*

Unfortunately, not long after I settled into my room, Elsa came and said there was a man to see me in the mess hall.

*"Was that Horst?"*

*Mom frowned.*

Am I telling this story or are you?

*"I'm sorry. You are."*

I'll get to Horst in due time. So I went over to the mess hall. It was next to the dorm. The right men could come in there, and the man who wanted to see me was the girls' team coach, Mr. Daughters. Ray Daughters — like sons and daughters. Right away, he said, "You better sit down, Sydney," and when I did, he said, "Look, I'm not gonna beat around the bush." He took a breath, and I swear, I thought someone had died, before he blurted out, "I'm sorry, Sydney, but you can't swim. You're not eligible."

Of course, that hit me like a ton of bricks. It didn't make any sense. "I'm not?" was, I think, all I managed to say.

"No, I'm afraid Mr. Brundage put the cart before the horse. He thought he could just substitute you for Eleanor, but it doesn't work that way in the Olympics. We'd already sent the names of the team in, and you weren't on the official list, so you aren't eligible. Mr. Brundage thought he could pull some strings, but even though he's in like Flynn with the Germans, there wasn't anything he could do."

"Oh," was all I said, Teddy.

"Then," Coach Daughters told me, "that means you can go home anytime you want, Sydney."

"You mean, go back to Chestertown? Take a boat right back across the ocean?" He nodded. Can you imagine, Teddy: go all the way to Germany and just turn around and go home like you'd just been over to Dover, Delaware? That was the nuttiest thing I'd ever heard. "Do I have to?"

"Oh no, you can stay. You're on the team. Here." He handed me a credential, with my name on it. "You're in the Olympics. You just can't compete."

"Well, Coach, I think I'll stay."

"Good. You can come to practice, maybe help out — whatever the other girls want."

"Sure."

"One thing, though. Did you bring a suit?"

"A bathing suit?"

"Yeah. See, we've already handed out all the suits we had on the ship and Eleanor kept hers, so if you don't have a suit, we have to scare one up for you."

Well, that was the Depression for you, Teddy. The United States of America didn't have the money for any extra bathing suits for their Olympic team. If President Roosevelt had known, there would've been hell to pay, but, obviously, he was in the dark. Luckily, though, I had brought my own — my sexy see-through silk number.

So Coach Daughters said, "Well, then, you're all set. Come on over to practice with the other girls tomorrow." He got up then. "I'm really sorry about this, Sydney. But I guess sometimes Mr. Brundage can act like a bull in a china shop."

"It's okay, Coach," I said. "I'm just glad to be here at all."

*Mom stopped and took another big sip of her Bloody Mary.*

See, Teddy, that's one reason why I was never very keen to talk much about being in the Olympics. Because I wasn't really. I was something of a fraud. As an Olympian, I was ersatz.

*"But, come on, it wasn't your fault."*

Oh, I know that. But still, it's a little embarrassing.

*"Well," I said, "you got a running start here."*

And I'm fortified some, too.

*So she put down her glass and picked up the thread.*

The next morning, when it was our turn to practice, we all walked over to the pool. After all, it wasn't even a half-mile away. The pool was part of the main complex — so near to the stadium itself, you could sense the excitement over there, it was so loud. As for us swimmers, though, we all just hoped that it got warmer by the time our races started in another four days. It was so unbelievably chilly for August. You can imagine what the water was like. Then, once you did get in, you didn't want to get out because the air was so cold.

But it was a magnificent pool for racing, and there must've been twenty thousand seats around it. Teddy, I'd never seen any stadium so big in all my life. I don't mean swimming stadium, you understand. I mean any kind of stadium.

Well, at practice I was just gonna swim with the other backstrokers, Edith and Alice, maybe race 'em a lap or two. But all of a sudden here comes these three men with a rubber raft and some cameras. They slipped the raft into the pool, and then one of 'em went over to speak to Coach Daughters.

I was way on the other side of the pool, but we could tell Coach wasn't very happy. He was gesticulating furiously. But it was clear he wasn't gettin' anywhere, because he finally just threw up his hands in disgust. "All right," he said, "just make sure you leave us some of the pool. We gotta practice." Then, he blew his whistle and, of all things, called me over. "Look, Sydney," he told me, "just do whatever they say so the other girls get a good practice in."

Well, Teddy, the three men were fixing the camera on the raft, and when the cameraman got on it, the one who'd been talkin' to Coach Daughters came back over. "All right, her," Coach told him. "She's the odd one out." That meant me. Then he walked away. And there I was left alone with this guy, and Teddy, I was, well, I was just a silly goose. He was so handsome. I mean, he sparkled, and when he smiled, I couldn't stand it. I couldn't even bear to look at him.

*"This must be Horst."*

Yes, Teddy, you can relax because we have

indeed gotten to Horst. We are down to where the rubber hits the road. Sure, I'd heard about love at first sight, but this was Exhibit A, and it was happenin' to me. All the boys I'd met in the United States, nothing, and then the first boy I meet in Germany, I'm a wreck. An absolute wreck. "Hi," he said, "I'm Horst Gerhardt."

I looked up. I had to make myself do that, but as soon as I saw him looking back at me, it was the funniest thing, Teddy. Even though I was this foolish little ninny, I suddenly had the feeling that he liked me. I had my sweatshirt on, because it was so cold, you know, so it wasn't like he could give me the old once-over, so he was just lookin' into my face, and of course I didn't have any lipstick on or anything, but dammit, Teddy, I looked back at him, and I smiled the best I could, and I just said, "Hi, I'm Sydney Stringfellow."

"Good to meetcha," he said. I remember that exactly. Good to meetcha.

"Yeah," I replied. It was amazing. My heart was going pitter-patter-pitter, but all the while I knew I was behaving like one cool customer. It was like I was an actor playing Sydney Stringfellow.

"Whereya from, Sydney?"

"The Eastern Shore of Maryland."

"Hmm. Don't think I know that."

"It's between the Chesapeake Bay and the ocean." I could see him kind of sortin' that out on the map in his mind. So I asked him, "Where you from?"

"Oh, right here. I'm a Berliner."

Now that threw me for a complete loop. He didn't speak any different from anybody in Chestertown. I couldn't help myself. "You're German?"

He put his hands on his hips, screwed up his mouth and said, "Ya got somethin' against that, sister?" You know, like he was a gangster in a movie — and perfectly.

And you know what I did, Teddy? I mean reflexively? I'd learned about five words of German in my guide book, but I pretended to cower like the mean gangster was holding a gun on me, and then I used three of those words: "Nein, herr. Dankeschoen." Which means —

*"No, sir. Thank you."*

You know German, Teddy?

*"Ja, about the same five words."*

Well, Horst laughed at me and said "Willkomen, huebsch," and I said, "All right, what's that?" and he swept his hand down like he had taken a big hat off and was bowing before the queen, and said, "Welcome, good-lookin'," which, of course

185

made me blush, but then we just stopped and looked at each other, and all I wanted was either to find out all about him or kiss him. And I was pretty sure he felt exactly the same way. However — darn it — just then the cameraman called something over to Horst, which I took from his tone of voice to mean: All right, stop talking to the girl and get over here.

So Horst kind of steered me in that direction, explaining as we went along, "Look, here's the deal, Sydney. We're working with Leni Riefenstahl on her film." To that point I'd never heard of her, but I gathered I was supposed to, so I kept my counsel. "Now, obviously, Leni's shooting over in the stadium today, but she wants to do some really original stuff with the swimming. We've got this amazing camera. I mean, Sydney, it can shoot underwater and over, both. It's unbelievable. You should see the film she's made already."

"I'd like to."

"Maybe I can show you sometime."

"Sure," I said. It was incredible how at ease I was — we both were. I mean he was absolutely the cutest, dreamiest, sexiest boy I'd ever met in my life, but on the other hand, we talked like we were old friends who'd known each other all our lives.

But then, the cameraman barked at Horst again, "Schnell! Schnell!" Horst whispered to me, "Quickly, quickly!" before he turned and answered him. Then he turned back to me. "Sorry," he said. "I told him you've got to understand what we're up to."

"Okay. Tell me."

"All right. What Leni wants is for us to get a close-up of a swimmer racing. I mean we want to be right in your face. We want the person watchin' the film to feel like they're actually gettin' wet. You got it?" I nodded. "So we'll start down at that end of the pool. You swim. Pretend like we're not there. There's no camera. You're just racin'. You see where Hans is?" I looked over. He was in the front of the raft, with his camera perched right over the side. "Hans, this is Sydney."

Hans deigned to give me a little wave. "His name is Hans Ertl. Trust me, you're being photographed by the best. You could be on a Hollywood set." And then he folded his arms and smiled devilishly at me. "Well, you know, you could be on a Hollywood set."

"Don't lay it on too thick," I said, blushing a little.

"So sue me," he said, smiling. Then he went right back to business. "Okay, now I'll be in the back of the boat, almost over Hans' shoulder, and I'll be holding that rope." He pointed to the third guy, who held a length of that. "That's Fritz." He nodded to him, and Fritz waved back. "Now, Fritz'll be at the far end of the pool holding onto the other end of the rope — taut — and I'll pull us back toward him, hopefully just fast enough to stay ahead of you. You get the picture? You wanna do it slowly once to get the hang of it?"

"No, I get it."

"Okay, then hop in, and I'll paddle down to you." And for just a moment more, he held his glance on me. So then, Teddy, I did something. Now, I told you it was chilly, so under normal circumstances I would've walked down to the end of the pool and taken off my sweatshirt there, but what I did was, I stood right there before Horst, and I reached down —

*And Mom reached down and pantomimed taking a sweatshirt off, the way women do, their arms crossing at the waist.*

— and very slowly, very deliberately, I raised that sweatshirt over my head. Now listen to me, Teddy. Inasmuch as I was married for decades and inasmuch as I bore two children, it has probably occurred to you that I have been naked in the presence of a man before.

*"Yes, Mom, that has indeed crossed my mind."*

Well, just for the record, never in my long life as a woman did I ever do anything as downright sexy as I did standing before Horst Gerhardt when I took my sweatshirt over my head that morning of August 4, 1936, at the Olympic pool in Berlin, Germany.

*And, for good measure, just in case I didn't get it, Mom pantomimed doing the bit with the sweatshirt again.*

I mean for all intents and purposes, it really didn't make any difference that I had a bathing suit on underneath. It was the single most brazen thing I ever did in my life. I am not a brazen woman, Teddy.

*"No."*

But that was just plain old-fashioned brazen.

*"And what, may I ask, did Horst do?" She winked — which I hardly remember Mom ever doing.*

Well, thank the Lord, he did just what I expected. He looked, and it was obvious he liked what he saw, and then I even gilded the lily, because I held that pose a bit longer, as I casually brushed my hair back —

*And Mom pantomimed brushing her hair*

*back, slowly, intently, teasing, her arms held
high, so that her chest popped out. My mother,
the strumpet!*

— and then I went down to the other end
of the pool and jumped in. Didn't even feel
cold. Felt like I was right back in the Chester River. Meanwhile, Horst got into the
raft and paddled down. He held the rope
tight from Fritz. Just naturally, I took my
usual position for the backstroke, but Hans,
who could speak a little English, immediately shook his head and cried out, "No,
no, no. Ozer way."

Horst spoke up. "You're a backstroker?"

"Yeah. But I can do all the others."

"It'd be so much better if we could really
see your face."

"You want freestyle?"

Hans held onto the camera with one hand
and made a sweeping motion with the other.
"Breaststroke?" Horst asked, making the
breaststroke motion himself.

"Ja, ja."

"Okay, Sydney, can you do the breaststroke? That way, your arms will go out to
the side and we can really see your face up
tight."

"Sure," I said. "It's not my best, the
breaststroke."

"It's okay," Horst said. "It's a great face."

Funny the way he said that, Teddy. It wasn't flirtatious at all. It wasn't like a man saying "you're beautiful," you know, playing up to you. Even if he means it. No, it was just like a statement. The way he said it, it was the best compliment I'd ever gotten. Honest to God, I was so glad when I could start swimming, so I could move. If I'd just stood there any longer in the pool, I think I would've melted.

*She shook her head at the wonder of the memory, and reached down and took a nice big gulp of her Bloody Mary.*

Well, I started swimming. The breaststroke. Hans worked the camera, and Horst pulled on the rope. The girls in the other half of the pool stopped practicing and watched. Even Coach Daughters had to watch. It was pretty interesting, actually. I had to swim with the camera just in front of me — hardly a foot, maybe. I splashed Hans pretty good. They do all sorts of camera tricks now, of course, but this was downright revolutionary for that time. And when we got to the other end of the pool, Horst asked me if I'd do it again. Tell you the truth, Teddy, I would've done it all day long just to be there with him, so besides the breaststroke, we did a couple lengths butterfly and a couple freestyle.

Hans seemed pleased, so Horst told me that'd be enough, and I hoisted myself out of the pool and took off my cap. I'd quickly brushed my hair back, trying to look as pretty as I could before Horst came over and handed me a towel.

*"And correct me if I'm wrong, Mother, but you're in that kinda see-through suit."*

You are not wrong at all, Teddy. And you can also read into the record that I took my own good time putting that towel around me.

*"You vixen, you."*

Yes, Teddy, your old mother was a regular she-devil on this occasion. But after I thought I'd given him enough of the peep show, I wrapped myself in the towel. And Horst said, "That was great."

"You got what you wanted?"

"For now." Well, he just meant it vis-à-vis the shooting, but it was funny, we were so in sync already, Teddy, we both sort of took it to mean something else, and we smiled, shyly, together. Now understand, Horst wasn't the least bit fresh.

*"Come on, Mom, give the devil his due."*

Well, all right, perhaps he'd been a bit cheeky. But I do think you could say I was leadin' him on.

*"Yes, I believe you could."*

Well, we won't split hairs, Teddy, because right away, Horst said, "Wouldja like to come over to the place tonight?"

"What place?"

"I'm sorry, I guess that didn't sound right. I mean the big place, the headquarters where we're makin' the film. It's not far from here."

"Sure. I'd like that." And then I remembered. My heart sank. "No, look, I forgot. Some of the girls asked me to go out tonight, and I really gotta do that. See, I just got in yesterday."

"Whatdya mean 'yesterday'? I thought you'd all been here a week."

"Well, not me. It's a long story."

"I'd like to hear it."

"And I'd like to hear how come you're a German but you speak English like an American."

"It's a long story."

"Well?" I said.

"Okay, tomorrow night we'll tell long stories."

"Ja. Danke."

"Not bad."

"It's the only German I know."

"I'll teach you some more."

"Like what?"

"Oh, like" — and he gave me this mouth-ful.

So I said, "Okay, gimme that slow."

And he said, "Wie . . . bist . . . du . . . nur . . . so . . . schoen . . . gewoden."

And I repeated it till I got it right (which is why I still remember it, even though it's been a coon's age). So then I asked him: "Well, what's it mean?"

And he said, "It means 'How'd you get so pretty?' "

So I blushed a little and said, "Come on. I can't say that."

"Yeah, whaddya wanna say?"

"I wanna say, 'Thanks for the swell com-pliment, but go easy on the sweet talk.' "

"Oh, all right. That's . . ." and he rattled it off. And then he said, "Okay?"

And I laughed. "Okay. What time tomor-row?"

"How 'bout seven o'clock?" I nodded. "But Sydney, just hang on if I'm a little late. Leni works us pretty hard." And he looked at me longer and kinda smiled. Neither one of us stuck out our hands, because I guess it's sort of foolish shakin' hands with someone you know you're gonna be kissin' soon enough.

*"You knew that, huh?"*

"Teddy, trust me. It didn't take any ESP. I

might've been a little outta my element, but, the Eastern Shore or Berlin, Germany, I knew a thing or two about physical attraction between members of the opposite sex."

*"You could feel the electricity, huh?"*

*Mom held out her hands, stiff, and wiggled her fingers like Frankenstein's monster getting the juice.*

Oh my, yes, Teddy, I was lit up like Times Square. So I just said, "Don't worry, I'll wait for you."

It's funny, isn't it, Teddy, how well we used to operate before there were cell phones so we always know where someone is. We got along just fine then even though we didn't have everybody's co-ordinates every second of the day. Didn't we?

*"Yeah."*

Well, it didn't matter. I knew I was onto somethin' good. I'd've waited for that boy till the cows came home.

The waitress came and Mom told me to go ahead. I ordered a Cobb salad. "Fine," she said. "I'll have a bacon cheddar cheeseburger, and don't scrimp on the fries." She smiled, shaking her head at me. "Under the circumstances, there's no sense me holding back."

"All right," I told the waitress, "eighty-six the salad, and I'll have what the lady's having."

"Live large, Teddy. Live large." She took a generous sip of her Bloody Mary. "I'd have another one of these monkeys, too, but it'd make me sleepy, and I'm just gettin' to the meat of the story."

"Horst," I said.

She grinned puckishly. "Oh, the girls just razzed me somethin' awful as soon as he left. Coach had to scream at 'em to get back to practicing. But you could tell how envious they all were. I mean, he was the cutest thing you ever did see. These kids today do all this internet dating, where they get matched up so perfectly. I guess it works. They all hop into bed so fast now I'm not sure it matters anyhow. But I don't know, Teddy, I think it's better when he comes outta the blue."

"So, I take it Horst did indeed take you out the next night."

"Even better than that." She paused for a second, pondering, then held up her drink glass. "Oh, miss," she called out to the waitress, "let's do this again. And one for my friend, too." She turned back to me. "What the hell, Teddy, I can sleep all afternoon, and then I'll be wide awake for the Olympics tonight. Natalie Coughlin's in the medley relay."

Mom drained what was left of her inaugural Bloody Mary, told me to start the tape recorder again and then resumed her story.

You must've seen that movie, *Cabaret.*

*"Mom, I directed a production of that a few years ago."*

Of course, Teddy. Well, you remember that joint where the goofy girl sang where they had all the telephones on the tables —

*"The Kit Kat Club."*

Exactly. Well, there actually were places

like that in Berlin. The guy who wrote that —

*"His name was Christopher Isherwood."*

Oh yeah. Well, he must've gone to one of them. So did we. It was called the Femina, and several of the gals on the team had already been there before I got to Berlin, and they wanted to take me. It was very European, very sophisticated, very — well — naughty. Most of us even had a beer. We nursed them, of course, but it seemed quite daring. I was sitting at a table with a few of the girls, Iris and Dorothy and Katherine, I think, and you'll never guess what happened.

*"Your telephone rang."*

Teddy, how in the world did you guess that?

*"Let's just say you telegraphed your punch, Mom. And a little birdie tells me it was Horst calling."*

Well, if you're gonna take all the suspense out of this, I guess I don't hafta tell you the rest.

*"Oh, don't be so sensitive. What'd he say?"*

Well, Dorothy answered. That's Dorothy Poynton, the diver — remember I told you: Dorothy was married. She was a little more savvy than the rest of us, so she answered the phone and listened for a second before she handed me the receiver and cooed, "Be still my heart."

I didn't get it right away, Teddy, but the other girls sure did. They started giggling. I just said, "Hello?"

And, of course, yes, it was Horst, and he said, "Hey, Sydney." And then he told me to look over my shoulder, and there he was at a table with two other guys, up in this sorta mezzanine, and I almost died. The other girls had already spotted him, so even before he said anything, Dorothy said, "Well, I guess we'll see you back at the dorm, Sydney." So then, when Horst asked me to come up, I knew it was okay with the other girls if I left them. And I did. In a July minute.

He rose when I got to his table. You see, he was a gentleman, Teddy. As it was, most everybody had better manners then, but that's neither here nor there, and if I got into that, it would only make me sound like an ancient scold. Which, of course, I am.

*"Really, Mom, I think you're very up to date."*

Well, that doesn't stop me from gritting my teeth at the antediluvian behavior I encounter these days, but let's get back to Horst.

*"I'm all ears."*

Good. Well, there were two friends of his

at the table, and they both shook my hand and then departed forthwith.

*"Forthwith?"*

Yes, pronto. Itsky-outsky. So there I was alone with Horst. He said, "Can I getcha a beer?" Remember now, he spoke just like the boy next door. And even though I'd already finished almost one whole beer, which was pretty much my limit, I threw caution to the winds and accepted. "Try a Rothaus," he said.

"What's that?"

"It's my favorite, but you have to be German to know about it. It's been made for centuries somewhere down in the Black Forest. I think monks used to make it. They had a lotta time on their hands when they weren't praying, so they learned how to brew a damn good beer."

"Sounds fine with me." So he picked up the phone and ordered two of those Rothauses. I'll tell you, Teddy, I thought the Empire Room at the Palmer House was something, but this was beyond anything I'd ever imagined. Of course, you gotta remember, when I'd been to the Empire Room I was not in the company of Horst Gerhardt.

We looked at each other and smiled, and I believe both of us would've been delighted to continue that arrangement ad infinitum, but finally I sorta regained consciousness and reminded him that he was gonna tell me a long story. He said, "A long story?"

"You know, how you learned to talk English like an American."

"Oh yeah, we both had long stories."

I nodded. "You first. Didja spend time in America?"

"No, never, unfortunately. But I'd really like to come over there." My heart leaped, Teddy. Just the thought that this dreamboat might actually cross the Atlantic and become a "to be continued . . ." in my life.

"So," I said, "if you never — ?"

"It's really not that long a story. My father's a diplomat, and when I was a little boy he was posted to the embassy in Tokyo, and when it was time for me to go to school, my parents decided to send me to the American school. There were a lotta Americans in Tokyo, and they ran the best foreign school there. My mother had spent some time in England before the war — actually, she's something of an Anglophile, speaks veddy British — and she also thought it would be a good idea for me to learn English. Dad agreed, and so little Horst in his liederhosen went to study with all the Yanks. Almost right away, they started calling me 'Ger.' "

"Ger?"

"From Gerhardt. They didn't like Horst."

So I blurted it out: "Everyone used to call me Trixie." Immediately, I was sorry I'd volunteered a name Eleanor had advised me to ditch, but Horst thought it charming.

"Trixie? I like that. It's just so . . . American. You prefer that or Sydney?"

"Oh, I'm all Sydney now."

"All right. But I'll surprise you sometime and call you Trixie — just 'cause I like it."

"All right, Ger."

He laughed and reached over and put his hand on mine. I remember what struck me was how natural it was, Teddy. How naturally he did it, how naturally I felt. Usually, you know, especially when you're young, every move a boy makes seems so . . . well, studied. Horst just did it and right away, I felt . . . well, that my hand was where his belonged. And he kept it there, tellin' me his story:

"So I was with all these American guys, and the teachers were all American, too. I told Mom the liederhosen had to go. My God, I even learned to play baseball. Hey, there's a game next week. Wanna go?"

"A baseball game? In Berlin?"

"Yeah, an exhibition in the Olympic

stadium. Show the Germans what the Americans are so crazy about."

"Sure, I'd love to go."

"Good, it's a date. Anyway, I hung out with American boys mostly, and you know how it is: what you learn when you're young makes the greatest impression on you. I even had to be Germanized some by the time I came back here to live."

A waitress in some sorta faux Alpine outfit brought the beers, and Horst took his hand off mine long enough so we could raise our glasses. Then he said, "There were a couple kids who came from down South in my class, and I even learned to talk with a Southern accent." I cocked my head, like okay, show me, and he put down his glass and took my hand again and said, "Honey chile, Ah'm jes so dang glad Ah met y'all."

He had it exactly right, too, but best of all, I could tell he meant what he was saying. I didn't try any accent back to him. I just said, straight up, "Me too, Horst. Thank you."

We drank up, but I didn't do a very good job of pretending I liked the beer. It was awfully bitter. "Aw, you don't like Rothaus?"

"Well, it's, uh . . . sharper than I imagined."

"Want me to getcha somethin' else?"

I shook my head. "No, this is fine." And then I said — oh Lord, I remember this word for word, "Anything's wonderful with the present company." Now, was that a line? I mean for a kid to just toss it off? I thought to myself: look to your laurels, Noël Coward. And lemme tell ya, Teddy, it sure passed muster.

Because . . . Horst cocked his head and stared at me and said, "You know, I'd really like to kiss you, Sydney."

And I just said "Yeah," and we kinda stuck our heads forward over the table and kissed. Just like that. On the lips. Right there before God and everybody in the Femina bar.

"Thank you," he said. "That was lovely."

Of course, right then, the phone rang. I'd forgotten the girls could see us, but right away we both figured who it was, and Horst gestured for me to go ahead and pick it up. It was Dorothy. "Well," she said, "those Germans sure work fast." Let us just say, Teddy, that I did not deign to honor that with an answer. I just said, "Oh, hi."

"Okay, Sydney, we're gonna be leavin' soon. The consensus is that very possibly you would rather not come with us."

"Yeah, that's pretty accurate."

"All right. And we all say: your German's one awful cute fellow."

204

"I know that."

"Well, have a good time, and don't be too late."

"Okay." I hung up the phone. I could tell Dorothy'd been ready to add something about me taking care of myself. Well, I didn't need that, thank you very much. "They're gonna take off and get a cab," I told Horst.

"Don't worry. I'll drive you back." He took another gulp of his beer, so I took a sip, too, and it was better than the first time. "I think it's an acquired taste," I said.

"You're not," he said.

"I'm not what?"

"You're not an acquired taste. There was somethin' about you right away."

"Yeah."

I'm afraid, Teddy, that the Noël Coward repartee deserted me when he looked at me with those big baby blues. So, since I was no longer brilliantly holding up my end of the dialogue, Horst went on: "After Tokyo, my father got posted to run a consulate in Manila for a year, and most all the foreigners in the Philippines were Americans, and so we not only spoke almost exclusively English — even at home — but my language was completely Americanized. To my mother's despair."

"You got any brothers or sisters?"

"One older sister. Liesl. She's married." He paused, and I thought he was gonna tell me more about her, but instead he decided to go back to his own story. "Then, after Father got posted back to Berlin for a couple years, he made ambassador, and we went to Lisbon. And trust me, in Portugal, nobody but the Portuguese speak Portuguese. It was all English. By the time I got back here, it was almost like German was my second language." He paused then and held out his hands. "There — that's my linguistic history. And you?"

"Me what?"

"What's your long story?"

"Oh yeah." So I explained to Horst about Eleanor and why I happened to show up after the rest of the team, and how I found out I wasn't allowed to swim.

He took a long pull on his beer and shook his head. "Aw, that's a raw deal, Sydney."

"Oh, I dunno. Right now, I think I got a pretty good deal."

"Yeah, me too."

We were, of course, talking about being with one another.

*"I gathered that, Mom."*

Yeah, I just didn't want to leave, Teddy. I mean, I'd completely forgotten about swimming. But I knew it was getting late, and so I asked him to take me home. He had a silver Opel roadster, and I remember driving back, how I noticed everything all around — things I hadn't paid any attention to on the way over. All that stuff about I only have eyes for you — I never felt that, Teddy. I think that when you're falling in love you see everything brighter and clearer. Everything is more vivid. That's what love does to the whole world around you.

*"Mom, you're already in love with this guy?"*

Teddy, I thought I had been crystal clear on that subject. What part of "head over heels" don't you understand? Do you think I'd be wasting all this who-shot-John if he was just a passing fancy?

*"Well, it's just that —"*

It's just that I had never felt like this in my life. Never. All I wanted was to get back to the Friesenhaus so he could kiss me goodnight. I was all scrunched up as close to him as I could get, and when he stopped the car out front he turned to me and put an arm around me. It was hard for a guy to drive a car with his arm around a girl in those days, Teddy, because you had to shift gears. So he turns to me, and he says: "Look, if you can't swim in the Olympics, wouldja like to come out to Grunewald,

207

where there's this beautiful lake, and you could go swimming there . . . with me?"

"Sure."

But then he shook his head. It was a set-up. "No," Horst said. "I don't know. One time at the Rot-Weiss Club —"

"The what?"

"The Rot-Weiss Club. That's red and white, rot-weiss."

"Oh, okay. Now I know two more words."

"Right. It's our best tennis club, and I got back from Lisbon, and I thought I was a pretty good player, so the pro suggested I play this girl, and I said, 'C'mon, I don't want to play any girl,' but he said she was pretty good, so I played her and guess what? She beat me straight sets. She was somethin' like the national junior champion."

"Yeah?"

"Well, it was humiliating. Getting beat by a girl. So I don't know if I wanna go swimming with you and get shown up."

"That's okay. I'll pretend I can only dog paddle, and you can rescue me."

He shook his head. "No, I don't know. Because now that I think about it, Sydney, I already know one other thing you do better than me."

He had me there. "What's that?"

"Kussen."

"What?"

"Kussen. You kiss better than me."

"No, I don't. You kussen much better."

He drew closer. "Well, let's see if we can settle the argument." I mean, can you believe it, Teddy? Every other boy I'd kissed had just sorta moved in and planted it on me. This was like being in a movie. Dialogue, Teddy — dialogue! And, boy, we really did some kussen this time. And after a while I could sort of feel his hand around me kinda hovering, and so I reached up and took it and steered it right down, smack onto my bazoom.

*"Oh, come on, Mother, I really don't think —"*

Oh, for God's sake, Teddy, don't be such an old woman. Have no fear, I'm not gonna get graphic. My tongue is just loosened up a little by the vodka. And besides, is there no poetry in your heart? You can't listen to an old lady recounting the sweet memories of young love? Besides, I stopped kissing him long enough to say, "Just for a moment."

*"Well, I'm glad to hear there was some display of ladylike restraint."*

Yeah, wise guy, but I also added: "For now." And then I tore myself away from him and outta the car and ran through the gate of the wrought-iron fence and inside the Friesenhaus, and I just delighted — just delighted — in all those other girls in their night gowns giving me those looks of censure . . . or envy. My, did I give it back to them.

*Mom beamed, took a healthy swallow of her Bloody Mary and then actually smacked her lips.*

Talk about a Cheshire cat, Teddy. Talk about a Cheshire cat.

Mom finished her bacon cheddar cheese-burger and — more to the point — her second Bloody Mary, and, true to her assumption, she was ready for a good nap. As soon as we got home and she went into her bedroom, I went to the garden to call my sister.

Now, I must admit, there was a part of me that was upset, even angry, for here was Mom absolutely radiating in this luminous story about her love for this sweet-talkin', sharp-kissin' German hunk. I felt hurt for my poor father, that he'd spent fifty years as an adoring husband, but it had all been a chimera, he some sort of afterthought.

But then, there was also a part of me that was absolutely beguiled by the whole fascinating story that Mother had suddenly chosen to reveal to me. I'd certainly never myself had any adventure of the heart like this — nothing so romantic nor so thrilling.

211

I had to admit, as hard as I had fallen for Jeanne, that first great blush of my true love had certainly not reached the poetic peaks of sheer ecstacy that Mother's own romance had attained.

In this frame of mind, I called my sister. Naturally, right away, when I told Helen that I was alone, outside, she assumed something must be wrong with Mother. "Oh no, in fact she's on a roll. We just got back from lunch, and she had two Bloody Marys."

"Jesus, Teddy. What's the occasion?"

"Memories."

"What?"

"She's just having a ball telling me about her whole Olympic experience."

I could almost visualize Helen shaking her head on the other end of the line. "That's amazing," she said. "She'd always skip over that. I'd press her, and she'd pretty much skim over the Olympics, just suffer me in that way of hers, maybe talk about Jesse Owens and Hitler, stuff you could read in a book. Very impersonal."

"Well, trust me, she's not leaving anything out now."

"I'm jealous, Teddy. I always thought mothers were supposed to share the skinny with daughters. And fathers with sons."

"Well, it's cross-germination time, I guess. But, Helen, here's a question. All the time she's talked to you . . . I mean, I know she never got into the Olympics, but did Mom ever mention a guy named Horst?"

"Horse?"

"No, no. German. Horst — with a *t*."

Right away, Helen said, "No. That's a new one."

"Horst Gerhardt."

"Sorry, Teddy. What's the deal?"

"Well, the fact is, she's really not telling me about the Olympics per se. They're only the background for this Horst. She could be in Fort Wayne, Indiana, for all she talks about the Olympics. It's just mein Horst."

"Who the hell is he?"

"Well, in the word of my new confidant, he was a quote dreamboat unquote."

"God, dreamboat. I haven't heard that in years. Not since we were girls, and we'd say to some stuck-up guy, 'Hey, dreamboat.' And when he'd smile, we'd say, 'Not you, shipwreck.' "

"Oh, you girls were mean."

"It's a cruel world out there, Teddy. But, go on, tell me about Mom's dreamboat."

"Well, trust me: Horst sure fit the bill. Suave. A gentleman and a scholar. Delightful and charming. Silver-tongued, too."

"Jeez, why couldn't I ever have met a guy like that?"

"You did. But you just kept throwing 'em back and then casting the net again."

"All right, smarty-pants."

"Of course, it's also possible that the dreamboat might've been a dirty rotten Nazi. I haven't had the nerve to interrupt her reverie and ask that rather rude question. But —"

"Is Mom okay, Teddy? I mean this isn't her mind playing tricks?"

"Oh no, she's absolutely as sharp as ever. She's incredibly vivid. It's even a little embarrassing."

"Embarrassing?"

"Let's just say it's a little more than I wanna know. Granted, this was into the second Bloody Mary, but she made a point of describing how Horst copped a feel off her the first time."

"Oh, come on, Teddy."

"No, I'm serious. Let me ask you, Helen: have you ever in all your long life as a mother felt inclined to describe to any of your children how somebody copped a feel off you?" Helen just answered that with a laugh. "No, I didn't think you'd ever shared that delicate information. But, more seriously, I feel sort of embarrassed for Daddy.

I mean, I know he wasn't in the picture until after Berlin, but the way she talks about this Horst, it's like she's forgotten the lifetime she just happened to pass with the dear father of her children."

"Come on, Teddy, she's just reminiscing. Everybody idealizes their first love — and she's abroad for the first time, and it's the Olympics, and the guy's a dreamboat. Mom's dying, Teddy."

"I know that, Helen."

"You watch. She'll get around to Daddy. Just because she let some German kid feel her up once — hey, you know how much Mom adored Daddy. Come on, was there ever a sweeter marriage?"

"I know. I know. It's just I had to wonder if she'd ever mentioned Horst to you."

"No. Never. When I was first dating, she'd laugh about a couple of boys who took her out on the Eastern Shore. You know — 'just us girls' stuff. But Horst — no. Hey, now you got me interested. Lemme know how it comes out."

"Oh, don't worry, you'll get the full treatment. I'm taping her."

"You're what?"

"Yeah, she bought a tape recorder and makes me take it all down."

"Wow."

"Yeah. She's actually written the whole story out, but she wanted to tell me the fun part. Which basically seems to mean the Horst part."

"Horst," said Helen.

"Jawow, Frau Emerson. Herr Horst Gerhardt. Handsome young gentleman of romance, charm and mystery."

After her nap, Mom got all wound up, in the negative, about something President Bush did or something he said or both, and that put her in such a foul mood she didn't want to talk about Berlin. She even sulked while we watched the swimming that night. But by the next morning, the storm clouds had drifted away, and she was a-rarin' to go again. She all but shoved the tape recorder at me. "You like a good love story, don't you, Teddy?" she snapped.

"Of course I do."

"Well, this one's picking up steam."

"I thought Daddy was the love of your life."

She shook her head at me. "God, you directed all those plays. You'd think you, of all people, would understand drama. A love story is different from the love of your life."

"Okay, but this Horst —"

"Excuse me: This? He wasn't 'this' Horst,

thank you very much. He was Horst."

"Okay, Horst. But Mom, this is Germany, 1936. They were a bunch of pretty nasty folks. I'm sorry, but . . . was Horst a Nazi?"

She leaned back in her chair and templed her hands, more thoughtful now. "That is, of course, a very legitimate question. And I'll come to it. But you gotta remember somethin', Teddy. Here we are in 2004, and we have the wonderful benefit of hindsight. Now, let's go back to 1936, and put yourself in my shoes. Sure, we all knew Hitler had been terrible to the Jewish people and the homosexuals and the gypsies, too. That was no secret. But here the authorities of the world — of the world, Teddy — had said it was fine for Germany to hold the Olympics, which is supposed to be this great celebration of the brotherhood of man. Okay?

"And I'm eighteen years old, wet behind the ears, just off the boat from the Eastern Shore, and it sure all looks hunky-dory to me. And to just about everybody else, too. Among other things, Hitler had kinda cleaned up the joint. All the ugly anti-Semitic signs were removed, and on the surface it's all peaches and cream. Keep in mind, too, to most of us, Hitler was just another dictator, because the world was rife with dictators in those days. Dictators were a dime a dozen. Besides, everybody was raving about what a great job Hitler was doing. We still had breadlines in the United States. And Mussolini had the trains running on time. So put it in perspective."

"Please, Mom, I'm not being judgmental."

"Oh, I hate that word, Teddy. I can't believe my own flesh and blood used it."

"Judgmental?"

"It's so oily. The only thing worse than that is when somebody pretends to be apologetic and says 'with all due respect,' because that's simply an excuse to be judgmental and criticize." She shook her head and pursed her lips. "With all due respect . . ."

"Okay, Mother, with all due respect I won't be judgmental. I was just asking."

"Thank you. And if you ever call me 'inappropriate,' I'll cut you out of the will. Inappropriate — please!"

"Hey, Mom, let up on me. That's terribly inappropriate."

In response, you know what my own mother did then? She gave me the finger, shot me the bird. And we laughed like a couple of old buddies.

"Sorry, Teddy. I'm loaded for bear this morning. You see, the point is, it's easy to say now that I was suckered. But good night, nurse, I had a lotta company. And look — right now, right now, any fool can see that this jackass in the White House is the worst excuse for a president we've ever had, and yet you know the polls — half the people living in these United States in the here and now still plan to vote for him. So go easy on my crowd back in '36."

"That's very well said, Mom."

She nodded smugly, but then put a more pleasing expression on her face, and leaning forward, downright grinning, she said, "That's the general, Teddy. But there was also the specific, which was I'm head over heels in love with Horst Gerhardt, who is the best lookin' thing ever to come down the pike — certainly down my pike — and I'm snuggled up next to him in a car and it's a moonlit night, and excuse me if I didn't say, 'Just a minute, Horst, before I fall passionately into your embrace, what are your views on the Sudetenland?' Assuming, of course, that I'd ever heard of the Sudetenland."

"I get the picture, Mother."

"Good. Yes, I wasn't living completely in a vacuum, and we'll get back to some of that." She paused. "In fact, more than you might possibly imagine. You really have no idea."

"No idea?"

"You have no idea at all, Teddy." She said that with such authority that it sounded a little ominous — and so completely out of character. Maybe she realized that, because she quickly got back to the subject. "Listen, of course I was already wondering some about things. Not dwelling on them, you understand, but even a naif like me couldn't help but wonder a little. But for now, let's get back to the love story."

"Okay," I said, waving my arms before me in surrender. "Love story."

And she began again to talk into the tape recorder.

Well, that next evening Horst picked me up and took me out to dinner at a little café. I had my first glass of schnapps, Teddy. But just one. I behaved myself. I was a good girl. We just talked. I didn't care about my dinner — wienerschnitzel, I think — because I just wanted to listen to Horst tell me about his life and to tell him about mine. I didn't want food to get in the way. I wanted him to know everything about me, even though his life had been so much more interesting than mine. But he seemed to hang on my every word, mundane as they were.

Then, as we were finishing dinner, he

asked if I wanted to go meet Leni Riefenstahl, and, naturally, I said I'd love to. By
now, I'd heard a great deal about her. She'd
been a dancer, and then a movie star,
especially in a bunch of movies that took
place in the mountains. I gathered Leni was
quite the athlete. But, above all, she was
very determined. In fact, Teddy, she was
what you men used to call a "hard broad."
Now, you have to understand, there were
also dames then. Dames and broads both.
But there's a difference. Eleanor Holm, for
example. She was more what you men used
to call a "tough dame." Leni was a hard
broad.

*"What were you, Mother?"*

That's a good question, Teddy. I think I
was a tough dame, I really do. But there
were times when I had to be a hard broad,
and I think I pulled that off.

*"I never saw you that way."*

Nah, by the time you were old enough to
notice that stuff, I was just a lady. You could
only be a dame for so long. You could be a
broad longer. But only so long. Of course,
nobody can use words like that anymore.
It's inappropriate. It's a visual world now,
Teddy. Tattoos and toplessness. That's okay.
It's tacky, but it's okay. Because you can see
them. In this world, anything you can see is

222

just fine. We're back to paleolithic times, when painting pictures of the animals on the cave walls was what passed for sophistication. But, you call some girl with tattoos and her bazooms hanging out a broad and everybody has a fit.

Anyway, Leni Riefenstahl. Hitler asked her to direct a propaganda film for him. And Leni certainly knew which side her bread was buttered on. She made Hitler look like a demigod, a regular avatar. So then she got the job as director for the Nazis' Olympic film. And now she was bossing everybody around. Oh, Leni Riefenstahl was a pistol. Everybody and his brother said that.

So we walked to Horst's car, and he opened the door for me, and I noticed, standing there, that he was taller than me — but only by a few inches when I had my heels on. Remember Winnie the Pooh?

*I nodded. You never knew where Mom was headed, how stuff came from nowhere.*

I think it was Christopher Robin. Well, either him or Pooh himself, talking about Piglet, said, "Just the size of Piglet, my favorite size." Horst was like Piglet in that respect. He was my favorite size. And so, when he opened the door for me, we looked into each other's eyes for about a tenth of a second and then he took me into his arms and we started kissing. Big time.

Now, Teddy, don't get nervous again when it comes to your mother's lust. I'm just bringing this up to make a point, because that was the exact moment when I realized that the best kissing is standing up. I never wavered from that point of view from that moment on, that time when I was standing by the side of a car, kissing Horst Gerhardt. You see it in the movies. Stand-up kissing is just the best. Sitting down, it never works as well. It's never even as sexy. And when it comes to lying down, there's so much other stuff going on that the kissing becomes small potatoes. But standing up . . . I never forgot.

*"I won't dispute you, Mom."*

Good. So, after the kissing, we got into the car, and I tried to tone the electricity down, bring more of a sedate atmosphere to the proceedings. Besides, I was curious. I asked him how he got involved with Leni Riefenstahl.

"Well," he began, "a few months ago, I was at the Rot-Weiss Club —"

"Red-White."

"Ja, Fraulein Stringfellow. Very good." I snuggled a little closer to him, Teddy.

*"What happened to the more sedate atmosphere?"*

Well, the boy had to drive the car, after all. I could listen to him and snuggle at the same time. So Horst went on: "Liesl, my sister. She's married to an, uh, army officer, and he was on maneuvers, so she was living back home, and the four of us went to the club. Leni was there. Everybody knows who she is, so we were surprised when she suddenly came over to our table. I assumed she'd met my father somewhere, but no, she'd spotted me across the room, and it was me she wanted to talk to." Horst paused then. He said, "This is a little embarrassing, Sydney, but she wanted to know if I'd be in her movie."

"Really?"

"Yeah. Leni said I was just the type she wanted."

"What type is that?" I asked. "The same as you're my type?" (I could be a little arch in those days, Teddy.)

But Horst let that go. He just said, "Well, see, she was gonna start the movie with the torch comin' from Greece, from Olympia."

"What torch?"

"It's something new. An Olympic torch. They lit it on Mount Olympus, and then runners brought it here. Literally — passing the torch."

I hadn't heard about this, Teddy, as I'd

been on the ship when they'd lit the flame in the Stadium at the opening ceremony. So I asked him, "You carried this torch in Greece?"

"No, no, Sydney. Leni used lots of runners. Like Greeks when we were in Greece. But she wanted a special type when the torch got to Germany."

"And you're the type?"

"Yeah. Tall, fair. You know, that's supposed to be the classic German type."

"Handsome."

"I didn't say that."

"I did." And I was pretty sure that Leni Riefenstahl was on the same page.

"Well —"

"So she filmed you?"

"Yeah, Leni wanted me to carry the torch precisely when it came over the border from Czechoslovakia into the Fatherland. So I went down with her —"

"Oh, just you and Leni Riefenstahl, the big, sexy movie star, together down by Czechoslovakia?" See, I was just teasing him, Teddy, but he reacted very, well, I would say, viscerally.

"Oh, come on, Sydney, there was a whole camera crew there. It was all business."

Even by then, Teddy, when I was still a kid, I had a pretty good idea that whenever anybody said that something was "all business," with a great deal of emphasis, it probably wasn't. So I kept at it. "She's really pretty, isn't she?"

"Leni?"

"Yes."

"Not as pretty as you."

That brought me up short. "Oh, come on."

"No, you're really beautiful, Sydney."

I snuggled a little closer. "Thank you, Horst. That's the sweetest thing anybody ever said to me."

"It is? What's the matter with the American boys? Are they blind?"

Instinctively then, I scooted away from him, over to the far side of the seat, but I kept my eyes on him when I spoke. I wanted to say it unencumbered by being up close, snuggling. I wanted the words to carry the weight. "No," I said, "it's just the sweetest because you were the one who said it." He only smiled at that, watching the road, so I asked him how the filming at the Czechoslovakian border went.

"Well, pretty good. I think she'll use a few seconds of me in the film, but she chose another fellow to actually carry the torch into the stadium and light the flame."

"The nerve of that hussy!" I said.

"Come on, Mom, you didn't actually say 'hussy.' Did you?"

Well, in fact, Teddy, people did say hussy then. It was different from either broad and dame. Hussy meant sort of a slut, but with an attitude. Horst knew I was just having fun, though. Him from Berlin, me from the Eastern Shore — still, everything was right as rain between us from the word go. That was the magic of it. So he just shrugged and said, "Yeah, I was almost famous. But if I was the type, I wasn't the perfect type. Leni wanted a guy with blond hair."

"You're blond, Horst."

"No, I'm more of a light brown. She wanted an absolute blond. And you don't argue with Leni. So I didn't get to run into the stadium. But anyway, then Leni asked me if I'd help with the filming. She could use my English, and I could do the odd jobs —"

"Like when you came out to the pool in the raft."

"Exactly. But thank God I'm only helping out. Leni's working everyone to death."

We were driving on the west side of town, in the section called Charlottenburg. That was the high-rent district, and it wasn't too far from the stadium and my dormitory. Horst pulled the car into a parking lot in front of a large manor house — almost a castle, you could say. I started to open the door, but he stopped me and moved closer. I thought he wanted to kiss me again —

*"Even sitting down, Mother?"*

Now get it straight. I didn't say kissing was bad sitting down. I just said kissing standing up was better. And trust me, I was not adverse to kissing Horst, irrespective of whatever physical geometry might be involved.

*"Thank you for clearing that up."*

Well, he didn't want to kiss me. Not this time. What he wanted was for me to check and see if any of my lipstick from the standing-up kiss was smeared on his face. Which it was. "You don't want Leni to see another girl's been monkeying around with you, do you?" I asked.

"Put a sock in it, Sydney." He knew I was just teasing him. I took out my handkerchief — we carried handkerchiefs back then; Kleenexes were still just for hoi polloi — and put some spit on it and wiped the lipstick off, and we were ready to proceed into the castle. "It's called Haus Ruhwald," he told me. "That means Peaceful Woods. But I'm afraid, with Leni, it usually isn't very peaceful."

"Is she working this late herself?"

"Oh God, she's the worst. She doesn't sleep, so she doesn't let anyone else either. You'll see." And I did. It really was all business. As magnificent as the building was outside, it was spare inside, almost spartan. They even had cots in the halls, and here and there some poor, exhausted worker had flopped down, trying to steal a little shut-eye.

"You really think we should be here?" I asked him. My curiosity about meeting Leni was battling my fear of having her meet me. But Horst tugged me along, down the hall.

In fact, I heard Leni before I saw her. It was a woman's voice, barking German, that poured out into the hallway. Thereupon, some poor fellow slunk out of the room where the shouting was emanating from. As he passed us, he shook his head, moaning to Horst.

"What'd he say?" I asked.

"He said she's like a dragon tonight, spitting fire."

"Oh, great."

"Don't worry," Horst said, taking my hand and leading me into the room from whence cometh the Gorgon flames. A projector was on, and the film was showing a relay race from the day before. Horst and I stood in the back, unobtrusively, but I could make out Leni, sitting in her chair, watching along with a couple of men. When this particular section ended, she muttered disagreeably, and then she ordered one of the men to do something or other, and when he seemed to protest — and rather mildly, I thought — she hit the ceiling, screaming God knows what.

German is very guttural, you know, Teddy. It can sound downright nasty even when it isn't. The funny thing is, too, it's a very rigid language. Not much to move around in. There's not even many cuss words in it. But it just has a tone to it, you know? So when the German is really and truly mean, it knocks you back on your heels. This was such an occasion. I kinda scrunched down alongside Horst.

Someone flipped the light switch on, and as the man she'd berated left, Leni turned her head just enough to spy Horst standing in the back. Well, let me tell you, Teddy, all of a sudden it was bluebirds and lollipops. "Horst! Mein schatz!" she cooed. Schatz sounds awful, doesn't it? If I called you schatz you'd think I was mad at you. That's German for you. But in fact schatz means something like treasure. Horst was her treasure. So then she stepped over to him and smiled and touched him.

It was merely a light finger to the shoulder, but it's been my experience, Teddy, that some women — and a few men, but not many — instinctively know how to touch a person of the other sex exactly right. It's not important where they touch the other person. They just have the knack. Well, that was the way Leni Riefenstahl touched mein schatz, and then they stood there and had a little chitchat, which, of course, I didn't understand word one of.

And the way they looked at each other. It was adoring and sly, and it occurred to me that this must be the way people who have slept together look at one another when they meet again with other folks around — thinking no one else is the wiser. Of course, myself not having slept with anybody up to this point, I was not yet personally privy to this knowledge, but, nonetheless, I believe to this day that it was an accurate supposition on my part.

*"Mother, you were jealous." She actually stamped her foot.*

No, Teddy, I most assuredly was not. Why? Because I knew that nothing in our lives mattered before we'd met each other. In fact, I rather felt superior to Leni Riefenstahl, because I was sure that Horst loved me now, and she would never have him again.

She still was looking at him, too, flirting with him — and, yes, he her; it takes two to tango, even when it's just innocent foolishness — so Leni really hadn't taken notice of me. It gave me the opportunity to look her over carefully. She was tall — taller than me — wearing gray slacks, but she was not as pretty as I'd supposed. Certainly, she could not hold a candle to Eleanor Holm. But she had a wonderfully expressive face, and large doe eyes of that color you so seldom see. A sort of gray-green, I think it is. And yes, for the record, yes, Teddy, she had very large bazooms. They were beneath a white buttoned blouse. But they were not bursting, Teddy. They were strictly under wraps. Tonight she was all business.

Finally, Horst was able to direct her attention to me and introduce us. Leni looked me over with a filmmaker's eye, more like a man than another woman, and then she pointed a finger at me, and in English — she spoke a very accented English — she cried out, "Oh yah, yah. I know zis vun."

It rather frightened me, but she smiled and held up her forefinger, waggling it, and said, "Yes, of course, ze girl svimming in ze pool zat Hans filmed." And back to Horst: "Ya, Hans told me vut a naughty boy you are. You are dere to pull boat, but all ze time you are making eyes at zis beauty."

Horst just said, "Did Hans get good film?"

"Very." And to me: "Ya, you vere qvite

good mid za svimmin', sank you. So, no, I can't be mad. Besides, Horst ist always eyeing ze girls."

"Just the pretty ones, Leni."

She cocked an eye at him and then went over and whispered to the other man who had been sitting by her. He left post haste. "So," she said, turning back to me, "you haf been mid Horst?"

He started to interrupt, but she shooed him away. "You stay out of zis, Horst. I vill talk to her now."

"Yes, I've been with Horst," I said.

"And he has shown you Berlin?"

"Some of it, yes."

"It's very beautiful city, no?"

"Yes, it is."

"Ve are showing ze whole vorld, are ve not?"

"Yes, you are."

"And Horst . . . ?"

"Yes?"

"He's very beautiful boy." I smiled, a little embarrassed. "You get beautiful city and beautiful boy, bose. Not bad, no?" I only nodded. The man who'd left the room returned with a film cannister. "Ah," Leni said, "so now I vill show you somesing else much nicer."

Horst didn't say anything, but he must've

guessed what was coming because he slinked back against the wall. Leni beckoned me to take the chair next to her, calling over her shoulder, "Von't you be vatching closely, too, Horst?"

"I'm watching," he called back, but not, I thought, with much enthusiasm.

And then the film came up, black-and-white, and there Horst was, dressed in white shorts and T-shirt, carrying the torch, running along some sylvan road, past leafy trees and a babbling brook. It was so lovely that any moment I expected adorable little woodland animals to appear by the side of the road to cheer him on, as Walt Disney would have them do. Leni applauded, nudging me, "Nice, no?" I nodded. It was nice. And Horst was especially nice, so trim and strong, running along, holding the torch proudly, as if it were some pennant, some battle flag to follow after. Leni certainly knew what she was doing, because Horst was the epitome of youth and strength and beauty, that very Teutonic icon. Aryan, Teddy. Okay, maybe not perfectly blond. But no one could look at Horst Gerhardt and not think well of Germany.

The road he ran on wandered out of the woods, to the outskirts of some little village, and there, waiting, was another German boy, just as fair, just as lithe, and I'm sure most anyone else would say just as gorgeous as Horst. But, of course, I could only think: almost as. Horst handed him the torch, and the new boy took up his journey.

"Stoppen!" Leni called out, and the projectionist halted the film. She turned around and beckoned to Horst. "All right, dear Horst, you haf seen it now. Vhat you sink?"

He stepped forward. "It's very pretty footage, Leni. Willy did a fine job."

"And you are very pretty boy, no?" She smiled devilishly, nudging me again (even as I realized she'd forgotten my name), before she looked back up at him. "But still — you von't go to Baltic?"

"Come on, Leni, I told you no."

"Oh, vhat shame."

"What's the Baltic?" I asked.

"May I tell her?" Leni asked.

"Yes, of course. But it won't change anything."

She turned to me. "After ve are finished vid Olympics, I am sending Villy — Villy Zielke, he shot vhat you yoost saw — up to zis . . . zis . . . Vhat vould you call it, Horst?"

"Bleakness. A very barren beach, Sydney. Up to the east, almost to Lithuania. Leni wants to shoot there because it's so lonely, primitive, and the sun will be lower then, later on in the summer, so it'll have wonderful shadows playing across the background."

"Danke, Horst. You see, Sydney . . ." (Now that Horst had reminded her of my name.) "You see, I vant to make it like ve haf gone back to vay Olympics zey vere, ancient time. And I vill haf my boys, running, yoomping in ze mist, yoost as it vas. Old Greek Olympics, you know, athletes vere vithout clothes."

"Naked?" I was stunned, Teddy. The idea, then, that someone — never mind Horst — that anyone would appear naked on a movie screen was simply beyond my comprehension.

Leni loved my obvious innocence. "Ya, ya, nacht — naked." She practically shrieked it. "Ze men. Vomen could not even enter stadium. Greeks luft bodies, men's bodies, and I vant to show zat, show how it really vas, vere ve have come from ze past, to Berlin, now." She sighed, looking at Horst. "But Horst vill not be one of my Greek athletes. He ist too bashful for vorld to see him. Only vants you for zat, I sink."

Oh, Teddy, I can tell you I lowered my head at that, and probably blushed terribly. I didn't dare look up at Horst. But Leni laughed and clapped her hands. "All right. Ve haf work to do, Horst, vhile you yoost go entertain your pretty girl. You must leaf now."

I rose immediately. Horst said, "Thanks, Leni, I appreciated that."

"Vell, ve all needed little break. But remember, Horst: Friday, I vant you in stadium for five-sousan' meters."

"I haven't forgotten."

"Goot." She turned to me. "You vill let him go for avhile?"

"Yes, of course. And thank you."

"Next time, perhaps, ve will show you doing your svimming."

"I'd like to see that." And then Leni leaned forward and kissed me on the one cheek, which surprised me, Teddy, but all the more so when she kissed me on the other. I wasn't familiar with that kind of European kissing. Leni Riefenstahl was the first person to kiss me on both cheeks. It's a little bit of trivia about your old mother.

*"Like kissing Horst standing up by the car."*

No, Teddy, that wasn't trivia. That was just plain kissing.

Unfortunately, there really wasn't a great deal for me to do when the team practiced. Coach Daughters gave me a stopwatch, so I timed the gals when they swam heats, but apart from that, I was pretty useless. Besides, the weather had remained chilly, so the last thing I wanted to do was get in the water unless I had to.

Then, on Thursday, we suddenly got some lovely weather — just a honey of a day. The swimming competition wouldn't start till Monday, but it uplifted our spirits, and we were all clowning around with the American boys. Usually, they worked out at another pool near their Village, but today they had the chance to practice in the Olympic pool itself.

I was standing down by the deep end, talking with Adolph Kiefer, who was the champion male backstroker. He was a really nice guy, from Chicago. I'd met him at the Lake

Shore Club. We all called him Sunny Boy. That's "sunny" with a *u,* Teddy, because he always saw the bright side of things. Everybody liked Sunny Boy.

All of a sudden, there was this big commotion, and we look up, and here comes some soldiers, and right after them, old Hitler himself. You knew him right away. He had his army uniform on, and that silly mustache of his. A civilian was with him, who I realized was an interpreter, because I heard him ask where Adolph Kiefer was, and they pointed over our way, and here comes Hitler, big as life, short as he is, right up to where the two of us were standing, chewing the fat.

Well, here was the deal. Hitler specifically wanted to meet Sunny Boy because he was of German descent and because he was another Adolph. I know that's sounds ridiculous, but it's true, because I was standing right there the whole time. Actually, I think Sunny Boy took it more in stride than Hitler did. The Führer, of course, was used to everybody saluting him and making a big fuss, but Sunny Boy just stuck out his hand as if he was meeting a mayor or an alderman or some such character, and then, through the translator, they chatted for a couple minutes about how Sunny Boy had

German ancestors and what a coincidence it was they both had the same name — zwei Adolfs!, imagine — and what a nice day it was and what a nice pool it was. Et cetera.

I was standing right there, Teddy. I mean, it was just Sunny Boy and the interpreter and Hitler and me, even if nobody paid any attention to me. But I was as close to him as I am to you right now. And frankly, he wasn't very impressive. He was just an ordinary Joe with a foolish mustache pasted on his face passing the time of day with a kid swimmer.

So then, when this rather garden variety conversation ended — and I don't think anybody ever gave Hitler credit for being much of a conversational whiz — he turned to go, and he found himself facing me. Adolf Hitler and me, cheek to jowl. It caught me off guard, Teddy, so before I knew it, I found myself saying, "Hi." I laugh everytime I think about it. The kid from the Eastern Shore meets the Prince of Darkness, and all I said was "Hi."

Well, here's the thing, though. Since he was so used to everybody kissing his behind and saying "Heil," I'm sure that's what he thought I said, so he gave me that standard bit of his where he crooked his right elbow and held his arm up straight. It was a real hoot when you think about it, but you know how those things are, Teddy: you don't think about it when it's happening. And so then off Hitler went. Bye. (No, I didn't say that.)

Years later, Sunny Boy said if he knew then what we all eventually learned, he wouldn't've shaken hands with Hitler, he would've punched him right in his stupid mustache and pushed him into the pool. But, of course, that was years later when he said that.

In fact, at the time everybody was pretty impressed, and even after Hitler gave the pool a once-over and left, we all kept on buzzing. I mean, Hitler was one of the most famous people in the world. It would be sort of like going to the United States and bumping into President Roosevelt or going to London and running into the Prince of Wales and Mrs. Warfield. That was the context. Nobody got into the politics of the thing. And, like I said, everybody was in a good humor, because we finally had such a lovely day.

After practice, I walked back to the Friesenhaus with a bunch of the girls, and as we came around this corner toward our building, I saw Horst's silver Opel roadster parked there and right away, to borrow the words, verbatim, from an old song: "Zing, went the strings of my heart."

Horst was standing by the side of the car in the sunlight. He had sunglasses on and was wearing tan slacks and a green sport shirt, leaning up against his car with his legs crossed down by the ankles in that show of studied casualness that very few of you men can pull off, because, well, it usually looks too studied. But Horst had it down, natural. There was a kind of what I'd call a Continental Yank to him. He was a vision, Teddy. He was an absolute vision.

The other girls kidded me, but sticks and stones — right? I was walking on clouds, immune to that sort of badinage. They couldn't touch me with a ten-foot pole. I just do-si-doed over to Horst. "Well," I said, "this is quite a morning for me. I just met Hitler and now you."

He said, "Did Hitler ask you to go around town with him?"

"No. I think he had other fish to fry."

"Well, good, then you can come out with me instead. It's a perfect day to see Berlin."

"Lemme just change."

"And bring a bathing suit."

"I've been in already. It's wet."

"That's what bathing suits are supposed to be."

And so I got into my best casual outfit,

which was a tropical print dress — mostly blue, with a big red belt. I'd been saving it for a nice day. I'd've felt silly wearing a tropical print when it was all grim and gray. And after all, you hafta understand I didn't have that much of a wardrobe selection. I hadn't expected a courtship in Germany.

But today, the tropical print with the short sleeves was just the ticket. At that time we called those sorts of clothes "gay." You know, it didn't have anything to do with sex; it meant light and festive. And this particular gay dress worked with my coloring and showed me to best advantage, which was the point. And I wrapped up my wet bathing suit in a towel, and we took off around Berlin in Horst's roadster.

I will spare you the travelogue, Teddy, especially since I can't remember all the names of this street or that plaza. Strasses and platzes. But Horst was so proud of the way his city looked, and he wanted to show it off to me. It was so fresh and clean, too — but not bright, you understand. Berlin was a gray city, so you couldn't say sparkling clean, the way we do. But it was spic and span. A lot of the Berliners had window boxes, where they grew vegetables. Times in Germany had really and truly been desperate only a short while before, so every little bit helped. But, for the Olympics, to make things prettier, the Nazis had made everybody grow flowers instead of vegetables. The Nazis were very good at spin, Teddy, although, of course, nobody called it that then.

All the buildings were scrubbed. If a store was vacant, they dressed it up as if it was thriving — Potemkin shops, if you will. Horst made a point of taking me to some plaza where the United States had bought a big building for its embassy, and that one building stood out because it was all drab. The Germans were really ticked off because after we bought the building, we didn't have enough ready cash to spruce it up. I mean, if we didn't have enough money for bathing suits, we certainly didn't have enough for spit and polish. That was the Depression, Teddy. People nowadays have no clue. They think you can just put anything and everything on a credit card, ad infinitum. The Germans actually wanted to buy the building back and put a shine on it, but we wouldn't sell. So that was the one eyesore, and Horst rubbed my nose in it a little, but only in a teasing sort of way.

Well, I do remember that the plaza that the embassy was on was a big boulevard called Unter den Linden. It was lined with lime trees. Oh, it was a magnificent thoroughfare, Teddy. There were banners looped along the trees, and every fifty feet or so, there were green flagpoles flying either the Olympic banner — you know, with the interlocking circles — or swastikas. One after the other. The snow-white Olympic flag played off against that harsh red and black. Every major street was the same: an absolute cavalcade of banners and flags. Every building, every shop. The Nazis must've adored flags more than anyone else. They never learned less-is-more when it comes to flags, did they?

Then we turned down one side street, and it was very striking because suddenly there were no swastikas at all, just a profusion of the Olympic flags. That brought me up short, because after seeing so many swastikas, their sudden absence was all the more striking. So, naturally, I asked Horst about it. I could tell right away that he was uncomfortable, that he regretted coming this way, and he barely glanced over when he answered. "Well," he said, "those are all Jewish stores."

"So?"

"Jews aren't allowed to fly the swastika."

"Oh, I see." It cast a momentary pall in the roadster. In fact, I think it was the first time when our conversation had wilted, even for an instant. He made a quick turn at the next corner, though, so once again we were on a street that was flying both the rings and the swastikas. I tried to think of something to say, but, of course, at times like this anything you say comes with a big stupid sign over your head that says: "I'm changing the subject," which is worse than saying nothing.

Horst was no better. He just stared ahead, pretending to concentrate on driving. Luckily, though, I suddenly heard: "Achtung! Achtung!" You see, Teddy, they'd also set up loudspeakers along the main streets, and whenever an event concluded in the stadium, the results would be announced. "Achtung! Achtung!" Then the results. And if the Germans won a medal, everybody would stop and cheer to beat the band.

It sort of bugged me at the time that they could get so worked up over the javelin throw or some such thing, but, then, when it comes to sports, we're all brothers under the skin, aren't we? We beat up on Bolivia or Mongolia or some little pissant country in basketball, and we all go nuts screaming, "U!S!A! U!S!A!" and "We're Number One."

Anyway, Horst eventually figured out a way to get us back into a natural conversation. "At night," he said, "they play marches and Viennese waltzes. You wanna come here some evening?"

"Yeah, sure, great."

"There're clubs and cabarets. We could dance, Sydney."

"I'd love that," I said. "I'd love to dance with you, Horst." The way he'd said "we could dance," I knew he must be a good dancer. Boys don't bring up dancing unless they're good at it. Men don't. So, I knew: one more thing he was good at. One more thing to love him for.

*Well, that's fine, I thought, but I just couldn't resist taking the magnificent Herr Gerhardt down a peg. So I interrupted her. "You always said Dad was such a wonderful dancer."*

*That caught Mom off guard, and she pondered it for a moment.* "Well, you're absolutely right about that, Teddy. Your father certainly was." *But then, very quickly, she was back in the car with lover boy.*

So Horst said, "Then it's a date. But now: it's time for a picnic."

I said, "A what?"

"A picnic, of course. It's a perfect day for a picnic. Look in back." Sure enough, when I picked up the beach towel there, it revealed a lovely picnic basket beneath it.

Horst turned the car toward Charlottenburg, west of the city, and then he drove down toward Grunewald, which was the next fancy suburb. We passed the Rot-Weiss Club, and then, a bit further along, we came upon this large forest. I mean, we are still in what I'd call greater Berlin, but all of a sudden here we are in a regular forest — dark green, rich in these tall fir trees. It was like any minute we were gonna come upon Hansel and Gretel following their bread crumbs. But then, only a bit further, everything opened up and there before us was this perfectly lovely lake. You could see large mansions ringing it, speedboats, and people swimming off this pretty beach. All the beaches on the Chesapeake, I'd never seen anything like it. Even Easton, as fancy as it was, couldn't hold a candle to it. "This is Lake Wannsee," he said.

We found a table, and I opened up the basket. Horst had provided quite a spread: sandwiches, cheese, sausage, and even apple streudel for dessert. He bought us a couple beers at the concession stand, and we laughed and exchanged stories. I told him all about Eleanor, and when he told me about living in Japan, I decided I'd let him in on my dream. "I want to go there," I said.

"Tokyo?"

"Yeah. The '40 Olympics. I think I can be the best by then, Horst. I think I can win a gold medal. That's what I'm gonna work for."

He smiled and cocked his head, but made me drop mine because he kept looking at me. "I'm sorry," he said. "You're so beautiful, Sydney, and I can't believe someone so beautiful is so wonderful too." He reached over and took my chin with his hand and raised it up so that I'd look into his eyes. "Will you let me come to Tokyo and be your guide? I can still remember a few words in Japanese. Let's see: Arigato. Sayonara. Gaijin . . . uh . . . kimono. Of course, that wouldn't be much help."

"But you'd come?"

"Sydney, I'd go anywhere with you." That made me blush all the more. "Besides," he went on. "Nineteen-forty. I'll have graduated from college and finished my military tour by then. We all hafta serve in the army for a couple years. It's a nuisance, but Hitler's very conscious of what happened to us after the war. So we all hafta learn to be little soldiers to make sure we're not conquered again."

He shook his head at the nonsense of it all. Remember now, Teddy, the First World War was The War To End All Wars, so anybody with his wits about 'em was sure there wouldn't be any more wars. Because wars had ended. Finis. "Well," he said, "would you let me come?"

"To Tokyo?"

"Yeah."

"Horst, I'd go anywhere with you." I was repeating, of course, exactly what he'd said to me earlier.

He reached across the table and took my hands in his. "What will happen to us, Sydney?"

"After I leave?"

"Yes. This can't end. I've fallen in love with you. Did you know?"

I just shrugged and said, "Yes."

Such an abrupt answer took him up short. "You know?" he asked.

"Uh huh."

"How?"

"Well, I've fallen in love with you, and you act the same way with me that I do with you, so I figured it out from there."

"You are amazing. I can hardly understand it . . . you . . . us."

"Me neither. I always wanted to believe in love at first sight, but it scared me because I thought, well, maybe it'll be first sight for me, but not for him."

"Well, it was." He squeezed my hand. "Could you live here?"

"In Germany?"

"Yes."

"Oh my god, Horst."

"You couldn't?"

"No, no, it's just — I never thought I'd ever live much beyond the Eastern Shore. Wilmington, maybe. Baltimore. But Germany. Wow. That's a stretch."

Now, you gotta understand something, Teddy. This wasn't just a lot of idle lovey-dovey. I was only eighteen years old, and he was only twenty, but back then, if you could scrape up the money, people got married at those ages. You couldn't just live together WBOC.

*"WB — what? What's that, Mother?"*

WBOC. Without benefit of clergy. That was sinful. There weren't any halfway houses you could move into together. So you got married. I mean, we mighta been skirting the heart of the subject, but we really were talkin' about marriage. Marriage! It was all going so fast, I got scared. "Come on," I said, "let's go swimming."

There were changing rooms. He came out in a navy blue bathing suit with yellow piping. Remember, he'd seen me in a bathing suit before, but this was the first time I'd seen him in one. Oh boy, Teddy! What a doll! Now, remember, this is a long, long time before bikinis. The bathing suits now would make what I had on look like Old Mother Hubbard, but, for that time, between the two of us there was plenty of skin to go around. A lot of men still wore tops, like basketball shirts, but Horst was bare-chested. And here was the thing: by my exacting standards, he had just the right amount of hair on his chest. Not too much, but just enough. I mean, he was picture perfect, lemme tell you. "Come on," I said, and I ran into the water.

When Horst followed me in, he kidded me. "Now don't swim too fast, so I can't catch up with you."

Fat chance — right, Teddy? I ducked down and swam underwater, and he came after me and took me in his arms. Hey, I'd been doing a lot of swimming these last couple years. I'd been in the water a whole lot, all over, but now, this — this was like all of a sudden I was swimming in champagne. I mean, the water just didn't feel like water anymore. We came up for air, and when we did, he kissed me.

*"Standing up, Mom?"*

Oh yes, it wasn't that deep. We were standing on the lake bottom, and he said, "Ich liebe dich," and I said, "What?" And he said "That's 'I love you' in German," so I asked him to repeat it, and I said it to him, "Ich liebe dich," and then we kissed again, and I said, "I feel like I'm swimming in champagne," and I broke away from him and swam on my back a ways, looking up to the blue sky, just like I did back home, but thinking, how can this be the same blue sky that I looked up into when I was alone in

the Chester River? How could that be possible?

Oh, Teddy, what a honey of a day that was.
What a honey of a day.

The next day was Friday — Friday, the seventh of August, 1936 — and Leni had given Horst a job that morning in the stadium. She'd had some railroad-type tracks built down a straightaway just to the inside of the running track, with a camera placed on a little tram on the track. The idea was, a cameraman could keep up with the runners, filming them abreast as they raced. It would be a new angle altogether. She'd chosen the five-thousand meters, since the runners ran slower in a long-distance race, so it'd be easier for the camera to stay up with 'em. Unfortunately, the motor that drove the tram made too much noise, so it'd been disallowed as a nuisance. So, Leni needed someone to push the apparatus, and she asked Horst to take on the task.

I couldn't see him working, though, because that particular morning Coach

Daughters had scheduled a trial race in the backstroke. The swimming competition would officially start Monday, with the first heats in the backstroke the next day, so Coach wanted Alice and Edith to have an intramural race in preparation. Then they'd tail off their workouts and be primed for the real thing. Since I was standing there, Mr. Daughters said, "Well, Sydney, you might as well race, too." And you know what, Teddy?

*"No."*

I coulda won.

*"Whatdya mean you 'coulda'?"*

I mean, Teddy, I lost on purpose.

Edith usually started out fast, and I found out early on that I was keeping up with her. I was breezing, Teddy. I'd never swum so easy in my life.

*"Ah, I guess that being in love can be a magic carpet ride, Mom."*

There may be some truth in that, Teddy. But it was also the case that even though I wasn't gonna swim in the Olympics, Coach Daughters had given me a couple tips — you know, when he happened to see me working out with the other girls. Just little stuff — but it did make a difference. Maybe more than anything, though, I swam so much better because there was no stress, no

258

pressure on me.

I knew then what I could do, Teddy. I realized that now that I knew how easily I could swim — how fast I could swim — that I could win the gold medal in Tokyo. I knew it!

Only suddenly, after I made the turn against Edith and Alice, going into the last fifty meters, it occurred to me what the implications were if I did win. Which I knew I was gonna do. Easy. I wasn't even in the Olympics, and here I was gonna beat the two American girls who were. Just think what this would do to their confidence, Teddy.

I was even with Edith, but she was starting to fade. And Alice, who tended to finish well, was coming up, but Teddy, I had plenty of gas left in the tank. So I did what I had to do for the old red-white-and-blue. I began to slow up. Imperceptibly, you understand, but just enough.

*"You threw the race."*

Exactly. I took a dive. The last thirty or forty meters I put on a pretty good act and let 'em both pass me. And now I knew Eleanor was right. I was absolutely gonna be the next Queen of the Backstroke. I almost ran all the way back to the dorm and stayed in my room, because I really didn't wanna face

259

the other girls.

After awhile, Elsa, the interpreter, came in and said that Herr Gerhardt had called and would pick me up a little earlier than we'd planned. Of course, by now, I was all the talk — the gossip — of the Friesenhaus. I'd even found out that, behind my back, the other gals called Horst "The Red Baron" — he, of course, being the dashing German pilot who'd shot down several of our planes in The Great War. (I'd kept that little nugget away from Horst.)

Elsa, too, was as curious about Horst as my teammates were, so when I merely said "Danke," after she delivered the message from Horst, she took that as the little opening she needed to pry. "Ah," she said, "your young man is teaching you German."

"Ein bisschen," I replied. That means "a little," Teddy. Well, you could see Elsa figured she had carte blanche now, if you will excuse me for also meandering into French.

*"Your linguistic skills are overwhelming me, Mom."*

All right, you wisenheimer, silencio, por favor. So then Elsa said: "Ah, and is Herr Gerhardt from Berlin?"

"Well, he is, but he's studying architecture at Heidelberg."

"Ah, isn't that nice?"

"Yes, Elsa, he's very nice."

"He speaks such perfect English."

So I explained how his father was a diplomat and how Horst had learned English abroad. And we chatted on, but, of course, every innocent little tidbit I told her soon spread throughout the premises. It also, by the by, got on a resume they were keeping of all the girls. Horst and I weren't just an item, Teddy. We were on file. But, who knew?

In any event, after I finally got nosy Elsa out of the room, I put on my best cocktail dress. Well, it was also my only one — a red and green borderprint number that my mother had bought for me when I went to the Trials. The dresses in the thirties were extremely attractive, Teddy. They pinched in at the waist and had a slim bodyline that showed a girl's curves to the world. There weren't as many fat gals, then, either. There were more real curves by the bushel.

*"Hourglass figures?"*

You bet, Teddy. And my sand was in all the right places, then.

Now the men dressed elegantly, too. We liked to dress up then, in the Depression. Maybe because we didn't have much, we wanted to be stylish whenever we had the chance. It seems like the reverse nowadays, that the more people have, the worst they want to appear. Casual. But when did "casual" become a synonym for "sloppy," Teddy? I might have come from the Eastern Shore, but damnit, I didn't forfeit grace when I was casual.

Oh my, excuse me, now I sound like an old scold, don't I?

*"No, you don't, Mom. I like it when you express your mind."*

Why, thank you, Teddy. Now that you're also getting to be a, excuse me, *senior citizen*. God, isn't that an awful phrase, senior citizen? The only thing worse is "up in years." Everytime I hear somebody refer to me as "up in years," it's all I can do not to say, "oh, speaking of up — up yours." But, you'll be pleased to know that your dear old mother has so far resisted that urge.

*"I am duly relieved, madam."*

Oh, what the hell, Teddy. What's the use of being old if you can't be crotchety? What's the use of living all these years if you can't remind the present-day idiots that just because they're knee-deep in technology, it doesn't make the here and now any better than the past? The young people today think they're so smart, but our forefathers were so much smarter than we are.

*"They were?"*

Of course they were. They understood the world they lived in. We're really strangers, Teddy — strangers to the everyday. We don't know how a damn thing works. We just push buttons. That's an indication of intelligence? Please. In the olden days, people were in control of their lives. They had to know the world to survive in it. They knew how to plant food and harvest it and how to cook it and how, like, if they were going somewhere in a wagon, they knew how the wagon worked. But us — the more things we just turn on, the dumber we get . . . en toto.

*"That sonuvabitch Edison ruined it all for us."*

Absolutely. Now, go to the automatic ice maker and put some cubes in a plastic glass and pour me a nice tall gin and tonic.

*"But, Mom, it's only quarter past four."*

I know what time it is, Teddy. I can read a watch as well as the next dummy who doesn't know how a watch works. I know I'm jumpin' the gun, but the next part of the story requires a little lubrication, I think. Don't worry, I'm not gonna get hammered. We'll just move the time frame up this evening, then be stupider and have something from the microwave for dinner. It's the last night for the Olympic swimming, so

I'll try to finish up my bloviating in time for us to watch it. And if you think you can hold your liquor like a gentleman, then please make yourself a drink, too. A woman of a certain age shouldn't drink alone, Teddy. It casts her in a bad light.

*So, I fixed two gin and tonics and picked up the tape recorder and we moved down to the garden. There, Mom began once more, taking me back to the Friesenhaus. Horst arrived right on time again, looking like a million dollars, of course, and as soon as they got into the roadster, away from the prying eyes of Elsa and the girls of the Friesenhaus, he drew her, in her red and green borderprint, to him and they kissed a passionate hello.*

*I kept thinking to myself: couldn't they at least have a lovers' quarrel, maybe just a little spat? Couldn't a little rain fall on their parade? But, of course, I kept these captious thoughts to myself and only listened as Mother went happily back in time again with her dreamboat.*

After we'd torn ourselves apart, Horst asked me to close my eyes, and when I opened them, I saw him looking at me with this silly expression on his face. That's because there, perched on his brow, was a laurel wreath. "Nice," I said, taking it. "Who'd you steal it from?"

"Leni keeps a few in case she needs one for a close-up or some kind of a retake, and she grandly presented me this one for my efforts today." As we pulled away, he took his hand off the gearshift and made a muscle. "I worked harder pushing that damn camera on the tracks for the five-thousand than the guys did running in the five-thousand."

I reached over and pinched his cheek. "Leni's really got a thing for you, honey . . ." I believe that was the first time I'd ever used a term of endearment like that with Horst. You know, Teddy: honey, baby, darling, that sort of thing. But it just came out, naturally. He looked over at me when I said that with a sweet smile of satisfaction. Little things mean a lot. There was a song by that title, and it's very true. I said, "I'll bet she's jealous of me."

"If she is," Horst said, "you better watch yourself. Leni thinks she was an Amazon in a past life."

"An Amazon?"

"More'n that. A queen. An Amazon queen."

"So, I'm just hangin' by a thread, huh, waitin' for her to strike?"

" 'Fraid so, liebchen."

"What? What'd you say?"

"Liebchen. Like 'sweetie.' You call me honey, I call you liebchen."

I made a muscle, then, just like he had. "Well, mein liebchen, if the Amazon wants to fight me over you, I'm ready for her."

Horst laughed. He turned the car off the main street, the Kurferstendamm (which I knew by now that if you were in the Berlin in-crowd, you called it the "Ku'damm"). I hadn't really been paying any attention to where we were, though, until suddenly I realized we'd turned onto that street where only the Olympic flags flew — the one with all the Jewish shops. Horst surprised me — not just that he'd brought me back here, but that now he slowed down, pulled over and parked.

I'd already had a question in my mind, so I went ahead and asked it. "Is she a Nazi, Horst? Leni?"

"Why'd you ask that?"

"Well, you said how much Hitler likes her."

"Yeah, but Leni — I don't think Leni cares about politics. She's her own political party. Reincarnated Amazon queens don't have to join. Now my father, though — he's in the party."

"He is?"

"Dad's a realist. That's what diplomats

266

have to be. He couldn't very well be in the foreign service anymore if he wasn't."

"Are you?"

Horst laughed. "Please. My father made me join the Hitler Youth when we got back from Portugal, but I couldn't stand that. It's all rock climbing and camping out, make-believe soldier stuff. As soon as I went to college, I got the hell outta that. It's bad enough I'm gonna have to go into the navy for a couple years." And then he suddenly turned to look directly at me, moving closer, too. I'd never seen Horst so intense. "You were upset when we came down here yesterday."

"Well, not upset. Mostly surprised, I guess."

"You think I hate Jews, Sydney?"

"What?"

"Do you?"

"No, Horst. I don't think you hate anybody."

"Thank you, liebchen." Then he held out his hands, palms up, sorta shaking them, trying to put his thoughts together. "Look, let me try to help you understand. You can't believe how bad it was here. My family was so glad to get to go to Japan — and it wasn't easy there, either. The Japanese had taken our islands in the Pacific after the war, and so it was pretty sensitive for Dad. For all of us. Hell, nobody liked the Germans then. But just to get out of Germany. I mean, people were starving here. It was awful — chaos. And Hitler brought us back. He did. Not just economically, Sydney. We got our pride back.

"But I guess sometimes you need a villain to bring people together. The Nazis think so, anyway, and they said the Jews were responsible for everything bad. The Jews and the Cosi."

"The who?"

"Cosi — Communists. But look, they weren't any prize, either. There were fights, riots. And some of the Nazis were really bad guys — you know, bullies, thugs, riding the wave. And especially after they took care of the Cosi, they could run wild. And so that was the bad that came with the good." He stopped and thought for a moment before going on. "You know, though, we're not all that different from other people."

"I don't think you're different at all."

"Ah, no, I didn't mean me. And I don't mean you, but look at the way you are with the Negroes." I lowered my head and fiddled with that laurel wreath that I still had in my hands. "You go to school with Negroes, Sydney?" I shook my head. "You go to church with 'em?" I shook my head. "They live in your neighborhood?" I started to mention Gentry Trappe, but I knew he was a special case thanks to my father, so I just shook my head again. "And there's some Americans who even kill Negroes, aren't they? What do you call that?"

"Lynching," I said — very softly.

"Yes." Then he grabbed the laurel wreath from me and threw it into the back and took my hands. "I'm sorry. All that is so bad. But you're not bad. And I'm not bad."

"No."

"I wish I could stand on the street corner and shout about how we're wrong about the Jews, Sydney. I wish I could do something. But I can't. It would end my father's career. And the thugs would probably beat me up."

"Really?"

"Oh yeah. They would. But in your country, you — I don't mean you. I mean anybody. You have all your freedom. You can say something. You can do something about how the Negroes are treated. But who does? So who's worse? Us because we can't protest? You because you can, but you don't?"

"I don't know, Horst. I don't know." This was all rushing at me, Teddy, and I wasn't ready for it, and, anyway, Horst was right.

Back then, we didn't think through the situation with black people. Most of us. It was just the way of things. Segregation. Jim Crow. We white kids went to Chestertown High, and the black ones to Garnett. They all lived in their section of town. Away from us. And I'd just gone along with that, all my life. It took Horst to make me feel guilty. I had to go to Germany, where they were starting to kill the Jews, to see the beam in my own eye. That's from the Bible — Jesus himself — Teddy. Don't worry about the speck in somebody else's eye, when you've got a beam in your own.

But then Horst let go my hands and drew back a little, leaning away from me, speaking conversationally. "You know Max Schmeling?" he asked.

"The boxer."

"Yeah. He and his wife like to go to a place, the Roxy Bar, over on Joachimstalerstrasse. My father'd met him a couple times, so one night he and Mom joined them for a drink. The Schmelings. At the Roxy. This was just a few weeks ago, after he came back from knocking out Joe Louis in New York, and Mr. Schmeling said that everybody over there had called him a dirty Nazi and worse, but when he started pounding Louis, suddenly he could hear some of the Americans screaming, 'Kill him, kill him.' He'd never heard anything like that before when he was beating up some white boxer. And, Mr. Schmeling said, so many people over there were against him, just because he was a German, but he could walk into places — restaurants and hotels and so forth — that Joe Louis wouldn't be allowed in. So maybe we're all the same — all crazy."

He looked away, then, out the window, toward all those Olympic flags. I didn't know what to say. He turned back to me. "Am I talking too much?"

"No, no, Horst, you're not."

"Well, then, let me say this one more thing, that life is so much better here now. We don't need villains anymore. And now the Olympics have come, and it's been so wonderful, and what I want to think is that the Führer will see how it can be, how wonderful it can be when people are all together, and start to act on that. It was so awful here for so long, and, okay, if his people had to be tough to get on top, and some of them got out of control, that's terrible, but now the Nazis can make their bad people behave and concentrate on the good things. I think maybe the Olympics have done that for us."

With that, he broke out into a great big

smile, and although he looked at me when he talked, it was almost as if he was really talking to himself. "When I was carrying that torch, when I was down there with Leni, and Willy was filming me, running along, holding it high" — he pantomimed holding a torch up — "I just felt so wonderful. It was like my whole body was being lifted up and swept along. It was like that torch was magic, and it was carrying me — not the other way round. Does that make any sense, Sydney?"

I didn't know what to say, so I just nodded. "All my life, I was so self-conscious to be a German, to feel somehow weak and yet bad, too. All my life. But suddenly, I just felt so proud to be . . . German. I can love Deutschland now, Sydney. I can love it just like you love America."

He reached out and took me by the shoulders. "And now, these Games. Everyone must see how we can be, how it can be. I think — I know — it'll be so much better now." He took me into his arms then, but not to kiss me — only to hold me. To hold us together. I put my arms around him, too. We hugged for the longest time, and when he finally let me go, and I could look into his face, I could see that his eyes were misty. He took his fingers and rubbed them under his eyes, clearing them up. He managed a smile then, and he shrugged, and he said, "Of course, maybe that's all just a big wish, and it's only because I'm so happy because of you. Liebchen."

"Liebchen," I said. "I'm happy because of you, too."

"Good," he said, changing his tone completely. "Because the reason we're here is we're gonna go to a swell party."

Horst took my arm and steered me toward the nearest shop. The sign on the window said simply: ROSENTHALER. The name alone — that was obviously enough for its clientele, for the window displays were filled with mannequins dressed in the finest, loveliest gowns.

"Mother's always bought her best clothes here," he told me. "She swears by it. Liesl bought her wedding gown here."

"But why are you — ?"

"Because I told you, Sydney. We're going to a party. And you need a gown."

"But I can't afford —"

He reached into his pocket and flashed a big bankroll of marks at me. "I'm buyin', doll," he snarled, in that best movie gangster imitation of his.

"Horst, you can't —"

"Yes. I can. You know where this came from?" He held it up. "This is what I got for being in the movie. So, if you want, look at it this way: Leni Riefenstahl is buying you a gown." He waved at the store windows. "You like any of those? Which one do you want?"

I was utterly flabbergasted, Teddy. A boy is buying me a gown? The only gown I'd ever had, my mother bought for me for the senior prom. My God, that was only two months ago. It seemed like another lifetime, a yellow prom gown from Miss Margaret at Jefferson's Dress Shop on Cross Street in Chestertown, Maryland, and here I am now, a lady on the Continent being treated to a gown in a fancy store by her new beau.

For just a second — just an instant, Teddy — it passed my mind that there might be a quid pro quo here. I buy you a gown, sweetie pie, and I'm expecting some payback. You know. Liebchen, smeechen. But, no, I couldn't believe that. I could tell from the expression on his face how much Horst wanted me to have a beautiful gown and how much he wanted to look at me in a beautiful gown. How could I say no?

*Then Mom winked at me.*

Besides, Teddy, I was kinda warming to that idea of a quid pro quo.

Anyway, I pecked him on the cheek, but I told him he had to tell me what party we were going to. Well, it turned out that it was *the* party. The hottest ticket in town. He reached into his pocket and handed me the invitation: all embossed in gold, with swastikas adorning the four corners. You see, the party was being given by no less than that creepy Joseph Goebbels, Hitler's propaganda major domo — Sunday night at his estate. All of Germany's medal winners from the first week were being honored, along with the who's who of Germany and the Olympics both — well, you get the picture: everybody who was anybody. The crème de la crème, Teddy.

Now, I know you wanna know how my young Lochinvar made the cut for such a grand soiree. Well, it was somewhere in here that I finally began to appreciate that Horst's father was something more than just another run-of-the-mill cog in the foreign service. It was he and Frau Gerhardt who'd been invited, but they were headed out of town. Klaus Gerhardt had been in the navy, so he was serving as one of the host muckety-mucks at the sailing races up at Kiel, on the Baltic. So, with a little diplomatic legerdemain, he'd prevailed on Goebbels to transfer the invitation to his son and his guest, which, of course, was yours truly. Only, then the poor Cinderella from the

Eastern Shore needed a gown for the ball.

We entered the store to be greeted by an older gentleman, who I took to be Herr Rosenthaler. Horst introduced himself, and immediately, as soon as she heard his name, Frau Rosenthaler materialized, and there was a great deal of chitchat, which I took to be about Horst's mother and sister. Then he introduced me, and explained how I needed a gown for an Olympic party. If Horst mentioned that we were going to the Goebbels' bash, I never heard the name. I took note of that. I knew enough to know that no Jewish people ever wanted to hear that name.

Then Horst turned to me. "Okay, Mrs. Rosenthaler will take care of you." And just like that, without so much as a how-do-you-do, he headed toward the door.

"Wait, Horst, where you goin'?"

"I'll be right outside. What do I know about gowns? They do. This has been in their family forever."

"Wait, wait, Horst. What type do you want me to get? What . . . ?"

He came back and took my hands. "Listen, Sydney, you get what you like, you put it in a box, and Sunday night, the first time I see it, it's on you. And then I'm gonna take the prettiest girl in Berlin to the Goeb

—" He stopped. ". . . the prettiest girl in Berlin to the grandest party."

Then he was gone. The Rosenthalers looked me over politely, but rather as if I were some kind of specimen. It was apparent that they spoke no more English than I did German. I smiled back stupidly, but by now I knew enough to say, "Hallo. Wie geht es Ihnen?" — "how are you?" Frau Rosenthaler only replied, "Goot," then brandished a tape. That did speak a mutual tongue, so I told her "size eight" in English, and when even that didn't seem to register, I simply submitted my body to measurements. Now, Teddy, now we had something to go on, and she steered me over to a rack, where, apparently, there was a confluence of my size and Horst's price range.

Frau Rosenthaler held out a couple gowns for me. One was a sky blue, the other what I'd call an ivory. It was absolutely lovely. But then, just as I reached for it, another one at the end of the rack caught my eye, and I immediately brushed the ivory aside and turned to it. "Is that my size?" I asked. "Size? Size?" I placed my hands over my busts and then on my hips. Frau Rosenthaler got the idea, and quickly checked the tag. She pulled the gown out. "Yes, ja, yes," she said, beaming, taking the dress and holding it up before me.

Oh God, Teddy, it was the most beautiful thing I'd ever seen in all my life. The idea that I could be encased in such glorious attire was beyond my comprehension. It was magnificent. I saw the price tag, too: ninety-five marks. That was almost fifty dollars, which doesn't sound like much now, but trust me: it was a fortune for a gown at that time. I almost ripped it away from poor Frau Rosenthaler and held it out before me. "Ja, ja," I said. "Wunderbar, wunderbar!"

*"What color was it, Mother?" She didn't answer me, only hurried away. When she returned, she held her purple acetate folder. Beaming, she reached inside.*

This is the only souvenir I have left from that time, Teddy. The only thing I saved.

*"Why just this?"*

Oh, I brought a few other things back with me from Berlin, but over time I simply lost them or they disappeared, the way things you don't care about go to a place you don't know. But this I saved, because all I had to do was glance at it, and all the wonderful memories of that time would come flooding back. I couldn't sit somewhere and tell these things to myself, Teddy. I needed you for that. It would've seemed dotty, talking to myself. But, whenever I wanted to — just to look at this was enough to remember it all.

*And, with that, Mom pulled the swatch out of the folder and held it up for me. "Red," I said. "Wow. That's some red."*

Well, technically, Teddy: magenta. And all these years, I've kept it in dark places and it's hardly lost any of its color. Look at it.

*It was, I would suppose, about four or five inches by eight. It was a brilliant red. All right, magenta. I held it, touched it, giving it more care than I normally would've for any mere piece of fabric, because I understood the value Mother placed on this keepsake — this artifact.*

*There were some raised stitches. I ran my fingers over them. "What are these?"*

Cording. Trapunto cording is the proper term, I believe. You see —

*She took the swatch back and placed it up above her bust.*

You see, Teddy, visualize. This was the top of the bodice.

Oh, if you could have seen me in that little changing room. After I put it on, I just ran my fingers over it all. And this was the top. It was a high top, with magnificent wide sleeves. I think that's what made it so special. Why, Ginger Rogers could have climbed right into it and started tripping the light fantastic with Fred Astaire — right there in Rosenthaler's boutique.

*She fingered the swatch again, caressing the cording.*

And that cording, Teddy. The trapunto cording ran all across the front, and out over my shoulders and down under the arms.

*She traced all that with her fingers, as she described it to me.*

Then, there was a large bow in back.

*"The same color?"*

Oh yes. The whole gown was magenta. The back was low, where the bow was. That was often the style then, that the back was very low and the front high. There was no cleavage at all. Just a little dip in the bodice beneath my neck. And a neck could be important, Teddy. I wore my hair short, which was pretty much the fashion, curled up at the nape of the neck. My neck was on display.

And then I ran my hands down my sides, where the gown came in at my waist. So, yes, maybe there wasn't any cleavage, but the way it was cut — well, I can assure you, Teddy, it displayed my . . . my rack to best advantage. Besides, if you could see a lady's bare back, it served to emphasize the mystery of the front. And remember now, my hair was short. There was a lot of back. Cleavage is a tease, Teddy, but a bare back is more sensual in its own way. It is bare, after all, isn't it? There's much to be said for a high front and a low back, even though most men wouldn't say it.

*Holding the swatch close to her, she swirled a little, seeing it all in just the right light of her mind's eye.*

And remember, Teddy, there were dinner parties then. It wasn't a fast-food world. A lady would sit at a table, and it was important that the front of her dress be attractive, because that would be on exhibit. If it was just a couple of straps and some cleavage, even the best of that physical display might begin to wear thin on the other guests by the main course. I know that may be hard for a discriminating gentleman such as yourself who has spent decades peering at cleavage and that which abuts it on either side, but in a genteel world, there really were other, more stylish considerations.

*"A point I will acknowledge, Mother, reluctant as I may be to concede it."*

All right. And so, in the changing room, I saw how wonderfully the gown clung to me, just flaring out below my knees. It was cut on the bias, too, which, of course, made it all the more special.

*That lost me. "I'm sorry: what's that?"*

Cut on the bias?

*"Yes. I never heard of that before."*

Teddy, how old are you now?

*"You know, Mom. I'm sixty-one."*

And you have never, in all your life, sixty-one years of a relatively sophisticated life — you have never, in all this eon, heard of any clothing being bias cut?

*"No, I have not."*

Then, given that this has escaped you for sixty-one years, it's reasonable to assume that it's unlikely you will encounter any discussion of the subject in what remains of your sojourn on this planet, and so therefore we are not going to interrupt this reverie of your dear old mother's for any further technical explanation. Let's just leave you with the basics: that the gown is tight on me in here —

*She slapped her thighs.*

— and then flared out, so, if you can envision this, Teddy — try now — you have the wide shoulders and the wide skirt, top and bottom, and me in between.

*"I can envision."*

Good. And so I emerged from the changing room, and I stood there, nearly breathless, and, well, hallelujah: the reaction was all a gal could desire. Frau Rosenthaler clasped her hands before her bosom and sighed, and Herr Rosenthaler simply said,

"Schon, schon, schon," over and over. I didn't know what that meant, but I knew it was damn good, whatever it was. And that was that, Teddy. That gown fit like it had been cut for me alone. They had only to take in the tiniest pinch under my arms, and that was it. There was Cinderella in magenta.

Mr. Rosenthaler folded the gown up and put it in a box. I hated to treat it that way, but Horst didn't want to see the gown till he could see me in it. In that respect, it was sort of like a wedding gown.

*She paused, wistfully.*

All the more so, from hindsight, since it turned out that I never would have a wedding gown.

And so, clutching the box, I glided on air out to the car. Horst went back inside and settled up. When he came back, I thanked him and kissed him. Then I said, "You spent too much."

"No, I didn't, Sydney. And don't ever bring it up again." So I let that slide, Teddy, even though that gown was terribly expensive. It was the most expensive present I'd ever had in my life.

But Horst wasn't done, because then he took me to the Rot-Weiss Club for dinner. Everyone was elegant, dressed to the nines. It must've been obvious how impressed I was, for after dinner, when we were strolling on the veranda, Horst asked me, "Do you really like it here?"

"Of course I do. Can't you tell?"

"It's important to me," he said.

"Come on, Horst." I swung my arms wide and whirled around. "This place is absolutely beautiful."

"No, no, Sydney, I don't mean just here. I mean Berlin. I mean us — Germans. Have you liked us?"

"Yes, I have."

It had started to get chillier again. The beautiful day before had been the exception. He took off his jacket and put it round my shoulders, took my hand and walked me down to the tennis courts. "We play our Davis Cup matches here," he said. "Have you heard of Gottfried von Cramm?"

Actually, Teddy, the name only dimly rang a bell, but, in the context, I figured correctly that he must be a tennis player, so I said I had. "He's a member here," Horst said. "The Baron — he's old royalty. He made the Wimbledon final last month. He lost, but he was injured at the very beginning of the match. The Baron played on, though. He simply wouldn't give up. And then he apologized for playing so poorly. Everyone admires him so. We'd never had a German do so well at Wimbledon before. And no one — no one from any country — had ever played so nobly. The Baron made us all so proud."

There was a bench there. It was quite dark, because there was no moon. You could barely see the courts before us, from the lights of the clubhouse we'd left behind. When we sat down, I thought he was going to kiss me, but instead he actually leaned away, putting his elbow up on the far arm of the bench. He looked out toward the courts, into the dark, and began to speak as if from a script. "Remember, Sydney, remember I told you how my mother sent me to the American school in Tokyo in lederhosen?"

"Yes. You told me that."

"Well, it was mortifying. Of course, none of the other boys wore them, and not only that, I didn't speak English that well yet, and I stuck out like a sore thumb. I was seven. It was 1923, and the war had only been over five years. Now, the other boys didn't remember the war at all. They'd been too young. But, oh, they all sure knew that we Germans had been the enemy. They knew that. And they knew they'd won the war, and Germany had lost. And so, right away, I was an outcast. No one wanted anything to do with the strange duck in the funny pants."

Horst stood up and put his hands in his pockets, but he kept talking. It's a little bit the way I've been talking to you, Teddy. I just have to say these things, and I may be saying them to you, but, really, I just need to say them. I thought at the time that it was more important for Horst to say what he wanted to than it was for me to listen. I thought I was just an excuse for him to talk.

*"I'm just an excuse, Mom?"*

In a way, yes. Don't take it personally.

*"Don't worry, I don't."*

Good. But I do hope you're listening.

*"Of course I am."*

Well, I listened to Horst then, out by the tennis courts. I could tell what he was saying mattered a great deal to him. He told me that at recess, several boys teased him, called him a "kraut," and one of them, a bully named Andy, began to jab at him, and then he grabbed Horst and threw him to the ground and started punching him.

Horst turned directly to me, then. I was still sitting on the bench, wearing his jacket. And he said, "He beat me up pretty good, Sydney. Andy was much bigger than me, and I didn't have a chance. And the other boys just watched. I don't know about girls, but boys can be very cruel, honey. They're kinda like those brownshirts, you know, the really awful Nazis, who're suddenly very emboldened, very mean when they're all together. A teacher finally heard the ruckus and pulled Andy off me, and told us to stop fighting. Only, of course, there was just one of us responsible for the fighting. But I didn't say it wasn't my fault. I just looked around at all the other boys who'd just stood there watching me get beat up, and I let it go. I think it made some of them ashamed. A couple of them, anyhow.

"So I got beat up just because I was a German. In a way, I found out then what it was like to be a Jew. Or a Negro.

"When my mother came to pick me up and saw me all scratched and bruised, she wanted to go right to the headmaster and complain. But I wouldn't let her. I just told her never to make me wear those damn lederhosen again. Which she didn't. And I learned to speak better English, and to speak it exactly like the American boys. And I told you: I learned to play baseball. I caught on, Sydney. You live abroad, you adapt. I can be a chameleon. I can be an American.

"It drove Andy crazy, and near the end of the year he tried to pick a fight with me again. And guess what?"

"You beat him?"

"Oh no. That'd make a good story, but Andy was much too big for me to ever beat him. Besides, I've never liked to fight. No, but it was even better. You see, the reason Andy got so mad at me was that the more popular American guys had begun to accept me. After a while, they didn't care anymore that I was German. They'd forgotten that I was supposed to be a rotten person. By the end of the year, I was accepted into the right group. You know? And Andy wasn't part of that. That was much better than if I'd just beaten him up. The other guys stopped Andy from trying to pick on me. I got much more satisfaction that way. I'd found my way in, and Andy was still out.

"But I never forgot, Sydney. I never forgot how hated I was in the beginning just because I was a German. And I don't want anyone ever to look at us like that again."

I reached out and took Horst's hand. "That's a very nice story," I said. "I'm glad you told me."

"Yeah, I wanted to tell you, Sydney. I've never told another soul."

So I was wrong. It was important that someone had listened to him. "Thank you, Horst. That means a lot to me."

Then, after a moment, he said, "You wanna go back to our house with me?"

I said, "Sure."

Horst put on a very serious face then. He said, "You understand, Sydney. My parents are up in Kiel for the sailing. We'd be alone."

So I just said, "Yeah, you told me."

And, of course, Teddy, I'm sure you know that in 1936, a so-called nice girl, which is what I was, so-called and otherwise, was not supposed to go to a boy's house unchaperoned.

*"But still, you said 'sure.' "*

Yes, and as we used to say on the Shore: in a July minute.

Then Horst said, "You can trust me, Sydney," and I nodded that I knew that, and we got in his car. His house was also in Charlottenberg, not far away, on a lovely little street named Dernburgstrasse. It was a very nice area, a very nice house. Germany had come a long way since the terrible times after the war. Especially on this western side of town. To me it didn't look any different from some nice section of Baltimore or Wilmington.

He asked me if I wanted a schnapps, and I said yes, because I was suddenly a very sophisticated schnapps drinker, and while he got the drinks I started glancing at the various photographs of his family there in the living room. I was looking at one picture of three boys, standing on a dock somewhere, when Horst came back. "That's my father," he said, pointing to the boy on the left. "And those were his brothers — Henner and Max. They were both killed in the war."

"Oh, I'm sorry."

"Yeah, Dad was the only one of the brothers who survived, and he was wounded."

"Is he okay?"

"Oh yeah, he recovered. Almost entirely. He still has a slight limp, but most people can't even notice. He was lucky. His ship sank, but he got to shore safely." Then he pointed out more recent pictures of his parents. "That was in Portugal."

"When he was the ambassador?"

"Yes."

His father, Klaus, was as handsome as Horst was, with the same light coloring, the same smooth features that would be too pretty on most men, except for the sharp chin and eyes that had a hint of the devil in them. Herr Gerhardt was standing, smiling, with one arm around his wife. She was a beautiful little blonde. Inge. It looked like you could put Inge in pigtails and she would yodel. There was also a photograph of the sister, Liesl, at her wedding, and she was every bit as adorable. Her husband was in his army officer's uniform.

On the same table was another photo, this one of several men, standing together in some sort of garden. It took me a moment before I realized that it was Hitler himself in the middle; Herr Gerhardt was at the end. "Your father knows Hitler?"

"Well, he's met him a few times. That's in Bergdorf, the mountains. He'd get mad at me for telling you this, but Dad thought he had a chance to be the next ambassador to London, but it seems it'll be von Ribbentrop." That meant nothing to me, but Horst pointed to another man, the one standing to Hitler's right. "There. Hitler's crazy about von Ribbentrop, but Dad doesn't think he's all that bright." He waggled a finger at me. "Now, Fraulein, don't you dare repeat a word of that." Of course, he was smiling when he said that.

"Are you kidding?" I said. "I can't wait to

spill the beans about that down on the Eastern Shore."

"I hate a girl who can't keep a secret." He put the picture back in its place. "Anyway, Dad figures now that he'll probably get sent back to Tokyo, as the ambassador there this time. Mom's not crazy about the idea, but she likes being an ambassador's wife. And it's different now. The Japanese are pretty much our friends."

"Would you go, too?"

"Back to Japan? Oh no. Just the one more year at Heidelberg, and when I graduate, do my damn time in the Navy —"

"Why the Navy?"

"Oh, the Gerhardts've always been a naval family. Besides: better than the army. I don't want anything to do with guns, thank you very much. So get the sailor stuff outta the way and then go to architecture school." He picked up his drink and raised it to me. "Of course, now, I will go back to Tokyo in '40, so I can be there with you when you win the gold medal."

I said, "Then I'll never let you leave me again," and with that as a pretty good jumping-off point, Teddy, we began to kiss —

*"Ah, standing up."*

Yes, Teddy, but not for long. Pretty soon

we were on the sofa, and we were doing some heavy necking. We called it "necking" then. I don't know when "making out" came into the vernacular. And the necking was getting pretty hot, and suddenly Horst stopped, and he said, "I'm sorry, Sydney, I promised you that you could trust me."

And let's just say I did something then that upped the ante, and I said, "Well, I didn't promise you that you could trust me."

And he got this wonderful expression on his face — surprise and delight. It may be the most gratifying expression you ever see from another human being, Teddy: surprise and delight, together. And so I drew even closer to him, if that was possible, and I whispered: "I want to make love to you, Horst." I knew exactly what I wanted, Teddy. I knew exactly what I was up to.

And he said, "Somehow, I didn't think you ever had."

And I said, "No." Just that. But then I said, "Only not here. In your bed, Horst. Because when I'm gone, I want you to think of me every time you go to sleep."

Well, I've gotta be honest with you, Teddy. That poetry wasn't exactly spontaneous. I'd thought of that when he was out of the room, getting the drinks. I told you I knew what I was up to. I didn't want to be a so-called nice girl anymore. I decided that I'd rather have it be nice instead. So I got up and put out my hand, and he took it, and we went upstairs to his room. I wasn't the least bit nervous. I mean, here I was about to go to bed with a guy who'd screwed Leni Riefenstahl, the big movie star. But you know what? I figured he knew a lot of men had screwed Leni Riefenstahl, but I'd be very special.

So we made love in his bed. It was wonderful. You always hear how the first time isn't so good. Well, I can't speak for any other girl, but it sure was wonderful for this girl. So, in a while, of course, we made love again.

Don't you hate it, Teddy, the way everybody nowadays just says "have sex" instead of "made love"? What a terrible devaluation of the language on the one hand and love on the other. I didn't think at all: I'm having sex. I thought: Wow, I'm making love.

And we were lying there, then, and Horst said, "I better get you back to the dorm."

"Why?"

"Isn't there a curfew?"

"Not really," I said. "They just sort of expect you back. But what're they gonna do with me? Not let me swim in the Olympics? I'm not allowed to anyway."

And so I went to sleep in his arms, in his bed. And I remember so well, Teddy, when I woke up the next morning, looking over at him, my own liebchen, lying there, his hair splayed out over the pillow. He was so handsome. And I thought to myself, Lord, but you sure are different now, Trixie Stringfellow. Only I didn't mean that I was different because I was a woman now, because I'd had a man. No, I thought how different I was because I'd learned how to love, and I knew that someone magnificent loved me too, with all his heart and soul.

I turned off the tape recorder and said no more, departing, leaving Mother alone in the garden with her reveries — thinking back to the time of her life. That, I realized was what Berlin had been. People always say: I had the time of my life. But I guess some people only have that one time that qualifies. And Mom did. And now that she was back there, I left her alone.

I was somewhat relieved, too, that she had come to what I concluded must be the romantic denouement of this saga. Of course, I remembered that the mysterious contents of that purple acetate folder were yet to be revealed. But what could be left? After all, young Sydney Stringfellow would have to be returning home from Germany in another week or so, and what further role could the incandescent Horst Gerhardt possibly play in her life? He had wooed my mother, given her the time of her life, fallen just as hard and fairly for her as she had for him, and acted with perfect honor even as he deflowered her and, to boot, escorted her to ecstasy.

Good grief, no wonder an old woman who was dying remembered this glorious idyll of her youth so vividly and so tenderly. Indeed, now I was able to restrain my earlier anger toward Horst. I knew that my mother had dearly adored my father and been devoted and true to him in her love for a half-century, till death did they part. It would be nothing short of spiteful of me to resent this one gloriously romantic interlude that my mother shared with another man in another time and place before my father material-ized in her life.

Besides, by comparison, it made me recall my own ragged and unsatisfying admission into the realm of sexual congress, and I could only be envious that my dear mother had chosen so well for her debut and orches-trated the performance so neatly, down even to her dialogue that would have done justice to the most lush French novel. Only, how had she forgotten to hire the violins to play "Love in Bloom" and the cherubs to toss rose petals upon the bed?

Then, too, how could you — how could any man or woman — not be taken with young Herr Gerhardt? As my mother had wanted to be his lover, I wanted to be his buddy, his chum, his pal. The guy was quite special, that's for sure, a grand co-star in the epic my mother had starred in.

So I waited upstairs and returned to the garden only when Mom called for me to bring her a couple more ice cubes. When I reached her, she began by offering some apology.

"Sorry if I told you more than you wanted to know, Teddy. I suppose I was almost in something of a trance there for awhile."

"Oh, that's okay, Mom. It's about love, and there's always room for more of that in this tawdry twenty-first-century world of ours."

"Well, thank you for indulging me, but I suppose if I'm going to tell my story, I might as well not censor any of it — especially the sweet spots. I warned you there'd be a little sex."

"Mom, you were fine. You were very decorous. I give it a PG-13."

She accepted that assessment, but then couldn't resist: "I spared you the full-frontal nudity."

So, okay, if she was going to be flip now, I'd pay her back in kind. "Of course, if you'd told me that you'd first given it away to Frankie of Easton, Maryland, parked by a corn field in the back seat of some jalopy, I wouldn't've been as approving."

"That's no way to talk to your old mother."

"All right, I'll give you the megaphone back." I flipped on the tape recorder. "Where do we go from here?" She only grinned at that, and answered by simply reaching back into the purple acetate folder to pull out the swatch of magenta, which she placed on her lap, where she could pat it occasionally for either emphasis or affection. And so she began again.

You've heard that phrase about the Nazis: "the banality of evil?"

*"Yes, of course."*

Well, Teddy, the Goebbels party would be the beauty of evil. Of course, I saw only the former. That evening I was myself a microcosm of almost every German. They said that for as long as Hitler had the economy humming and was winning battles, most people in Germany simply ignored the other terrible, obvious realities. And like that, this evening, I was so blinded by how perfectly gorgeous it all was, that I never stopped to ponder what horror paid for this sumptuousness. Not for a moment did it cross my mind.

*"Oh come on, Mom, you said yourself: you were eighteen years old. You'd only been abroad for a week — the first time in your life. You'd just fallen off the turnip truck. You didn't know Germany from Peru. You don't have to be hard on yourself."*

I said: I was Germany in microcosm. I knew enough by then, Teddy. I wasn't completely blind. Horst had told me things. No, I'm not flagellating myself. I'm simply saying that, looking back, I see how easy it is for any of us anywhere to go along. That's all. And Horst was Exhibit B. He, who had told me how he wanted to shout from the rooftops about injustice, ah, when the chance came to enjoy the fruits of that terror so that he could impress a pretty girl, he bought her a gown and pleaded with his father to get him inside the tent, and then he forgot all the complaints he'd had and drank the hemlock just like everybody else.

It worked, too. The pretty girl wasn't just in love anymore. She was in his thrall.

We pick and choose so, don't we, Teddy? We are the most selective of creatures.

And so we arrived at the Goebbels, amid spotlights crossing the heavens like a Hollywood premiere — Horst in his white dinner jacket, me in my scrumptious magenta gown.

*For emphasis, she patted the old swatch from the gown that she'd laid in her lap.*

We were obscenely handsome, all the more so that we were, I'm sure, the youngest couple there. I realized — smugly — that everyone was looking at us with envy. Why, Teddy, they were all Ponce de Leon, lookin' to drink from our fountain.

The Goebbels' estate was on an island in the Havel River, on the way down to Potsdam, not far from where Horst and I had gone swimming in Lake Wannsee. I forget the German name of the island, but it means "peacock," and, yes, the birds roamed the gardens. Kings had lived there. But Goebbels had dressed it up beyond what mere royalty would have been satisfied with. In a way, Teddy, this was his coming-out party for international society, and all of us embroidered his respectability.

You reached the island by walking over pontoon bridges, and once there, there were two lines of pretty girls — the best looking dames from the night clubs in Berlin. Goebbels had them gussied up like male pages from the seventeenth or eighteenth century — the wigs, the knickers. And at the end of this sexy gauntlet, there stood the Goebbelses to receive us. They both had deep tans and were decked out all in white, head to toe.

Of course, Goebbels didn't know us from Adam, but as soon as Horst gave his name to the attaché standing there next to mein hosts, Goebbels understood that Horst was Klaus Gerhardt's son, and he greeted him warmly. Then, when Horst introduced me, Goebbels kissed me on both cheeks. He was the second person to do that. That's quite a distinction, isn't it, Teddy — in the double-cheek-kiss category? First Leni Riefenstahl, then Joseph Goebbels. He closed a little too tightly onto me, though, making sure his white suit could press a bit on my bodice. God, but Goebbels was such a smarmy little bastard.

Anyhow, there were champagne bars set up everywhere, and a buffet the size of the Chesapeake Bay and over a ways, beyond a high curtain, they'd built a regular mini-amusement park. And I don't mean just skee ball and some guy guessing your weight. It was quite a production. Keep in mind, it was a big island. Goebbels wasn't gonna appropriate some dinky sandbar.

Near to where we came in, too, there was a large dance floor, with a full orchestra playing. Mostly, in fact, it was playing

American pop hits. They were into "Begin the Beguine" when Horst and I reached the dance floor. We just stood there, taking it all in. Only a few couples were dancing. Everybody else was, like us, simply so dazzled by the whole business. Then, all of a sudden, there was this sort of glimmering apparition at my side, and whoosh, like that, Horst was gone, swept away. Presto — he's out on the floor, holding the apparition in his arms, whirling. Well, guess what? It was Leni Riefenstahl, in this shimmering silver gown, that if it was any tighter would've had to be painted on. And I believe I told you, Teddy, that the lady had some curves.

*"You made that point, Mom."*

Well, she'd just abducted Horst, and they were gliding all over the floor. I told you, when a guy suggests maybe you can go dancing, then you can bank on it that he's a good dancer.

*"Yes, you made that point, too."*

Well, Horst was, as I expected, just a honey of a dancer, and as the other couples on the dance floor looked up and saw that it was Leni Riefenstahl herself in the arms of this handsome young Astaire, they began to evacuate the premises post haste. I mean, at this point in the Olympics, after Hitler himself, Leni Riefenstahl was the cynosure of everyone's eyes. Then the band moved into "Just One of Those Things." Remember that? "It was just one of those things, just one of those crazy flings . . ." Boy, I remember that, Teddy. I loved it. Great lyrics. But it really picked up the tempo, so all of a sudden it's just *mein liebchen* and that vixen in the clinging silver gown sweeping around the dance floor.

But, luckily, it's at this point that I realize I am not the cheese, standing alone. Next to me, likewise gaping at Leni and Horst, is this very nice-looking fellow. I did sort of a double take before I realized it was none other than Glenn Morris, the hot-shot American who'd won the gold medal in the decathlon only yesterday. His picture was in all the papers.

*"You told me Leni had taken more than just a filmmaker's interest in him."*

Exactly. In fact, Teddy, if you ever get a copy of *Olympia,* and really you should —

*"I will Mom, absolutely."*

— well, you will see Mr. Morris prominently displayed. He's on screen more than old Hitler himself. Leni had fallen ass over teakettle for the guy.

Now, at the time I was unaware of this, but knowing Leni's interest in the younger set, I put two and two together very quickly.

I nudged him. "You're with Leni?" I asked.

I think he was irritated that I was so nosy, but he acknowledged that he was. "Well," I said, "I'm with the guy she's dancing with." That brought no pro-active response from him, either, so I stuck out my hand. "Hey, congratulations on the gold." He shook it and mumbled thanks. Nothing more. Obviously the strong-silent type. So then I said, "I'm Sydney Stringfellow, from Maryland. I'm swimmin' the backstroke." And now that I had his hand I kinda yanked on it. "Come on, let's us dance, too."

"I don't know," Glenn said. In point of fact, Teddy, he was downright reluctant. He even tried to unhinge my hand from his. He said, "That's pretty fast stuff they're playing."

Luckily, though, right then the band switched to "I'm in the Mood for Love," so I said, "Come on, that's a slow one," and I tugged him out onto the floor, and we began to move with the music. Approximately. Now, the decathlon, as you know, Teddy, is a very demanding event. It was multitasking before anyone came up with that expression. You have to run and jump and throw the discus, and a bunch of other things I've forgotten, and Glenn Morris was the best in the world at them, altogether.

The renaissance man of sport. But, one thing I can promise you that is most assuredly not in the decathlon is dancing, because he was certainly no prize at that. A terpsichore Glenn was not.

But as I was despairing, over his shoulder, I see Horst steering Leni our way. Glenn and I were sorta holding to one spot, tiltin' back and forth. That's what passed for dancin' with the decathlon-champ-slash-renaissance man. A real cement mixer. But Horst — my hero! — tapped Glenn on the shoulder and said, "Double cut," and Leni gave me a little wink and fell against Glenn, taking my place in that stationary spot, while Horst whisked me away, gliding, Teddy, gliding. I was back, swimmin' in champagne again.

I was so enthralled, in fact, that at first I didn't hear a little buzz from the crowd. It was just as the band switched to "East of the Sun (and West of the Moon)," which I adored, so I glanced over Horst's shoulder and saw that a third couple had come onto the floor. That was what had occasioned the buzz, you see. Horst just happened to whirl me around at that moment, though, so I couldn't immediately see who it was, but in another instant, they swung by, and in a loud voice, I heard: "Sydney!" and the girl leaves her partner and runs over and kisses me and then runs back to him. She hardly missed a step. Guess who?

*"Mom, come on."*

Eleanor Holm! She was dancing with her husband, Art Jarrett. The vocalist. As soon as he'd heard how that jackass Avery Brundage had kicked Eleanor off the team, he'd taken the next ship to London and then flown to Berlin to protest. Lotta good it did him. Brundage wouldn't even see him, and, for good measure, he banned Eleanor from swimming in all the other meets in Europe, too. She'd gotten a job as a reporter, covering the Olympics for the International News Service, so Brundage decreed that writing about swimming made her a swimming professional.

Well, naturally, Horst's interest was piqued. "Who's that?" he asked me.

"Eleanor Holm." (I knew he meant the girl.)

"No fooling. She's really pretty."

"Yeah, I know," I said. Eleanor was in this beautiful black backless gown, with a spray of bright red and sky blue down her left side. And, of course, not only were she and Art Jarrett wonderful dancers, but he was crooning along. Right there in the middle of the dance floor, sans microphone, he started singing "East of the Sun" to Eleanor.

"Up among the stars," and so forth and so on. I forget the lyrics. Songs all had such great lyrics then, Teddy. They had words that meant something. Songs even had little prefaces, introductions before you got into the meat and potatoes of the chorus and the harmony. It says something that the decline of the written word may be illustrated by music. Of all things. But songs had clever lyrics then; they had meaning. But now that nobody is familiar with the English language anymore, you have to see everything, so even music has to have videos. You have to see music to appreciate it now. Isn't that something? Beethoven is probably rolling over in his grave. Not to mention Cole Porter.

You probably don't remember Chester A. Riley on television, do you?

*"No, that doesn't ring a bell." Mom was off on one of her tangents now, so I just relaxed and went along for the spin.*

He was the star of a show on the radio called "The Life of Riley," and halfway through every show, when things came to a pretty pass, he would wail to his wife, who was Peg. He would say, "Peg, what a revoltin' development this is." And that's the way it is with lyrics. They're a lost art. What a

310

revoltin' development this is.

Anyhow, because Art Jarrett stopped to sing, the band was smart enough to do another chorus of "East of the Sun," so Horst whirled me around some more. I could see everyone looking at us and whisperin'. Like: that's Leni Riefenstahl herself with the guy who won the decathlon. And that's the infamous Eleanor Holm, with her husband, the vocalist. But, achtung, achtung: who in the world is the great kid dancer in the white dinner jacket with the girl in that gorgeous magenta gown? Who are they? I just knew that's what everybody and his brother was sayin', and I adored it, Teddy. I drank it all in. And let me tell you, I didn't miss a step. Horst and I coulda stepped right outta a Busby Berkeley musical.

There are times in your life when you rise above, don't you? When you do something you couldn't possibly imagine that you could. You know, like the guy who lifts up the two-ton truck when the little child is trapped under it. You just do it.

Then — well, you know how you men try to explain it. It's because of . . . come on, now. You know.

*I hadn't realized I was about to be tested. I came back to attention. Finally, I ventured:*

*"Adrenaline?"*

No. Come on, Teddy: balls. Balls, Teddy. When some man does something exceptional, you men always say: he's got balls. Typical man talk. Because you've got balls. You possess them. And of course, we gals don't. Oh, it's so tedious what you guys say. God knows I've heard it enough. Oh, he's got a big pair. Oh man, made o' brass. Stuff like that. Well, it isn't balls, Teddy.

*"No? What is it?"*

It's neck!

*"Neck?"*

Yes. As in: you stick your neck out. And maybe you don't even realize you've done it till your neck's already out to here. I had to stick my neck out to dance around with all those big VIPs watching, to dance out there without showin' any fear and gettin' it right. Now, that was neck, Teddy. I probably only had neck a few times — well, only two times for sure in my whole life.

*"What was the other . . . the other time you had neck for sure?"*

Don't rush me. We'll come to that, don't you worry. What did I tell you about surprises? And for God's sake, let me savor all this. I mean, when the band finished "East of the Sun," they paused, and everybody applauded. It was better'n winnin' a race. I just fell into Horst's arms. "God, I love you," I said. And for good measure, I said it in German, too: "Ich liebe dich." He hugged me to him and whispered the same thing into my ear. Yep, both languages. Double your pleasure, double your fun.

And Eleanor ran back over and reminded her husband about how he'd met me at the Palmer House. Then she said, "Well, Sydney, aren't you gonna introduce me?" I explained who Horst was, and I was kinda hangin' onto his arm, and the way Eleanor was lookin' at me, I knew she knew we were sleepin' together, 'cause she was lookin' at me the same way I'd looked at Leni and Horst when I'd first seen them together. Now that I'd been there myself, Teddy, I knew. As we used to say on the Shore: you don't know how you look till you get your picture took.

So, we're standin' in the middle of the dance floor, chitchattin', Eleanor cursin' Avery Brundage, me tellin' her about the pool and the Friesenhaus, and so on and so forth, when who should come over but Leni Riefenstahl with her new enamorato. She was lookin' great, too. When she was working, she eschewed make-up, Teddy. She said Hitler didn't like it, and she never knew when she was gonna run into him, so she just left it off. But she knew the Führer wasn't gonna make an appearance at the Goebbelses. He was no party boy, Hitler. So tonight, Leni had pulled out all the stops. She was as dolled up as Eleanor. Or me, for that matter.

And now we're old pals, Teddy. Leni gives me the double cheek kiss again. But then it hit me that, of all people, I was the only one in the group who knew everybody else, even if my relationship with Glenn Morris could only be described as fleeting. So I introduced him and Leni to the Jarretts. Immediately, Leni touched Art perfectly, the way she touched all men perfectly, and then she turned to Eleanor. "Oh, I am so glad to meet mitt you, Eleanor," she said. "I so much vanted you to be big star ov my film."

And Eleanor said, "You're not as sorry as me, honey. I've already been in movies, you know."

"But not svimming."

"No. That SOB Brundage wouldn't allow that." Eleanor stamped her foot. "God, I'd give anything just to get in the pool here."

Horst picked up on that. "You wanna swim in the Olympic pool?"

"God, yes. I've come this far. I was in L.A. four years ago and Amsterdam in '28. For cripe's sake, I'd just like to try it here, too."

So Horst turned to Leni and said something to her in German, which, I gathered, was along the lines of: you can handle that.

Leni beamed. "Yah, ve vill film you svimming tomorrow. Hokay?"

Eleanor was flabbergasted. "You can get me in the pool? It's that easy?"

"For me, yah," Frau Riefenstahl said. She turned to Horst and said, "Schatzi, vhat is . . ." and she asked him something roughly like how do you say I'm in charge of the whole situation in English?

Horst thought for a moment, then shrugged and said, "Oh, how about, 'I'm holding all the cards.' "

Leni liked that so much she repeated it. "Yah, yah. I am holding all ze cards."

Now that the track and field was finished, Leni had primarily moved her base of operations over to the pool. She was something to see, Teddy. She'd always come in gray slacks — reminiscent of Katharine Hepburn, if that rings any sort of fashion bell with you — and if the weather was bad, which invariably it was, she wore this white waterproof greatcoat, which was all the more impressive because her assistants all wore dark coats. Why, it was like a singing group with a lead singer. I don't know what exactly the men around her did. Maybe they were her bodyguards. Maybe they were just there for show. That wouldn't've surprised me. After all, Leni also had a personal photographer, some fellow named Rolf, who also followed her all around.

*"You mean, his job was not to photograph the Olympics, but to photograph the woman photographing the Olympics?"*

316

Exactly. Oh, Leni Riefenstahl was some piece of work. She'd run from camera to camera, barking orders, and if any of the still photographers — you know, the newspaper boys — got in her way, she'd dispatch one of her bully-boys over to the guy with a pink piece of paper — a real pink slip — which said essentially get out of my way, Buster, and one more time, you're gone for good. And he would be. Yes, indeed, Hitler had given her all ze cards.

He came back out to the pool one day to see the races, Hitler did. There was a German guy named Ernst something in the breaststroke he wanted to cheer for. Of course, it was a big deal when he arrived with his entourage. Everything ground to a halt, and they raised his special Führer's flag above his box, and all the Germans gave him the Heil Hitler business, but once he got settled in, everything pretty much went back to normal. With Leni, though, normal was a constant circus. I mean, Teddy, you got an actress who thinks she's a reincarnated Amazon queen running the show with thousands of people watching. Oh, she played it to the hilt.

But Monday evening, after the day's races were over, the pool was deserted, and, as promised, Leni came back. She brought

Hans, the guy who'd filmed me from the dinghy. Horst was designated to pick up Eleanor and her husband, and since Horst had suggested that Eleanor might want some company in the pool, I grabbed my little travel bag with all my swimming gear in it and moseyed over to the pool.

By the time I got there, Eleanor had already changed into her official U.S. bathing suit. Remember, she'd been given one of the team suits — and the nice blue team robe with white trim, as well — but by now she'd taken off her robe and was posing all around the pool for Hans. They were more what you'd call cheesecake shots than anything else, and Eleanor was really enjoying herself. "Wait'll Avery sees this," she kept saying. It gave her a small measure of satisfaction that she'd be on display in the official Olympic film, in her official U.S. suit at the sacred Olympic pool itself. Take that, Avery Brundage. It was a coup for Leni, too — exclusive photos of The Exile right there in the actual Olympic pool!

I stood there awhile with Horst and Art Jarrett, watching as Leni barked orders to poor Hans, shooting Eleanor in various fetching poses. That wasn't hard. Eleanor could do fetching very well. After awhile, though, Leni glanced up to the evening sky and decided she better get Eleanor into the pool itself. Action!

So Eleanor jumped in, but first she called to me to go change. "Hey, Leni," she said, "you gotta shoot some of Sydney, too. She's gonna be the next Queen of the Backstroke." I could tell, though, that this didn't interest Leni one bit. All she wanted was the controversial Miss Holm, the incumbent queen. Still, something started turning over in Leni's mind, because after I returned in my bathing suit, she said, "Vell, ve got two svimmers. Vhy don't ve haf race?"

I didn't know what to expect from Eleanor, but she called out, "Sure. Whaddya say, Sydney?" So, I thought, why not? I jumped in, and Leni started screaming at Hans to get the camera where it had the most light. Eleanor really got into it. "Hey, Sydney, this'll be the real Olympic final," she said, and that reminded me that I'd brought the stopwatch, so I called to Horst to go get it out of my bag.

"How many times you go?" Leni asked.

"It's a hundred meters," Eleanor said. "One down and one back."

"Ve do two more," Leni immediately declared, "so Hans ist sure to get better film."

Typical Leni. It had gotten a little cooler,

so she'd put that big white coat on, which seemed to give her even more authority. But Eleanor wasn't taking any bossing about svimming. "No, down and back. A hundred. Right, Sydney?"

Naturally, I went along with Eleanor. Leni frowned, but she could see Eleanor was steering this ship. Myself, I took a little while longer to warm up, which PO'ed Leni even more — "Get your girl to hurry, Horst. Ze light, ist going!" — and then Eleanor and I took our places.

"Hey, this is fun," Eleanor said.

Horst was the starter. He had the stopwatch. He held his hand up. Hans started filming. "On your marks," Horst said. Then, just when he was about to say "Go," he dropped his arm and said, "Wait a minute."

Leni went nuts. "Vhat ist zis quatsch, Horst?"

"Just a second, Leni. I gotta talk to Sydney." And he leaned down to me by the side of the pool.

"What's up?" I asked.

"Liebchen, are you sure about this? When Avery Brundage sees this, maybe he'll get so mad he'll ban you too."

That thought hadn't occurred to me, but now Horst had put the bee in my bonnet. "You think so?"

"I don't know," Horst said. "The man sounds pretty mean."

Instinctively, I turned back to Eleanor. Meanwhile, Leni was going nuts. She was crouched behind Hans, ready to direct him, and she had no idea what we were talking about. "Vhat ist dis, Horst? Schnell, schnell! Ze light! Ze light!"

"Eleanor?" I asked.

She'd relaxed her grip on the backstroke hand holds, so we were both just standing there. "Sydney," she said, "if you think this could jeopardize your future, then don't do it."

I mulled that over, then turned back to Horst. "No, look: I'm not doing anything wrong. I'm on the team. I swim here every day." He just shrugged, helpless. I turned back to Eleanor. "I'm not doing anything wrong. He couldn't —"

"Yeah, well, he threw me off the team just because he felt like it, didn't he?"

"But that wasn't right."

This time, Eleanor shrugged.

I thought about it some more. If Avery Brundage was gonna bar me just for swimming innocently against somebody else he'd barred, if it was crime by association, then, dammit, Teddy, it was plain downright un-American, and if that was the case, well, I didn't even want to race anymore. That's what I thought. And so, Teddy, I turned back to Horst, and this is what I said: "Fuck him."

*I couldn't help but laughing. "You said that, Mother?" In all my life, I had never once heard my mother use that word. Not once.*

Yes, I did. To this day, I have no idea where that came from. Of course, I knew that word, and of course, I'd heard it enough (although not nearly so often as you hear it nowadays, when it's replaced "damn" as your everyday adjective), and yes, I'd probably said it myself, tittering with Carter, but never, never in my life, Teddy, had I uttered that word emphatically, and in mixed company, to boot. But it came from somewhere, and that's what I said, loud and clear. "Fuck him." Quote. Unquote.

Horst looked astonished, and Art Jarrett — well, I could see he was taken aback because he kinda ducked his head — but Eleanor. Eleanor just roared to beat the band. She brought her hands down, slapping the water hard, splashing it all over. "Sydney," she said, "you really are gonna be my successor." And we both began to laugh — which only made Leni scream some more. "Schnell, schnell! Ve are vasting light."

Finally, Eleanor and I composed ourselves, and Horst threw his arms up. "Okay, we're ready now, Leni." Hans started the camera up again. "On your marks," Horst called out. "Go." He clicked on the stop-watch.

Well, Teddy, it was a completely different feeling than back in Astoria, Queens, at the Trials. I was so loose, it hardly felt like swimming. It felt like I was back, driftin' down the Chester River. Easy, easy. Don't press.

Understand, though, for all that, from the first, Eleanor was in front, and she eased ahead bit by bit as we came to the pool's end. I'd been monkeying around with my turns a lot since I got to Berlin, trying to improve them, and now, when it counted, I managed to flip back better than ever. Eleanor was the master at that, though, and she extended her lead. I'd say she was almost two body lengths ahead of me when we headed for home.

It was sort of weird, too, because of course, no one was cheering. I mean, it would've been tacky for either Horst or Art to root, so it really was like being back home on the river. Here I am, racing alone against the most famous swimmer on the planet in the Olympic pool itself, and it's dead silent.

But suddenly, a few meters into the second

lap, I realized I was catching up with Eleanor. Intellectually this shouldn't have surprised me. She must've been so out of shape. Still, emotionally, it was shocking. I glanced over and saw that my head was even with her kick now. I'd cut her lead about in half. And I felt strong, Teddy. I wasn't in the best condition myself, you understand, practicin' a little with the team, but mostly doin' the town with Horst. But I was flowin'. Another few meters and I wasn't but a half-length behind. I was gonna beat Eleanor Holm!

I could feel myself edge up some more. Each stroke, I drew closer. My head was about the level of her chest now, and there were still ten meters to go. I pushed it into my highest gear. And you know what? You know what?

*"Mom, come on, I'm all ears."*

Well, Eleanor Holm whipped my ass. I don't know where she got it from, Teddy, what reservoir of strength she drew from, but in those last few strokes, instead of me catchin' her, she thrust herself forward. Her out of shape, partyin' every night all over Berlin. There I was, at just about her chest and ready to fly past her, and a few seconds later she's touchin' the wall, and I'm back there around her knees. Close, but no cigar.

324

That just shows you what a champion Eleanor was.

*"She had a big neck, huh?"*

A big brass neck, Teddy.

It did take her a while to get her breath back, but as soon as she did, right away she hugged me. "Sydney," she said, "that's the best you ever swam. I really thought you had me." She looked up at Horst. "What'd I do it in?"

"One minute, seventeen and eight," he said.

"Way to go, honey," Art called out.

"Not even near my best," Eleanor said. "But I'll take it." Then Eleanor looked straight at me. "But you, Sydney — you really are comin' along. You must be doin' all the right things."

I got a devilish smile on my face then, Teddy.

*I could see what was coming, but I didn't say anything.*

And Eleanor saw something in that expression and said, "What, did the cat eat the canary?" So I leaned over to her and whispered how I'd followed her advice and made love with Horst the night before. And she just hooted and slapped the water again. "See, what'd I tell ya, Sydney? What'd I tell ya?"

"What's all that?" Art asked.

"Just girl talk, Art. Just girl talk."

So then we started to climb out of the pool, but Leni came running over in her great white coat, screaming: "Von more time. Von more time. Vile still haf golden light."

Eleanor just waved her off, though, and headed to the locker room. "Sorry, honey. Just one take. Art and I are goin' to the Konigin Café tonight." And off she went. The Konigin was a fancy dance place on Ku'damm.

Leni just stood there, fuming. She was fit to be tied, Teddy, but she'd met her match. She couldn't cry here and play the poor wounded woman put upon by men, because, well — Eleanor wasn't a man. Takes one to know one, doesn't it?

That night, I fixed dinner for Mom. I make a mean spaghetti bolognese. Honesty compels me to admit that it is the only mean dish I make. In fact, it's the only dish I can make, mean or otherwise. But Mom and I ate hearty and then watched the last night of the swimming. It was something of a letdown, though, because Michael Phelps gave up his place in the men's relay so that one of his buddies could win a medal. Mom thought that was uncommonly generous, but, she said, it was rather like going to the theater and having to see the understudy replace the lead.

"You wait, though, Teddy. In four years in Tokyo, Michael will do even better. He still hasn't reached his peak."

"Beijing," I said.

"Beijing what?"

"You said Tokyo, Mom. In 2008, the Olympics are in Beijing."

"Oh, my, yes — the wish was father of the thought. Tokyo was my Olympics. My alleged Olympics." She shrugged then. "Well, that just shows you. So much can happen in four years. Maybe Michael will have quit swimming by then. Maybe some new super-duper swimmer will have come along. Do me a favor."

"Shoot."

"If he does do even better in Beijing, put a rose on my tomb — in honor of me and the Tokyo Olympics of 1940."

"Okay, will do." And I did. When Phelps won eight gold medals at Beijing, I put a whole bouquet on Mom's grave. Well, I pulled one rose out and put it on Dad's, next to her's.

So the swimming ended with a whimper, and in another day, I'd be flying back home to Montana. "I'm gonna miss having you to tell my story to," she told me the next afternoon, when we repaired again to the garden.

"It's been really wonderful for me. You made it worth waiting for all these years."

"You're not disappointed in me, Teddy?"

"In what way?"

"You know. Your dear, sainted old mother throwing her lustful self unconditionally at a boy she hardly knew."

"No, Mom, I think after, uh . . . let's see . . . sixty-eight years, the statute of limitations on any of your libertine teen-age behavior has run out. I'd have to say: what happened in Berlin, stays in Berlin."

"Hmm. I'd call that a rather qualified dispensation, but I'll take it. And I'll try to finish up the rest of my memoirs today."

"This is the end?"

"Of the oral part. I'll give you the rest of what I've written to take home. Maybe you better read that after you leave. You may not be so forgiving of me then."

That took me aback. "Sounds rather ominous," I said. Mom gazed away. Once again she seemed a little tired, a little older, a little sicker. Maybe looking forward to watching the swimming had buoyed her for a while, but now that that was over, her spirits had fallen and taken her body down a bit with them. I was almost prepared to say that perhaps we should postpone this final session till later on. Or that I could stay another day or two.

But, instead, she glanced back at me, then beckoned imperiously at the tape recorder. With that, some of the sparkle came back into her eyes, and a bit more of zest returned to her voice, and she was off and running again.

■ ■ ■ ■

Well, Teddy, I'd have to say that the rest of the time in Berlin was more of the same. But remember now, I was grading on a curve. More of the same was more of heaven.

*She stopped and shook her head.*

I'm sorry. Excuse the hyperbole.

*"Forgiven."*

Thank you. I'll try to limit the overkill. But, my, it was wonderful. Horst's parents returned home from the sailboat competition, so that took away our love nest, but Horst had some friends with bachelor apartments, so we never had any trouble rendezvousing for l'amour.

*I shook my head. She got the picture.*

Did I go over the top again?

*"Skirted it, anyhow."*

All right, I'll assume a less poetic tack, Teddy. I went to the swimming every day, cheering on my teammates. It was very exciting — twenty thousand people screaming at a swimming meet. The first heats in the backstroke were Tuesday, with the semis on Wednesday, where Alice and Edith did well enough to make the finals for Thursday. There was a young Dutch girl named Nida

Senff, and she had a sensational heat. She swam a 1:16.6, which was only three-tenths of a second off Eleanor's world record. Nida was clearly the one to beat — she and another Dutch girl named Rie something.

When the racing wasn't on, Horst and I would just go off. You know, hither and yon. One day we drove up to Grünau, to the river where the Olympic sculls were racing, and one evening we went to watch the exhibition baseball game in the stadium. That was like something out of *Alice in Wonderland,* a hundred thousand Germans watching Americans play a game they didn't understand a lick. Another afternoon we drove down to Potsdam, to the great castle there where the old Prussian kings had lived. They didn't hold any Olympic events in Potsdam, and so it was more like just being a tourist somewhere. And you gotta remember, the little girl from the Shore had sure never seen a castle before.

Tuesday evening, though, I had to meet Horst's parents. Klaus and Inge. That was not something I would've voted for, but Horst had been a bit too effusive in talking about this strange American girl he'd been running around with, and so they'd grown curious. Also, between you and me and the lamppost, I think maybe I hadn't hidden my tracks completely, and Frau Gerhardt had a pretty good inkling that somebody else had been sleeping in baby bear's bed. Whether she shared these suspicions with her lord and master, I don't know, but Horst's father certainly went over me with a jeweler's eye when we met.

Now let me clarify that for the record, Teddy. Men can give you very admiring looks — very admiring, indeed — but there's two types. The one is the salacious. Even when that guy is looking you in the face, you know where his mind's eye is. But then there's the other. You don't mind him giving you the old once-over, because you can sense that he's more of a connoisseur. Probably just as randy as the other fellow, but you can tell that he really does like women.

*"As people?"*

Well, I wouldn't go that far, Teddy. That's giving you men a bit too much credit. But the second type, which was clearly Herr Gerhardt, does deign to accept us for what we are and not just for what we can deliver. It's a fine line, I know, but I've always put you on the right side of the line, so be thankful for small favors.

*"I appreciate your giving me the benefit of the doubt, Mother."*

Of course, you'll probably slip back now that you're long enough in the tooth to be a dirty old man. But let's get back on track:

Frau Gerhardt served tea, which, as you know, I've never much liked. It's just so thin, tea is. It's not that I dislike it. Some drinks are simply unpalatable. Scotch, for example. How does anyone like Scotch well enough to become an alcoholic? Beats me. And Dr Pepper. Yuck.

*She even made a face and stuck out her tongue some. "That's an interesting pair," I observed.*

Well, they just happened to come to mind in tandem. I haven't touched either of them in eons, but some distasteful memories stay with you in perpetuity. Or I can honestly say: I will take those memories to the grave, the grave being imminent enough for me nowadays.

But certainly, Teddy, I don't find tea abhorrent, and I sipped it politely with the Gerhardts while we chitchatted about where the hell the Eastern Shore was and how I came to swim and what-have-you. Then Herr Gerhardt leaned in a bit —

*"Still giving you the old once-over?"*

No, he had another target in his sights. "Now Sydney," he began nicely enough. Like Frau Gerhardt, he had only a bit of an accent, and his English was more British than American. "Stringfellow," he went on. "That's an interesting name."

I said, "Well, it's certainly a long name." He nodded, smiling. The subject of my name invariably came up whenever I'd meet people, so I'd developed a pat routine about it. "My father told me that it probably derived from the craftsmen in the middle ages who prepared the strings that fit in bows. The fellow made strings to shoot arrows with. String-fellow." That was the second part of my schtick on my maiden name, Teddy, and that usually was enough to satisfy anybody. But Herr Gerhardt wasn't finished.

"And what sort of name is it, exactly?"

"You mean, its heritage — that sort of thing?"

"Precisely."

"My father told me it was British. It's an odd name, I know, Herr Gerhardt, but there's more Stringfellows around than you might imagine. Especially in the South. I guess you could say we're more the Yankee end of the Stringfellow clan, although no one would ever call the Eastern Shore Yankee territory."

I don't know if he followed all that inside American stuff, but he said, "I see," and then he went on: "And your mother's side?"

"Oh, that's easy. Mom's a DeHavenon. That's French Huguenot."

"Ach."

"Of course, sir, you have to understand that it's been a coon's age since any of our crowd came over from France. I don't think I've ever met a DeHavenon who knew a single word of French. Not even merci beaucoup."

At that point I noticed that Horst had a disagreeable expression on his face, and I thought perhaps I'd said something out of line, but both his parents chuckled politely. Herr Gerhardt sat back comfortably in his chair, and Frau Gerhardt said, "That's very charming," and she held up the teapot to see if I wanted more, which I didn't, of course. Quite frankly, Teddy, at this point, this would've been one time when I would've been delighted to have had a shot of Scotch.

Horst seemed to come back to life then, speaking up to explain how I'd come to be in Berlin because of Eleanor's expulsion. Naturally, the Gerhardts had heard all about Eleanor Holm. Everyone had. So that produced a fertile conversational gambit, especially since I could provide some humorous anecdotes and explain how Horst had met her too. Then I added: "So you see, it's really something of a fluke that I'm here. I think my Olympics will be in Tokyo."

"Indeed," Frau Gerhardt said.

"Yes, and, of course, Horst has told me . . ." I paused and looked over at him at this point, because I was teasing him, making him think I was about to spill the beans about how I knew Herr Gerhardt might be going to Tokyo as ambassador. But then I quickly added: ". . . that you all lived in Tokyo for several years."

And Horst gave me one of those you-got-me looks, and I winked at him, but right away, Herr Gerhardt said, "Well, Sydney, it appears that Mrs. Gerhardt and I will be going back to Tokyo very soon ourselves."

"You got the job?" Horst asked.

"It should be announced as soon as the Olympics are over."

Horst promptly rose, clapped his father on the shoulder and shook his hand. "Congratulations, Father. That's wonderful." It was quite a lovely moment to see between a father and son. You could tell there was both respect and rapport there.

"Danke, Horst." Then Herr Gerhardt turned to me. "You see, Sydney, it seems I will become ambassador to Japan, so should I still be in Tokyo in '40, I will be cheering for you" — and then he lowered his voice in mock conspiracy — "so long, of course, as there are no German girls in the race."

"I understand, sir. And congratulations."

Since Horst was on his feet now and we'd all shared a fine moment of camaraderie, I could see he was ready to try and pull the plug and gracefully usher me out. I was preparing to take his cue, when Herr Gerhardt said, "So, Sydney, will you Americans have your black auxiliary in Tokyo again to dominate the athletics?"

Well, I was lost, Teddy. On two counts. First of all, I hadn't a clue that the Germans had been calling Jesse Owens and our other sprinters our "black auxiliary." And second, I didn't know that the Europeans called track and field "athletics." So I was totally out to sea.

Horst jumped in. "Father," he said, "I don't believe that any Americans think of their colored athletes as a 'black auxiliary.' It's just not so." He spoke that rather evenly, but it was immediately crystal clear that Herr Gerhardt did not like being contradicted by his son.

He looked up at him and, I thought, speaking as if I weren't even there, he said, "Perhaps it is good, though, for Sydney to know how others may feel about her country. God knows we have had to endure our share of criticism long enough."

I wanted to say something, but I was still a bit unsure about the nature of the whole discussion. Horst looked over to me, his face pained, fearful that I'd been hurt. I tried to signal to him that I was all right, just a bit tossed. Happily, into this breach, Frau Gerhardt — ever the diplomat's wife — tried to patch things over. "It's only too bad, Sydney, that should you come to Tokyo, Horst shall not be there. Alas, we must be leaving my baby behind here to continue his studies."

"Well," I said, grinning, "he's not a baby anymore."

"My baby — always, I'm afraid," she said, smiling at him. Our exchange was light. Her goal had been achieved, the brief squabble put past us.

Unfortunately, though, Horst then said, "Well, I may be seeing Sydney before that. I'm thinking of perhaps studying in the United States."

As blithely, even cheerily, as he said this, both his parents looked as horrified as they were stunned. And believe me, Teddy — I was just as stunned myself. This was news to me.

Frau Gerhardt said, "You've never mentioned this before."

"It's just something I've been thinking about, Mother. After my naval service."

More sternly, Herr Gerhardt said, "We have discussed, of course, some sort of apprenticeship with Albert Speer."

"Yes, Father, of course, that certainly remains a possibility."

This time, Herr Gerhardt turned to speak to me as if Horst were the one not present. "Albert Speer is the most influential architect in Germany, Sydney. The Führer himself has designated him the prime architect of the Third Reich. And I have personally spoken to Mr. Speer about Horst. To not accept the golden opportunity of working with him would be as if someone in your country turned down a chance to apprentice for Frank Lloyd Wright."

I nodded.

Horst tried to put a little oil on the waters. "Father, going to study in the United States is simply an idea I've had."

Herr Gerhardt replied, "And one that seems to have sprung up only very recently." With that, he turned and smiled at me, indicating very neatly from which bewitching wellspring this idea must have sprung. But it was a fond gesture in the way he managed it, so then, the diplomat again, he rose and, smiling upon me, continued: "Sydney, you are as beautiful and as bright as Horst promised us. And I see now, you must, as well, be just as influential."

"But, Father —" Horst began.

Herr Gerhardt held up his hand. "No, no. We can discuss these matters at some future time. For now, you and Sydney should go enjoy this glorious time in Berlin." And with a sly emphasis: "You have so few days left together."

So that Horst couldn't continue the conversation in any way, I quickly stood before Herr Gerhardt and thanked him. He took my hands and kissed me upon both cheeks, as did Frau Gerhardt. I made sure to take hold of Horst and cling to him, so he couldn't step back and try to keep things going. Then, as sweetly — but emphatically — as I could, I said my auf Wiedersehens.

As soon as we stepped outside, Horst made a point of putting his arm about me, and he kissed me sweetly as he helped me into the car. He knew his parents were watching, and he wanted to make certain that they understood the way things were. I'll tell you, Teddy: I sure would've liked to've been a fly on the wall back in the house at that moment, though. My ears were burning, I can guarantee you that.

We drove back into Berlin, to the great park called the Tiergarten, which used to be the royal hunting grounds. Horst didn't say anything, which was unusual. I could see he was a little unnerved by the encounter with his father, so, for diversion, I just prattled on about Edith and Alice and their chances for medals. He responded only in a cursory fashion, so I was especially glad when he parked the car. Isn't it awful being cooped up in a car when somebody isn't being communicative — especially in those ancient days when cars didn't have radios to turn on?

Now the Tiergarten, Teddy, is sort of the Berlin version of Central Park in New York, which I'd been to at the Trials. Only in Central Park, you hardly ever lose sight of the skyscrapers. In the Tiergarten, though, there were these tall sycamore trees that completely separated you from the city.

Maybe it's different now, and maybe Berlin has skyscrapers that loom all up, too, but back then there was a sense that we'd left the city completely behind and were far out in the country. It was downright sylvan, and we strolled along by a little lake, Horst still silently communing with his thoughts, me trying to figure out exactly what his thoughts were.

About then, we came round a bend in the path and were jarred somewhat because four or five stormtroopers — what they called "brownshirts" — were striding toward us. These were the Nazi thugs. I didn't know it at the time, but Hitler had ordered them to lay low during the Olympics, to behave themselves for the benefit of the foreign visitors. But, you know, they just plain looked nasty, Teddy — perhaps especially because, simply by their martial presence, they soiled the serenity of the park. As we passed them, they smirked at us, and it certainly wasn't lost on me that Horst didn't acknowledge them in any way, shape or form.

No, I didn't feel threatened at all, but there was just such an ugly impression about them. In fact, it stood out from all my other memories of that time. I would look back to when the war started and remember that one brief moment, and think, "Ah, that's the Nazis." All the good stuff when I was there, but I could never forget that one passing incident. Of course, at the time, in the Tiergarten, in this lovely haven, it seemed as if the brownshirts were the ones out of joint. But, of course, it wasn't that way. Those SOBs were just lying in the weeds, biding their time.

Certainly, though, I could immediately sense that these creepy guys stirred up something in Horst, because right away, he gripped my hand harder and guided me over to a bench that overlooked the little lake. I sat down, but he only put his foot up on the bench and bit his lip for a moment. "Horst?" I said.

"I'm just so sorry," he said.

Teddy, I still didn't know what was eating at him. "What about?"

"You know. My father."

I reached up to take his hand, but he wouldn't let me. "Honey, he didn't upset me. Really."

He leaned forward then, on his knee. "You didn't get what that name business was all about?"

"Oh, shoot, that's nothing. People are always asking me about my name. It's a funny name. They used to kid me in school."

"No. You don't understand, Sydney. The

whole thing was just to find out if you might be Jewish."

Only then, as the Bible says, did the scales fall from my eyes. "It was?"

"Yeah." Horst took his foot down from the bench and knocked his one fist into his palm. "My father is getting so bad about that. It didn't use to mean anything to him, but now that he's in the party, and —" He stopped, and shifted about. "I mean, Dad doesn't have to get involved with domestic stuff. He's a diplomat. But now I see him losing some perspective. And he's too smart for that." He paused. "And too nice."

"You love him a lot, don't you?"

"Yes, I do, Sydney. I'm very proud of him, too." Suddenly, he sat down next to me. "Look, I'll tell you. There's a certain amount of tension in the family because of Liesl. Well, not because of her, but because of her husband. Walter is an officer, a Standarten-führer in the SS."

I knew so little, Teddy. I'd never even heard of the SS. "What's that?"

"SS — Schutzstaffel. Oh, never mind what it means. It's Hitler's own police force, sort of a second army. And Walter is a very . . . uh, dedicated Nazi. Very passionate. And I think it affects Dad — and, frankly, I haven't had the courage to say anything. And, I'm sorry, it really got to me when he started on that name stuff with you."

"Hey, please don't get upset because of me."

Horst took both my hands and looked right at me. It was so abrupt and so dramatic, it took me aback. "Could you live here, Sydney?" he asked. "Could you?"

"Remember? You asked me about that."

"Yes, of course." And at that he got up again and crossed his arms. He was so squirmy. He just couldn't stay put. "No, no, I know it would be so much easier for me to come to the United States. I mean, just the language."

"Yeah, the language."

"That's why I thought about going to school there."

"That was kind of a surprise — for us all." And boy, that was an understatement.

"Well, it's a possibility."

"Yeah."

"It's just, I don't want to leave here. I don't. It's like it's all coming together for Germany now. And, yeah, some of the stuff isn't right, but we've come a long ways, and I know these Olympics have made such a difference. Everybody can see that. My father should see that." He sat down next to me again, and for the first time in awhile, he smiled. He hadn't smiled during any of this. "I'm just so excited, Sydney. It's all happened so fast. The Olympics. And you just drop in from off the moon or somewhere, and all of a sudden I'm completely in love with you."

"From the moon."

"Yeah."

And then, you know what, Teddy? You would have thought we'd've fallen into some passionate embrace at this point, but we didn't. Not at all. We didn't even look at each other. We both just stared out at the lake in front of us. And neither of us said anything for the longest time. I knew what he was thinking, because I was sure he was thinking exactly what I was, that we had found each other, and it was perfectly amazing, but, of course, I knew he was also thinking about Germany and how that affected things.

Only after quite a while I started to cry. Very softly at first, and then harder and harder. It took him by surprise. Well, it took me by surprise. I mean, it was completely involuntary. "Sydney? Why?"

"Because I'm so happy," I said, and I fell into his arms.

"Oh," he said.

"But also because I'm sad."

"You are?"

"Because I have to leave you next week."

"Please don't think about that."

So I tried not to, but I didn't succeed altogether. I kept crying because I was so happy and so sad at the same time, which sounds like a crazy thing, Teddy, but which was absolutely the case on this occasion when I was in the Tiergarten. We both stared out at the lake again, for the longest time.

The next night I took Mom out to dinner. She chose a different little restaurant nearby. It was French and very highly regarded, but I think Mom picked it largely for the name — it was either a *le* or a *la*. When it came to restaurants, Mom much preferred the ambiance to the cuisine. Names mattered. She made sure to get us a table by the window, because it offered a good view. Views mattered.

For September it was especially warm, as if summer had gone into an overtime, but it was our last evening together. Mom had plans, though. Helen would be visiting her in another week or so, and then she wanted to come back to Missoula to, as she put it, "see my old friends one last time . . . above ground." She knew her days were running out, but she remained markedly calm and held to her good spirits.

We both ordered a gin and tonic, and

Mom raised hers in toast: "To G and Ts," she proclaimed. "Last one of the year. You can't drink gin if it isn't warm."

"Why?"

"I really don't know, Teddy. My father absolutely subscribed to that rule. He used to call tonic 'quinine water,' so maybe it has something to do with the tropics — heat. Don't you drink quinine to ward off malaria?"

"Or the tsetse fly," I said.

"Anyway, you shouldn't be caught dead drinking gin and tonics once the frost is on the pumpkin. I adhere to that principle in life." And she took another sip, then quickly dove into her purse and hauled out the tape recorder and placed it on the table.

"You brought that?"

"Well, I thought I'd tell you about the race while we were waiting for the meal."

"The race?" I asked, clicking the recorder on.

My race, Teddy, for goodness' sake. The Olympic one-hundred meter backstroke. Thursday, the thirteenth of August, in the year of Our Lord, nineteen hundred and thirty-six.

*"If only you could have been in it," I said, and Mom sighed.*

349

Yeah, more's the pity. But it was a honey of a race to watch — even if it was another nasty day. The weather just never got consistently nice that whole two weeks. Just those few odd good days, like the time Horst and I went to the beach. He wasn't at the race, though. Leni had him doing something somewhere else that afternoon. Of course, Eleanor came. She was brandishing a press pass, but she chose instead to sit with us, her erstwhile teammates. Just to stick it to the blazers. She plunked herself right down next to me.

*The waitress came back then and tried to talk us into Pellegrino instead of good Oregon tap water and, failing that, distributed the menus and asked if we wanted to know about the specials. Mom listened, but said we'd get around to ordering in due time. She shook her head when the waitress left.*

The older I get, the more damn specials. I swear, if I lived another ten years, there'd be so many specials, it'll be easier for the waitresses to hand you a sheet with the specials on it and then recite the menu. Less is more, Teddy. Nobody ever learns less is more anymore.

*I commiserated with her.*

But you let me wander off again, Teddy. Now where the hell was I?

*"Eleanor Holm had just plunked herself down next to you."*

Oh yeah. And here came the seven gals, who were the backstroke finalists. There weren't any Germans in the race, so the stadium was relatively sedate, but anybody who knew anything knew the two Dutch girls were the ones to beat. Rie Whatever had already won the freestyle, and Nida Senff had the best time in the heats.

Eleanor wasn't impressed, though. She had on a bright rose outfit with a picture hat, because she knew people would be watching her, and before the race she told me, "I could handle this bunch pretty easily, Sydney, but I've got to cheer hard, so everybody'll think I'm a good sport." So right away, she stood up and yelled, "Yea, Edith" and "Come on, Alice" — things of that nature.

That was for Edith Motridge and Alice Bridges, the two American gals, you understand. And I'll tell you, Teddy, until the gun actually went off, I think more people were watching Eleanor than the swimmers. It made me downright self-conscious just sitting next to her, because I knew all eyes were trained on her and therefore a lot of them couldn't help but see me, too. Peripherally. If I'd known that ahead of time, I'd've paid more attention to my attire. I was pretty drab compared to Eleanor in that snazzy red ensemble of hers.

Of course, no one zeroed in on Eleanor more than Leni. She was there, in the usual Riefenstahlian get-up, the slacks, the white greatcoat, with the usual entourage — they call that a "posse" now, don't they?

*"Yes, they do."*

Well, I like to be au courant, Teddy, even as my clock winds down. So Leni had her whole posse, and she had two cameramen. Hans was shooting the race, and she had Willy shooting the crowd — which, when push came to shove, mostly amounted to concentrating on La Holm.

And then the race started. Edith got off well, as always, and she was in the lead with Nida Senff. And when the Dutch girl made a bad turn, damn if Edith didn't get in front.

I said to Eleanor: "Maybe she can do it," but Eleanor just shook her head. "Nah, she always fades, Sydney," and sure enough, by the time they got halfway through the last lap, Nida had moved back ahead. Now here came both Rie Whatever and Alice moving real fast, though. Alice had on a yellow cap. It stood out, and for just a second there, I thought maybe she might win, but the two Dutch girls were too good. It was pretty close, though, all four of 'em — a honey of a race — so the crowd got into it even if there wasn't any German to root for.

*"Well, come on, Mom, who won?"*

Oh, Nida held on, and Rie Whatever was second, and Alice touched out Edith for third. Poor Edith. She just couldn't last. There were no big scoreboard clocks then, so we had to wait for them to check with the judges with their stopwatches. Then came the announcement: "The gold medal goes to Miss Nida Senff of the Netherlands in the time of one minute, eighteen and nine-tenths seconds."

Eleanor stood up to cheer — you know, still playing the good sport — but out of the corner of her mouth, she said to me: "Sydney, that is so piss poor. I could've beat 'em all by ten feet." She clapped some more, and then she turned back to me and said, "And you would've beat 'em by five."

Well, she was absolutely right, Teddy — based on that practice race I'd had with Alice and Edith when I let 'em win, and then the one I'd had with Eleanor a few nights before. I swam much faster than the winner, so I took some pride in that, but it was cold comfort. That and a nickel would get me a cuppa coffee. I certainly never went around saying, well, I was really faster than the Olympic champion.

*"But you're saying it now, right?"*

*Mom sipped her gin and tonic, considering.*

Sure, Teddy. I might as well air it out now. Damn straight: I was already the Queen of the Backstroke, even if nobody knew it but me and Eleanor.

The waitress came back then, and when I flipped off the tape recorder, Mom said, "Can you tell us the specials again, please?" After she heard them all, she said, "I think I'll order off the menu."

Now that I think about it, I can't ever remember Mom going for one of the specials. She was always pretty much a meat-and-potatoes lady.

Mom was tired after dinner, so as soon as we got back to her place, she went into her bedroom. I sat down and picked up a magazine, but before long, I heard her call for me. She was propped up in bed, with a light quilt jacket over her pink nightgown. She'd taken off her wig, but wore some sort of nightcap. Next to her, lying on the bed, was the purple acetate folder. She patted it. "I guess I can give you this now," she said.

"I'll know where to find my place?"

"Oh, it's easy. Just look for the part when I get back from the Olympics."

"So, nothing much else happened in Berlin?"

"No, after the backstroke was over, it was mostly just me and Horst being lovey-dovey. I'll spare you that."

"Oh, go on and tell me the rest, Mom," I said. "You haven't left much to my imagination."

"Well, then, just for a minute more, Teddy," and she patted the sheets. I sat down there, on the edge of the bed, just as she used to sit next to me on my bed when I was a little boy about to go to sleep. But then she crossed her arms and made a bit of a face.

"What's the matter?"

"Well, actually, Coach Daughters got a bit put out with me because of Horst."

"Why was that?"

"He told me that even though I hadn't been able to compete in the Olympics, I could walk in with the American team for the closing ceremony. But I told him that while I appreciated that very much, Horst had gotten real good seats from his father, and I was gonna watch with him. And Coach Daughters said, 'You know, Sydney, you're a very pretty girl, and I'm sure you'll have lots of boyfriends, but the Olympics is a once-in-a-lifetime thing.'

"I didn't want to contradict him and tell him that Horst wasn't just another run-of-the-mill boyfriend, but was the love of my life. I let that go, Teddy. Instead, I just said: 'No, Coach, I promise you I'll be at Tokyo — and I'll win you a gold medal there.'

"Coach Daughters shook his head and said, 'I hope so, Sydney, but a lot can

356

change in four years. Just look what happened to Eleanor. It's a wonderful thing to be part of a closing ceremony.'

"I could tell how much he wanted me to march in with the other gals, but that was going to be my last night with Horst, Teddy, and wild horses weren't going to tear me away from him, even for a minute. I told Coach I'd think about it, but I was just fibbing and he knew I was, so that was that."

"So you went with Horst?"

"Oh my, yes, and it was wonderful. Remember, I hadn't gotten to Berlin in time for the opening ceremony, so the spectacle was all new to me. Of course, nowadays everybody sees everything on television, so there's never anything new under the sun. Nobody just says: this is wonderful. This is absolutely breathtaking. Nobody ever says that anymore. No, everybody has seen everything, so they just compare whatever it is with something else. Well, sure, this is a nice ceremony in Athens, but it isn't as nice as the one in Sydney. Or Barcelona. Or Disneyworld was better. Or that dreadful Las Vegas. We're all so jaded, Teddy. We can't take anything at face value. All we do is compare things. Isn't it funny? I'm the old person. I'm the one who's seen so much, and I still marvel at new things. It's the younger people who don't possess that facility anymore. They've grown up different. They don't like surprises."

"Like when they take pictures and can see what they've taken."

"Exactly. I'm glad we discussed that." Of course, with Mom, there wasn't ever much discussion, but I let that go. She sighed. "At any rate, the closing ceremony was beyond my wildest dreams. Let me see now. Let me get this in the right order. There was a choir singing — all dressed in white, like angels — and a whole squadron of trumpeters trumpeting and a battery that fired a farewell salute, with rockets cascading across the sky."

She swept one arm in a rockets' arc.

"Of course, from hindsight we can say how typical it was of the damn Nazis to be so martial, but I promise you, at the time, that never crossed anybody's mind. You see, that's a metaphor for it all. There's so much we don't put together even though it's right before our very eyes. It's so easy to say: well, couldn't you see what was going on, Sydney? And what was the matter with Horst? Was he blind? But very few catch on, Teddy. Very few.

"There was this old comedian. I forget his name. He was what they used to call a 'baggy-pants comedian.' But he had a famous line — and with a German accent. German accents were cheap laughs, because the language sounds so pompous. He'd just say: 'Vas you dere, Charlie?' and everyone would die laughing."

" 'Vas you dere, Charlie?' "

"That's right. He'd just say it and everyone would break up. Lord knows why. But as much as people laughed, it had some wisdom to it, because if you weren't there, wherever the there was, you couldn't get it. What do they say now: 'You don't know jack.' Right?"

"Yep. That's what they say."

"Well, if you weren't there, you didn't know jack. But you see, here's the point: even if you were there you still probably missed it anyway." She sighed again, and slapped my leg. "Oh shoot, Teddy, I got off the track. You're not supposed to let me get off the track."

"Well, I just didn't want to interrupt. I mean, it certainly sounds like the ceremony was a sight to behold."

"Oh my, yes. It's imbedded in my memory. Now, let's see. Oh yeah, the band — well, it wasn't a band; that makes it sound like Tommy Dorsey or Ted Weems or somebody. It was the Berlin Philharmonic. The Philharmonic began to play a hymn by Beethoven. And I just snuggled up to Horst, and I never wanted it to end. Never.

"We always remember the wonderful times we had, don't we, Teddy? Of course we do. And, much as we hate it, we can't put some of the horrible moments out of our heads, either. But you know what're the most memorable moments of all in our lives?"

I shook my head. Another discussion.

"They're at a time like that was. It's when you're part of something wonderful, you're so happy, you're exhilarated . . . but you not only know it's gonna end — hell, everything ends — you know it's gonna end very soon, and that sadness will follow. That's the way it was with me. Because here I was with Horst, and we were so incredibly in love, and we were together at this amazing spectacle, and yet I couldn't drive it completely from my mind that soon it'd be over, and I'd be torn away from him, and no matter how much we professed that we'd meet again and be together forever, no matter how much we wanted to believe that, we knew we didn't know for sure.

"And, Teddy, we weren't even thinking about something like a war. That wasn't on anybody's radar, even if they'd had radar then, which they didn't. It was just that he was in Berlin, Germany, and I was in Chestertown, Maryland, and it was the Depression. I only knew that despite my ecstasy, I'd soon be paying with just as much sadness. The extremes, juxtaposed, Teddy — that's the most memorable of all." Quickly then, she looked right at me. " 'Parting is such sweet sorrow.' "

"Yes?"

"Who said that? Shakespeare?"

"Of course, Mom. That's *Romeo and Juliet.*"

"I should've known. Shakespeare said everything the Bible didn't. But that's just nonsense. That's just the poet showing off. What's sweet about parting, Teddy? Huh?"

"Well, you know, Mom, kissing goodbye. That's a sweet part: kissing."

"Oh stop it. You're just defending Shakespeare because all you theater people have to defend Shakespeare. I knew damn well I wasn't gonna feel anything sweet about parting from Horst. Damn well.

"But, before that, at the stadium, oh my — all that majesty. It just made being with Horst that much more joyous." She paused and glanced away, wistfully, and then, still without looking back at me, she reached over and squeezed my hand. She took a

361

breath and began again.

"The hymn. The Beethoven hymn they played was entitled "The Flame Dies." Talk about on point. And as they played it, the searchlights came down lower and lower until it was like a tent of light. A veritable tent, Teddy. Then, from down at one end of the stadium, here came fifty-two tall German gals, all dressed in white. They must have scoured the land to come up with this bunch, all tall, all blonde, all about the same size. Maybe Leni Riefenstahl found them when she was out looking for the cute boys. Or that creepy Goebbels.

"Anyway, they marched in by twos, like Noah's Ark, and went over to where the flag bearers were holding the flags of the Olympic nations. Fifty-two of them. That's why the fifty-two girls in white. Of course, that's like a drop in the bucket now, fifty-two, what with all those countries that used to be Yugoslavia and all the jack-istans and mack-istans and so forth, but fifty-two seemed like a great deal of countries to me at the time. So the flag bearers lowered the flags, and the girls put laurel wreaths on the flag poles.

"And then they lowered the Olympic flag itself, and there was this whole procession, with about a dozen German fencers as the escort, their sabers drawn, takin' the flag over to the burgomeister of Berlin, who was sittin' there with Hitler. The idea was that the burgomeister would take care of the flag till Tokyo. That was the tradition. God only knows what happened to that poor flag. But anyway, when the music ended, everybody rose, and there was dead silence. A hundred thousand souls, and you could hear a pin drop. And the lights began to dim. And that was when, down at the end of the stadium, by the Marathon Gate, the flame began to go out. Down, down, down. Then poof — it was gone. Extinguished. You had to get goosebumps. I snuggled up closer to Horst.

"I know you're not supposed to say anything good about the Nazis, but let's give the devil his due: those SOBs could put on a show, Teddy. They were great at massing multitudes. Nobody ever did multitudes better than the Nazis, except maybe the Chinese, but they've got the advantage when it comes to multitudes because there's just so damn many of them, the Chinese. The Nazis could do great multitudes without as many multitudes.

"Then, in the silence, here came the voice of the head Olympic pooh-bah, the chief blazer of them all. He spoke in English. He said" — and here Mom intoned again, like an announcer: " 'After offering to the Führer, Adolf Hitler, and the German people, our deepest gratitude, we call upon the youth of every country to assemble in four years at Tokyo, there to celebrate with us the twelfth Olympic Games.'

"You bet your sweet life I remember that. I was the youth they were calling.

"I couldn't help myself. I just hugged Horst and whispered, 'We'll be there.' And he answered by kissing my forehead. Oh, it was all so sweet and lovely. I was so happy, Teddy. I was suddenly absolutely sure that whatever would happen to us, me back in America, him at college and then in the navy, by 1940 we'd be there in Tokyo together and I would win my gold medal and Horst and I . . . then, then somehow we would never be apart again.

"My eyes began to mist up just as the choir started to sing the finale. They sang in German, of course, but the lyrics were up on the scoreboard in English. 'Friends, farewell,' it said. 'Even if the sun should sink for us, others will beckon. Friends, farewell.'

"And the music faded away, softly, softly, until it was quiet again. I was breathless from all the beauty, Teddy. In fact, at first, I don't think I even noticed it, I was so lost in my own reverie, but somewhere in the stadium a chant began, and it grew and grew and grew: 'Sieg heil,' it went. 'Sieg heil, unserem führer, sieg heil." Over and over, all these right arms outstretched and raised. And louder and louder until it became a roar. 'Sieg heil, unserem führer, sieg heil.' "

I dared ask: "Did Horst join in?"

"Yes, he did. He even took his arm from round my waist so that he could raise it in salute with all the others. He was proud, Teddy. At that moment, he was so proud to be a German. And it went on and on for quite a while. But here's the thing: as soon as it died out, I pretty much forgot that part. It's like: who remembers 'The Star Spangled Banner' after the ballgame is over? When it was done, it was gone, and I only kept thinking about everything beautiful that'd come before. 'Vas you dere, Charlie?' Ya, I vas dere, Teddy, but I still didn't get it. And neither did anyone else.

"You see, the irony was that as far as the future was concerned, the only part of that whole beautiful evening that'd ever mean anything was the end. 'Sieg heil, unserem führer, sieg heil.' The rest was just cotton candy. But who knew? Pass the cotton candy. Oh my, Teddy, what a glorious time it was for a girl to be in love with a boy."

She let a big smile play across her face

and then, after a moment, reached over and picked up the purple acetate folder and handed it to me. "Now, take this home with you, and after you read it, if you can still stand me, call me."

"Stand you?"

"If you can."

I let that pass. "Okay, Mom. I will." I took the folder and stood up, then leaned back down and kissed her on the forehead, just as Horst must have done that night at the stadium.

I was almost to the door when she called to me, waving for me to come back. She held out her hand, and I gave the purple acetate folder back to her. She unsnapped it, reached inside and pulled out the swatch she'd saved from the magenta gown with the trapunto cording. Without another word, she handed the folder back, and after softly fondling the swatch, she placed it on the table next to her bed. By the time I reached the door she'd already turned out the light.

■ ■ ■ ■

# Part Three:
# Jimmy

■ ■ ■ ■

Could Mother possibly think that I would simply put that purple acetate folder in my suitcase, not to pick it up and read it until, oh, a week or so later when I had some spare time? I'm quite sure she knew exactly what I would do, which was to immediately sit down there in her living room and begin to read.

I slipped the pages out. There was one handwritten page on foolscap on top. It said simply: "HOW MUCH WILL YOU DO FOR LOVE?" — which was, of course, that curiously strained philosophical question Mother had posed a few days before.

I put that aside and found two other pages, typewritten. They were held by a large paper clip to the cover of an old seventy-eight record album (the edges cut a bit so that it could fit into the folder). It was an album of songs of Vera Lynn. The pages were dated fairly recently, May 7,

2003 — my father's birthday — and it read:

Jimmy & I loved listening to Vera Lynn (now, of course, Dame Vera Lynn — & she is still alive & kicking!) during the war. I suppose people would think her songs were very sappy now. There was even one entitled "Be Like A Kettle and Sing." Cheer up! Like that, most of her songs looked forward to the end of that awful war — or at least tried to put the best face on things, e.g. "When The Lights Go On Again (All Over The World)" & "Wish Me Luck As You Wave Me Goodbye" & "Goodnight Children Everywhere" & several others we'd play on the old 78 record player. (Did we still call them gramophones then? I can't remember.)

Anyway, our favorite was called "There's A Land Of Begin Again." I think you could call that our song. I don't know who wrote it, & it's certainly not the sort of song people like anymore, but I think it'd be an apt title for our story. And, if anybody cares, here are the words:

When all your troubles just surround you
And around you skies are grey
If you can only keep your eyes on
The horizon, not so far away.

There's a land of begin again
On the other side of the hill
Where we learn to live & love again
When the world is quiet & still.

There's a land of begin again
And there's not a cloud in the sky
Where we'll never have to grieve again
And we'll never say goodbye.

And then Mom began her story. Accustomed to neat, clean twenty-first-century word-processor copy, I had to adjust to her old typewritten words on onion-skin paper. While it was not a terribly messy draft, words — sometimes whole sentences — were crossed out, with corrections made by pen. It was clear that Mom had just wanted to get this down, on the record, and wasn't worried so much about neatness so as to take the time to type whole pages over.

More to my surprise was the date she had typed at the top: August 9, 1984 — and then, on the next line, in parentheses, she had added, "upon our return from the Los Angeles Olympics."

I remember when Mom and Dad had gone there. That Olympics obviously must've brought back memories of '36 and Berlin, inspiring her to tackle this when she got home. And, indeed, she began by explaining:

I am 66 yrs old now & have thought for a long time that I should write this "memoir," since I am at an age when death is certainly a real possibility from now on. I do not want Jimmy to see this, should he outlive me, so I will not place it in the safe deposit box, but leave it with my "effects" for Teddy &/or Helen. Perhaps if I grow more courageous I will give it to one of them while I am still upright &, as they say, being of sound mind & body. Or mind anyway.

At that point, Mom began writing her story out, much as she had told it to me. I skimmed through the pages until I found her at the end of the Olympics and began reading there, which was her Chapter Five, Part I.

## CHAPTER FIVE

### I.

I returned home on the good ship SS President Roosevelt with many other Olympians. I roomed in 3rd class w/ Mary

Lou Petty. She was going to meet her fiance in N.Y. A fine pair of moonstruck gals we were. Mary Lou was just counting the hours till we docked, while I was bemoaning the hours since we left. I wrote Horst a love letter every day, but as we neared N.Y. I realized I was carrying coals to Newcastle, & so I took the whole batch & excerpted the best parts & boiled it down into one absolutely fantastic love letter.

When we arrived in N.Y. there was no one to meet me, but by now I felt quite comfortable in Gotham (nobody called it "the Big Apple" back then). So I got a taxi at the pier & asked the cabbie to 1st take me to a post office, then to Penn Station, so I could get a train to Wilmington (& connect to the "Bullet").

Luckily (!), the main p.o. in Manhattan was right across the street from Penn Station, so I took that as a good omen & mailed the letter to Horst, then got a train very quickly.

The amazing thing was that I was only home for 2 days when I got a letter from Horst. How? Well, he had managed to get it on the Hindenburg, the great dirigible, which would explode a year or 2 later. I took that letter, held it to my heart & went down to the dock & read it there alone, crying all the while for happiness, worried that my expressions of love that I had written him had not attained the heights he had achieved. Among his other many good attributes, Horst was a wonderful romantic. Oh, what letters. They verged on poetry. Well, certainly I thought that at the time.

I wrote him back, that obviously neither English or German was his 1st language. No: the language of love was.

(Forgive me the excess, but was I a goner!)


So, right away, I was irritated again. I had been foolish enough to think that once Mother left Germany, the rest of her story would be Horst-free, but here she was, decades later, still prattling on, still completely infatuated by this teen-age heartthrob. I had to keep telling myself that however much her young swain had meant to her way back then, I had been an actual living, breathing witness to so many years of the wonderful marriage my parents had together. I could take comfort that the evident reality of that true love — day after day, year after year, decade after decade — overwhelmed even the most romantic memories of that brief summer's interlude of youthful infatuation.

Satisfied that I was upholding the honor of my dear, late father, I turned the page:

It was still every bit my intention, after a month or 2, to pull up stakes & move to N.Y. to join the Women's Swimming Association. But the best laid plans . . .

When I missed my period, I thought to myself "uh oh," & then I began to get ill in the a.m., & altho at 1st I simply refused to believe what had happened, it didn't take Sherlock Holmes to tell me what the score was — especially when my 2nd period was also gone w/ the wind. I cried a great deal & simply could not believe that I'd let myself get into this situation that only happened to stupid, vulnerable girls in bad cautionary novels. On one rare occasion when I could laugh, I asked myself: would Nancy Drew get knocked up?

But, so it seemed, was I.

I shifted uncomfortably on the sofa as I read this, and while I didn't yet know the outcome of what certainly was my mother's teen-age pregnancy, I wanted to cry for her that she had been feeling guilty about this for all these years, sufficient to write it all out as a confessional. Not "stand you," Mother, simply because you got pregnant?

Come on, Mom.

But, of course, I was now absolutely furious at that sonuvabitch, that silver-tongued German dastard who had done this to her. Surely, at last, she would see him for the flawed and thoughtless predator that he was. And so, enraged, I read on:

Of course, it would've helped if I could blame Horst & feel sorry for myself, but without going into detail, let me simply say that I knew exactly when this must've happened & that it was my responsibility altogether. (Well, for the most part. It takes 2 to tango.) Yes: the wages of sin!

Okay, so I gave up. The rotter Horst Gerhardt could still do nothing wrong in my mother's blind eyes.

Against all odds, I kept hoping that maybe, just maybe, I wasn't pregnant, but I was terrified to go to my family dr. & have him be privy to my situation. So I went to see Gentry Trappe, that dear old black man who lived in the tenant's house on our property.

I felt very ashamed about my predicament, so I approached him gingerly, inquiring if there might be a "colored" dr. I could see, because it involved a "delicate" matter.

Notwithstanding how circumspect I was, I believe the old gentleman got my drift. Uneducated tho he might've been, Mr. Trappe was nobody's fool. "Miss Trixie," he said, trodding on very careful ground, "would this involve a, uh, woman's thing?"

"Yes, in fact it would," I replied, as if I was shocked he'd made such a good wild guess. Mr. Trappe suggested I might see a lady named Miss Victoria, who, altho not an actual MD, expertly handled these female matters which were ever such a mystery to men. I suppose she was a midwife.

The next day, Mr. Trappe insisted that he personally drive me to see Miss Victoria, because, of course, she resided in the black area of town, & he did not believe I should venture there on my own. He said, "Your father, God rest his soul, wanted me to live in the old house so's to keep an eye on you & your mother, & Mr. Stringfellow would be upset w/ me if I didn't escort you myself."

So he took me there, &, of course, once I described my symptoms to Miss Victoria & she examined me, she immediately officially confirmed what I already knew, that

I was, yes, as the expression goes, more than a little bit pregnant. I thought I was prepared for this news, but actually hearing the finality of the diagnosis was sufficient to cause me to break down.

Miss Victoria hugged me to her, rocking me some, as if I was more a baby than somebody having one. How especially comforting it was, in this 2nd worse moment of my life (the 1st being when I heard my father had been killed), that this stranger was so caring. We are so lucky sometimes that people who know us might succor us in distress, & here this nice lady, who had never set eyes on me before, was my angel of mercy — plus: we 2, of different races, different worlds. I've never forgotten that kindness after all these yrs.

I finally stopped sobbing. Miss Victoria had, of course, seen that no wedding ring adorned my finger, and w/o drawing attention to that, she simply said, "What are you gonna do now, child?"

I just shook my head and said, "I don't know."

"Well," Miss Victoria said, "let the Good Lord guide you." Which was probably the best advice anybody could have proferred at that particular moment.

I pulled myself together then, as best I

could, all but forced a dollar upon Miss Victoria as fair payment for her services, & managed to put a brave face on things all the way home w/ Mr. Trappe. Since he had been the beneficiary of my father's largesse — that made me think about Daddy & how disappointed he would be in me for being stupid or loose or both at the same time.

I went down to the dock & sat there, w/ my arms wrapped round my knees. There, I assessed my situation, & decided that I had 3 alternatives, which was whistling past the proverbial graveyard, because only 2 were valid. The one that wasn't was getting Horst to marry me. Obviously, given where he was, that was entirely out of the question. I didn't even see any sense in revealing my condition to him. So I actually had only 2 alternatives, & here they were: I could either tell my mother, then go discreetly away somewhere, have the baby & put it up for adoption. Or I could get an abortion.

When I got back to my room, I wrote Carter Kincaid at Towson St. Teachers, down near Baltimore, & told her I was "in trouble," & maybe she could help me. Dear Carter! The instant she got my letter, she called me long distance, person-to-person, given the private nature of the matter, & told me that another girl in her dormitory had also found herself in the family way, as we referred to that circumstance then, & so she knew she could arrange for my predicament to be safely & expeditiously resolved.

When I told my mother that I was going to visit Carter for a few days she got a little cross at me. She said, "Trixie, you've been home 2 months, & as far as I know, for all your talk about going to live in N.Y. to practice with that swimming club, I haven't heard boo from you recently on that subject."

Well, obviously, finding myself pregnant had, shall we say, put everything else on the back burner. Nonetheless, I had received a letter from L. deB. Hadley, who always wrote his name that way. People in swimming even called him L. deB — you know, like: Eldeebee. He was the famous coach of the Women's Swimming Assoc., often referred to as "the father of women's swimming." He had practically invented the freestyle stroke, or at least, the correct breathing part for it. In his letter, which he had carbon-copied to Eleanor Holm, L. deB. officially invited me to come to N.Y. & be a member of the WSA.

Normally, of course, that would have put me over the moon, but given my being great (or, shall I say: soon to be great) w/ child, it didn't mean beans to me.

Nonetheless, I fished the letter out now & showed it to Mother. "Well," she said, "the least you could've done was mentioned this to me."

"I'm sorry, Mom. It's just that everything had been so exciting, that I just had to calm down &, you know, find my bearings. So I thought I would put off N.Y. till the spring."

"Well, that's fine, honey, but I'm not having you just lollygagging around till the flowers bloom again."

"Oh no, Mother, I understand that. I was going to talk to you about this."

And I was. But now, the rubber had hit the road, so I broached my idea. That was: that I would work in the insurance office as what we used to call a "chief cook and bottle washer." Or a Gal Friday, some would call it. A factotum, others.

"Well," Mom said, "that's fine w/ me."

"I could practice my typing, too, which would help me get a better job in N.Y. And you wouldn't have to pay me anything, Mom, just give me my old allowance."

Instead, she said she would pay me $8

a week, plus dry cleaning money, inasmuch as I would have to look correct & neat every day in the office. We agreed that, #1, I would write L. deB. & fib a little, tell him that because of a family matter I'd be unable to come to N.Y. till the spring (that would be '37) &, #2, that I would start working regularly at the insurance office as soon as I returned from visiting Carter. As I started to leave the room, however, Mother called back to me. "Yes, ma'am?"

She sat down on the sofa & patted the seat next to her. "Trixie, take a load off for a second." When I was settled, she began: "Now this good-looking German boy . . ." And my heart sank, because I thought she must've somehow put 2 + 2 together, what with my a.m. sickness & general mopey attitude, but, happily, no. Instead, she said, "Listen, honey, we all know what it's like to have your 1st real romance. And, you know, somehow summer romances are the most, well . . . romantic. I met your father in Nov., but there was a boy named Mike Carey from Fairlee I'd fallen head over heels in love w/ the summer before that, & somehow that all seems so much more vivid — altho it was over by Labor Day, & I was married to your dear father for 18 wonderful yrs.

"But I can so remember the songs Mike Carey & I used to dance to & kiss to & whatnot. I can remember those better than the songs that were popular when your father & I really fell in love. Summer songs, Trixie. You remember them. That's the way it is with summer romances." She paused. "That, & it's hot," she added.

"Yes ma'am."

"And to meet this boy on your 1st trip abroad. A foreign boy in a foreign land. And, my gracious, that snapshot you showed me. Why, he would turn any girl's head. Good nite, nurse, he's an absolute dreamboat."

"He's awful nice too, Mom."

"I'm sure he is. I'm sure you wouldn't just fall for another pretty face, Trixie. But the point is, the summer is over & so is the romance, & given where he is, he might as well be the man on the moon, so it is absolutely over & done w/. I appreciate that your heart may be breaking, but you have got to stop mooning about & get on w/ things."

"I know that, Mom."

"To tell you the truth, Trixie, there's been times you looked so peaked I thought that missing that boy had made you physically ill. I mean, honey, I know the poet wrote that absence makes the heart grow fonder, but that's only to a point."

"Mom, look: it wasn't just a summer romance."

She hugged me then. "Honey, we all think that the 1st time we really fall in love. But he is w/ that awful Hitler man, & you're here on the Shore, & it's time to find someone new. Now, how 'bout that nice boy from Lancaster, Penn., at the college, who was your beau last yr?"

"Mom, he wasn't my beau."

"Well, he certainly could be."

"I'm just not that interested in him, Mom."

"Well, please, get interested. In someone. There must be one boy in the whole U.S. of Amer. who is up to your high standards." She released me from her embrace then, her sympathy for me evolving into a bit of annoyance.

"I'm sure I'll meet someone new," I said. "Maybe Carter will introduce me to someone I like."

"Well, Carter always has good taste. I thought sometimes she might be a little fast, but you're a girl w/ your feet on the ground, Trixie, so I wouldn't worry if she were to introduce you to some boy who presumed you were easy pickin's."

"Mom, please, Carter isn't fast. She's

just sophisticated."

"Well, I didn't mean to demean her, & if she can find a nice young gentleman to take your mind off that good-looking German boy, she would forever be in my debt."

"Yes ma'am."

So, w/ what little $ I'd saved up, I took the train down to Balt. I borrowed the rest of the $ I needed from Carter, & she took me to the house where I got my abortion. You hear about coat hangers & so on & so forth, but this man was a regular MD. He just performed abortions in his house at nite in order to stay clear of John Law.

He was a nice older gentleman, w/ a little mustache, which was unusual on professional men at that time, & he was kind to me & happy to let Carter stay in the room w/ me during the operation (which we call a "procedure" now, altho God knows why). I appreciated that, & when it was all over & done w/ & I was leaving, he said (in the gentlest way), "I don't want to see you back here, miss."

And I said, "No sir, you won't."

He gave me an envelope then, altho w/o saying anything. When I opened it up later, it had some condoms in it. Of course, we didn't say "condoms" then. We said "rubbers." I didn't mention it to Carter. I just put the rubbers in my pocketbook.

Carter took me back to her dorm room. I don't remember crying, but I was just so terribly sad. We talked & talked, but every time I'd start to talk about Horst, she'd tell me to cut it out. "You have got to forget him, Trixie."

I said, "You sound just like my mother."

"Well, sometimes mothers know better than you think they do."

That was the last thing I expected to hear from Carter Kincaid, so I told her about how I was going up to N.Y. in the spring. That impressed her mightily. But in the meantime, I went to work in the insurance office.

The letters would come from Horst like clockwork. It would take about 2 wks for a letter to go from C'town to Berlin & vice versa, so as soon as I got one from him I'd write him back & as soon as he got mine, he'd write me, so I could pretty much set my watch to it: once a month I would hear from Horst.

This served to completely inhibit any burgeoning interest I might've developed for other members of the opposite sex, especially including a nice young potential agent my mother had hired who really had his eyes on me. He was named Chipper,

& he was studying for the state insurance test. I'd help him out, going over the materials w/ him — altho all too often I caught him glancing up from the books, trying to sneak a peek down my front. Since I was not likewise distracted, what is called "the result of unintended circumstances" occurred, & I learned more than he did about becoming an insurance salesman.

Horst's letters were full of love. Besides that, he'd tell me all about his life at college, his friends, classes, etc. He'd teach me a little more German, too. His parents left for Tokyo in Nov., & so Liesl & her husband, Walter, the SS officer, moved into the Gerhardt house in Charlottenburg.

Pointedly, tho, Horst would never write about the political situation in Germany. However, when he'd visit home in Berlin, he wouldn't make any bones about how he disliked his brother-in-law. I could certainly read between the lines there. I devoured all I could about Germany in the Balt. Sun & on the radio. You didn't have to be an Einstein to get the drift that Hitler was up to no good. And here Horst was having to go into officer's training for the navy after he graduated from Heidelberg.

# II.

So the winter passed, with me measuring time by the letters from Berlin. When Chipper passed the state exam, I took a certain amount of pride. I knew they didn't much have female insurance agents, but I knew that if Chipper had the stuff to qualify, then I could damn well be an agent myself.

But the main thing was, I was lonely. Carter was away in college & since nobody wanted to take me out (or vice versa) because I was in love w/ Horst, basically I just worked at the office, practiced swimming at the college pool, & waited for Horst's next letter.

Easter fell pretty early that year, & that seemed like a good time to get on w/ it, go to N.Y. & join the Women's Swimming Assoc. So after church, I told Mom. She was not surprised in the least bit. "Trixie," she said, "I could see you were getting jumpy, so I took it upon myself to look into some things."

Our little agency billed a lot of insurance w/ Metropolitan Life, & via the telephone, Mom had become friendly w/ a Mr. Edgar Schooley, who was the general agent of a Metropolitan branch in Brooklyn. Mr.

Schooley was not only prepared to hire me for $22.50 a week as an office girl, but inasmuch as he and Mrs. Schooley's children were grown & had gone to greener pastures, he was delighted to take me in as a boarder. This still being very much the Depression, people were certainly not adverse to having boarders to help w/ expenses. I was going to pay $7.50 a week back out of my salary.

Mother explained that the Schooleys owned a town house in B'lyn Heights, which she had on best authority was the deluxe territory for B'lyn. This was important, for you've got to understand that at this time B'lyn was something of a standing joke w/ the rank & file of Americans. If anybody in a movie said he was from B'lyn or if anybody on a radio show said they hailed from B'lyn, this immediately prompted a chorus of guffaws & what have you. Mr. Schooley had assured Mom that not everybody in B'lyn said such things as "dems" & "dose," & that, notwithstanding the yuk-yuks from would-be comedians, B'lyn was actually a fine, upstanding, family place, that was even esteemed for its numerous churches.

Not only that, but Mr. Schooley had really done his homework. The pool the

WSA used to practice in was located on the west side of Manhattan in an apartment bldg called the London Terrace, but he'd assured Mom that it was easily accessible from the Metropolitan office in B'lyn on the subway so long as I was not uneasy about negotiating a change of trains.

Mom said, "Trixie, now this arrangement is not written in stone, but this gives you a good job & a lovely place to stay w/ fine, upstanding people. After you get your feet wet, so to speak, you could make new arrangements, & Mr. Schooley would understand completely."

I agreed, so I wrote L. deB. that I would soon be on my way. I arrived in B'lyn on the 1st of May, 1937. Sydney Stringfellow: have bathing suit, will travel.

The Schooleys certainly were lovely people. They called each other Mr. S & Mrs. S, & as a consequence, so did everyone else. Mrs. S's name was Vivian. A great many women then had Christian names that started w/ V. I don't know why. Velma, Vera, Vicky, Veronica, Violet, etc., besides Vivian. They've all gone, haven't they? I guess there's just no accounting for taste. Be that as it may, the Schooley house was attractive, albeit (to call a spade a spade) somewhat threadbare in the furniture dept., but I had what had once been the maid's room on the ground floor, which afforded me a great deal of privacy, including my own back door for entrances & exits. I don't think I could've asked for anything better right off the bat in B'lyn.

Mr. S showed me where to get the GG train, which was only a couple blocks from the house, & I rode that up to the office, which was in the Greenpoint neighborhood. In the movies, everybody pronounced it "Greenpernt," but in real life, only a corporal's guard of the folks I met actually did. B'lyn was not nearly as exotic as the legend at the time would have it.

Our office was at 877 Manhattan Ave. The agents worked out of there, but, of course, they were usually out & about trying to sell insurance, so mostly the office was populated by girls a bit older than I who sat at rows of desks typing out policies & form letters. It was not very scintillating work, but everybody was delighted to have a job, starting at $27.50 a week. The gals were nice & when they found out I came from "the sticks," they were fascinated, so I regaled them w/ quaint stories of the Eastern Shore, crabs, oysters, etc.

You would've thought I came from darkest Africa the way some of those city girls carried on.

Actually, my job was simple as pie, but probably more interesting than being chained to a Smith-Corona typewriter all day. I spent a great deal of time filing & sorting thru potential "leads" for the agents, & I can say, in all modesty, that I distinguished myself early on w/ a # of the agents, because, after all, I already knew so much about the ins. business. In today's lexicon I was "overqualified" for my job, but that was alright w/ me because I looked upon swimming as my real job. Then, too, whatever special tasks Mr. S had in mind usually added a little spice to my life. A prime example: in the course of most every day I ran errands outside the office.

Mr. S had an unfortunate, if perfectly benign habit of prefacing many of his remarks w/ this phrase: "You wanna know something?" So, on one of my 1st nites in B'lyn, he said: "Sydney, you're a swimmer — you wanna know something?" Naturally, I bit, so he told me that only a few blocks away from the Schooley residence was the finest indoor pool in all of N.Y. Of course, I was fascinated, so off we went to inspect it.

The pool was in the St. George Hotel, which was on Clark St. It was the pride of the area, if not all of B'lyn. "You wanna know something?" Mr. Schooley asked me. "There's nothing like this pool in all of Manhattan."

And you wanna know something? That was the God's truth. The pool was absolutely magnificent, surrounded by tiled piers that reached up 2 stories. It was more than a football field long & filled with salt water. The instant I saw it I wanted to jump right in, & Mr. S was delighted w/ how impressed I was at this certified B'lyn landmark.

But here's why I'm digressing: would that the Women's Swimming Assoc. had such a pool! Instead, it was a poor cousin to the St. George's. The pool at the London Terrace was only 25 yds. long. Good grief, the one back home at the College was longer than that! And here it was home for the premier female swimming club in all America, if not the whole world. It would be as if the N.Y. Yankees practiced on some sandlot that didn't even have an outfield.

But, as they say (or did then), every cloud has a silver lining, & that would be

L. deB. Handley. On my 1st day of practice, he greeted me in such exquisite attire that I thought he must've just come from some special affair. He wore a bespoke gray pin-striped suit w/ a blue striped shirt (he always said "stri-PED, w/ 2 syllables, not just old "striped" as we did on the Shore) w/ a magnificent bright yellow tie, complete w/ stickpin & a fancy pocket handkerchief. He told me one time, "Sydney, a man who would be seen in public w/o a pocket square might as well be naked." Words to live by!

You see, here was the thing: L. deB. — or Coach Handley, as we girls, of course, called him — always dressed as fashionably as when I met him on this 1st occasion. Not only that, at the pool he somehow could stay comfortable in his stylish get-up for what seemed like forever. Remember now, it gets exceptionally steamy in an indoor pool room, but L. deB. seemed utterly impervious to the elements. He was practically sweat-proof.

He was also a wonderful teacher & since some of the wealthier girls had other more-or-less private coaches at pools where they came from, L. deB. concentrated working more w/ me & the other girls who didn't have personal coaching. The WSA gals were a nice bunch, but while some of them came from the suburbs, especially up in Westchester County, the more wealthy environs, I was the only one who'd actually moved from out of town. Unfortunately, no one else on the team resided in B'lyn, so, only seeing one another at practice, we were like ships passing in the nite.

So, I was basically lonely again, but Mom always forwarded my monthly letter from Horst, & I took advantage of being in The Greatest City in The World, going hither and yon on the subway, which only cost a nickel, seeing all the sights. It cost 60¢ to call C'town and 65¢ to call Balt., so I paid Mr. S & made 3-minute calls to Mom and Carter every couple weeks or so, & of course they returned the favor. "You wanna know something?" Mr. S asked me one day. "You could call your young gentleman friend in Berlin for $24." He had looked it up. But, of course, that was out of the question.

Horst wrote me that he would graduate from Heidelberg in July, then begin his cadet training. At least he was going to be an officer, but, still, he made it crystal clear that he had no interest whatsoever in the military. He wanted to study architecture,

& he wanted to marry me. It was as simple as that. His letters were as passionate as always, & his love for me remained as strong as ever. As I was utterly faithful to Horst, I knew that he was to me, even tho he was a boy & even then I recognized that males of all ages do not always subscribe to the same rules as we do.

But I simply believed w/ all my heart that Horst remained true, even tho I kidded him, asking him if he would be a sailor w/ a girl in every port. He wrote back that ports were out of the question because his love for me was as deep as the ocean. I cried in my bed that nite, thinking for the 1st time in a long time about how beautiful our child would've been if only we hadn't been separated by that deep ocean & could be married.

Meanwhile, when my mother wrote me, she never failed to ask: "Have you met any nice boys up there in the Big City?" She couldn't believe that my "thing" for "the good-looking German boy" persisted. (She always identified Horst as "good-looking," I knew, because it implied that I was a starry-eyed ninny who'd just fallen for his looks.)

At the office, most days Mr. S would give me the premium payments that had come in. Most were checks, but there were a lot of money orders & some people actually foolishly sent cash thru the U.S. mail. The bank we used was the Bank of Manhattan, which had a branch located right next door at 875 Manhattan, so Mr. S would bundle everything up, put it in a canvas bag & dispatch me next door to deposit it. It was a pretty easy routine, which I enjoyed because it allowed me to get out of the office & away from all those clattering typewriters.

On this particular occasion at the bank, early in June, I was surprised to find a new teller, &, in a word, he was awfully cute (excuse me: 2 words). He even bore a passing resemblance to Horst. (Well, the blue eyes!) I smiled shyly at him, he smiled back, but it was all business, no banter. Nonetheless, the next day when I came to the bank, I kind of hung back, pretending to be filling out slips or some such thing, till I saw that the cute blue-eyed boy's window was free. Then I strolled up there as if by dumb luck.

This time we chatted some. He asked, "You come here every day?"

"Most," I said. "I'm w/ Metropolitan Life next door. I never saw you before."

"Well, I was a runner. I just got promoted

this week."

So that explained his presence. We conversed some more in the days that followed. I have to be honest, that this was the 1st boy who had turned my head even a smidgeon since I fell in love w/ Horst, but innocent chatter hardly qualified as unfaithfulness. Inevitably, altho he was very shy, he told me his name, which was James Branch (but call me "Jimmy"), & I told him mine, so then he asked what time I got off, & while I shouldn't have responded to that, I did, & sure enough, he was nervously waiting for me at the door of #877 when I got out.

Hallelujah! I almost threw the pages up in the air. At last Mom had met Dad, and surely now that infamous Teutonic lothario, Herr Gerhardt, would recede into the mists. So, relieved and thrilled, I read on:

Jimmy asked if I wanted to get a soda, but I explained how I had to go to swimming practice. That fascinated him, so he suggested maybe the next day, & I explained I went to practice 5 days a week & sometimes more.

"Where do you go?" he asked, & I told him about the pool at the London Terrace.

"You go into the city?" That impressed him even more than the swimming itself, because you should understand that even tho B'lyn was every bit a real city, & was laid cheek by jowl with Manhattan, B'lyn people possessed something of an inferiority complex & referred to Manhattan as "the city."

"Look, Jimmy," I said, "you're a really nice guy, but I have to tell you, I have a very serious beau."

"Oh, I see."

"We're going to get married."

"He's a very lucky fellow."

"I'm a very lucky girl."

After that, when I brought the deposits over, most days I'd make sure to go to different tellers, because I didn't want to lead Jimmy on. Well, then he outfoxed me. Usually I'd swing by the bank right before lunch. I'd bring a sandwich & thermos to work, so I'd go over to McCarren Park & read a book while I ate. Wise to my routine, one day Jimmy switched his lunch hour, so he was waiting for me outside my building. He had his sandwich & thermos, too. "Would you at least have lunch w/ me?" he asked. "Your beau couldn't get mad at that."

And so we did, & I must say we enjoyed

learning about one another (although I kept Horst off limits in our tete-a-tetes). In fact, I agreed that we could eat together in McCarren Park once a week, on Thursdays, when he could change his lunch hour. So I learned that Jimmy came from upstate N.Y., from poor, unhappy circumstance, that he had left home after high school, taken odd jobs & whatnot, worked in the CCC for a year & then come to try his luck in the big city.

Shy as he was, he was not at all lacking in confidence, but because he'd had such a difficult life, Jimmy was as unsure of the world as he was sure that he could make his way in it. Everything had been such a struggle for him, & he was very much alone. That scared me a bit, for he needed someone so terribly much, & I realized that he wanted me to be that someone. But despite his bashfulness, he was bright & funny, &, it is worth noting again: he was awfully cute — or cute as a bug's ear, as we were wont to say then. But, at the end of the day, none of that mattered. I still waited as anxiously as ever for Horst's next letter & went to sleep every nite thinking of him alone.

# III.

The national championships for '37, which were scheduled for Jones Beach, were fast approaching. L. deB. was not only convinced that I'd win, but that I could very possibly break Eleanor's record. He presented me w/ my black WSA silk suit w/ the big S in the middle of my chest, & let me tell you, the 1st time I put that on, I was so proud I would've busted my buttons if I'd been wearing any. Back in my room at the Schooleys, I put it on again, even tho it was still damp, & I just stood there, admiring myself, turning this way & that in front of the mirror as if I were a lingerie model. The championships were only 2 wks away.

Then, a few days later, I came out of my bldg on the way to the bank. It was the middle of July, extremely hot, so I just had on a blouse & skirt (& the obligatory slip & stockings). I took about 2 steps toward #875, when all of a sudden this big, burly guy came out of nowhere & jumped me. At 1st, I was so taken by surprise that I didn't appreciate what was happening, but then I realized he was trying to steal the canvas bank bag from me. He'd obviously been watching my routine.

He also probably figured that I was a frail little vessel, so I'm sure he was shocked when he wasn't able to yank the bag away from me right off the bat. I just instinctively hung on. But it all happened so fast, you see. I don't think it even occurred to me to scream "help." But then, there were lots of people all around me — within feet of me! — & they were just as stunned themselves. Everyone just stood there, gaping. I couldn't blame them. You just don't expect a thing like this to happen in front of you, much less to you.

All the while the big guy — we called such scoundrels "yeggs" in those days — tugged at the bag. I tried to hold on for dear life, but he gave one last big yank, & he was so strong that he not only pulled the bag out of my grasp, but he caused me to lose my balance. My momentum jerked me forward, & I tumbled hard, headfirst, onto the sidewalk. I was able to stick out a hand to break my fall, but then it was almost like I skidded along on the pavement.

Finally, a couple of people did yell, reaching out to try to grab the mugger, but he eluded them & dashed away, heading south. I'd banged my head when I fell, but not enough to get knocked out, & as I lifted my head up to watch the robber run away, suddenly, who did I see materialize but Jimmy. He'd just come out of the bank next door, to where I was headed, & had actually seen the scuffle. When he realized that, yes, it really was me being attacked, he'd immediately run towards us.

The thief had planned to make his getaway in Jimmy's direction. A subway station was up the other way, at the big intersection where Manhattan crossed Greenpoint, so obviously it made sense for him to run in the opposite direction, where there were fewer people & less likelihood of police. He might've gotten away, too, but here came Jimmy, absolutely unafraid, running right at him. So the thief ducked across Manhattan Ave., dodging the traffic. Jimmy went right after him, cutting in front of a trolley. They were maroon & cream. Isn't that funny? I haven't thought about that in yrs, but now, as I write this, I can see it all as plain as day, Jimmy running right in front of that maroon & cream trolley car.

By now — & you know, this has hardly taken only a few seconds — a couple of nice people came over to attend to me. I just wanted to watch the chase, tho, so I kind of raised up, trying to look across the street. It was no contest. Jimmy was like a jackrabbit. Before the thief had even reached the next corner, at Milton St., he could see that Jimmy was going to catch him, so he dropped the bag in hopes that his pursuer would be satisfied to stop & recover the loot.

But Jimmy didn't go for that dodge. A couple steps further on, right where the guy turned down Milton, Jimmy leapt onto his back & brought him down. Then he started pummeling him. By now, of course, all sorts of people had joined the chase. One of them picked up the bank bag, while some others pulled Jimmy off the thief & held the culprit till a couple of cops ran down from Greenpoint Ave. About time!

Jimmy just turned away & ran back toward me. I saw him coming, & I was scared he was going to get killed crossing the street. It didn't seem like he even looked side to side for the cars. He only had his eyes on me, screaming my name. "Sydney! Sydney!" I think back, & it doesn't seem like I can remember any other sounds the whole time, just Jimmy screaming my name.

When he got to me, I was sort of up on my knees, & he kneeled down before me. That's when all of a sudden the whole thing hit me, & I began to cry. "Oh, Sydney — you all right?" he asked. I tried to answer, but I was having a delayed reaction, & now — now that I had my wits about me — now I realized what'd happened. Now I was scared. My face was cut from where it had scraped on the sidewalk, so I knew I looked a sight, but Jimmy was just gazing upon me w/ the greatest concern.

I thought he might even start to cry for me, so I reached out to hug him, because I needed to, & also because, knowing him, I knew he didn't dare try to hug me himself because it'd be just like him to think I'd feel that he was taking advantage of the situation. There was such a sweetness to Jimmy Branch.

It wasn't until that second that I felt the pain in my wrist. It had been such a to-do I hadn't even realized that when I'd put out my right hand to break my fall, it had done something to my wrist. I just stared at it. Now I hurt like hell, but now was when I stopped crying. That was because I was suddenly in disbelief. "My wrist, Jimmy, my wrist!" I didn't know whether it was broken or strained or sprained or what, but I knew I wasn't going to be doing any swimming for a while. Just like there wasn't any Olympics for me in '36, there wouldn't be any national championships for me in '37. I would've felt cursed, but the wrist hurt too much for me to feel anything but the pain.

Well, suddenly, it seemed like the whole world descended on us. There were policemen, & one man who said he knew 1st aid gingerly looked at my wrist & said "oh my," & then the guy who'd retrieved the canvas bag appeared, & then there was a police siren, & the people who weren't being solicitous to me were congratulating Jimmy, patting him on his back, helping him dust himself off, etc. A trolley had stopped dead in the middle of the street & all the passengers were staring at me. Not only that, but the fuss had brought everybody running out of their offices & shops to see what all the commotion was. Remember, there was no air conditioning then except maybe in movie theaters (where it said: "IT'S COOOOL INSIDE" w/ icycles coming off the letters), & since it was one of the hottest days of the summer, all the windows were wide open.

In fact, suddenly, there was Mr. S himself & most of the girls from the office — all part of the crowd hovering around me. I told whoever it was who'd picked up the bag: "Give it to him" — meaning Mr. S.

Then a cop said, "What happened exactly, miss?" but even before I could answer, a woman said, "Officer, this young man is a hero."

Jimmy kind of ducked his head, because he was quite modest by nature, but I was so proud of him, & even tho I was holding my wrist, I said, "The lady's right, Mr. S. If it wasn't for Jimmy that guy would've gotten away w/ all the day's premiums."

So right off the bat, w/o missing a beat, Mr. S said, "You wanna know something? You're gonna get a reward!"

And all the people standing around began to clap & cheer in the most heartwarming fashion. Jimmy told me later that he'd never felt so good about himself in all his life — notwithstanding how worried he was about me. "But," he told me later, "you're tough for a girl, Sydney, so I knew you'd be all right."

I put Mom's pages down and just shook my head, absolutely flabbergasted. It was one thing for my father not to want to talk about Guadalcanal, but I found it simply incomprehensible that neither he nor Mom had ever told me this lovely little story before. I mean, this was an absolute "My hero!" moment. Surely, this must've been the very instant when Mom began to turn her affection away from the self-assured Horst to the sweet and humble Jimmy. My father was stepping up! Pleased, I went into the kitchen and got a ginger ale and a couple of cookies, and returned to turn the page:

Well, the episode made Jimmy Branch an absolute celebrity, B'lyn division. Not only did Mr. S immediately give him a $10 reward, but when he reported the incident to the home office, they doubled it. The irony was, too, that there really wasn't that much $ in the bag, because, as I've explained, very few people were so naïve as to send cash thru the U.S. mail. Still, had the stupid robber gotten away, it would've been a real nuisance going back to all the folks who had sent in checks & $ orders. So the reward was richly deserved.

The Bank also gave Jimmy a dollar-a-week raise & a letter of commendation & the manager took him out to a very fancy lunch & told him he had a bright future at the bank. Not only that, but the B'lyn Eagle took Jimmy's photo & put it in the paper, making him "Good Citizen Of The Week."

Neither was I forgotten. I not only enjoyed a great deal of sympathy for suffering the broken wrist & the other cuts and bruises, etc., but I was also recognized for being such a brave girl & not just swooning when I was attacked. On my 1st day back to work, brandishing my cast and bandages, etc., Mr. S presented me w/ a lovely bouquet, then led the entire staff in a round of applause for me. "You wanna know something?" he asked the assembled. "If Sydney hadn't fought so courageously when the yegg attacked her, he would've gotten away before the courageous young man could give chase & save the day."

I tried to be a good sport & not let on how disappointed I was that I couldn't compete in the national championships, but, of course, I was absolutely crushed. I wanted a good race. I was never one of those athletes who thrived on practice. If there hadn't been a pot of gold at the end of the rainbow (that's the Tokyo Olympics in my case), I wouldn't have swam and swam and swam all those damn laps. So I have to admit that, alone in my room, I brought out my new WSA bathing suit & held it up before me w/ my good hand. And I cried.

Another offshoot of the incident was that

now all the single gals in the office, having discovered Jimmy, #1, fell for him themselves, &/or #2, could not believe how I could be resisting his advances. "What is your story, morning glory?" Iris asked me, uncomprehending of how I could be so cool to such a honey of a guy. Jimmy's picture from the Eagle was posted on the office bulletin board, there for all to see & rave about (particularly) in my presence.

And, of course, it was impossible for me not to accept Jimmy's invitation to go out on a dinner date w/ him, especially since he told me that besides getting a new suit, that was how he wanted to spend the $20 reward. On me. Under the circumstances, I knew this could in no way be construed as cheating on Horst. Mr. S — for he and Mrs. S were also both firmly now on the Jimmy Branch bandwagon — even suggested a restaurant that he felt sure would advance Jimmy's cause in his pursuit of my heart.

It was a place on Montague Street called Mammy's Pantry, which doesn't sound like much, but for some reason, there in the bosom of B'lyn, of all things, it specialized in seafood from my own Chesapeake Bay. Jimmy had never even heard of crab cakes before, but he adored them. He walked me back to the Schooleys, & I told him that I'd had a lovely time, which was true.

"So when can I take you out again?" he asked.

I shook my head. "I'm sorry, Jimmy."

"Don't you like me?"

"Of course I do. Can't you tell that, dopey? I think you're aces. But I'm in love w/ another boy, & I'm going to marry him. Come on, you KNOW all that."

"But, Sydney, he's in Germany."

I'd had to tell him that much about Horst by now. But I just replied: "Jimmy, it doesn't matter whether he's in Timbuctoo. So please, do yourself a favor & forget about me. Why, there's at least a doz. girls in my office who're crazy about you. And I mean some of the prettiest gals at Metropolitan."

Jimmy just shook his head. "I don't care, Sydney. I've just fallen for you like a ton of bricks, & —" I could tell that bashful as he was he'd really gotten his nerve up & was going to try to kiss me. I wanted to escape the embarrassment of rejecting him, so very quickly, I just stuck out my good hand, even if it was the left one. He sighed & took it in both of his & held me there. "Just tell me ONE thing, Sydney."

"Okay."

"Suppose — just suppose — you'd met me 1st."

"1st what?"

"You know, before the German fellow. Could you have fallen in love w/ me, then?"

"You can't change things, Jimmy. You can't change time."

"Just suppose."

Well, I had to put an end to this. "No, Jimmy, I can't suppose. You're the nicest person, but I love Horst."

So very quickly, I reached up & pecked him on the cheek, & then I dashed inside. In B'lyn Heights at that time, as in most of the U.S., nobody felt it necessary to lock their doors, so I could make my escape w/o prolonging the agony.

### IV.

I didn't even go to Jones Beach, to the nationals. I simply couldn't bear to be there, sidelined, watching the other girls swim. But when my cast was removed, dutifully I started practicing again. At work, Mr. S had initially been reluctant to let me start carrying the checks & $ back over to the bank, but I assured him that "lightning doesn't strike twice," & that I retained no fears of being assaulted again. I did, however, continue to make a point not to go to Jimmy's window, even tho I could see him eyeing me. And so, soon, I was back to my routine, & I even swam in a small meet in Sept., winning my race easily.

L. deB. said, "If you hadn't lost all that time w/ your wrist, Sydney, you would've set the record today. There's no question in my mind that right now you're the best backstroker in the world."

There was, however, one little black cloud that now unexpectedly appeared on the horizon. Horst's monthly letter didn't arrive, as it always did, like clockwork. I knew he'd begun his training as a naval cadet, so I decided it was a difficult time for him. But another week went by, then another. I began to worry, so I wrote him again, saying that I understood how arduous military life must be, but if he could just drop me a line, I'd feel so much better.

And, sure enough, a couple wks later, my heart skipped a beat when I came back from practice & there was a letter from Horst. Clutching it to my heart, I moved to my bed & tore it open. I could see right away that it wasn't very long. In fact, it was very short — & it certainly was to the point. Read it and weep:

Dear Sydney,
I hope this won't come as too much of a surprise, but I've decided that it would be best for us to go our separate ways. It is just too difficult for us to continue this way, with me here, you a whole ocean away. Good luck, Sydney. I'll never forget you.
Love,<br>Horst.

I held the letter in my lap, studying it. I think you could say I was in shock. Then, of course, that passed & I began to cry — 1st only ordinary, run-of-the-mill tears, then great gulping sobs. It made no sense to me at all. "I'll never forget you"!!! Well, then, why couldn't we at least talk about it, Horst? It was terrible. Finally, I ran a bath & sat there till the water turned lukewarm, then even cool. I got out & took the letter & tore it up & got into bed &, yes, literally cried myself to sleep.

I think it's fair to say: my heart was broken.

The next morning, when I came up for breakfast, Mr. S had already left. Mrs. S was walking on eggshells, I could tell. My eyes were red because I'd already cried some more, & I had a pretty good idea that Mrs. S had put 2 + 2 together, because she'd seen the envelope & knew how happy I was when Horst's letters came. Yet, instead, here I was, a complete mess.

"I'm sorry if you got bad news, Sydney," Mrs. S said, which was just enough to trigger another deluge of tears from me. I fell into Mrs. S's arms & sobbed some more. When I was relatively composed, she said, "I didn't mean to pry, but I heard you crying last nite."

"Yes," I said.

"So Mr. S said he didn't want you to come to work today."

"No, really, I —"

"No, Sydney, that's the dr.'s orders. Go out & try to do something to keep your mind off things — even tho I know that's probably impossible."

Well, it was, but I did try. The whole time I'd been in N.Y., I'd never been on the Staten I. ferry or up the new Empire State Bldg, so I did both of those. But I saw nothing, enjoyed nothing. (Didn't I tell you you saw everything when you were in love? Well, this was the reverse. In spades.) All I could see was Horst, & all I could think of was him & his letter.

This may sound goofy, tho, but after a while, I convinced myself that I wanted to believe his letter. You see, altho I was altogether new at this, I decided that there was a saving grace having the man you love tell you that he's ditching you, but you're still wondering exactly why.

It would be far worse to have him write & say, well, Sydney, the reason I don't want anything to do with you anymore is because I am sleeping w/ Miss Germany, 1937, who I am desperately in love w/ — & she's better than you in every which way.

But if it really was only that there was a stupid ocean between us, well, that's just a hurdle & it only made me mad that Horst could be so easily defeated by something as simple as distance. I thought, well, I can be a linear Rapunzel & let my locks grow, then spread them out across the sea so he could catch ahold & pull himself across to me. I mean, if it's just a case of so-&-so many miles: come on, Horst!

So that's why I decided that I wanted to believe the letter, because then he would obviously come to his senses & we would only look back upon this as "a bump in the road."

It was in that frame of mind that I showed

up at practice. I walked all the way down from the Empire State Bldg & all the way over to the London Terrace & by the time I got there, I was loaded for bear. I mean, I swam w/ a vengeance. I was an absolute naiad, & a dorsal to boot. I could've beaten the best men backstrokers in the world. L. deB. couldn't believe his eyes. "Whatever you got today, Sydney," he said, "bottle it & pass it round to all the other gals." I just gritted my teeth.

But then, as soon as I got outside, by myself, I started crying again. So I tried to dry them, to at least look halfway presentable, & —

I couldn't believe it. I refused to believe it. But there he was. Jimmy, of course.

Mr. S had obviously spilled the beans to him. Jimmy was waiting for me outside the subway. It was early in Nov. by now, a chilly nite, & he had his overcoat all buttoned up. He had his fedora on, too, because in those days if you worked in any office you were absolutely expected to wear a hat. He was just standing there, waiting, smoking a cigarette. It made me very mad that he would try to move right in on me in my lovelorn grief.

So I walked right by him as if he wasn't there.

"Sydney," he said softly. "Sydney, I'm sorry."

"No, you're not," I said.

"Yeah, I am. I don't like to see you hurt."

"Well, I am, so leave me alone."

I was striding away, leaving him in my dust. He called after me: "I just thought maybe you'd like to go to a movie." I had to stop. I mean, I knew I was being rude. I still didn't turn around, tho. But I heard him say, "We could go to the Roxy. I've never been to the Roxy, have you?"

That was the biggest movie theater in N.Y., up in Broadway. " 'Thin Ice' is playing, w/ Tyrone Power and Sonja Henie, & it's supposed to be real good. They have a stage show, too." I didn't say anything. "It might take your mind off things."

I still didn't speak. Except I probably made a face. He said, "Sydney, I'm not so stupid as to try to get your mind on me now. I just thought if you went to the movies, you'd get your mind off . . . you know, things."

Well, I did turn back then. "I don't want to talk," I said.

"Fine. You're not supposed to talk in a movie."

Well . . . "OK," I said — which I think, in fact, was the last thing I did say to him.

We got on the subway, went to the Roxy & watched "Thin Ice." Then we took the train back to B'lyn — but I just didn't want to talk to him. I didn't want to talk to anybody. Well, I did say, "No, thank you," when he asked me if I wanted anything to eat. Actually, I was starving. But I couldn't face looking at Jimmy Branch or anybody else across a table.

When we got to B'lyn, he walked me home. Well, I wouldn't actually say, he "walked me home." He just walked along w/ me. I didn't want him to, so I just sort of suffered him walking next to me.

At the Schooleys', I started down to my room. I did say, "Thank you for the movie."

I guess that standard bit of civility on my part gave Jimmy an opening. "Sydney . . ." I paused, sighing deeply, making it obvious that I was still only indulging him. "Sydney, I know how you must feel."

"No, you don't. Nobody you loved ever did this to you."

"Well, I never really had anybody love me much, but I can imagine." That sort of gave me pause. He was, after all, being very sweet, & I knew he was telling the truth about never having had anyone really love him. So I let him go on: "Listen, you have to talk to someone."

"No, I don't."

"Yes, you do. And you know, Sydney, all we've ever done is talk, but I think we've done that real good together, so, if ever you do want to talk, I'd be happy to. OK?"

I just nodded, so he began walking away. I started to go in, but then I stopped, & I turned around, & softly I called after him. "Jimmy?"

He turned back, & when he did, I walked up to him & tilted my face up. When he didn't get it, tho (which was perfectly understandable, given the circumstances), I got up on my toes, stuck my lips out & kissed him. It surprised him so much that at 1st he didn't even think to put his arms around me, but finally he remembered that you should hold a girl close when you kiss her.

I think Jimmy knew it was mostly a kiss of revenge, that I was kissing him just because I was so mad at Horst. I think he knew it wasn't even a very good kiss on my part. But also, I think Jimmy realized: OK, you've got to start somewhere, & this is a pretty darn good place to start.

V.

As opposed to how it'd been w/ Horst, it

was so entirely different going out w/ Jimmy. In Berlin, it'd been such a glamorous whirlwind. Sometimes later I even had to wonder: did all that really happen? It was like Horst must've been a vision, that I must've gotten pregnant thru some kind of immaculate conception.

In B'lyn, tho, it was nice, because Jimmy was nice, but otherwise it was really very pedestrian. We pretty much only had one another, because neither of us had any $, &, if anything, things weren't getting any better. Most people nowadays think the Depression was just one big flat line on a graph, but, in fact, it got better after the worst of it, only then that summer I moved to N.Y., the economy got worse again, & by '38, there we were smack in a recession in the middle of the Depression.

Jimmy & I were working all day, then I was swimming. Not only that, but CCNY, which is the City College of N.Y., had opened a new branch downtown at Lex. & 23rd, & inasmuch as tuition was free, Jimmy had started taking some nite courses there. Now that he'd been promoted, he wanted to get a college degree & make something of himself in the banking world. So, when we had the time, mostly we did free stuff, like parks & museums.

If we saved up a little $, we'd do a movie, and come spring, we went to Ebbets Field once, sat in the bleachers and watched the B'lyn Dodgers play. Also, when Mom sent me $5 as an Easter present, instead of buying a new "bonnet," we splurged & went to Coney Island, riding the great Cyclone roller coaster, the bumper cars, etc. About once a week we'd "dine" in some nice, clean — but (always) pretty cheap — little cafe. Dutch treat. I don't think people say "Dutch treat" anymore, do they? Maybe it's one of those things like Indian giver or French leave where the nitpickers think it might be insulting to the Dutch people.

Anyway, Jimmy was right. We did talk well together. He even told me that I was the 1st person he could really talk to, so, hard as it was for him, he opened up to me about all the bad stuff he'd had to endure. Now understand, he didn't want just to TALK all the time, but I wouldn't go to bed w/ him. Here was the problem: Jimmy was doing a pretty good job of helping me forget Horst, but, at the same time, when I was w/ Jimmy, that would make me think about Horst. See: going out &

doing stuff w/ one boy reminded me of going out & doing stuff w/ the other boy. I wish it hadn't been that way, but it was. And, of course, it wasn't fair to Jimmy.

Also: it wasn't fair to me.

No, no matter how sweet Jimmy was, no matter how much I liked him, I couldn't COMPLETELY forget Horst Gerhardt. There wasn't a day when Mrs. S brought me a letter forwarded from my mother that I didn't think: well, maybe this is it — maybe Horst has finally seen the light. But no, none of the letters were from him. And I wouldn't write him, either. I wouldn't beg.

One day, though, I fibbed & told Mr. S that I had a dr.'s appointment. Instead, I went into Manhattan, where I changed lines to get way down to Battery Place, where the German consulate was located. At the consulate, I said that I had a letter for Frau Inge Gerhardt, the wife of the ambassador to Japan, so could they please give me the address of the embassy in Tokyo.

It was certainly a simple enough request, but it threw everyone into an absolute tizzy. You could tell how sensitive the Germans were getting. All I wanted was a lousy address! I finally got to some junior officer, tho, & he believed me after I told him in detail how I'd met the Gerhardts at their home in Charlottenburg. So, finally, he gave me the address, & I wrote it on the envelope that already had my letter in it.

I may not be completely accurate in my memory, but this is approximately what I had written:

Dear Frau Gerhardt,

I think you will remember me. I came to your house with Horst one day during the Olympics. As you probably know, Horst and I have broken up, and it has been a long time since I have heard from him. But even if the romance has definitely ended, I was curious if you could tell me if he is well and how he is doing.

Thank you, and I do hope to see you and Ambassador Gerhardt in Tokyo at the 1940 Olympics.

Yours truly,<br>Sydney Stringfellow

I read the letter over and over at the post office. I thought it was very important to put in that part about how the romance had "definitely ended." I'm sure that just as my mother didn't want me to be involved w/ a German boy, Horst's mother didn't want him having anything to do w/ an American girl, so I let her know I wasn't trying to get my claws back into her darling son.

(This also makes me wonder why we say relationship now instead of romance. Why is that, do you suppose? I had a ROMANCE w/ Horst. "Relationship"? Excuse me, it's such a cold word. You can have a relationship w/ your butcher or the gal at the beauty parlor, can't you? Oh well, let me get on w/ my story.)

I tried to forget about the letter after I wrote it. It was such a long shot. Besides, as the summer approached, I was concentrating more & more on my swimming, determined as I was to set records in the backstroke at the nationals.

L. deB. was quite sure I'd break the 100-yd. record at a little meet we had scheduled the 1st week in June called the "New York Inter-club." We — that is, the WSA — were so much better than all the other clubs around that it didn't amount to any real competition, but, if you will forgive a very bad pun, it was good for us "to get our feet wet" w/ some real races before the nationals.

Then, that Tues., out of the blue, after I returned from practice, Mrs. S had a letter waiting for me — a reply from Frau Gerhardt. I opened the envelope nervously in my room. The letter was certainly very polite, however she was not gilding any lillies.

Dear Miss Stringfellow,

Thank you for your interest in Horst. He is quite well. He is a proud member of our Führer's Kriegsmarine. Horst has just been promoted from Fähnrich zur See to Oberfähnrich zur See.

The Ambassador and I are looking forward to seeing you swim against our German girls here in 1940.

Sincerely,
Inge Gerhardt

I remembered, then, in one of Horst's last letters, that he had told me he was training to become a Fähnrich zur See, which, he said, was the equivalent of midshipman. So now, he must have graduated into the regular navy, & I supposed his new position was like an ensign.

The letter only made me wonder more, tho, where he might be. Could he be standing (so handsome in his uniform), peering out over the bridge of some great battleship, or might he instead be crammed into one of those submarines that the Germans had used so effectively back in what we'd called the Great War? But whatever ship he was on, I knew he just wanted to get the heck out of the Kriegsmarine so he could get on w/ being an architect. OK, he'd broken my heart, but I still couldn't wish Horst anything bad (as much as I wanted to).

The next evening we had a lite practice, because L. deB. had us tailing off for our Inter-Club meet. As a consequence, I got back to the Schooleys' earlier than usual. But Jimmy was already sitting there on the steps that led down to my room, smoking a cigarette. I wasn't expecting him, & for that matter, even tho he was on my steps, he seemed almost surprised to see me. "Hey," I said.

He looked up, so forlorn that right away I knew something was wrong. Jimmy had one of those faces that was incapable of hiding emotion. In fact, it would've been an altogether bland, forgettable face except for the fact that it was such a good-looking face. "Sit down, sweetie," he said, pointing to the spot next to him. I mean, it was so unlike Jimmy not to immediately pop up when I arrived — or any lady. Despite his upbringing, he had somehow learned how to be every inch the gentle-man.

So, I sat there & put an arm around his shoulder. "Okay, kiddo, what's the matter?"

He couldn't even look at me, just stared away. "They let me go," he finally said.

I didn't understand. "Who did?"

"The bank."

"The Bank of Manhattan?" He nodded. "They fired you?"

"It's hard times, Sydney. They had to let a bunch of us go."

"Just like that?"

"Well, a week's notice."

"That's white of them," I said.

"Yeah, well, they had orders from the main office to let 2 tellers go, & me and Harvey were the newest." He just shook his head.

"OK then, come on, let's go get a beer, & we'll talk about it," I said, but he put his hand on my knee, kind of to hold me down.

"Nah, Sydney, I'm almost broke, & now I've lost my job."

"It's OK, Jimmy, my ship just came in." That was a little white lie. But I did have a bit of rainy-day $ tucked away, waiting for the next sales at Lerner's or Lane Bryant's, so I ran into my room & grabbed a few dollars & we went down to the nearest bar we liked, which was an Irish joint called McDougal's.

We took a booth in the corner & ordered a couple of Schaefers on tap, which was the loyal thing to do for anybody in Greenpoint, because the brewery was right there on Kent St. It still didn't much cheer Jimmy up, tho. "Let's have another couple," I said.

"You shouldn't, Sydney. You got a race this weekend."

"Jimmy, for Pete's sake, it's just Interclub, & if a couple Schaefers can slow me down, then I'm in a lot of trouble."

"Well, OK," he said, but he just held his head some more. "The thing is, Sydney, I've been thru so much crap in my life, & I was always able to take it, but I finally thought I'd come up aces. The bank, going to college, you —"

"I'm still your girl."

But even that didn't cheer him up. "What girl wants a fellow who can't even hold a good job?"

"It's not your fault."

"You know the worst?" I shook my head. "Mr. Bancroft said I could go back to being a runner. Then maybe, when things got better, I could be promoted back."

"Is that so bad?"

"I can't do that, Sydney. I can't go back.

429

I'm sorry. All the things I've had to do in my life, I've never once gone back. No." He banged his fist on the table. "No, whatever I do, I'm going forward." I patted his hand, but he only shrugged. "All right, I'll get us a couple more beers." I slid him a quarter, but that only reminded him he was broke. "I'm just a damn tramp again."

He slumped over to the bar. It hurt me just watching him, because I knew how unlucky he'd been all his life & how hard he'd fought to overcome everything, & how happy he'd been lately, how proud of himself he'd become — but now this. Didn't that Mr. Bancroft at the Bank of Manhattan remember that it was only a few months ago that Jimmy Branch had been B'lyn's "Good Citizen Of The Week"? How quickly people forget the good stuff (but how long they remember the bad things — that's the corollary, isn't it?). It made me mad.

But it made me care all the more for Jimmy, too, so when he came back with the Schaefers, I just said, "I've got another idea."

"What's that?"

"Well, my idea is that after we're finished these" — I held up my schooner — "we should go back to my room & you should spend the nite w/ me."

Jimmy almost choked on his beer. It made me laugh. "Are you serious?" he finally said.

"I wouldn't joke about that."

He reached across & took my hand. "God, Sydney."

"But we don't have to rush the beers."

Jimmy smiled & put his down. Then, suddenly, his expression changed. He took his hand away from mine & shook his head. "No," he said.

"No what?"

"Just no. You know how much I want to make love to you."

"That's for sure."

"But, no matter, I don't want you to do it just 'cause you feel sorry for me. It's bad enough that you're buying the beers."

I folded my arms, & I probably spoke too loud, because I have a tendency to do that when I get my dander up, especially when I fold my arms in the process. "Jimmy Branch," I said, "you listen to me. You bet I feel sorry for you. You're a real honey of a guy who just got a very bum break. But that doesn't mean then, OK, I'm gonna let you go to bed with me just for that. It's not like I'm just another beer on tap."

"Come on, Sydney, you know I didn't

mean that."

"Just shut up, Jimmy. But, here's the thing" — & this is when I leaned forward & looked him dead in the eyes. "Sometimes you don't realize how much you care about somebody till something bad happens to that person, & tonite, when I learned that even more bad stuff happened to you, I realized how much I DID care. So yeah, I feel sorry for you & I want to go to bed with you, but it's not because I feel sorry for you, but because the feeling sorry for you made me feel a lot more for you. Do you understand that?"

Jimmy just nodded.

"Good," I said. "Then that's settled." I hadn't had any dinner, but mere food was certainly out of the question now, so after we finished our beers, we walked back, hand in hand, to my room. We spent the whole nite together, & not only did it make Jimmy feel a lot better, but me too.

## VI.

That weekend, in the Inter-club match, I swam the 100 yds in 1:09 flat, which left me a bit short of Eleanor's 1:08.4. L. deB. told me, "You know, Sydney, I'm kind of glad you just missed. Now, when you break the world record at the nationals, you'll get a lot more attention."

But whatever pleasure I got from my swimming was tempered by poor Jimmy's mood. He was so melancholy. There just weren't any jobs to be had, &, no matter what, he wasn't going to accept being a runner for the bank again. He didn't eat enough, & he smoked entirely too much. He smoked Old Golds.

On one occasion, we were sharing a pizza pie. I'd never even heard of pizza till I got to B'lyn — tho they called it "apizza" then. I told Jimmy (again): "It isn't your fault, honey. It's the Depression."

"You'll never even think about marrying a bum like me."

"Well, I don't know how many times I've told you, but I'm not marrying anybody till after the Tokyo Olympics, & I'm sure you'll have a job then."

"You mean you'll marry me then?"

"I didn't say that, Jimmy. I just said I'd be prepared to marry you then."

That buoyed him some. "Go on, eat another slice of apizza," I said. "Your appetite is lagging."

So he did. But everytime I saw him, he was more down in the dumps. Then, one day — in fact, I know exactly: it was June

27th — he was waiting for me again outside the London Terrace, just leaning up against the bldg there, smoking, per usual. "Hi," he said, but not w/ the sort of enthusiasm you'd expect from somebody greeting their serious girlfriend.

"What's with you, Gloomy Gus?" I said.

"I got something to tell you, Sydney."

"Okay."

"Let's get a beer."

"Seems to me you've already had a couple beers."

"I've been waiting for you," he said. "I came over to Washington St, so I've been waiting."

"What's on Washington St?"

"The Marines, Sydney. I signed up for the Marines."

I took a big breath. It was like I'd been hit by a 2 × 4. "You did what?"

"You heard me. I signed up for the Marines. It's a job, Sydney. A girl isn't going to marry a guy w/o a job."

"Oh, Jimmy," I said, grabbing his arm. "You didn't do this for me?"

"No. Don't worry about that. I did this for me. I couldn't stand me anymore."

"I wished you'd talked to me 1st."

"That's why I didn't. Because then I'd've let you talk me out of it. Because I love you, & I don't want to leave you."

"I love you, too, Jimmy."

He turned & faced me. "You never said that before."

He was right. I'd been scared to tell him that. But I'd been thinking: why wait till after the Tokyo Olympics to get married? Eleanor set world records when she was married. So he held me tightly then, & we kissed very passionately, standing right there on 9th Ave. I always liked kissing standing up & invariably threw myself into it, as I did now.

In fact, just as we broke apart, I saw L. deB. come outside after practice. He was in a pale blue-striped seersucker suit & had on a straw boater, so he was easy to spot. He looked over at us, but I wasn't embarrassed about my indecorous behavior in public. I just asked Jimmy, "Well, when do you go?"

"I go to boot camp next week."

"Next week!?"

"Yeah. I was the last one to make the July allotment. We can't go before the holiday, so I leave the 5th. That's next Tues."

"God, only a week."

"Yeah."

"And how long?"

"Four yrs." I swear, I almost swooned. He grabbed me. "It's not so long, Sydney. It's like between Olympics. Think how fast that goes. You're halfway to Tokyo already. I'll be out July in '42. Or maybe if the Depression is still on & I like the Marines, I'll make it a career. I found out: Marines guard embassies all over the world."

That was not my idea of being a wife, going from pillar to post, the world over, but I didn't get into that. I was too shocked. Jimmy was just so proud he had a job, tho, that nothing else mattered — not even me. And I did understand, as much as I hated it, why he signed up. But you had to've been around then, in the Depression, to know what it was like, without any jobs, when you had your pride & ambition, but you couldn't do a darn thing about it.

Maybe you can appreciate, then, how I felt on July 12th. That was 2 wks later, or exactly one week after I saw Jimmy off from Penn Station to go to Parris Island, S. Carolina. I was in the office, filing, when Mr. S spotted me. Every day, when he'd go out for lunch, he'd buy a copy of the New York World-Telegram, which was his afternoon newspaper of choice. He'd glance at the headlines, read the sports, then finish it on the subway home & give it to Mrs. S to read while he had an Old Fashioned before dinner. That was his routine.

This day, as soon as he got back from lunch, he came right over. "You wanna know something, Sydney?" he said, handing me the paper, pointing to a headline down toward the bottom of the front page. It read:

Cite Chinese War
JAPANESE GIVE UP '40
TOKYO OLYMPIC GAMES

I hardly managed to read the article. I was in such a complete daze. I couldn't even make myself go to swimming practice that afternoon or the next day either. I couldn't concentrate at all at work, & that 2nd day, afterwards, I went to McDougal's & sat in the corner & drank 3 drafts. Like I was a rummy, drinking by myself. But the more I thought, the more I knew I had my mind made up. So, the next day, as soon as I walked into the office, I gave Mr. S my notice & then I called Mom & told her I was coming back to the Shore.

That afternoon, I went to the pool to tell L. deB. of my decision. I remember, for the 1st time, I called him L. deB. & not Coach, because this really didn't have anything to do w/ coaching. "I'm sorry, L. deB.," I said, "but if there's not going to be any Olympics, I just don't care enough."

"Sydney, Sydney," he said, beseeching me, "I know you're upset, but don't you worry. They'll be an Olympics. Helsinki, Finland, wants to jump in."

I shook my head. I didn't believe that for a moment. Europe was coming apart at the seams worse even than Asia. Hitler had already taken over Austria, & any dumb-bunny could see he wasn't going to be satisfied just w/ that. But L. deB. was such a gentleman. I let him take me by the hands & steer me over to where there were a couple of chairs. He kept holding onto one of my hands, looking right into my eyes. He had on a white linen suit, w/ a blue shirt & a yellow tie & handkerchief & a daisy in his buttonhole. I remember that distinctly. He was so stylish, I can always recall exactly what L. deB. had on at any particular time — even when I was so upset, like now.

He said, "Look, Sydney, I know it's none of my business, but one of the other gals told me that that boy I saw you smooching w/ a couple wks ago has left you."

"No, he didn't leave me, L. deB. He just left town for a job."

"I see. But he's gone away from you, Sydney, & I can only imagine how that hurts. But don't let that affect your swimming."

I took my hand away from him. "I'm sorry, I know you don't understand, but I just don't care all that much about swimming anymore."

He took my hand back, in both of his, holding it tighter still. He meant so well, I knew. He loved swimming so much, so he just couldn't fathom how I felt, because it never meant all that much to me. "Listen, Sydney, you swim at the nationals, you'll win, you'll set a world record & all those newspaper photographers will be taking your picture, & boys opening up the paper, getting a gander of you in your WSA suit — you'll be swatting fellows away like flies."

"I'm sorry," I said. "Even if Jimmy is gone, I still love him."

"Well, please, take a couple days to think about it."

"I've already done that. I promise, you, that's all I've done is think about this." And now I patted him on his hand. It was suddenly me, the kid, comforting him, the grown-up. "I'm sorry. I just don't care that much anymore. I'm going back to the Shore to sell insurance."

L. deB. slumped back in his chair, confounded by me. I would've been, too, if I'd been in his place & he in mine. But he could tell there wasn't any more to say, so he just lifted his eyes & watched me get up. Forlornly.

"Look," I remembered to say. "I forgot to bring my WSA bathing suit. I'll mail it back."

L. deB. waved that off. "No, keep it, Sydney, so if you ever change your mind, you can just come on back & slip it on & pick right up where you left off."

I leaned down & gave him a kiss on his cheek, & then, w/o looking back, I walked away. I never practiced swimming again, never swam a race again, &, to tell you the God's truth, I never had a moment's regret. It'd been exciting at 1st, & I know I was happy that I'd done something to make Daddy proud of me, but I honestly was never sure that I wanted to swim all that much FOR ME. You have to care so much, like Eleanor did, to be the Queen.

The funny thing is, when I walked away that day, I knew I was the Queen of the Backstroke, the best in all the world, so I really didn't care if I had to prove that to anybody else — well, unless there'd been an Olympics. That's what had really kept me going all along: to swim in the Olympics in Tokyo in '40. I wanted to win a gold medal there, but I think maybe in my heart of hearts what I'd really wanted most was to win a gold medal w/ Horst watching me.

That was the vision. It was sort of a package deal in my mind. I didn't just want people to say: there goes that Sydney Stringfellow, who just won a gold medal. I wanted people to say: there goes that Sydney Stringfellow, who just won a gold medal, & she's w/ her fiance, Horst Gerhardt. Aren't they a honey of a couple?! I'd always connected Horst w/ the Olympics so much that I guess I never really cared deep down about swimming after he left me. Maybe it still had more to do w/ him than it did w/ Jimmy.

Now — not that I hadn't come to love Jimmy.

## CHAPTER SIX

### I.

Back on the Shore, I threw myself into studying for my insurance accreditation & passed w/ flying colors. Even before I

441

could officially sell policies, tho, I had to take on more responsibility around the office, because my mother had gotten a beau herself. He was Elliott Parsons, who was a lawyer in Centreville, which was the next town down Rte. 213, over in Queen Anne's County. Mr. Parsons was in the process of a divorce, which would've normally scared Mother off, as divorced men on the Shore were regarded notoriously. However, Mr. Parsons' ex-wife-to-be had behaved so scandalously that word of her indecorous exploits had even reached C'town, so Mother was assured that Mr. Parsons was the aggrieved party, & thus could be legitimately comforted.

Mom was, however, on tenterhooks around me at 1st, *vis-à-vis* her budding relationship, fearful that I'd think that her attentions being paid to another man would insult the memory of my sainted father. When she finally broached the subject, tho, I promised her that I understood how time marched on in these matters. Given my blessing, Mom then began, *sans* impunity, to throw propriety to the winds in order to spend most of her nites in Centreville.

This left me holding the fort at home, where I became a veritable Miss Lonely-hearts. Here I was, once again, pining for my lover, waiting for letters from him. (Well, at least this time they didn't have to cross an ocean!) Jimmy was a faithful correspondent, too, if more given to cataloging the minutiae of Marine life than in elaborating, poetically, on his love for me & what a perfect human being I was, which had been more of Horst's modus operandi. But Jimmy never failed to wrap things up by telling me that I was beautiful & wonderful & that he loved me & missed me & spent all his spare waking moments thinking of me. A girl couldn't ask for much more than that.

Jimmy himself was an outstanding Marine. Why should I be surprised? Jimmy always succeeded at whatever opportunity he was given (not just vocationally, you understand, but also w/ my heart) whenever those rare occasions for opportunity came his way. It was just that after every success, every time he opened a door to march thru, he'd then find another door closed in his face. That was the Depression for you. But at Parris Island, he was named a squad leader & given a certification declaring him "Marine Of The Cycle." Also, altho he did not immediately apprize me of this, he became a devotee of poker,

& was soon so accomplished that his fellow Marines began to call him a "card shark."

This mattered because when boot camp was over & he had a furlough, he had enough $ from his poker winnings to pay for bus fare. So it was, when I came home from the office one afternoon after work, to my absolute amazement (and delight), there was Jimmy on the front porch, just rocking away as if he owned the place. And, then, to his amazement (and delight), Jimmy learned that my mother was bivouacking at Chez Parsons in Centreville, so we had a love nest all to ourselves! Needless to say . . . well: needless.

I introduced Jimmy to my mother the next day, & that nite Mr. Parsons took all four of us out to Bud Hubbard's Restaurant, where you could get the most sumptuous crab feast in C'town. Mother came into the office next morning & told me 3 things:

#1: Both Mr. Parsons & herself were tremendously impressed w/ "my young man."

#2: I should go home post haste & take some time off, to be with Jimmy on his furlough.

#3: She was going to "look the other

way," thus to ignore the fact that I, an unmarried young lady of good breeding, would be alone under the same roof w/ a young gentleman. What w/ her cohabiting w/ Mr. Parsons, tho, I think this was a case of: what's sauce for the goose is sauce for the gander (even if, in this instance, we were both geese).

For Jimmy, it was more than just being w/ me, making love to me; for him, the whole experience was idyllic. Never had he had any existence like this: actually being in a real home w/ love. I was only part of his package deal, but it didn't bother me at all not being the whole kit & caboodle. He said, "I don't ever want to leave, Sydney." By the time he returned to duty I knew I'd marry Jimmy Branch, &, I was sure, live happily ever after.

On his last afternoon, we went down to the river to take a dip. After we came out of the water we lay down on our towels, & Jimmy closed his eyes & sort of 1/2 dozed off. He was always built magnificently, but now, from that rugged boot camp, he was in the peak, the sun glistening off the droplets on the muscles of his body — pearls on ermine. I just gazed at him there, this Adonis of mine, & when he opened up one eye & caught me staring at him I felt a little embarrassed.

"Whatcha lookin' at, Sydney?"

"Just you. You're beautiful."

"Girls are beautiful. You're beautiful."

"No, boys can be too. You are. And this is the way I'm always going to remember you." And I made my hands like a Kodak & pretended to snap him, only as soon as I did that, he reached up & pulled me down & kissed me, & after that, it was Katie bar the door. Imagine if Gentry Trappe had been around or some boat (w/ children!!) had come by on the river! There we were, in another moment, naked as the day(s) we were born, rolling around on the grass in the bright sunshine. When we were thru making love, we still didn't care, & just lay there holding each other, absolutely oblivious to the world, especially to the Depression & the Marines . . . & Germany. We were prelapsarian.

PRELAPSARIAN! What in God's name was that? I know Mom liked to show off her vocabulary, and she never came across a word she didn't understand that she didn't immediately put down whatever she was reading and thumb through the dictionary. Myself, I'd usually just go on, trying to figure out the mysterious word on the fly (or to hell with it), but prelaparsian? I had to look it up. Surely it had to be high-class, elegant pornography.

So I found Mom's dictionary, and:

pre•lap•sar•i•an    adj relating or belonging to the biblical time before Adam and Eve lost their innocence in the Garden of Eden.

All right, so there was my Venusian mother and my Adonian father, at the height of their beauty, unashamed, upon the grass in their own Chesapeakean Valhalla, not a fig leaf to be seen. So I was glad when I put the dictionary down and returned to reading the onion-skin pages to discover that Mom had spared me any further post-prelapsarian detail and had then taken me, her son, the unbidden voyeur, onto some less sensual reporting.

When Jimmy's furlough was up, he was posted to Quantico, Va. w/ the 1st Marine Brigade. He remained there for the next 2 yrs. W/ his poker winnings, he was often able to visit me — altho starting in the fall of '39, the size of the Corps was greatly increased, & what w/ all the new recruits, Marine life became more urgent, Jimmy's

447

fuller of responsibility.

The reason the Corps — & the other services — were enlarged is because that's when Germany invaded Poland. That was when World War II really started, altho most of us Americans were loath to admit it. Myself, I wasn't surprised. Not because I was any wiser than the average Joe, but because I'd been there, in Germany, so every time something would happen like Munich or Kristallnacht, when the Nazis ran amok & beat up all the Jews, I would look back & see, from retrospect, that this was bound to be what the Nazis would do. It had all been there to see during the Olympics, as plain as the nose on your face, if you weren't blinded by all the hoopla, all the fun & games (or in my case, by also falling head over heels in love).

It was on those sad occasions, whenever Hitler & his crowd perpetrated something terrible again that I would think of Horst w/ SORROW. Poor Horst! I could only imagine how upset he must be, how distressed he surely was for his Germany.

Then I could not help but picture him on some ship & pray that he was safe. When the British fought that huge German battleship, the Graf Spee, I imagined Horst being aboard it. I eventually convinced myself that, yes, he must be, because when it was sunk none of the Germans lost their lives. I even imagined that somehow Horst had escaped when the ship was in port, at Montevideo, & now he was safely out of the war, being an architect in Uruguay. It was around Christmas when all this happened, & I thought to myself: what a wonderful Christmas present that would be, if Horst were alive, out of harm's way.

Then Jimmy came home on Christmas leave, & I was able to forget Horst again.

Jimmy was such a fine Marine. He advanced 2 grades, to Lance Cpl., & it was clear he could make a successful career as a soldier. Happily, however, that possibility no longer interested him. He had found his dream, the place he wanted to be — which was w/ me, in C'town. He adored my little town. And it was mutual w/ whomsoever in town met Jimmy, for everyone found him to be a honey of a guy. In particular, Mr. Parsons took a special liking to him.

He told me that one day he took him aside & told him, flat out, "Jimmy, we need new blood here on the Shore. Now, when's your tour up?"

" 'Bout 2 more yrs, sir. July of '42."

"Well, I speak not only for myself but for Trixie's mother as well when I say that we both hope you marry Trixie then & settle down here."

"Sir, I wanted to marry Sydney the day I set eyes on her. I've just never had 2 nickels to rub together."

"Times'll get better. Thank God we're not going to let ourselves get involved in that mess in Europe, so that'll only make the U.S. stronger while the damn Europeans go at it hammer & tong & never even mind what all those billions of Japs and Chinese are up to over that way."

"I certainly hope so, Mr. Parsons. If there's trouble, they've told us: the Marines will be the 1st to go."

Mr. Parsons let that unlikely possibility pass. "Now, I don't know if Trixie has told you, but, at long last, my divorce is going to be final, & as soon as that happens I'm going to make an honest woman out of Marian. However, as you know, my practice is in Centreville, so it doesn't make any sense to keep the place by the river."

"Mrs. Stringfellow will sell it?"

"Well, that's the plan. I mean, poor Trixie is out there by herself, rolling around like a marble in that big place. But . . . & this is a big but, Jimmy, if you're coming here to settle down, then that's where Trixie should live & raise her family."

"That's what I'd like, sir, w/ all my heart."

"That's what I wanted to hear. Now, have you thought what you'd like to do when you're out of the Marines?"

"Yes, sir, I have. I got into banking when I was in B'lyn, & I seemed to have an aptitude for it. I'm good w/ figures, so I thought I had a future in that line."

Mr. Parsons took that in. "Well, Marian & I have a better idea, if you're open to hearing it."

"Yes, sir. Absolutely."

"How 'bout insurance? Talk about figures. Insurance is a 1st-cousin to banking. From what I've seen of you, you could pass that insurance exam in jig time, you could help Trixie take over the agency, & let Marian relax & take care of me. I'm sure they'll be the pitter-patter of little feet in your house not long after you march down that aisle, & you'll want Trixie home as a mother. There's no reason why you couldn't be in charge of the office — tho Marian could pitch in to help you now & again. What do you say?"

Well, Mr. Parsons told me, it was all Jimmy could do not to cry — & he was of that generation of men who believed that it was sissy for a man to cry. He just rubbed his eyes. "Mr. Parsons," he said, "I never had anything drop in my lap before. Ever. I can't believe this."

So Mr. Parsons patted him on the back & said, "Jimmy, welcome to the Shore." And they had hooters of Maryland rye together to seal the deal.

Not only that, but after a couple ryes, Mr. Parsons showed Jimmy an absolutely gorgeous diamond ring. "Wow," Jimmy said.

"This was my mother's. She left it to me when she died 3 yrs ago." Jimmy nodded, not having the foggiest where this was heading. "Now, both my boys had already been married by then. You don't know them. They both left the Shore — damn them. Had to be hot shots, go to the city." Jimmy shook his head, commiserating. "I was going to give this to Marian when she accepted my proposal."

"Yes, sir."

"But she told me something. She told me that I hoped I didn't take it the wrong way, but she wanted to keep Bob Stringfellow's engagement ring on. And I did understand. I knew Bob, he was one fine fellow & I can't be jealous of the wonderful yrs he & Marian had together."

"That's awful nice of you, sir."

Mr. Parsons just shook his head, modestly.

By then, I was very glad he was marrying Mother. He wasn't my father. No one could be that. But he was one good man. I think a lot of men would've gotten their nose out of joint if their wife-to-be had wanted to keep her 1st husband's ring. But not Elliott Parsons. And then he absolutely bowled Jimmy over. "So, I want to give this to you for Trixie's engagement ring."

Jimmy was flabbergasted. "Oh, no sir, I couldn't —"

"Bullshit, son. There's no sense letting it sit in a safe deposit box collecting dust till hell freezes over. Besides, it's a nice symbolic way of bringing both you & me together into this wonderful Stringfellow family w/ these 2 beautiful Stringfellow gals."

That's when Jimmy did absolutely break down, crying. He was so embarrassed till Mr. Parsons grabbed the back of his neck (because he'd bowed it in shame), squeezed it & said, "On the Shore, Jimmy, we have a saying that the way you tell a gentleman is that he'll never let himself fart in mixed company or be afraid to cry w/ good friends." So Jimmy cried some more.

Then Mr. Parsons asked him, now that he had a ring, when he might propose, & Jimmy said, "I actually was thinking in a few wks. See, this is on the QT, sir, but that's when the Brigade's leaving Quantico for maneuvers."

"Where you going?"

"It's a place in Cuba called something like Geronimo."

"How long you be gone?"

"Months, I think. We're going to start practicing amphibious landings."

"Well, you're right," Mr. Parsons said. "Just before you go — I think that'd be a good time to hand Trixie this & pop the question."

Of course, that Geronimo place in Cuba was Guantanamo Bay, which nobody had much heard of at that time, & on his last leave before the Brigade shipped out, Jimmy did give me that ring, which was the most beautiful thing I ever saw (& which I've worn to this day). It had what seemed to me to be an absolutely monstrous diamond in the middle & 2 smaller (but not that much!) teardrop diamonds on either side, so I cried & Jimmy did, too. He was getting to be a regular crybaby, but he wasn't the least bit ashamed of that anymore.

For her part, my mother gave Jimmy the material for him to start studying for his Md. insurance exam, which he took w/ him on the ship to Guantanamo.

We decided we'd get married in Aug. of '42, right after he got out of the Marines. That really wasn't that far off, hardly more than a yr and a 1/2. Of course, I'm not giving anything away to say that by the time we did get to Aug. '42, the U.S. was fighting the Jap. Empire in the Solomon Islands at the Battle of Guadalcanal.

## II.

Going to Guantanamo was the start of the serious business for the Brigade. It never came back to Quantico again. It relocated to Parris Island, then it went to Camp Lejeune, which is in N. Carolina. There were whole months when Jimmy couldn't make it up to see me. Then, late in '41, the Brigade sailed down to Culebra, which is a little island off Puerto Rico. That's where Jimmy was when the Japanese attacked Pearl Harbor, & all of a sudden, the work the Marines had done w/ amphibious landings made all the sense in the world.

Of course, even before Pearl Harbor I understood he wouldn't be getting out in July, & now I realized that he'd be going to the Pacific, and sooner rather than later. I read about the Marines who had to surrender on Wake Island, & all I could think was: there but for the grace of God goes Jimmy.

He did come back from Culebra in Jan., &, irony of ironies, the Brigade now held maneuvers on none other than Chesapeake Bay — but C'town is way to the northern end & the Marines were at Bloodsworth Island, which was far south, down by the Va. line. We knew for sure by then that he'd be shipping out for the Pacific pretty soon, so we decided to get married the next time Jimmy could get home.

It was early in May when he got his final leave. He had 10 days. Corregidor had just fallen in the Philippines, & here he was going to war. It was a very grim time for 2 young people to get married, but that's what we wanted — especially because I told Jimmy flat out that I wanted to try to have a baby. I was obviously very fecund (although, of course, I kept that to myself), & he said, well, if that's what I wanted, he did too, & we would try our damndest.

He came up to C'town on May 9th, & the next day we took the train up to Elkton. If you haven't heard of it, it's a little town up by the Pa. and Del. lines, which was something of a marriage mill. It was like: Take a ticket. Next. Dearly beloved . . . I do. I now pronounce you man and wife.

But it was sweet enough for me. Elliott Parsons was Jimmy's best man, & Carter Kincaid came up to be my matron of honor. Carter had found a nice fellow in Balt., which is what she'd always wanted. She'd been Mrs. Roger Cochran for a year now. He was in real estate, but he was going to officer's training for the Army Air Corps. She was 6 months pregnant, so it was especially wonderful that she made the effort to come up.

This was all the more true because it turned out to be the last time in my life that I'd ever see Carter. But we certainly didn't know that then, & we all 5 — of course, my mother was there, too — toasted our marriage w/ a bottle of champagne Carter had brought. Then we all went to the train station, & we hugged each other. The worst part of war, besides the carnage, of course, is how you're always saying goodbye to people you love.

Jimmy & I spent our wedding nite at my

house on the river, the very house I had grown up in. How many girls get to do that? Gentry Trappe came over to congratulate us & promised me the summer's first peaches as a wedding present. The next morning, Jimmy & I left on our honeymoon. My car was that old Ford that we'd gotten with the insurance way back in '34 after Daddy was killed, so Mr. Parsons lent us his '39 Buick. Gas rationing had just begun, & you were only supposed to use 3 gallons a week, but Mr. Parsons had a full tank saved up, so, with my rationing points too, we were able to drive down to Rehoboth Beach and back.

Rehoboth is in Del. on the ocean — tho, on the Shore, we always pronounce it "ayshun." We stayed at the fanciest hotel there, which was called the Henlopen. It'd just opened for the summer season, so there was almost no one else in the place. That was fine w/ Jimmy & me. Purposely, we didn't buy any newspapers or listen to the radio, because we wanted to forget about the war as best we could & just have a normal honeymoon.

The Rehoboth boardwalk wasn't open yet, so one day we drove down to Ocean City, which is a larger resort, just over the Md. line. Back then, there wasn't much in the way of civilization between Rehoboth & Ocean City. Just sand dunes. But along the way we noticed that every 1/2-mile or so, these towers were going up right on the beach. I'd say they were about 75/80 ft. tall, made of concrete, no windows, but w/ one big slit near the top. We stopped at a filling station, & the old man who pumped gas told us that the towers were look-outs for German submarines out in the "ay-shun."

Hearing that, I couldn't help but right away think of Horst, just imagine that he might be in one of those U-boats out there, only a few miles offshore. After all, stranger things have happened. In fact, as we drove off, Jimmy noticed me musing. "Penny for your thoughts," he said. I managed to smile back, but honestly, I felt a little guilty thinking about Horst on my honeymoon w/ Jimmy.

Three days later, our idyll was over, & we drove back home. I was holding up pretty well, too, but when Jimmy actually put on his uniform to leave for good — he was a full corporal now, a squad leader — I began to babble like a baby. He had to hold me for a long time to calm me down. I just kept telling myself that at least I must be pregnant. God knows we'd put enough (pleasant) effort into that.

When the bus came, though, I wouldn't let myself cry because I didn't want tears to interfere w/ our goodbye kiss. Standing there right by the bus door, I kissed Jimmy with all my heart & soul until I finally had to break away.

People say "take care" all the time now. I think then, as a matter of fact, we tended to say "take care of yourself," but that seemed like a foolish thing to say to someone going off to fight a war, so instead I just said, "I love you, Jimmy. I'll love you forever."

He said the same & got on the bus. I waved till the bus turned the corner, but then I broke down completely, sobbing all over my mother's shoulder.

The 1st Marines — by now it was called a "division" & not a brigade — shipped out of Norfolk 3 days later. Nobody knew it then, but it was headed for New Zealand. We only knew it was going thru the Panama Canal, somewhere into the Pacific. That was May 19th when Jimmy sailed. It was on Aug. 7th, in the morning, when they landed on Guadalcanal.

By that time, I was very much pregnant w/ who would turn out to be my beautiful Teddy. I had decided not to tell Jimmy that in my letters, tho. I didn't want him to worry about me, &, even better, I thought: what a wonderful surprise it would be for him out there in the middle of nowhere when the baby was born, & I could send him a picture of our gorgeous new child!

The last page was slightly stuck to the one before — perhaps, I thought, from Mother's tears as she'd been reading over what she'd written. But I turned the page quickly, for now I was totally confused. In her telling, it was already the summer of '42 and Mom was happily living and working on the Eastern Shore, waiting for Dad to return from war so they could both settle down together in that place right there that my father had come to adore.

And yet I was born just a few months later, on February 12th, 1943, in Missoula, Montana. Why such a complete change in such a short time? I could only guess that perhaps when Dad was wounded on Guadalcanal he was sent to some military hospital out West, and they fell in love with the place and decided to stay.

In any event, I was completely hooked now (not least because I was about to be born and enter this saga). I began the next chapter.

## CHAPTER SEVEN

The Battle of Guadalcanal began on Aug. 7th. We weren't engaged in the European war yet, so it was the only game in town, & the coverage was huge. Every day I read the Sun voraciously, listened to all the news on the radio. The 1st Marines were trying to hold onto the airstrip they'd captured after they'd come ashore. That's all I knew. Except:

There were a lot of casualties. Everyone who knew me knew that, too, so no one, except perhaps my mother, dared ask me about Jimmy — even tho I knew they were looking at me as if I had "GUADALCANAL" stamped on my forehead.

Each day I waited for a letter. The last I'd received from Jimmy was dated July 30th. He wrote that he couldn't tell me anything, except he was safe, & they were steaming to somewhere. That somewhere, of course, would be Guadalcanal. That letter didn't reach me till Aug. 21.

Then nothing more. Of course, what did I know? I didn't know any other wives or sweethearts in the whole 1st Marine. Were any of the guys allowed to write? And if they could, could the mail get out? And if it did get out, did Jimmy's letter go down w/

one of the many Amer. ships that were sunk by the Japs (we said "Japs" then, so I think I can write that now because that's what they were to us then)? I thought about all these things more than the other obvious possibilities, which were that Jimmy was either too wounded to write or he'd been captured or even . . . killed.

Anyway, each day I read what news there was about goddamn Guadalcanal, & each day there was no news from dear Jimmy. It was excrutiating. I was glad for Sundays, because there was no mail to worry about NOT getting then, & the same for Mon., Sept. 7, which was Labor Day.

Mom & Mr. Parsons had gone to Atlantic City for a week's vacation, so I was alone. Mom had Gentry Trappe drop by to check on me, & he promised he'd come back w/ a few of the last ears of the summer's corn. I was almost 4 months along in my pregnancy, but I had only barely begun to show, & really I felt fine, so that afternoon I went down to the river & swam awhile, then lay some in the sun, mostly simultaneously wondering about Jimmy & trying not to wonder about what might be happening to him.

Afterwards, I put on a ratty old housecoat. I certainly wasn't taking any care with my appearance because I wasn't expecting any company, when all of a sudden, what to my wondering eyes should appear but a car coming down the driveway. It was a C'town Taxi. I couldn't even remember the last time anybody had come to the house in a taxi.

I watched from behind the curtains in the front parlor. I knew the driver, Mr. Remley, & I could make out that he was taking the fare from the person in the back seat. I could tell the passenger was a man & see, when he got out the far side of the car, that he had on a hat & was dressed in a suit. But that was all. Only when Mr. Remley's cab pulled away could I see clearly — him just standing there, holding a valise.

It was Horst.

I was completely discombobulated — as I think anyone in my place would be. It didn't even occur to me right away that he was a German & we were fighting a war against the Germans & here he was arriving at my house in C'town, Md., in a taxicab. I just was so amazed that it was him. After 6 long yrs.

I don't remember leaving the window & going to the front door & pushing the screen open & stepping out on the porch, but I must have, because, in my mind's eye, even now, I can see myself standing there by the front steps, dazed, looking out at him.

He stood there, waiting in the driveway as Mr. Remley drove off & then, when he saw me come out, he took off his hat &, just like it'd been only the day before yesterday he'd seen me on Cross St., he said, "Hello, Sydney."

And you know what I said? The first thing? I said, "Horst, I have to change." I knew I looked awful.

I heard him call to me, "No, no, it's OK," but I was already back inside, rushing up to my room, where I put on a white blouse & a green striped chambray skirt that I loved. I also tried to quickly fix my hair & put on some lipstick. Then I came back downstairs, a part of me thinking this must've been a dream, that Horst really wasn't there. But, of course, he was. He'd come up the steps & was leaning back up against the porch railing, waiting for me — that same way I remembered him leaning up against his Opel — casual & poised & (just so there's no mistake) every bit as handsome as ever.

Well, he wasn't that cool. Neither one of us knew what to do at this point, how to behave, so I finally sort of shrugged &

said, "Would you like to sit here?" There were 2 old rocking chairs; he took one. "You can take off your jacket," I said, which he did. Then I asked him if he'd like something to drink. He said he'd love a beer, & I said I'd like one, too.

As I started to go back inside, he said, "Sydney."

I turned back.

"I know you're married."

"How'd you know that?"

"The cab driver. He said you were Mrs. Branch now."

"I am," I said. "And I'm having a baby, Horst."

"I didn't know that."

"My husband's in the war. He's on Guadalcanal."

"I hope he's OK." Then he paused a moment. "I mean that." I just nodded. "Look," he said then, "I've waited all these years for this, so maybe it's not right, but I just have to say it, Sydney, that I've missed you all this time, & I'll love you . . . always." And he held out his hands in a gesture of futile supplication.

I suppose I blushed a little. I placed my palms on the front of my chambray skirt, pressing down on my thighs because otherwise I felt that I might've reached out to take his hands. "Well," I said, "thank you, but we can't talk about that anymore."

"No," he said. "I only wanted to be sure to say it."

So I went to the ice box for the beer, but after I opened it, I just stood there awhile & let the cold blow over me. I was scared & excited & curious, but no matter how I tried to compose myself, my anxiety overwhelmed my nerves. I brought the 2 beer bottles back. I still didn't know what to say, so I lapsed into more small talk: "I guess you won't like this as much as German beer. It's just a Md. beer."

"Gunther," he said, looking at the label. "Well, that's a German name." He didn't know what to say, either, & for goodness' sake, he'd had time to prepare for this. Some things in life you just can't script, tho, can you?

"Yes," I said. I sat down in the other rocking chair, & then, again, there was that awful dead silence that comes when people are either too bored or too confused (this being the latter), until finally I got ahold of myself & just laid it on the line. "All right, Horst, what in God's name are you doing here?"

He didn't answer me. Instead, he raised his beer bottle to me and said, "You're as beautiful as ever, Trixie."

"Horst, I told you we can't get into that sort of thing."

"I know. But I just wanted to tell you that one more time. And I don't know if you remember, but I told you I was going to call you Trixie once, & this'll probably be my last chance, so I just wanted to say it."

"Why'll this be your last chance?"

"Because," he said, shrugging, "because tomorrow I'm going down to Washington & turn myself in to the FBI."

You can imagine: as shaken up as I already was, that threw me for a complete loop. "Why?" was all I could manage.

"Because I'm a spy & I have some information I'd like to hand over &, of course," — very matter-of-factly — "then I'll be arrested."

"You're a spy?"

"Yes, I am, Sydney. I'm a spy for the Third Reich."

## II.

The words only hung there. In an odd way, it was even easier dealing w/ the fact of Horst being there — I mean, after all, I already knew Horst, flesh and blood — than in that revelation. I can't remember

468

what exactly I did at that point. I guess I managed to take a deep breath. "Well," I finally said, "it'd probably be easier for me if maybe you started at the beginning."

"All right," he said. It would take 3 Gunther beers for him to get through it all, but he began by going back to '36:

Soon after the Olympics, Horst had grown even more disillusioned w/ Germany. Whatever hopes he'd had for a change in the Nazis' attitude because of the good will of the Games quickly evaporated. After his parents went to Japan, he even thought about trying to somehow get out of the country, follow me to America.

He paused there & rubbed the cold beer bottle over his forehead. "Sydney," he said, "I can't tell you how much your letters meant. I read them over & over, then I'd rush to write you back."

"Well fine, Horst, so then . . . why'd you break it off?"

"Please listen. I'll tell you exactly." He'd finished college in Heidelberg & started his naval training. He hated it. He hated his country. He grew ashamed that his father could be an official of the Reich, & he couldn't even bear it any longer to have anything to do w/ his sister, Liesl, who, married to the SS officer, had become a

Nazi fanatic herself. "I really thought I was going crazy, Sydney. Here I am, an officer in the navy, commissioned to fight for my country — but it's a country I can't abide anymore. Pretending, day after day. It was maddening. I'm not cut out for that sort of split personality."

Right after he was commissioned & was about to be assigned to specialized battleship training — he really could've ended up on the Graf Spee — Horst was unexpectedly called to Berlin, there to meet w/ an army col. in intelligence. Apparently, someone had come across his records, which showed how much time he'd spent abroad & how well he spoke English. Horst Gerhardt could be more valuable in some intelligence capacity than as a mere naval officer. For the glory of Adolf Hitler, would he accept this greater responsibility?

"Yes," he said, & then he snapped out his arm before me &, in a loud, sarcastic voice, he all but hollered: "Ja, oberst. Heil Hitler." He swung his arm back down, & then, to me, softly: "My chance, Sydney, my chance." You see, he explained, now he knew that he might be able to play some role in intelligence that could sabotage some Nazi plan.

He was reassigned to the abwehr, which,

he said, was rather like the Nazi version of the OSS, our own new spy agency. First, tho, his past was subjected to a thoro going-over. Given that his father was a party member & an ambassador & his sister was married to an SS officer & they had no evidence of Horst ever expressing subversive views, he quickly passed muster.

Indeed, he explained, I, the Amer. girl he'd courted, was the only real question mark on his whole record. "Liesl," he said. "I'm sure she told them about you. They checked. For example, they asked me if I hadn't taken you to Goebbels' party."

"Boy, they didn't fool around."

"Oh, I anticipated all that, Sydney. I imagined I'd be questioned about you. And since I knew then that there was no way I could be w/ you — at least till the war was over — I wrote you the letter. If it matters, it was the hardest thing I ever did in my life."

"But you had to?"

"If I was to try & be the patriot, yes. I couldn't take the chance they'd open my mail & find out I was still in love w/, well, an enemy."

I nodded. "All right, I understand."

"Do you really?" He didn't ask for another

beer, but I saw his bottle was empty, so I went for another. When I got back, he'd risen from the rocking chair & had turned away. He spoke that way, too, looking off from me. "I only prayed that somehow, somehow there wouldn't be another man — you know, that you wouldn't fall in love. But, I couldn't expect —"

He shrugged, turning back then, & when I handed him the beer, we were standing next to each other. "I don't want to talk about me, Horst."

He took hold of my arm, but only ever so lightly. It was the 1st time we'd touched at all, & I let his hand stay there. "I'm sorry," he asked, "but what's his name?"

"Jimmy."

"What did he do before the war?"

"Please."

"Just tell me that."

"He was a banker," I said, stretching the truth a little.

"I'll bet he's very nice."

I said, "Horst, after you, I was spoiled, & I could only love a very nice man."

"Thank you," he said, smiling, releasing that gentle grasp. "I won't ask anymore. I promise."

I just wanted him to pick up the thread again. "OK, Horst, so you were in intelligence — the ab—"

"Abwehr. Funny too, for a spy service, it really doesn't seem to be very accomplished. You see, most of the Nazis' efforts along that line are in spying on their own people. That takes lots of their most talented guys away from studying the enemy. Ironic, isn't it?"

But, he went on, they used him reasonably well at 1st, translating, reading English-language newspapers & other more confidential material, analyzing, etc. He was good at it & he was promoted, to hauptmann — Captain Gerhardt. As a translator, he was even chosen as a jr. member of the staff when Hitler went to Munich to meet w/ Neville Chamberlain in '38. The next year, he was almost sent to N.Y. to accompany some German emissary to the World's Fair. Horst's excitement mounted. He was planning to run off then, find me, somehow defect. But, at the 11th hour, some higher-up cancelled the trip. "That was my lowest moment, Sydney. That almost broke my heart."

"Eleanor was the big star at the Fair," I said, deflecting the personal stuff. "The Aquacade."

"Oh yeah, I read about that. Did you go?"

I sat back down in my rocking chair. "No,

but when she was beginning to rehearse the show, Jimmy was away on maneuvers, so I went up to B'lyn. Eleanor practiced at a hotel there, the St. George. It has this magnificent indoor pool, & when I saw the practice, it all looked very glamorous. I spoke to Eleanor afterwards, asked her if maybe I could swim in the chorus —"

"You wanted to?"

"Why not? Jimmy was away so much. I was lonely. Maybe I missed swimming. But Eleanor said she wouldn't let me. She told me I was too good & too pretty — laid it on thick —"

"No, she didn't."

"Come on, Horst."

"Sorry."

"Anyway, she said if there'd ever be a road show, then I could be her, be the star. But she wouldn't let me be a chorus girl. And she was right."

"And there never was a traveling Aquacade?"

I shook my head. "So I stayed here. Mom got remarried. I run the office. I sell some too. I'm a certified insurance agent, Horst — certified."

"I wouldn't be a good risk," he said. "They'll probably hang me."

"Stop it." He shrugged. "So, all right, go

on. Tell me."

"Can we walk?" he asked. "Can I see the river?"

I got him another beer, & we strolled down there. "Is this like what you envisioned?" I asked.

"Oh, I don't know. It's hard to imagine a place you've never been to — but I did try to picture you here, swimming. It is pretty." I couldn't tell whether he meant that or was merely being polite. His mind wasn't on scenery. Well, neither was mine.

By the dock there were a few Adirondack chairs, the kind that slope way back, & we sat down. He loosened his tie & I just let him look out over the river for a while. It was late in the afternoon, but it was still hot. "It's more humid here than Germany," I said.

"Yes. It sure is." He only said that mechanically. Then he stared back out again, silent for another long patch. Finally, he turned back to me & began once more: "All along, I figured — well, I hoped — that they'd give me some sort of real assignment. Undercover. The real thing. But when it happened, I was overwhelmed." He stopped. I waited. "Sydney, they wanted me to kill the president."

"President Roosevelt?" He nodded.

"Wow," was what I said. I mean, what do you say?

"Yeah. It's called Operation Hauptstadt. That means 'capitol.' See, they've assigned another spy to go to England to try & kill Churchill. Washington, London — capitols. I don't know if they really thought either one of us could actually pull it off, but, sure, it was worth the gamble. I was given a lot of target practice w/ a high-powered pistol. I played along. I just figured the mere fact that it was me instead of somebody who might really TRY to kill Roosevelt already made me a success."

"So, what're you going to do?"

He took a long pull on his beer. "Hold on, Sydney. Let me back up. Now, at that time, I figured I'd just come see you, maybe figure how to lay low till the war ended. The main thing was, I wouldn't kill the president.

"But then it got more involved. They asked me to bring some information to a guy named Jerry Goldstein in N.Y. Turns out Goldstein is their # 1 spy in the country."

"Goldstein?"

"Well, obviously, if you don't want anybody to suspect you're a Nazi, Goldstein is a very good alias. So now, I'm thinking,

I can kill somebody in America. I can kill Jerry Goldstein, then hand the secret papers they gave me over to the FBI."

It surprised me that Horst could speak so blithely about killing someone, but then, it was war. I'd never thought Jimmy could kill anyone either, but he'd been trained to kill Japs. I guessed you could learn. So I just asked, "What's in the papers?"

He shook his head. "No idea. It's in code. But maybe the FBI or the OSS could break it. Anyway, Goldstein — as important as he is, if I kill him, I'm performing a real service.

"So they give me a fake driver's license for identification, $3000 in U.S. currency & a small handful of diamonds I could sell if I had to."

I broke in. "But how'd you get here?"

"You know, Sydney, it was actually re-markably easy." He spoke in such an offhand manner about everything, it made it seem all the crazier.

"Really?"

"Yeah, they just put me in a U-boat. No. 518. We went out of Bremerhaven, crossed the ocean, & arrived here 3 days ago. We came into Maine. You know a place called Bar Harbor?"

"Maybe heard of it." I was thinking, tho,

of those towers I'd seen along the beach in Del., & how I'd thought at the time how Horst might be out there, just off our coast. And sure enough, he would be.

"Well, Bar Harbor — it's quite a ways north, almost to Canada. We anchored there in something called Frenchman's Bay, waited for nitefall, surfaced just off the coast, then some sailors rowed me to a place called Hancock Point. I got out of the boat, ambled over to the main road, & then shortly afterwards some Nazi sympathizer who Goldstein sent picked me up in his car. I got the next train to N.Y. It was like clockwork." He chuckled. "Really, Sydney, it's harder for me to get from Berlin to Hamburg. I took a room at the Statler, & the next morning I called Goldstein."

"This was just yesterday?"

"Uh huh. God, it was only 3 nitets ago I was still on 518." Horst shook his head. "Incredible." There was such an air of the unreal to it — all the more so to me. Horst went on, still reciting it all very casually: "Goldstein answered, & I gave him the password rigamarole in case the phone was tapped. He went to a pay phone, called me back, said I should meet him that afternoon at 2 on a bench in Central Park.

"By half past one I was on his street. He lived on the Upper Western Side —"

"Upper West Side."

"Right. A lot of Jews live there, I understand. He's playing his part to the hilt. I simply waited for him to come out of his apartment bldg. I'm a pretty good shot by now, Sydney. All the practice they've given me. I thought it'd be quite easy, really. Get him in my sights" — he pantomimed raising a pistol — "& fire. Bang," he said. "Easy."

"Jesus, Horst."

"Yeah. In Berlin, they'd shown me a photograph of Goldstein, so I knew what he looked like. And sure enough, a few minutes before 2, he comes out. I took a deep breath. Suddenly, I was scared to death. Not of being caught. No, that's wrong — it wasn't scared. Excited. I was thrilled, Sydney. Thrilled. I was actually going to do something important against the Nazis. I was actually going to play a role. Yes, I was excited. And, I'm sorry, but I felt no guilt about killing this man. None. So I took my pistol out of my little travel bag . . . & that's when I saw the woman."

"What woman?"

"His wife, I suppose. Little Frau Goldstein. She was w/ him. And that stopped me dead. Somehow, I just couldn't kill a man — any man — in front of his wife. I couldn't do it, Sydney. But I thought, well, maybe she's just out shopping or something, & she'll leave him before he gets to the park. So I shadowed them, staying back, on the other side of the street. After all, I'm pretty sure he knows what I look like, too.

"But she didn't leave him. She stayed w/ him the whole way, sat down on the bench w/ him. I guess it made him look less suspicious to be w/ a woman — just a husband and wife out for a nice little stroll in the park. I watched them awhile longer. I could see Goldstein begin to look at his watch when it got to be a few minutes past 2. I started to take out my gun again, but it was the same thing. I couldn't shoot him w/ her there." Horst stopped then & took another swallow of his beer. "Or maybe, Sydney —"

"Maybe what?"

"Maybe I couldn't have shot him no matter what. Maybe I just can't shoot a man. Maybe I'm not cut out for that." He sighed.

"Yeah, who is?" I said.

"I don't know, but when I realized I couldn't do it, I left the park, went back to the hotel, checked out & headed to the train station. I figured, okay, maybe it's just as good to tell the FBI about Goldstein. Maybe he's more valuable to them alive. You know, this is a guy who knows a lot."

"So, you were going to Washington?"

"Yeah. But I had to see you 1st, Sydney. You understand."

"Of course. And if I wasn't married?"

He just looked away. "I thought I was supposed to leave you out of it."

"I'm sorry. My fault."

"Don't ask me to dream anymore, lieb-chen."

I let it pass. I drank my beer. Finally I went on: "OK, so now you plan to go to the FBI, turn yourself in & tell them about Goldstein —"

"The whole plot. They have to alert the English about Churchill, too."

"And then you'll be in custody."

"Yeah, but hey, Sydney, I was just being dramatic. If I give myself up & give them Goldstein, they won't hang me. I'm pretty sure. You know about the Nazis who landed in U-Boats a few months ago to sabotage stuff?"

"Sure."

"Well, they hanged some of them already —"

"Yeah."

"But the guys who lost their nerve & turned themselves in — they only put them in jail."

"Horst, they got something like 30 yrs. You want to spend 30 yrs in jail?"

"They wouldn't sentence me to that much. Those guys just gave themselves up. I'm giving them the biggest Nazi spy in the country."

"OK. You get 10/15 yrs. That's crazy. You can mail them all the information & they'll never know you existed."

"I thought about that. But think of all the mail that comes into the FBI. It could sit around for days. Goldstein's already trying to figure out what happened to me. He's not going to stay put much longer. They could shoot Churchill tomorrow."

"So, OK, listen to me, Horst: we send it certified mail, then I call up the FBI & warn them to look out for a letter that tells about a plot to kill the president. That'll certainly get their attention."

"They'll trace the call."

"I'll take the train to Wilmington, make the call from a pay phone —"

"You?"

"Yeah, I'll do it. Horst, for God's sake, you've got to get lost."

"But then, maybe you'll get caught, & —"

"Horst, please. I'm a pregnant woman w/ a husband fighting for the country in Guadalcanal. The only possible thing they could want from me is to know where you are, & once you leave here, I won't KNOW where you are."

I couldn't imagine where I was getting all this stuff — all these ideas — from. I didn't understand how I'd suddenly taken command of the situation. Maybe it was simply because all these wks I'd been so helpless, just waiting to hear about Jimmy — waiting, unable to do anything myself. And now, I actually had the chance to DO something — to think, to plan, to act. I'll be honest: it was exhilarating.

But who was I fooling? It was the chance to do something FOR Horst. Not for an instant did I question anything he told me. Not for a moment did I doubt that I shouldn't help him. I just knew that anything I could do for him, I would. I must. So I did.

He was listening to me. He needed me. He took in everything I suggested. "OK," he asked, "what's certified mail?"

"Special treatment. Whoever gets the letter has to sign for it."

"So then it sits on a desk."

"I said I'd call them about it."

"I don't know, Sydney. Goldstein's bound to get nervous & run. Maybe he even thinks they captured me."

"So they'll find him. That's what the FBI does. It finds bad men."

"I don't know."

"I do," I said. "I know." All right, I would make him do what I thought best. I got up & came over to his chair & kneeled before him. "You love me?"

"Sydney, please. You know I do. Don't, don't —"

"Then do this for the girl you love. OK? Save yourself, Horst. For me, save yourself."

"But I can't have you."

"But you love me?" He nodded. "Then we DO things for people we love." I had to pull out all the stops. I couldn't let him go to jail for yrs & yrs. "Or do you just love me because you want me?"

"Come on, Sydney, that's not fair."

"No, come on, Horst. That's not love."

He looked down at me, & I knew he wanted to kiss me, & God forgive me, there was a part of me then that didn't know Jimmy Branch any more, didn't know I was married to Jimmy Branch, didn't even know I was carrying Jimmy Branch's baby — & that part of me, which was a bigger part of me than I wanted to admit, wanted Horst to reach down & take me in his arms & kiss me. And I think Horst knew that. But, God bless him, he didn't try. He just said, "Then what do I do, Sydney? Where do I go?"

"Come on." I stood up & took his hand & led him out onto the dock. "I used to come here just to think . . . of you. Mostly. Sometimes I'd go in the water, sometimes only sitting here, dangling my feet, wondering what you were doing. Sometimes I'd smile. Sometimes I'd even cry. But always, I'd think: someday Horst will be here w/ me."

"And here I am."

"Yeah. But I never thought it'd only be for just a little while."

"No."

"But that's the way it has to be, doesn't it?" He nodded. "OK, you're a smart guy, Horst. When you leave here, go to a city. People get lost in cities. Pick one, any one. You've got some $. You'll get a job. A war's on — remember? Companies are desperate for bright young men."

"They'll want to know why I'm not in the army."

"You're 4-F."

"What's that?"

"That's the designation for someone who's physically unfit."

"But I am fit. Look at me."

I did. "You don't have to ask me to do that." We both smiled for the 1st time in a while. "All right. You have a bad back. You have flat feet. Asthma. There's all kinds of things that aren't obvious."

"OK."

"And what I'll do is: as soon as you get a room, wherever, call me right away & I'll write a letter on Robert Stringfellow Insurance Agency stationary giving you the greatest recommendation a man ever had."

"So if I was so damn good at my job, what do I tell anyone about why I left?"

"You got tired of a little town. You didn't like selling insurance. Whatever. Come on, Horst, you're a spy. Spies should be good at this kind of stuff."

"I told you: maybe I'm not a good spy." We both laughed a little again. A small motorboat passed by in the middle of the river w/ a man & a woman out for a holiday spin. They waved at us, happily. You didn't see that much anymore since gas was rationed.

"Look," I said, "1st thing tomorrow, we'll take the train up to Wilmington. I'll mail the letter. Then you get a train to . . . somewhere."

Horst looked a little puzzled. "You mean spend the nite here?"

"Well, sure."

He shook his head. "I'm sorry. I couldn't do that, Sydney. I couldn't take it, being in the same house w/ you."

"Yeah," I said.

"Yeah."

I looked at my watch. "All right, the last train is another hour. I'll drive you to the station."

He asked one thing, then. He asked if he could just stay on the dock for a few minutes by himself. So I left him there. I believed that now that Horst was at my place, he wanted to dream a little about what might've been.

I understood. It was all I could do not to dream, too. And I was ashamed of myself for thinking that way, too, for, of course, I was another man's wife.

### III.

I hardly slept that nite. I'd wake up & see the envelope w/ the letter I'd written to J. Edgar Hoover himself sitting on my bureau. Along w/ it were the coded pages

487

Horst was supposed to hand over to Gold-stein, & on plain stationary, in my handwriting, unsigned, an outline of Operation Haupstadt, & Goldstein's address & phone #, & the notation that he was the top Nazi spy in the whole U.S.

Surely, I thought, as soon as somebody reads this, they'll be breaking down his apt. door. But then I'd think: suppose the letter just laid there in a pile? A diamond is forever. Bureaucracy can be too. Right? The commission studying Pearl Harbor had shown that we'd had ample indications of what to expect. Still, nobody had put 2 + 2 together. Maybe Horst was right. Maybe he had to personally show up & give himself up to bring enough attention to the plot.

At one point I got up & took out a box from my bottom bureau drawer. Once it had been mostly souvenirs of Horst, but I'd long since thrown out all his letters & the other remembrances of us. Now it just held remembrances of things Olympic. But there was one item that did relate to us that I'd kept: the invitation to Goebbels' party. It was embossed in gold, swastikas on the corners, so fancy & grand: ". . . erbittet die Ehre Eurer Teilnahme an dem Jubelfest zum Ruhmwe der Olympschen

Spiele." I pulled that out, & before dawn, when I couldn't even pretend to try to sleep any longer, I put it in my pocketbook along w/ my anonymous letter & the coded pages.

The 1st train to Wilmington wasn't till 8:30. I ate breakfast impatiently. My mind was racing. I checked my gas rationing book. I still had some stamps. So, a new plan: at 7, I got in the car & headed south. It wasn't all that far to the ferry that crossed the Bay. On the other side, when I got to Annapolis, I parked & took a bus into Washington. Even after I got there, I kept looking into my pocketbook at the letter. Mail it, you Dumb Dora.

Instead, I went to a phonebooth, looked up the # for the FBI, put in my nickel & started to dial to tell them about the letter I was going to mail. But I hung up. No matter how I tried to stop myself, I knew deep down that I'd go to the FBI. Well, I told myself, when I got there I'd just tell someone how important the letter was & then drop it off & leave. Yes, that's what I'd do.

I caught a cab. The FBI didn't have its own bldg yet. Its offices were in the Dept. of Justice bldg on Constitution Ave, between 9th & 10th. I walked in. There was a desk there at the entrance w/ 2 men in guard uniforms. I pulled out the envelope.

"Yes, miss?" the one guard said to me.

I started to hand him the envelope. And then I stopped. To myself I said: Oh, what the hell, Sydney: in for a penny, in for a pound. Before I knew it, I heard myself say, "I'd like to meet an FBI agent."

"Do you have an appointment, miss?"

"No, but this is very important."

"Well, you have to have an appointment."

"No, I just need to see an agent. It's about the president."

The guard shook his head at me, smiling snidely at my naivete. He was obviously not taking me seriously. It was still warm, in the 80s, & I had on a light summer dress, a patterned rayon crepe w/ a fairly deep neckline. It was tight in the belly. I wouldn't be able to wear it again till after I had the baby. The bldg didn't have air conditioning & Washington was very humid. The dress was clinging to me some, so if the guard really wasn't paying any attention to what I had to say, he was still paying attention to me. I could tell that. So I flirted a little: "Please, sir. There must be one agent who could see me for 5 minutes."

"It's about the president, huh?"

"Yes. The Nazis want to assassinate him."

"Is that so?" he said. Now he'd become downright patronizing. The SOB. But I kept myself in check.

"Yes, it is. Sir, I swear. Please, there must be one agent."

Maybe it was just that I remained so polite. Whatever, I could tell: he wasn't quite sure what to make of me. Still, he wouldn't bend. "Here's a # to call," he said, handing me a slip of paper.

But, by chance, at exactly that moment, a nice-looking young man in a tan suit came in & passed by the desk. "Hey, Charlie," he called over to the guard. He slowed down just enough to give me the sly old once-over.

Well, as I said: in for a penny, etc. I reached out & touched his sleeve. "Are you an FBI agent?" I asked, trying to make my eyes bigger.

The guard said, "I'm sorry, Mr. Anderson. She's —"

But Mr. Anderson held up his hand. "It's OK, Charlie." And then he turned to me, & rather like he was addressing a child, he said, "Well, yes, I am an FBI agent."

"I have to talk to you."

"Well, what do you want to talk to me

about, miss?"

I sighed. You know, it's one thing to use your feminine wiles to get something from men who're only interested in feminine wiles, but at a certain point: no more of the little girl lost. So I cut the big eyes, & as straightforward as possible, I said, "I happen to know that the Nazis are planning to try & assassinate Pres. Roosevelt. Now, that's what I would like to talk to you about, Mr. Anderson."

Well, that did take him aback. He looked me hard in the face to see if he could tell if I was blowing smoke. So, quickly, I added: "It'll only take 5 minutes. Tops."

It was apparent that he was still dubious, but, hey, why not a lousy 5 minutes w/ a lady in a clinging summer dress, even if she might be as nutty as a fruit cake? "Let her sign in, Charlie," he said.

Stupidly, I wasn't prepared for that, for signing anything, but I wrote down Joan — because the last movie I'd seen had been w/ Joan Fontaine & that popped into my head — & then you know what came to my mind? Gunther. For the beer I'd had yesterday w/ Horst. So: Joan Gunther. And for an address, I made up a # & a st. — something like 37 Elm St. — and wrote down "Hagerstown, Md.," because that

was in the opposite direction from C'town.
It was that simple. This was back before
you had to give your social security # just
to get a Coca-Cola.

I turned back to the agent. "I'm Joan
Gunther, Mr. Anderson. Thank you very
much." He nodded & led me to the eleva-
tor. His office was on the 3rd floor. We
headed down the long hall, past the stairs
& the restrooms & the offices, one after
another, lined up behind frosted glass
doors.

We came to his. It was hot & cramped in
there. He took off his jacket, revealing that
he had suspenders on. He hung up his
jacket & his hat & threw open the window,
then turned on a little fan. It didn't help
much. Mr. Anderson became very busi-
nesslike then, motioning me to take the
chair in front of his desk. I think he'd
decided on the way up that I really was
barmy, & so he wanted to get rid of me in
a hurry. "Okay, Miss Gunther —"

"Mrs.," I corrected him, holding up my
left hand.

That only irritated him more. "OK, Mrs.
Gunther, what is all this about the president?"

"Write this down, please," I said — but
very forcefully.

He kind of rolled his eyes, but he reached for his fountain pen & poised it over a legal pad. I gave him Jerry Goldstein's name & address.

"So?" he said. Like that.

"So, Mr. Goldstein is the biggest Nazi spy in the country."

"Oh sure. Goldstein."

I held my temper. "Obviously it's an alias," I said. "And a pretty good one if you're a Nazi spy."

That took him back a little, so I went on: "You want his phone #, too?" He grunted, & I gave it to him. It was a Trafalgar exchange — TR something. Telephones still had name exchanges in those days & weren't all #s.

"And he's a big Nazi spy?"

"Probably the biggest over here."

"And how do you know that?"

"I'm sorry. I can't tell you."

"Then why should I believe you?"

I reached into my pocketbook & handed him the pages that Horst was supposed to deliver to Goldstein. He looked at them, curiously, dismissively. And fair enough: they were simply a bunch of typewritten pages — and in German gibberish, because it was code. I said, "That was sent from the Abwehr in Berlin to Goldstein. You know what the Abwehr is, don't you?"

Reluctantly, he shook his head, so I told him: "The Nazi spy agency."

He nodded & said "Oh, yeah," like he'd just remembered that.

I gestured to the papers. "That's all in code, but maybe someone in the OSS can make something out of that."

"So where'd you get it?"

"That's what I can't tell you."

He frowned. "You walk in off the street, Mrs., uh, Gunther, you hand me a bunch of . . ." — he waved the pages in the air — "you tell me a guy's name, & I'm supposed to accept this pig-in-a-poke at face value."

"Look, I know it sounds crazy, but it's the truth. It's like I'm the lady in red."

"What about the lady in red?"

"Well, did the other guys in the FBI care who she was? She gave you a tip that John Dillinger was at the movies & that's how you got him."

"Let's leave John Dillinger out of this," Mr. Anderson said.

"I'm just saying it's apropos," I replied. "But if you don't do anything & Mr. Roosevelt gets assassinated, well, I'm sorry, but it's blood on your hands."

OK, I went over the top w/ that, & I knew

it even before he leaned forward & snapped his fingers right toward my face. "I don't appreciate that." He was irritated now, I could tell, & when folks get irritated, they don't tend to believe what you tell them. My mistake. So I backpedaled.

"OK, Mr. Anderson, I'm sorry, but Goldstein is involved in a plot to shoot the president. It's called Operation Hauptstadt. Hauptstadt means capitol — like Washington & London are the capitols. Because it's also part of the plan to try & assassinate Mr. Churchill."

He leaned back. "You know this?"

"I do." I paused. "Look, I'm sorry. I know I'm just a strange woman come out of nowhere, but that's the God's truth."

That threw him a little. I could see, every time he started to dismiss me as some ditzy girlie, I'd say something in a way that'd make him wonder again. Especially, when I'd said "Operation Hauptstadt." Foreign words give you an air of credibility. So he stood up & looked out the window for a few seconds, cogitating — or, anyway, appearing to cogitate for my benefit. Whatever, when he turned back to me, his tone was more conciliatory & polite. "Look, Mrs. Gunther, try to see this from my point of view. You come in out of the blue, &

you seem very sincere — you do — but if we chased every crazy —"

"Excuse me, I'm not crazy."

Good. That put him on the defensive. "I didn't mean that. What I meant was, if you put yourself in my shoes, this could seem crazy. I mean, who are you? Have you got, like, a driver's license?"

Of course I had it, but I lied. "I don't drive. I took the bus from Hagerstown."

"Well, have you got anything? A social security card?"

"Not w/ me."

"Have you got a darn library card? Anything?"

"I'm sorry. I only brought the information."

"OK, OK." He went to his coat, hung up behind the door, & pulled out a pack of Chesterfields. He lit up, then remembered to offer me one. I shook my head. "OK, OK," he said again. "Just tell me this. In general terms. In general, how did you come by this information? Now, please understand: you got to give me that. You got to help me a little here."

I didn't reply right away. I was thinking. #1: yes, I did have to give him some more information, but, I figured, so long as I didn't give him Horst's name, there was no real risk. Horst was gone. Besides, once they got Goldstein, he was probably going to blow the whistle on Horst, anyway. And #2: I'd been pretty innocent to think the FBI would just accept the information w/o dying to find out who I was. Now how was I going to get the heck out of here?

"All right," I said at last. "I see your point."

"Thank you."

I took a breath. "So I learned this from the Nazi agent who was sent over to shoot the president."

"Sent over from Germany?"

"That's right."

"So, you, up there in Hagerstown, you got it from the horse's mouth, direct from Berlin?"

"Yes, I did."

"And how exactly did he get here . . . from Germany?"

"I can tell you that — exactly."

"I'm all ears."

"Four days ago, he arrived on U-Boat 518." I pointed to his pad. "5-18," I said. He wrote that down. Curtly, like I was delivering expert testimony, I went on: "The submarine surfaced off Bar Harbor, Me., in Frenchman's Cove, & he was rowed ashore there at Hancock Pt. You can look it up."

"Just 'cause it's there, doesn't mean the U-Boat came there."

"No. But it did. You wanted to know how he got into the country. I've seen the watch towers they built down at the beach, down by Ocean City. So, we're on the lookout. Right?" He nodded. "Well, that's how he got here. I guess they don't have anybody looking out for U-boats up around Bar Harbor."

"And what's his name?"

"That's what I won't tell you."

He leaned forward on his desk, right into my face. "Excuse me, you say you know a Nazi spy, in this country, out to shoot the president, but you won't tell me?"

"Yes, that's right. Because he's not a Nazi spy anymore. Don't you understand, Mr. Anderson? He's the one who gave me this." I pointed to the papers on his desk. "He's the one who told me about Goldstein. Because he hates the Nazis. He's a hero, Mr. Anderson. Don't you understand?" I reached into my purse & took out a handkerchief, as if I was going to tear up.

"OK, OK. So why did this Nazi . . . excuse me, Nazi traitor —"

"That's right."

"Why did he tell you all this?"

"Because he loves me."

"Oh, I see. And you love him?"

"I did. Once. I'm married now. To somebody else. An American."

"Okay, so where did you meet him — the German?"

"I don't want to get into that."

That made him slump back down & put on a great show of exasperation. He took another drag on his cigarette. "All right, just a second." He picked up his phone and dialed 3 #s — obviously, an extension.

I was thinking fast. There was no more I could tell him. The ball was in his court now. So I reached back into my pocketbook &, very carefully, pulled out my driver's license & the little purse that held my money. I put them in my lap. Then I tried to think: was there anything else in that pocketbook that could identify me?

"Hey, Bobby," Mr. Anderson said on the phone. He whirled his chair around, to get the full blast of the fan, so that now he was pretty much facing away from me. "Ralph Anderson. Could you check out a name for me? Thanks." And then he read him Goldstein's name & address & phone #.

Then I remembered. I still had the 2nd

half of my roundtrip bus ticket to Annapolis in the pocketbook. And, of course: my keys. Mr. Anderson was still more or less looking away, reveling in the breeze from the fan, as he talked to whoever Bobby was. I reached back into my purse & started fishing around. I grabbed the keys, & put them on my lap, too. They jangled a little, but Mr. Anderson was still talking so he didn't pay any attention. "Just find out if we have anything at all on this fellow." And he chatted a little more about how awful the Wash. Senators baseball team was.

My fingers came across the bus ticket. Gingerly, I pulled it out, & when I was sure Mr. Anderson wasn't looking at me, I stuffed it down my front. I put the pocketbook right back on his desk & waited for him to get off the phone. After a few seconds more, he hung up & whirled back toward me. "Okay, you heard that," he said. "We'll just see if there's anything in our files on this Goldstein character."

"I don't think there will be," I said. "I think he lives a very respectable life."

"Double life?"

"Yes. There's a Mrs. Goldstein, too."

"She's also a spy?"

"Probably. But I don't know. I mean, she lives with him." I reached into my lap, then,

& w/ one hand I palmed the purse & driver's license & w/ the other, the keys.

"Okay," he went on. "So, let me get this straight —"

Suddenly I put a pained expression on my face. "Mr. Anderson," I said, "excuse me, just a second. I, uh —"

"Yes? You all right?"

"Well, yes, but, well, I'm pregnant."

"Oh, I see."

"And, I'm sorry, but I just HAVE to go to the ladies' room."

He looked distressed. Men don't know what it's like to be pregnant, so it's a wild card you can always play. I stood up, grimacing, holding the keys & the purse tightly. I made no effort to reach for my pocketbook. It sat smack on his desk, waiting for me to return. "Please, you understand."

He was solicitous. "Of course, Mrs. Gunther," he said. "It's that way, right down the hall."

"Thank you," I said, acting all the more uncomfortable. "I'll be right back."

"Take your time," he said, & he lit up another Chesterfield.

I smiled a thank you at him, then left his office, heading down the hall. When I got to the door of the ladies' room, I glanced back, just to see if he might be watching. He wasn't.

So I kept walking a few more steps, then turned down the stairs, hurrying now. In the lobby I resumed a casual pace. Going past the check-in desk, I smiled sweetly at Charlie & whispered a big thank you, as if he'd been a tremendous help. But I never slowed. I simply kept walking, trying to appear normal. Outside, I turned up 10th St. It was hardly a minute or 2 since I'd left Mr. Anderson's office, & my heart was still racing. Up the st., there was a Rexall drugstore on the corner, so I turned in to catch my breath.

In those days, if you'll remember, drugstores had fountains. I sat down & ordered a vanilla phosphate.

Another minute or so & Mr. Anderson was going to start to get curious. But my pocketbook was on his desk. He'd wait longer. Women DON'T leave their pocketbooks. But finally he'd have to get some secretary to go into the ladies' room. Then he'd check my pocketbook, but all he'd find, besides my lipstick, compact, etc., would be the letter I'd addressed to J. Edgar Hoover himself, which included the invitation to Goebbels' party. That was the piece de resistance, I knew. That was surely going to make him sit up & take notice. It was better than a foreign word — it was an authentic foreign artifact. Then he was going to call downstairs to the desk to find out if anybody had seen me leave. All that was going to take a few more minutes, so I sat there at the counter, sipping my vanilla phosphate, plotting the rest of my escape.

OK, I thought, just retrace your steps: grab a cab back to the Greyhound station, take the bus to Annapolis, pick up my car, drive to the ferry & go home. Safe. But then I thought: I'd told Mr. Anderson I'd come in from Hagerstown on the bus. Wouldn't the bus to Hagerstown & the bus to Annapolis leave from the same station? Probably. Wouldn't that be the obvious place for them to look for me? Probably.

Time was passing. I'd drained the phosphate. Maybe by now the secretary had gone into the ladies' room & discovered I'd gone. I really cogitated. Then I got up, went outside & hailed a taxi. "Union Station," I told the cabbie. That's the train station.

I bought a ticket to Baltimore, & when I got off there, I took a cab to the Balt. bus station & took the bus to Annapolis. Then: into my car, the ferry across the bay, home. Safe & sound.

I can only describe myself as excited. I felt like a master spy — master spyess? I'd accomplished exactly what I'd set out to do, outwitting the mighty FBI in the process. Surely, they'd send the pages over to be de-coded now, & they'd go right after Goldstein, & even if he'd gotten scared & taken off, they'd find him. And Horst was not only safe and sound somewhere, but his mission was accomplished. When he called, I'd tell him what I'd done. He'd be so proud that his efforts had been successful.

I only kept thinking: was there anything in that pocketbook I'd forgotten that might reveal who I was? You know the stuff every woman sticks in her pocketbook. Then you forget. But try as I might, I couldn't think of anything that'd be incriminating. Still . . . ?

I tried to sleep, but even tho I was tired, I was still so keyed up. I just wanted Horst to call me. I knew it'd take him a couple days to get settled, but I could hardly wait to tell him all about my adventure. I lay there in bed, thinking about him. I thought about Jimmy, too. No, I didn't. I didn't think about Jimmy. I only wondered about Jimmy, & that is different, & that made me wonder about myself & what sort of a woman I was. What sort of a wife.

## IV.

I went back to the office the next day. It rained all morning, which was good, because we needed that on the Shore, even if most of the crops were in. But what w/ Labor Day & then missing work yesterday, I had a lot to catch up on, so I threw myself into it, barely stopping to eat the sandwich I'd brought for lunch.

My mother called long distance from Atlantic City. It turned out that the Miss America contest was on that weekend, so she and Elliott were going to extend their vacation a couple days & watch the finals at Convention Hall, which was one of the largest auditoriums around at that time — quite the marvel to see. Otherwise, the day proceeded apace. The rain finally stopped, & it was steamy. My clothes clung to me, so I wanted to go home & get out of them & go swimming.

At 1/4 past 3, Gentry Trappe called. That was very unusual, so right off the bat I asked him if everything was all right. No, indeed, he said, everything was fine, but he just wanted to tell me that Western

Union had come by w/ a telegram & that he'd signed for it.

My heart leapt. Obviously, it was Horst, contacting me from wherever he'd gone to. It was all I could do not to leave the office right away.

Now, this was still only '42, the start of the war, & I didn't know yet that the government sent out telegrams to next of kin. And so, when I did get home & picked up the telegram where Mr. Trappe had left it & rushed out onto the porch & sat down there & ripped it open, I had no preparation whatsoever. I was just certain that it was from Horst. Who else would be sending me a telegram?

But there it was. It isn't hard to remember. It was pithy & to the point:

THE SECRETARY OF WAR DESIRES TO EXPRESS HIS DEEPEST REGRET THAT YOUR HUSBAND, CORPORAL JAMES L. BRANCH, WAS KILLED IN ACTION ON AUGUST SEVENTH ON THE ISLAND OF TULAGI.

That's all it said.

I let the telegram drop into my lap. I didn't cry right away. I was too shocked, I guess. I just sat there. Finally, I got up. I started taking my clothes off as soon as I got into the house. I was so clammy. They were sticking to me. I took everything off, letting them lay, one by one, wherever they fell as I climbed up the stairs. By the time I got to the top of the stairs I didn't have a stitch on, & I just walked into the shower. I stayed there forever, letting the water run on & on, all over me. Then I came out, still dripping wet, & I stood in front of the full-length mirror in my bedroom, stood sideways, staring at myself. You couldn't really see the little swelling in my belly when I had any clothes on, but it was obvious now when I was naked.

All I could think was: there's Jimmy's baby, & he's gone forever & he didn't even know he was going to be a father. I didn't see my face or my legs or my arms or my hair or my breasts or anything. I just saw that little swelling. This is what I thought: that's all in this world that's left of Jimmy Branch. A little bump.

And that's when I started to cry — not just cry, but those great wracking sobs, so much so that I just sank to my knees & held my head & said Jimmy's name over & over till I finally could get up & get dressed. I walked down by the river. I thought I would cry some more, but there were no more tears left w/in me.

I had to stop reading — just imagining the agony that my poor mother had gone through. God, think of it — being mistakenly informed that her husband had been killed. That must've been the cruelest experience. No wonder neither she nor Daddy had ever wanted to talk about Guadalcanal. I pondered this for a few moments more before I went back to Mother's story, turning one more onion-skin page.

But at that moment I heard a noise, and when I looked up, Mom was coming out of her room. She'd put on her bed jacket, but had, I suppose, simply forgotten to put her wig back on. I'd never seen her this way before, with just a frizzy bald head. In the dim light on that side of the room, in her nightgown and her light pink jacket, she seemed like a wraith, some pale apparition. But she was a friendly ghost, and she smiled at me as she stepped closer. "Aw, curiosity killed the cat," she said.

"Hey, come on, Mom, did you really think I couldn't read this as soon as I got it?"

She shrugged. "Well, where have you gotten to?"

"Incredible. They've just sent you the telegram that Daddy was killed. I simply can't fathom how the government could make a mistake like that."

Mom sighed, and her eyes seemed to go vacant. Then she shook her head, ever so sadly, at me. "Oh, Teddy, it was no mistake."

"But, Mom —"

"Come on, it's not that hard. You can figure it out now." I closed my eyes.

Oh my God. Of course, there was only one answer. It really was so simple after all.

"Can't you?" she asked.

"Yes. I see." And, in fact, it was at once so suddenly obvious and so incredibly shocking that I barely reacted outwardly. The news simply infiltrated me, and I slumped there, stunned, staring at Mom, unable to say anything else.

She sat down next to me and hugged me. "You all right, Teddy?"

I managed to mumble that I was.

"Well, I hope so, 'cause that's what you had to know."

"Yes. Thank you."

She rose and started to turn back to her room. "So, now that that's settled, I'll let you finish the rest alone."

At last, then, I began to regain some semblance of lucidity. I couldn't let her leave me now. "No, Mom, wait. I'll read it all later. You're still awake. Please. You can't just let it go like that. You gotta tell me the rest. Tell me it all. I wanna hear you tell it."

She paused only for a moment, for I believe she'd been hoping that I'd ask her that. "Well, all right, Teddy. But do me a favor. If I'm going back there in time again, there's a bottle of Old Crow in the liquor cabinet. Everybody used to drink Maryland rye when I was growing up. Oh my, did Carter Kincaid and I get so awfully tight on that one night when we were kids and her parents were out and we got into her father's bar. It was called Pikesville. I can't forget that poison. Pikesville Maryland rye. Oh my. That almost did me in for drinking for a lifetime."

"But it didn't."

"No, a lifetime is too long for most things. Now, of course, they stopped making Maryland rye years ago, but bourbon tastes the closest to it, so I have some for old time's sake every now and then. And I think this would be one of those nows and thens."

"Okay," I said, rising.

"But just a finger now, Teddy. Or a thumb since you've got skinny fingers."

"I'll make one for myself too, Mom."

"Well, that's fine. Lots of water: sippin' whiskey we called it."

"And, Mom?"

"Yes?"

"Don't you want to put your wig on?"

Her hand shot up to her head and she felt it. "Oh my, I was still half-asleep. I'm sorry you have to see me such a fright." I started to protest. "No, no, don't try and be polite, Teddy. But it squares the circle, I think. I came into this world as bald as a bowling ball, so I might as well go out the same way."

"Yes, ma'am," I said, and by the time I'd fixed us both a thumb of Old Crow, she was back, with her wig firmly in place, and even a little lipstick on for good measure. She made a point of going across the room and picking up the vase with the flowers in it that she'd brought in memory of Daddy. Carefully, she set it on the table, right in front of her. I had the tape recorder out, so I put a new tape in and turned it on. When Mom was sure it was spinning, she took a sip of her bourbon, and began again.

So, Teddy, the long and short of it is precisely what that telegram said, that Jimmy Branch, your dear father, was killed on August the 7th, 1942, on Tulagi, in the Solomon Islands.

*She let that sink in again. I took a sip of my drink and tipped my glass to the father I never knew. Mom offered a little salute at my gesture.*

He was one fine man, your father, Teddy. I'm so sorry you never got to know him. And I'm sorry he never got to know you. He would've been proud of his son. I should've told him I was having a baby, Teddy. At least he could've taken that to his grave. Poor, poor Jimmy.

*"Mom, excuse me: where's Tulagi? I thought it was Guadalcanal."*

Yes, Guadalcanal was the main target. The Japs had built an airfield there, and we wanted to take it from 'em. But Tulagi was a smaller island, just across the channel, so we had to take that, too. There were three battalions assigned to the task, under a colonel named Merritt Edson. They called him Red Mike.

*"Red Mike?"*

That's what they called him. They had better nicknames back then. They were descriptive. I knew two or three boys named Red myself. Well, one was Reds. And another boy we called Freckles. I knew a Fats and a boy we just called Noggin because he had a huge head. That would be "politically incorrect" now, I suppose. But back then, you were what you were, and it was Red Mike who led the Marines onto Tulagi.

*"Do you know how Daddy was killed?"*

Yes, as a matter of fact, I do. Exactly. Weeks after I got that telegram, my mother forwarded me a letter. It was from Jimmy's platoon leader, a second lieutenant — Daniel Carmody was his name. I'm afraid it wasn't complicated, Teddy. Just a bit of irony. The Japs were caught completely off guard at Guadalcanal. They'd been rolling through the war like you-know-what through a goose, and they weren't ready for someone to actually fight back. God Almighty, they took Singapore on bicycles.

So, anyway, the Marines just waltzed onto

Guadalcanal. It was days before the Nips —
we called 'em "Nips," then, so I'll let that
word pass my lips now, since we're talking
about the ones that killed dear Jimmy —
before they began to fight back on Guadalcanal. But the crowd on Tulagi had their act
together better, and as soon as Red Mike's
gyrenes landed they began to prepare to
throw them back.

The boys came ashore at Tulagi about
eight in the morning, and — this is what
Lieutenant Carmody wrote me — of all
things, the first thing they had to get across
was a cemetery. But just beyond that was a
little hill. Hill Two-oh-Eight. That's where
the Japs were dug in. Jimmy was not only in
the first bunch, he was the point man. He
volunteered for that, the damn fool. So he
started up the hill, and that's when the Japs
began their counterattack. That's when they
started firing. For all I could tell from that
letter, Jimmy was the first man they hit. I
guess he was ducking and running from one
spot to another, leading the way, and one
time he didn't make cover, and he took a
machine gun burst. Well, he didn't suffer,
Teddy. They ripped him to pieces.

I'm sorry to be so graphic, but now that
you know . . .

*Mom reached down and took a sip. So did I.*

*To tell you the truth, I didn't know how to feel. I'd just discovered that I'd never known this man who was my father — well, this man who had fathered me — and so I was filled more with curiosity than sadness.*

*Mom only shook her head.*

Lieutenant Carmody said he died bravely, a hero, in the service of the United States of America. I guess. Does just getting killed make you a hero? Maybe he was more a hero that time he took after the mugger in Brooklyn. But you know, Teddy, I've often thought that Jimmy might well've been the first American in all the war who was killed after we started to fight back. The very first. On the ground, I mean. There'd been Midway, on the sea. But when we finally did go on the attack, it was on August the 7th, 1942, and it was Jimmy Branch who was the first one to move up and fall. Your father. Jimmy Branch: killed first, Hill Two-oh-Eight, Tulagi, the Solomons. That was the start of us winning the war, and Jimmy . . .

*She shook her head, more mournfully now.*

. . . was the very first. It was so much like him, I have to say. All his life, Jimmy would go forward. Always moving up, moving on. He'd get blocked — he wasn't at all lucky, Jimmy — but then he'd just step sideways and go forward again. All his life. Right to the end — going up that damn hill. I can just see him having an Old Gold and saying, yeah, sure, lieutenant, I'll go ahead, I'll be the one out front. I can just see that. He deserved better.

*"He got you, Mom."*

Yes, I was the best he had in his life. I don't say that immodestly. There was so very little good he ever did have. It wasn't difficult for me to be his best thing. I'm just so glad I could give him the most joy in his life. Very few of us can say we were that to another soul and know it's true.

*"You still think about him, Mom?"*

Oh Lord, Teddy, yes. But with time, less and less. I'd always dwell on his memory on his birthday. And our anniversary. Horst came upon me crying once, and I had to tell him why, that Jimmy and me had been married this day. So, after that, on May 10th, your father would always gimme a little distance, you know. Maybe if you'd looked more like Jimmy that would've reminded me more of him, but you always favored me —

*"I know."*

— so when you got to be twenty-something, Jimmy's age when I knew him, when I loved him, there was none of that, seeing him in you. So, yes, he faded, Teddy, but no, I never forgot him. Bless his heart.

*"So then it was just a question of Horst taking his place?"*

*Mom nodded, but barely, and when she finally did begin to talk again it was one of the rare times when she wouldn't look directly at me. She said:*

Teddy, forgive me.

*"For what, Mom?"*

Well, for what I did to Jimmy. You know, I never cheated on Jimmy, and I never cheated on Horst. All my life, I never slept with another man. But if, for purposes of discussion, if Gary Cooper or Jimmy Stewart had shown up one afternoon in Missoula and said he had a room down at the Holiday Inn and he'd like me to come down there and roll in the hay with him, and I did, somehow I think that still wouldn't've meant that I didn't love your father — Horst.

But, oh my, what I did to Jimmy.

*"But he was dead, Mom."*

That's true. But o'course, I didn't know that then. Just the instant Horst got out of that cab that day and said, "Hello, Sydney." Well, I was a goner. God forgive me, when I opened that telegram, I didn't just think about poor Jimmy. I thought —

*She stopped and looked back at me.*

You get the picture, Teddy.

*"I understand."*

Do you?

*"I think so."*

Well, thank you, if you do. If you can understand, then maybe I don't even need your forgiveness. Anyway, let's call a spade a spade: the instant I read that telegram I was destined to be with Horst. Destined, Teddy, destined.

I had to get with him. I had to hide him. Somehow. You see, I knew it was only a matter of whether it would be Goldstein and the Nazis who'd find him and kill him, or the FBI would catch Goldstein, and he'd tell on Horst, and then they'd find him and put him in prison.

I remember, then, I began second-guessing myself that I'd gone down to Washington and told them all about Goldstein. Otherwise, who would have known, Teddy? Who would have known a man named Horst Gerhardt was in the United States? What I'd done for my country was against what I'd done for my love.

What would you do for love, Teddy?

*"I really don't know, Mom."*

Well, it turned out, it wasn't a conflict with me for very long.

*"Why's that?"*

You want me to tell you or you want to read it?

*"If you're still up to it, I'd like to hear it from you."*

All right, Teddy, but don't hate me when you hear.

*"Come on, Mom, I could never hate you."*

You have no idea what I did, Teddy. Not a clue in the world.

All right. That next day, which was Thursday, I couldn't bear to go into the office. I didn't want to talk to anyone. Late that afternoon, I went down to the river to swim. Just for the heck of it, sometimes I'd wear my old Women's Swimming Association suit, with the big S on my chest, and that day, because I was finally starting to show with my baby — that's you — I decided to put it on one last time. If you'll recall, Teddy, that was the suit that was very sheer, very revealing.

*"Yes, indeed, I do recall."*

Well, I was walking back up to the house, and all of a sudden I see this big black DeSoto coming down the driveway. I felt sort of naked, Teddy, but I had a big beach towel, and so I wrapped that around myself and approached to see who it was. The car pulled to a stop in front of the house, and a short man in a dark suit got out. He hadn't noticed me, so he went straight to the front door and rang the bell and peered in. Like always on the Shore back then, I'd just left the door open, except, of course, for the screen door. You had to keep the screen door closed or the flies would get in. It seems to me there were more flies back then. Everybody was always saying: close the door or the flies will get in, and you don't hear that anymore, do you?

*"No, now that I think about it."*

Anyway, flies aside, Teddy, as I watched the man up there on the porch, it naturally occurred to me who it must be. The FBI, of course. "Hello," he called out, looking through the door. "Anybody home?"

Damn it. I knew it. I'd left something in that pocketbook so they could trace me.

Well, obviously the jig was up. So I called out, "I'm coming," and I waved to him (making sure to keep that towel around myself).

As I got closer, the man walked over to the side of the porch where I was coming from and said, "Sydney Stringfellow?"

"Well," I replied, "I'm Sydney Stringfellow Branch now."

He reached into his jacket pocket and took out his wallet, flipped it open and flashed me a badge, which of course didn't surprise me, inasmuch as I knew he was the FBI. "I'd like to ask you some questions, Mrs. Branch."

"Okay," I said. "Just let me get out of this wet bathing suit." It was still damp, Teddy, and, anyway, if I was gonna be grilled by a G-man I at least wanted to be properly attired.

"I'd rather we talk right here," he said. Still quite polite, you understand.

"It'll just take a minute for me to change," I replied.

But this time, when he answered me, he was much sharper. "No, ma'am, I'd like to talk to you right here, right now, thank you very much."

Now that surprised me. It struck me as being so out of character. But by chance, at that moment, I happened to glance over toward his car, and I noticed the license plate. It was orange. I'd lived in Brooklyn long enough to recognize that license plate: New York State. And as much as my mind was whirling, I knew one thing: that the FBI would be coming up from Washington.

Maybe he saw me look at the car. Certainly he saw that my expression changed. He stepped right up to the porch railing, and this time when he spoke, his voice was full of actual menace. "Come up onto the porch," he said, staring at me with hard eyes. He had heavy eyebrows, too, which accentuated the harshness. "Right now."

You know, Teddy, every one of us has said things that we wish we hadn't.

*She looked at me for affirmation. "Oh yeah," I said.*

Well, I have too, I'm afraid, but never in my life, neither before or since did I ever say anything so stupid as I was about to utter. Just one word. And the instant it passed my lips — barely more than a whisper at that — I knew it was the dumbest thing I'd ever said. But just a reflex, Teddy. And it was done.

*"What'd you say, Mom?"*

I said: "Goldstein." And there it was. Now he knew I knew. In the next instant, he pulled a pistol out of a holster from under his jacket and pointed it right at me. "Now, come on up," he said. Naturally, I obeyed. I'd never had a gun pointed at me. It's a thing to make you shiver, lemme tell you.

So, I came up the porch steps and stood in front of him, lookin' down at the muzzle of that pistol starin' me in the face. I was surprised by how small Goldstein was. Horst hadn't mentioned that. For some reason, that irritated me. The little Nazi creep. Made me think of that awful Goebbels. Still, I was scared to death, but I did ask him again if I couldn't change my clothes.

"You're welcome to," he told me. "Only I'm afraid I have to be with you."

"What are you, a peeping Tom?" I asked. (I don't believe we said "pervert" back then, Teddy.)

"Look," he said, without taking offense, "you can turn your back on me, but I'm not lettin' you outta my sight."

"All right. Never mind."

"Have it your way," he said, beckoning me, with the pistol, to go inside.

"Make sure you close that door so the flies don't get in," I said, which was really an idiotic subject to bring up under the circumstances, but the damn flies were always on my mind. And he did close the door, and there I was, alone in the living room with him. I asked him if I could at least throw something on over the bathing suit. I don't know why, Teddy, but even if he killed me, I didn't want him to see the outline of my . . . you know . . . through that sheer suit. At least I wasn't gonna give him that little treat. So he let me go over to the coat closet, and I got out an old linen jacket that I'd wear when I was weeding and whatnot.

Then I crossed back and took the chair he

motioned me to. He sat sort of catty-cornered from me, on the sofa, so he could keep that pistol close on me and pointed right at me. "Okay," he said then, when we were settled, "where's Gerhardt?"

I shrugged. "I have no idea."

He immediately raised the gun up, pointing it right at my face. "Don't gimme that, lady. You know my name. He told you. So where is he?"

"Please lower the gun," I asked, and at least he did that; he brought it back down. But he still kept it pointed at me. At my heart, Teddy. I tried to figure out what I could tell him that would be the most innocent. You see, I could tell he really didn't know much himself, that he was fishin'.

"Go on, go on," he snapped.

"Okay," I began. "Horst called me."

"Where from?"

"He didn't say. This was a few days ago."

"When?"

I tried to calculate. "Sunday. I'm pretty sure it was Sunday." I said that because I knew that was the day Horst was in New York, supposed to be meeting Goldstein.

"So what did he say?"

I got a little sharp with him then. "Just relax and lemme tell you," I said. "He wanted to talk to me."

"Why?"

"Will you let me talk?" He nodded, grudgingly. "Well, obviously you know about me because Horst and I were in love at the Olympics, and he called me because he wanted to tell me that he wanted to see me again. Now you gotta understand, I haven't seen him since '36. He stopped writing me five years ago. I haven't heard one word from him in all that time, and out of the blue, he calls me. And once I got myself together, I explained that I was married and having a baby."

"You're having a baby?"

"Yes, I'm almost four months pregnant."

I thought that might soften him up a bit, but he just snapped: "So, okay, where's your husband?"

I paused for a second. Maybe I should tell Goldstein he'd just gone out to the drugstore or something. Maybe he'd leave then. But I took too long to respond, and he got wise. "He's not here, is he?"

Stupid me: I'd blown my chance. First I'd said something I shouldn't've said. Then when I should've said something, I didn't have the sense to. Now there was no use pretending. I just told him: "He's a Marine. He's . . . he's in Guadalcanal."

Goldstein only nodded at that. "So, then

what'd Gerhardt say?"

"Well, he said he wasn't surprised that I'd gotten married, but it disappointed him. So, naturally, I asked him what in the world he was up to? I mean, it's a little baffling, a German in the United States when we're fighting a war against Germany. And what he told me was that he was on an under-cover mission here, and he was supposed to meet a guy named Goldstein in New York, but his intention all along was not to carry out the mission, and so if he couldn't see me, he was just gonna get lost."

"That's all he said?"

"That's about it."

"You don't know where he was goin'?"

"Frankly, at that point, I don't think Horst knew where he was goin'. I mean, where he wanted to go was here, and when he found out that wasn't in the cards, I don't think he had any idea."

"And he didn't say anything more about me?"

"No. Well, when he said he was supposed to be meeting a guy named Goldstein, I remarked how that was strange, meeting a Nazi with a Jewish name, and he said, of course, it's an alias. So that was it. I don't really even know who you are."

I thought that was a good idea to put that

on the record. It was pretty apparent to me that Goldstein didn't have a whole lot of options, vis-à-vis me, Teddy. If he was used to killing people in cold blood, he'd just shoot me and be done with it. I thought that'd probably be his preferred option, because obviously, if he left me alive, the minute he drove off, I was gonna be on the phone to the FBI or the State Police and so on and so forth, reporting him.

Or, if I was lucky, and if he'd already abandoned his apartment and was headed for parts unknown, then, if he wasn't a cold-blooded killer who could shoot a pregnant woman, then maybe he'd just rip out my phone and screw up my car, something like that, and leave me be and take off.

Well, Teddy, I put myself in Goldstein's shoes, and, quite honestly, I figured it'd be a whole lot more likely that I'd just kill me if I was him. Don't they say "whack" now?

*"Yeah, I think that's the colloquial expression these days."*

Well, that's what I figured: he'd whack me. After all, how could anyone ever possibly connect him to my murder? But if he lets me be, and I blow the whistle on him, and he gets caught, they'd hang him in a July minute. Why take a chance on that? No, Teddy, I didn't like my chances at all. I was scared to death. I think I would've peed in my pants, except all I had on was my WSA bathing suit, and he would've noticed it, and I didn't wanna give the SOB the satisfaction of seeing me so scared. You understand?

*"I do."*

Well then, I thought, besides not peeing, what could I do? Just for the record, Teddy, since it happened to me, let me tell you: after a while of having a gun pointed at you, you relax a little. I don't mean it gets old hat, but you do regain some of your composure.

So, I kind of shifted in my seat, which gave me a chance to glance around without lookin' like I was. On my right, at the corner of the L between my chair and the sofa where he was sitting, was an end table. There were two things on it. One was a large lamp and the other was a cigarette box. Well, it really wasn't a box. It was a wooden duck that had a lid on its back, where you could stick cigarettes in. Somebody had given it to my father. Mother hated it because she had no interest in ducks whatsoever and thought that grown men going duck-hunting was the stupidest form of entertainment known to man or beast, but some buddy of Daddy's had given him that wooden duck, and after Daddy was killed, Mom felt guilty about removing it. So, there it was, still on the table, and I thought, well maybe if Goldstein drops his guard, I can pick up the duck by its neck and slug him with the duck body. It was not, I'm afraid, a very viable weapon — especially with a pistol pointed at me from about two feet away, but it was about all I had to make do. You see?

*"I guess."*

Well, Teddy, Goldstein was silent for a while, mulling. That encouraged me. Somebody who mulls might not be quick on the trigger. Finally, he spoke up. "Did he say he'd call you again?"

"Yeah, actually, he did." Goldstein brightened, but I took all the air out of that balloon. "He said he'd gimme a call when the war was over."

He frowned. "And you don't know anything else?"

"Look, I'm telling you, sir." (I can't believe I called him "sir," but I distinctly remember I did.) "I loved Horst once, but that was long ago and far away, and I haven't had any contact with him in years. He calls me, finds out I'm married, we talk for a couple more minutes, and then he's gone out of my life again."

Goldstein just glowered, so I thought maybe it was time to appeal to his better instincts — assuming that a Nazi might have any. I think you'd say now, Teddy, that I tried to play the sweet-little-thing card. I lowered my head and rubbed my eyes. "Oh, sir, please, won't you just leave me alone? I don't know anything else. I don't know who you are. I can't help you. Just please." And I tried to cry. In fact, I began to cry. Well, not really, Teddy, but at least I made as much noise as if I was crying. I mean, I really boo-hooed to beat the band.

*She smiled then, and did a little boo-hooing for my benefit.*

You see, at just that instant I was sure I'd heard the kitchen screen door open, and I had a pretty good idea who it was who'd opened it, and I wanted that person, who must be Gentry Trappe, to hear me cry, and then I wanted to keep on making enough noise so that Goldstein wouldn't hear the kitchen door close. Luckily, Teddy, Gentry Trappe never slammed a door in all his born days. He was the quietest door-closer I'd ever encountered in my entire life.

And Goldstein, with all his mulling and my faux crying, didn't hear a thing. "Come on, come on," is all he said.

"Well, you wouldn't let me get dressed,

and I don't have a hankerchief," I said. "Lemme get a Kleenex." And Teddy, I reached over to that duck, like it was a Kleenex box.

And sure enough, just as I did, I glanced up, and I could see Mr. Trappe coming into the room from the kitchen. He was to my right, but behind Goldstein. He was carrying a few ears of sweet corn he'd brought for me, and his eyes were wide open with confusion and fear at the scene he'd chanced upon.

Thank God for Gentry Trappe or I wouldn't be here today. And come to think of it, Teddy, you wouldn't have been any place any day, ever.

*And Mom paused and took a sip from the Old Crow. Then she looked back up at me. She said:*

Promise me you won't hate me, Teddy.

*I only shook my head, still completely unsure of what she was talking about, as she went on:*

I opened my eyes as wide as I could — on purpose. You see, now I wanted to make sure Goldstein did see that I saw something. I wanted him distracted. Sure enough, he turned his head a little, and when he did, I screamed out, "He's got a gun!" Then I grabbed that wooden duck, the cigarette box, by the neck, and I brought it down across Goldstein's arm. I hit him square on the wrist, where he was holdin' the pistol.

*Mom pantomimed the action. She had a pretty smooth range of motion. She never did, as we say, "throw like a girl." Maybe it came from all the swimming. In any event, I could imagine that she walloped Goldstein pretty good.*

Okay, Teddy, Goldstein turned back from spotting Mr. Trappe at that instant and pulled the trigger, and the gun fired, which scared the living you-know-what outta me. But because I bopped his wrist in the nick of time, his aim was off, and the bullet missed me. In another second, Mr. Trappe had sorta shoveled the ears of corn he was carrying into Goldstein's direction, and then he tumbled over the back of the sofa, grabbin' him round the neck, and I smashed Goldstein on his wrist again with the duck.

At that point, he managed to get off one more shot. It went through the screen door. I found the hole later. But that was when I fell forward onto his arm, just as Mr. Trappe had come all the way over the back of the sofa onto Goldstein's back, so he couldn't keep hold of the gun anymore. It dropped to the floor, and I snatched it up and pointed it right at his head.

"Okay, Mr. Trappe, I got it now," I said. By then, he had Goldstein in a headlock from behind.

Poor Goldstein, Teddy. I must say, he looked more chagrined than anything. Here he was, the top-dog Nazi in the whole United States, and an old man and a pregnant woman had beaten the crap out of him and taken his gun away. I was still scared out of my wits, but, at the same time, there was something comical about it.

Gentry Trappe, of course, was mostly just puzzled. "Miss Trixie," he said. "Who is this?"

"I'll tell you in a minute," I said. "First, go into the garage and get something to tie him up with. There's some clothesline in there."

He was reluctant to leave me alone with the guy, but I gave a little wave of the gun, to assure him that I was quite capable of handling the situation, and he hurried off to the garage.

At this point Goldstein turned a little sullen, trying his best, I think, to affect a tough-guy pose. "So what'r'ya gonna do?" he asked.

"I don't know," I said. "I guess I'll call the FBI." Then I got a little smug, Teddy. I couldn't resist lettin' him know the score.

"Actually, I already reported you to them. Your goose is cooked."

"I figured maybe." Then he pleaded a little: "Look, why don't you lemme go, and I'll just get outta your hair?"

"You think I'm born yesterday?" I said.

And then, Teddy, Goldstein said something every bit as stupid as what I'd said a few minutes earlier. He thought he was bein' so smart. He kinda snarled at me: "Well, have it your way, sister, because once you turn me in, the only name I'm givin' the bastards is your old lover boy. And they'll get that sonuvabitch traitor for sure. They'll find him." He shook his wrist then. It was pretty bruised from me clubbing him with that duck.

And I thought: yeah.

*"Yeah what, Mom?"*

Yeah. Of course, Goldstein was gonna tattle on Horst. I'd already figured that, but now my mind began to turn over, Teddy. I was very calm, very rational. I just thought to myself how Goldstein was as good as executed the minute the FBI got him. They hadn't even wasted any time hanging those saboteurs they'd caught who'd snuck in on the U-Boats — and those guys hadn't even managed to do anything. But that's what you do to spies. You hang them. In wartime.

you kill them.

And I thought about Horst, Teddy. I thought about Jimmy, too. I did. How he was gone, killed in the war. And I thought about Horst and how he still loved me and how much I'd loved him once and maybe I had never stopped loving him, but, anyway, I knew I'd love him again.

*Mom paused, and her eyes took on a thoughtful aspect, and I could see that she was framing the scene in her mind's eye. Then, without any drama at all in her voice, she simply told me:*

And so, Teddy, just like that, I pulled the trigger.

*And she crooked her finger before me.*

*She leaned back and folded her arms across her chest, letting that soak in. It all came so fast. Instinctively, I just said, "You what, Mom?"*

I pulled the trigger. I executed him. Actually, I pulled it a second time, but that was probably unnecessary. Remember, I was holding that pistol only a foot, maybe eighteen inches from him, pointed right at his heart, and Goldstein was probably dead even before I pulled the trigger the second time.

*"But, Mom . . . how?"*

*She did not change her expression, only tried to do her best to help me understand.*

*She was more illuminating than emotional.*
*There were no dramatics at all.*

Oh, understand, Teddy, I knew exactly what I was doing. It wasn't like shooting a duck or a dove. I knew I was murdering another human being. Thou shalt not kill — right? But I did it without blinking an eye. I'm sure I didn't feel any different than the Jap did who mowed Jimmy down on Tulagi. It was just a bit of the war, Teddy. In a strange place. But . . . just a bit of the war.

*She stopped and looked me right in the eye.*

So, do you hate me now? Do you hate your mother now that you know she's a murderer?

*I managed to shake my head, and reached out and took her hand. "No, I don't, Mom. I mean, there were extenuating —" But then I stopped and grabbed for my glass, and I swigged — I mean, swigged — my bourbon. As for Mom, she merely resumed talking again, without any particular tone to her voice, quite evenly, bordering on the matter-of-fact. I think she'd gone over this so many times in her mind, even talking it out to herself, that it came off as some sort of statement — testimony, in a way. It was almost as if she might call me "your honor" and conclude by signing her name and writing out the date to her confession.*

See, Teddy, I'd simply decided that he was going to be executed, so I might as well be the executioner. And, of course, not that it mattered, but it did spare him any agony. He never had a clue. Never in a million years did he figure this nice, young, pregnant girl from the Shore was gonna kill him in cold blood. You know, Teddy, I don't even remember any expression on his face. He was dead before he could be surprised. He just slumped back and then tumbled over to the side on the sofa, and the blood started to stain his shirt, sort of oozin' out. But I barely noticed.

I just kept sittin' there, holdin' the gun, and wonderin', did I do it to save Horst, or did I do it because I wanted Horst? Did you do it for love, Trixie, or did you do it for yourself? And you know, Teddy, I've never lost a minute's sleep over the fact that I killed that man. But I have spent all these years wondering what led me to do it.

*"Well, Mom, love and selfishness can usually be intertwined. We love someone, and we want her . . . him. I don't know where you can draw the line."*

*She nodded at that assessment, but only, I think, to be polite. It didn't seem to settle the issue in her own mind. Nothing could, not after all these years of wrestling with it herself. She just took another sip of her drink and went on.*

I did have the presence of mind to call out to Gentry Trappe that I was all right, so he came runnin' back into the room, and I told him that Goldstein had tried to take the gun from me, so I had to shoot him, and he commiserated with me, that a young lady had had to shoot someone in self-defense, but I assured him I was fine, and then he told me he'd call the police. That's when I finally got up outta that chair. I hadn't moved the whole time, Teddy. But I had to stretch, and I said, "No, Mr. Trappe. We're not gonna call the police. Or anybody."

"We're not?"

"No, we're gonna take Mr. Goldstein and dump him out here in the river. We're gonna deposit him in Davey Jones' locker."

*For the first time in a while, Mom smiled.*

My gracious, Teddy, but you should've seen the expression on Mr. Trappe's face.

Of course, Teddy, it was all very unreal — or "surreal," as everybody says now. For only at that point did it begin to seriously enter my consciousness that there was a dead man, who I'd killed in my bathing suit, lying on the sofa in our living room. My practical side kinda kicked in at this point, though, and I told Mr. Trappe I'd explain, but first I ran upstairs to get some towels so Goldstein wouldn't bleed all over the darn place.

I hurried back with the towels and covered up the body, but I'd noticed my shower curtain when I'd grabbed the towels, so I ran back up to my bathroom and yanked that off the rod and came back down, and we wrapped Goldstein in that.

"Miss Trixie . . . ?" Gentry began then. I mean, I did owe him an explanation. But the magnitude of what I'd done finally hit me, and I began to cry for real. I said, "Let's go in the kitchen," and we went out to the table in the pantry. There were pantries then, Teddy. My gracious, I haven't thought about pantries in a coon's age.

*"No, ma'am."*

So I got us glasses of ice water, and we sat down, and I said, "Now listen, this isn't going to make any sense to you, but that man is a Nazi spy." Naturally, Gentry looked at me like I had lost my marbles. So I went on: "Remember when I went to the Olympics in Germany?" And he nodded. "Well, I met some people there, and in a roundabout way, Mr. Trappe, that's what brought that man here. He was looking for someone I know. And I appreciate that might be hard to understand, but you just hafta trust me, because if we go to the FBI, it can hurt someone else. Someone who's good."

He nodded, sort of. So I went on: "I know this isn't fair, but I promise you, whatever happens, nothing will happen to you. All right?"

It was obvious that he was still pretty dubious — which I certainly would've been had our positions been reversed — but he managed to give me the benefit of the doubt, saying, "All right, Miss Trixie."

And, Teddy, I stuck out my hand then, and I said, "Sydney." He cocked his head, unsure what I'd meant by me just saying my name, so I explained: "Mr. Trappe, you and me've known each other for a long time, and I think it's time we got on a first-name basis. So I'm Sydney and you're Gentry. Okay?" And he agreed and shook my hand.

We couldn't get rid of Goldstein's body till it was dark, so we set about planning. First, I put on a pair of sneakers and some old overalls over my WSA bathing suit. Then we dragged the body out of the house, around back. There was an old anchor in the shed and behind it some cinder blocks that had been there for a million years. I asked Gentry to get a wheelbarrow and haul them down to the dock. Next, I moved Goldstein's car, hiding it behind the shed. Then I set about the incredibly unpleasant task of taking the clothes off the body. If it did somehow manage to pop up off the river bottom and float up, I knew that the fewer ways to identify him the better. Well, I did leave him in his underclothes. I couldn't imagine that they could possibly help identify him. Besides, as they say now, Teddy: I just didn't want to go there.

So after I got his clothes off, right before I was going to pull the shower curtain back around him, I couldn't help but stop and look at his face. It was quite placid, really. Remember, Teddy, I'd just shot him in his heart. And I couldn't help but study that face. It was not bad-looking. It was just another face. And it occurred to me that I'd be the last person on this earth who'd ever see that face, so even though I was the one who'd killed him, I couldn't help but take what I guess you'd call a sort of proprietary interest, so you know what I did, Teddy?

*Of course, I had no idea. I shook my head.*

Well, I kneeled over him and took my hand and smoothed his hair down. He was already stone cold, of course, and it was spooky, but I somehow felt that it was the least I could do. You see, it occurred to me that if some Japanese soldier had come across Jimmy's body before our boys got to it, I would've hoped they wouldn't've done anything disrespectable to it. Just because it was war, I didn't think you had to be hateful to the dead bodies.

And that made me think of Jimmy again, so I had to pause for a moment. I sat back down on the ground, looking away from Goldstein, and remembered my dear Jimmy. That brought on more tears — but not for what I'd done, you understand. Just for poor Jimmy. For your father.

*"Yes, ma'am."*

After a while, I composed myself again, and turned back and wrapped the shower curtain all around Goldstein. I got up then, and I looked down, and I said, "May God bless you."

*That took me aback. "You did?"*

Yes, I've never been much for that rot-in-hell business. He was dead. I'd made him pay for his sins here. I was just really sayin', 'Well, God, it's your business now.' I mean, Teddy, I never forgot that if Gentry Trappe hadn't showed up when he did, I'm sure Goldstein would've killed me. There but for the grace of God — right?

*"I must say, Mom, that was very generous of you."*

Oh, I don't know, Teddy. In a way it wasn't at all personal. It was just the war. Anyway, that was the end of that. I started goin' through his effects.

His wallet had a driver's license, which did indeed identify him as Jeremiah R. Goldstein, age forty-three. It was pretty easy back then to make up new names and such. He had $187 in cash, which was a lot of money to carry in those days. And he had a couple of blank checks and various notes and cards. No pictures — no photographs. I guess spies don't carry that sort of thing.

Anyway, I took all that there was back to

the shed, and with some strong scissors, I cut everything up but the money and put it in the garbage. I gave Gentry the $187. He was a little reluctant to take it, but it was such a considerable sum, whatever compunctions about the source of the filthy lucre were soon overcome.

We waited till well into the night. The only boat we had wasn't much more than a rowboat with an outboard, and it took us a while to figure out how to ideally position the body. Eventually, we decided that the best way would be to place it — still wrapped in my shower curtain, now — up near the bow, cross-wised, so that his head and shoulders hung over one side and his legs the other. See, once we got the anchor and the cinder blocks tied to him, that would be the easiest way to push him overboard without swamping the boat. Over the bow.

It was past eleven when we pushed off, Gentry up front, making sure the body didn't fall off before we tied the dead weights to it, me in the back steering the little putt-putt. I don't know how deep the river was, but we all knew the Chester had a good channel, because big ships used to dock in Chestertown in the colonial days. It had been a very serious port at one time

Certainly, it was plenty deep for our particular purposes. I knew that.

There was only very little moon and no other boats on the river at that hour, and when we got out to the middle of the river, I cut the motor and let us drift in the darkness. But just then, Teddy, at that very moment when we were dead in the water with a body hangin' over the bow, suddenly we had a terrible bright light shining right on us. It felt like the whole world could see us. Gentry whispered, "Oh Lord," and I just held my breath.

In another moment I realized it was headlights from a car on the other side of the river. High beam shinin' right at us. Bright as day, us caught red-handed with a body.

Gentry said, "Is it the po-lice?"

I tried to figure out where it was coming from, and then, just like that, I said, "It's okay, it'll go off in a second."

And just like that, it did.

*"How'd you know?"*

Because I'd figured out that the car must be on a little dirt road I knew that came down that way. It was where kids went to park and neck. I'd been there a time or two myself, double-dating with Carter Kincaid, though mostly fending off, rather than necking. But I knew that whatever boy was drivin' that car wasn't interested in anything on that river, and the instant he got to that parking spot, he was gonna turn those damn lights off as quick as you can say "Jack Robinson." Which he did.

So, phew, there we were back in the pitch dark again, and Gentry tied the old anchor and two cinder blocks to the body, and once we were sure they were secure, he just sort of rolled Goldstein over the bow. In a jiffy, he was beneath the waters and out of sight. Master criminals we were, Teddy. I wiped my fingerprints off the pistol, because I didn't know whether water affected finger- prints, and I heaved that into the river, too. Then I pulled the cord on the outboard, started her up, and brought us back to the dock. It all went like clockwork.

Where we split up, he to go over to his house, I said, "Thank you, Gentry. I can't tell you how grateful I am."

And he started to say, "Well, Miss Trixie —"

And I stopped him and said, "Sydney."

So he said, "You're welcome, Sydney."

And you know, Teddy, I do not hold much with people who allude with confidence to the minds of the dead — you know, like those who take their vacation to Jamaic<

right after their mother dies, because, they say, "she would've wanted me to," when I'm not so sure she would have. But on this occasion I felt it appropriate to say, "My father would be very appreciative for what you did for me."

He nodded and said, "I believe so, yes," and then spontaneously, we came together and hugged one another, which was very unusual in those days on the Shore — a black man and white woman of any age embracing in any way. We both knew that, too, but it was just the natural thing to do, so we did it. Then he turned and headed off for home. And because of the way things worked out, that was the last time I ever laid eyes on Gentry Trappe, who was one of the finest gentleman ever of my acquaintance.

When I got back to the house, I took a shower and put on my wrapper, and then I took my Women's Swimming Association bathing suit and went downstairs and cut it all up. There was blood on it. Besides, I knew I wasn't ever going to wear that bathing suit again. Even if being in the WSA had only been five or six years ago, it was a part of my life which seemed so long gone that it hardly seemed possible that that girl in the silk bathing suit had ever once been me.

So I put all the cut-up parts into the trash and went upstairs and got in bed and thought about what I had done today and, especially, as I said already, why I had done it.

*She took another sip of the bourbon.*

Now, tell me the God's truth, Teddy: are you ashamed of me for what I did?

*"No, Mom, I'm not the least bit ashamed of you. I'm just more amazed than ever."*

Yeah, I told you there was one other time when I had a big neck. That day, I had a big brass one. Didn't I, Teddy?

*I raised my glass to her in acknowledgment, and then she went right on with the very last story of the war.*

Mom and Elliott Parsons came back from Atlantic City on Sunday. They'd enjoyed the Miss America contest. If I recall, Miss Texas won.

Naturally, though, the first thing Mom asked me was had I heard anything about Jimmy, but I bit my lip, and when she saw the tears in my eyes, she assumed that it was from worrying about him.

Then I waited, Teddy. I just waited for Horst to call me from wherever he was. And it wasn't only impatience on my part that made me wish he'd hurry up and contact me. See, it occurred to me that Goldstein might've told his wife or one of the other Nazis that he was goin' to find me, so after a while, when they didn't hear from him, they might very well come lookin' for him. And although Goldstein was safely at the bottom of the Chester River, that big DeSoto of his was still parked out behind the shed, as big as day. I made up my mind that on Saturday I'd drive it somewhere — anywhere, Teddy — and abandon it.

But, thank God, on Wednesday night, Horst called. He was in a phone booth. I could hear him dropping the coins in as the operator requested them. "Sydney," he said, "I'm in Boston, and I've got an address for you."

I said, "Never mind." That was a little too abrupt. He didn't know what to say in return. So I just said, "Horst, do you love me?"

And he said he'd already told me that, and so then, as I fought back the tears, I told him Jimmy had been killed and consequently it seemed sensible to me that we should spend the rest of our lives together.

I don't quite remember how he answered, because he was obviously in shock, but it was most definitely in the affirmative. So I said, "If you want to be with me, Horst, we'll have to go somewhere new, and you'll have to be Jimmy Branch — at least till the war's over."

And I remember very distinctly then that he just said, "Okay."

You see, from the very first, Teddy, we always had a meeting of the minds, Horst and me.

*"Did you tell him about Goldstein?"*

Oh, good gracious, no. I never told a soul about that until I told you a few minutes ago. I just told Horst about my little adventure with the FBI, told him they'd assured me they'd get Goldstein. I understood that Horst would be a little wary — at least for the rest of the war — about the Nazis tracking him down, but the way I figured it, better he worry a little about that for a while than be burdened with the awful truth about what his wife had done for the rest of our lives. I don't think you want to go around telling people you love that you're a murderer.

*"Oh, Mom, please. I think you were just an instrument of the state."*

Well, Teddy, that is a wonderful euphemism. Why, that's like when the executioner apologized to Anne Boleyn before he chopped her head off, that it was nothing personal. I remember that. "Instrument of the state." Hmmm. I'm very grateful for that.

*"You're welcome to it," I said. "But, come on, tell me: how'd you get to Montana?"*

Oh, I understood that we had to go somewhere a long ways from the Shore, somewhere where no one who'd ever known Jimmy was liable to just sorta drop in, and also somewhere where none of Goldstein's crowd would ever find Horst. Basically, Teddy, I was inventing the witness protection program before it occurred to the government. So I just got out a map, and, in the full scheme of things, Missoula looked like the best bit of nowhere.

Of course, first I had to explain to Mother what was up. I told her about Horst and about him defecting and me going to the FBI — and then, then I told her about Jimmy being killed. She cried quite a bit at that. She loved Jimmy. Anybody who met your father did. He was a honey of a guy.

*"That's nice to hear, Mom."*

Yes, and it's the God's truth. No girl was ever so lucky as me to have two such perfectly wonderful gentlemen love her.

But, Teddy, the main point of me talking to Mother was to tell her that I was running off to God knows where with Horst, who was going to become Jimmy. She took this all in remarkably well, and just asked me where I was going. I said, "East of the sun and west of the moon." You may remember, Teddy, that the first time I danced with Horst, that was the very first song the band was playing.

*"At Joseph Goebbels' party."*

Yes, so that was kinda our song, and it

certainly seemed apropos at the time. Later, Horst and I fell in love with a new song that fit our circumstance even better. It was a song by Dame Vera Lynn —

*"I know, Mom, you wrote about it in there." I pointed to the purple folder.*

Oh, of course. "In The Land of Begin Again," on the other side of the hill. Yes, we went to Missoula, but we always thought it wasn't in Montana. It was in the land of begin again.

*"How'd you get there?"*

Well, after all the fireworks of the week before, it was actually pretty prosaic. I told Mom she couldn't tell anyone what had happened and where I'd be, and, of course, she said she had to tell Elliott, which I agreed was the natural order of things, and then I made her promise me that when she sold the place, she'd give Gentry Trappe enough to live on comfortably for the rest of his life.

Mom said, "Well, all right, Trixie, but it's not my intention to sell the place till after the war. Maybe you and your good-looking German can come back then when the smoke has cleared."

I said that was fine with me, but I knew, Teddy — I knew that once Horst and I got settled in the land of begin again, we couldn't ever come back to the Shore. And I was right about that. As right as rain.

So, the very next day, I packed a bag and put it in Goldstein's DeSoto. The car was registered to someone named Kornelia Steffen, with an address I recognized as being in Yorkville, in Manhattan, which was the German section of town. I imagine she was Goldstein's wife, or his lady friend — anyway, the one Horst had seen with him. I destroyed all that identification, and I took a screwdriver with me, and I drove up to Philadelphia. There were two main train stations in Philly, and I parked the car on the street near the one in North Philadelphia. It was residential up there, easy to park. With that screwdriver, I took off the license plates —

*"Why'd you do that, Mom?"*

Well, Teddy, when you're trying not to leave any traces behind, your mind starts working like a thief in the night. I also left the window open and the keys in the ignition, hoping someone nefarious would have the good sense to steal it. Good riddance.

*"Did anyone steal it?"*

I don't know, Teddy, but I do know I never heard boo from anyone about Goldstein. Maybe the FBI found Kornelia Steffen. I suppose they warned the president and Mr.

Churchill about the plot, about Operation Hauptstadt. Maybe they were able to decode the papers Horst had brought over for Goldstein. I don't know. All I know is, Horst and I had done our damndest for the United States of America, and now it was time for us to concentrate on ourselves. So we met in New York at Grand Central Station and were off to the land of begin again.

We rented a place in Missoula, and he got a job with a bank. Once he showed them Jimmy's "Good Citizen of The Week" citation and the letter of commendation they gave him at the Bank of Manhattan, they grabbed him. Good men were in short supply during the war, you understand. And he began to work his way up in the hierarchy, although I believe it's au currant, Teddy, to say "up the food chain" now.

*"Yes, Mom, that puts you with the In Crowd."*

Yes, and then you came along, Teddy. Baby makes three. We were a family. And we fit in.

*"Did Dad ever contemplate turning himself in? I mean, after the war?"*

We did talk about it. But I was the one who broached the subject, and, to tell you the truth, he simply wasn't interested. He said he was happy being Jimmy Branch and being with me. And you. It was probably

558

the wrong moment to even consider that, too, because that's about when we bought our first house, and I became pregnant with Helen. It was certainly no time to change horses in midstream. After she was born, I proposed that I go back to selling insurance in town, so he could get an architectural degree, but he waved that off, too. He was doing very well at the bank, moving up —

*"— up the food chain."*

Why, Teddy, I couldn't've said that any better myself. No, honestly, I'm sure he would've been happier as an architect, but he learned to like banking well enough. And he was good at it. As well we all know, you don't get everything in life. We were content. After all that had happened to separate us, your father and I were content just to be together.

*"Did he ever make any effort to find out about his family? Ever want to go back to Germany?"*

*Mom shook her head.*

No. I knew he had no interest whatsoever in his sister — "the SS moll," as he called her when she was still, however remotely, a subject of some discussion. But he had loved his parents. He was sure that both of them had just been swept along by the Nazis, that it wasn't their natural bent at all. But he was almost curiously incurious about what might've happened to them. He simply said, and I remember this so very well: "Sydney, the Nazis destroyed millions of families. Let us just accept the fact that the Gerhardts were one more of those." And that was the end of it. I never brought it up again.

After Helen finished college and we didn't have tuitions to worry about anymore, we took the trip to Europe. Do you remember?

*I nodded.*

It was 1970, Teddy, and we set up the usual grand tour — London, Paris, Monte Carlo, Italy. Once we got over there, I tried like the devil to get him to pop up to Berlin, but he wouldn't hear of it. Somehow, he'd just put all that out of his mind. It was quite amazing, really, how easily he'd become Jimmy Branch. In a way, it was harder for me — at least at first — because, of course, I had known the real Jimmy Branch. I had loved him. I had married him. But in time, I didn't think "Horst" anymore. I was able to accept it, too. Very soon, in fact, we never, ever talked about it.

*"But God, Mom, wasn't it hard being some-one else?"*

Oh, your father would hate you for being so dramatic. He was never anything but himself. Lots of people change their names. All those actors. Cary Grant was Archie Leach, but he managed just fine once he became Cary Grant, didn't he? It's just a name, Teddy. Didn't your friend Shakespeare say that about roses?

*"Yes, ma'am. He allowed as how they'd be just as sweet no matter what you called 'em."*

Well, Mr. Rose meet Mr. Gerhardt — the erstwhile Mr. Gerhardt. Trust me, the father you knew all your life was the same boy I fell in love with in 1936. It was really only his name that changed, and since no one but me — and, well, Mom and Elliott — would ever know both Jimmy Branchs, Horst was an original for everyone else who met him. He only fell out of character one time.

*"When was that?"*

The summer of '84. Remember, I got him to take me down to the Olympics in Los Angeles, and although he didn't care that much about swimming, he was a good sport, and we had tickets at the pool most every day. McDonald's had built the pool.

*"Mickey D's?"*

Yes, and a magnificent pool it was. That was their contribution to "The Movement." That horse's ass Avery Brundage I told you about always called the Olympics "The

Movement," like they were something sacred.

But anyway, 1984. Now because your father didn't follow swimming, he was quite surprised to find out that the best swimmer in the world then was a German boy named Michael Gross. He was sort of an early version of Michael Phelps, although, of course, not nearly so good. He was extremely tall, Michael Gross, and with arms so long they called him "The Albatross."

The first time we saw Gross win a gold medal it was in the two-hundred freestyle. He set a world record — absolutely blew all the others away. And there were all sorts of Germans there cheerin' the Albatross on. Remember now, Teddy, the Berlin wall was still up, and Michael Gross was a West German. The ones on our side. So it really pleased your old man. Well, a couple days later, Gross was swimming in the hundred-meter butterfly, and though he was by far the best butterflyer in the world, it sort of took him a while to unwind that long body of his, so he was an underdog in the hundred. In the short race.

But all these Germans — West Germans — were wavin' flags and leadin' cheers for the Albatross, and, in particular, there was a large group of younger ones down below us, near the pool, and shortly before the race started, your father turned to me, absolutely out of the blue, and he said, "Sydney, is it all right with you if I go down there with them?"

Well, you could've knocked me over with a feather, but, of course, I said yes, and he scrambled down to be with that bunch. Remember now, Teddy, he was a man of . . . uh, let's see, sixty-eight years then, but he was like a spring chicken for that moment. I looked down, and I couldn't hear what they were sayin', but I could see him chattin' with some of the Germans, and when Michael Gross was introduced, he started whoopin' and hollerin' in German just like all the others.

And Teddy, damned if Gross didn't set another world record, comin' up at the end and out-touchin' the boy from the United States, who was the favorite. So the air kinda went outta the whole stadium, except for the German contingent. And no one was makin' more of a fuss than your father, right in the middle.

After a good while, he came back up to our seat, and you know what, Teddy: he was crying.

*"And men aren't supposed to let women see them cry."*

Oh my, no, your father had experienced his consciousness-raising by then, and he wasn't the least bit embarrassed. He was smiling through his tears, just beaming. And he said, "I always hoped it would be like this . . . liebchen."

I didn't quite get his meaning. I said, "Whaddya mean?"

And he said, "You know, back in '36, I dreamed it would turn out that we Germans could be like the good people in the world. That the Olympics would show us that. That's what I wanted."

And that's when I started to cry myself, Teddy, because here it was 1984 in Los Angeles, but you know what occurred to me? You know what I thought?

*"No, no I don't."*

Well, what I thought was that this was finally my Olympics, too. My Tokyo Olympics of 1940 had finally arrived in Los Angeles.

And your father reached over and took my hand, and he squeezed it, and then he went back to being himself again. He only gave himself that one moment to be what he had been, to remember what he had dreamed that summer when we fell in love the minute we met, not having the foggiest

what lay just around the corner.
   Or ever after, for that matter.

The employees of Thorndike Press hope you have enjoyed this Large Print book. All our Thorndike, Wheeler, and Kennebec Large Print titles are designed for easy reading, and all our books are made to last. Other Thorndike Press Large Print books are available at your library, through selected bookstores, or directly from us.

For information about titles, please call:
  (800) 223-1244

or visit our Web site at:
  http://gale.cengage.com/thorndike

To share your comments, please write:
  Publisher
  Thorndike Press
  295 Kennedy Memorial Drive
  Waterville, ME 04901